THE
PRISONER

THE PRISONER

A Novel

OMAR SHAHID HAMID

Arcade Publishing • New York

First North American Edition 2015

This is a work of fiction. Names, places, characters, and incidents are either the products of the author's imagination or are used fictitiously.

Arcade Publishing books may be purchased in bulk at special discounts for sales promotion, corporate gifts, fund-raising, or educational purposes. Special editions can also be created to specifications. For details, contact the Special Sales Department, Arcade Publishing, 307 West 36th Street, 11th Floor, New York, NY 10018 or arcade@skyhorsepublishing.com.

Arcade Publishing® is a registered trademark of Skyhorse Publishing, Inc.®, a Delaware corporation.

Visit our website at www.arcadepub.com.

10 9 8 7 6 5 4 3 2 1

Library of Congress Cataloging-in-Publication Data

Hamid, Omar Shahid, author.
   The prisoner : a novel / Omar Shahid Hamid. — First North American edition.
      pages ; cm
   ISBN 978-1-62872-524-7 (hardcover : alkaline paper) — ISBN 978-1-62872-547-6 (ebook)
   I. Title.
   PR9540.9.H33P75 2015
   823'.914—dc23
                                   2014041346

Cover design by Saurav Das
Cover photo: David Ridley

Ebook ISBN: 978-1-62872-547-6

Printed in the United States of America

For my father, who gave his life for what he believed in

And for the men and women of the Karachi Police, who put their lives on the line every single day

And for my friend and mentor, Chaudhry Aslam

Author's Note

For the reader's benefit, a glossary explaining some cultural terms, slang, and occasional words and phrases in Urdu appears at the back of the book, on page 285.

THE
PRISONER

1

A cool breeze blew across the front courtyard of the prison, causing the solitary figure to shudder. The gentle rays of the winter morning sun were breaking through the early mist. The weather was chilly by Karachi standards, although it couldn't have been colder than a particularly crisp November day in London or New York. The balmy climate of the city was such that Karachiites only bothered to take out their sweaters and shawls barely for about fifteen days in a year. This year, however, had been different. A cold snap had hit the city and lasted for most of the month. Temperatures had been the lowest in recorded history.

The man at the gate coughed and stamped his feet. Having been a lifelong resident of the city, he was totally unprepared for the wintry weather. He was a tall man, and his muscular legs had the bearing of an athlete's. He wore a khaki-and-gray police uniform with the badge of the Elite Police Group on his right breast, certifying that he had been a police commando at one time. But his expanding girth and the way his service belt nestled under his paunch underlined the fact that his athletic days now lay in the distant past. Just below the badge was a black nameplate with the name CONSTANTINE etched upon it. Despite his slipping physical form, he was a man who still took pride in the smartness of his uniform. The khaki pants were starched stiff, the tan-colored boots polished like mirrors, and his ink-blue beret fell perfectly on his clipped hair. The shiny silver crescent and star that he wore on each shoulder stated his rank as a superintendent, but the lettering next to his ranks said "PRISONS" instead of "POLICE." The only personal touch to his uniform was the small gold cross that he wore around his neck.

"Bloody faujis," he swore under his breath. Trust an army officer to schedule a meeting first thing in the morning! Constantine D'Souza was definitely not a morning person. Most cops aren't. A policeman usually never leaves the police station before 3:00 or 4:00 a.m., and he is not inclined to be back on duty till at least midday. The faujis had fixed timings, clock in at 8:00 and out at 4:00. Unfortunately, the point they never understood was that crime doesn't follow a timetable. When the coup first happened, army officers would show up to monitor the police stations promptly at 8:00 a.m., expecting to find the in-charges at their desks. Usually, no one except the duty officer and the night sentry were present at that hour. Constantine hadn't met the young army captain monitoring his police station until a good ten days after the takeover.

The inconvenience of the early hour did not concern him as much as the phone call of the previous night. He had been woken by a voice he hadn't heard in years. Nevertheless, he recognized the crisp tone immediately. Colonel Tarkeen had served in Karachi's intelligence establishment for so long that there was hardly a police officer above the rank of inspector who did not recognize his casual, hail-fellow-well-met tone, spiced with just the right amount of steel.

"Constantine, how are you, my boy?" Tarkeen was one of the very few people who made it a point to actually pronounce Constantine's name correctly. Twenty-five years in the Karachi Police had seen it bastardized to "Consendine."

"Fine sir, and you? I heard that you had been posted again in Karachi but I—"

"Yes, and I'm *very* disappointed that you haven't come to see me. All the old boys had come over—Farooq, Waseem, Haider—and I ask them all about you, but they say Constantine doesn't want to come to Bleak House to pay his respects. They say you're trying to stay away from me, they say you think you don't want me to be your *friend*. That isn't *true* now, is it, Constantine?"

"Not at all, sir. Nothing like that. I've just been busy settling down here at the Central Prison. I came here just a couple of months ago.

Nothing like that at all, sir. Farooq and all are just joking with you, sir. I'll come by tomorrow if you like."

"Hahaha. Don't *worry*, my boy, I know you haven't strayed. We will meet, and *sooner* than you think, but for the moment, I need your help."

"Anything, sir."

"I'm sending one of my boys to you tomorrow. His name's Major Rommel. He will be with you at 0700 hours. I want you to assist him in *any* and *every* way possible. Thank you, Constantine."

And with that, the line went dead. The fact that the call had come out of the blue disturbed Constantine. Colonel Tarkeen never did anything impulsively. He was the ultimate spook. He had served for seven years with the Intelligence Agencies in Karachi, seven of the most tumultuous years in the city's history. He had overseen the bloody battles against the ethnic insurgents, the coup which removed the previous prime minister, the events following 9/11 and the ensuing crackdown on the jihadis. Normally, an officer would be expected to serve an average tenure of two to three years in the Agencies, but Tarkeen had been considered so indispensable that his tenure was extended twice. And now, after a short hiatus commanding an artillery unit in some small military cantonment town, he had managed to get himself posted back to Karachi. He had an encyclopedic knowledge of the officers of the Karachi Police and an expert understanding of who was good, who was bad, who was corrupt and who was weak. He had often used them to further his own personal agenda, in addition to his official directives. He also understood the intricacies of police work, rare for army officers who usually saw things in black or white. Constantine suspected that Tarkeen had viewed the world in nothing but shades of gray for a very, very long time. If Tarkeen had called him, he wanted something from him. The reference to Constantine's not paying his respects had been deliberate, to corner him. But the most disturbing thing was the last line about giving *any* and *every* assistance. It was the way he said it. He was after something very specific, and the underlying message was clear. No matter what it was or what it entailed or how much he disliked it, Constantine had to do it.

It was not uncommon for the Intelligence Agencies to send their representatives to the prison. The place was crawling with informers and turncoats, and everyone was spying on everyone else, like some latter-day Pakistani version of East Berlin in miniature. The Central Prison, or CP, as it was called, was a hive of information and a virtual university for crime. Jihadis, terrorists, activists of all the political parties, along with the average, run-of-the-mill murderers, rapists, and robbers—CP Karachi had them all. They were all living together, learning from each other. An offender would be locked up for a minor offence in the CP, and after spending a couple of years there, he would come out with a Masters degree in criminality. The concept of rehabilitation in prison went out the window with the CP. You came out of there a much bigger, better, and more dedicated criminal. When it had been constructed, at the beginning of the last century, it was meant to house between 3,000 and 4,000 prisoners. It now housed at least six times that number, in the same area. The only additions to the building had been the system of several layers of boundary walls and innumerable guard towers that isolated the old prison from the main road like some ancient, impregnable Byzantine fortress. Indeed, the front entrance of the prison, where Constantine now stood, very much resembled a medieval castle, with a massive iron gate, set in a yellow brick façade with turrets overlooking it.

Constantine shrugged his shoulders. There was no use worrying about what the faujis wanted. The damn Agencies would do things exactly as they pleased, and there was nothing to be done about that. Still, the timing was curious. They probably wanted to come in and question one of the jihadis who was locked up. Little good that would do them. Even if they knew, the jihadis would never talk. Yes. That had to be it. Couldn't be anything else . . . unless it was something to do with *him*. . . . But no, that couldn't be it either. After all, who even remembered *him*?

A bhishti—water carrier—threw water on the dusty ground. Slowly, the prison was coming alive. The first mulaqatis, the visitors, having cleared a couple of checkpoints, were slowly making their way towards the final checkpoint and waiting area on the right side of the prison entrance. They would have to wait a couple of hours until the little stall windows on the side of the prison wall were opened, through which they could meet their loved ones and briefly touch them for a few precious minutes. The stalls appeared like some kind of bank teller's window, behind which the prisoners sat and disposed of the customers in front of them in record time.

A Toyota Land Cruiser approached from the direction of the juvenile prison entrance. Its windows were darkened, and it had a police number plate. From behind the spare tire tied to the back of the vehicle, two tell-tale wireless antennae were visible. Constantine swore under his breath. The bastards kept one wireless for their own communications, and the other on the police frequency to listen in on them.

The jeep pulled up just in front of Constantine. The passenger door opened, and a young man stepped out. He couldn't have been more than twenty-eight or twenty-nine. He was a tall fellow with a very fair complexion, and sharp features which marked him as a Pathan. He also had a luxuriant, jet-black moustache waxed and tweaked to a fine point. He was in shirt and trousers, not in uniform, but his severe, short-cropped hair and Ray-Ban Aviators gave away his armed-forces background.

Constantine cursed the faujis again, and then he cursed Tom Cruise for having made that bloody *Top Gun* movie. Since then, an entire genera-tion of faujis had grown up thinking they could be like him just by buying those cheap rip-off sunglasses for 200 rupees from Zainab Market.

The man returned Constantine's salute with a nod.

"Consendine D'Souza? I'm Major Rommel. I believe Colonel Tarkeen told you I was coming."

"Yes, sir. Pleased to meet you."

The small gate of the prison opened, and Constantine led the major into the entrance. They entered a passageway, at the end of which was another gate, which led to the main courtyard of the prison. The pas-sageway served as the administrative nerve center of the prison. On one side of the passage was a spiral staircase, which went up to the wireless communications room and the turrets. On the other side was a tinted glass door. Two wardens sat behind a desk in the middle of the passageway with a huge register, logging everyone coming through the gates. Both rose from their chairs as Constantine and the major entered. One of them attempted to hand a pen to the major to sign the register, but Constantine waved him away.

"No, no, *this* sahib doesn't have to sign." Constantine guided the major towards the glass door. "Come this way, sir, this is my office."

The office was small, narrow, and badly lit, with no windows and cheap tube lights adorning the walls. A dirty rug, which must have been red in 1942, the year it was probably placed there, covered the floor. A large, battered desk, upon which was draped a green baize cloth, typical of government offices, dominated the room. Behind the desk was an equally battered cane revolving chair. In front of it were two slightly more modern-looking plastic chairs.

On the wall facing the door hung the standard, government-issue portrait of the Father of the Nation. The old man seemed to be staring down with faint disapproval. Next to him, a large oak incumbency board listed the names of all those who had been posted as superintendent of the Central Prison since 1895. Whenever Constantine looked at that board, it never ceased to amaze him that all the men the names stood for had been more than happy to fleece hundreds of thousands of rupees from this prison, yet none of them had ever bothered to spend even a little to improve this office. Cheap bastards.

"I'm sorry about the office, sir. I've just recently moved here myself. Haven't had a chance to spruce it up. Won't you take a seat?"

"Yes, you were posted here two months ago, weren't you?" Major Rommel eased himself into one of the plastic chairs and opened the file that he had been holding in his hand.

"That's right, sir." Constantine noticed that stapled to one corner of the file cover was *his* passport-size photograph. The major seemed to be reading from *his* confidential file.

"Please sit, Consendine. That's a very unique name even for a Christian." Constantine felt slightly irritated at the major's patronizing attitude. The bloody bugger had walked into *his* office. Who was he to offer him a seat in his own office? And what the hell did he think he knew about Christians? Typical arrogant, immature army officer.

"It's actually Constantine, sir. Yes, it's not a common name, even in the Goan Christian community. But my father was a great cricket fan. Named me after some old West Indian cricketer whom he used to idolize. Always told me he used to hit a lot of sixes. I haven't seen you around before, sir. Are you new in Karachi?"

"Yes, I just reported to the I Section five days ago. Tell me, I'm confused. My file shows your rank as a deputy superintendent in the Karachi Police. So what are you doing wearing the ranks of a superintendent?"

Although the question was a perfectly legitimate one, Constantine found himself growing more and more irritated at having to explain his position to the major. "Yes sir, I've been seconded to the Prisons service from the Karachi Police. I have not been formally promoted, but I have been allowed a shoulder promotion since I am holding the position of superintendent of the prison." Faujis were always obsessed with uniformed ranks, constantly comparing their own to the civil ranks of the police and always trying to lord it over the poor cops.

"Ah. I see," said the major with a faintly disapproving air. He began studying his file without any regard to Constantine. Any attempts at pleasantry had been dispensed with. There was no doubt that this was an interview, and the file the major was reading was Constantine's dossier.

"Constantine Michael D'Souza. Born 1959, recruited as an assistant sub-inspector in 1981. Promoted to sub-inspector, 1988. Topped the Elite Special Police Group commando course, 1991. Worked with I Section in Operation Clean Slate, 1992. Wounded in a police encounter with activists of the United Progressive Front in 1998. Promoted out of turn as inspector in the same year for arresting Ateeq Tension, a UPF activist who was wanted in seventy murder cases. Promoted out of turn again, as deputy superintendent of police in 2002 for tracing out the Shi'a doctors' killings. Impressive."

"I can save you the time of going through that lengthy dossier, sir. Just ask me what you really want to know, and I'll tell you straight away. I have no problems with the Agencies. You can ask Colonel Tarkeen."

The major seemed to have picked up on Constantine's annoyance, so he changed tack. "No, I just like to be thorough in my research. Tell me, what is your job description as *superintendent* of the prison?" Up till this point, the major had still not removed his Tom Cruise sunglasses. Now he did so, revealing a horrible scar that ran diagonally across from just under his left eyebrow to the ridge of his cheek. Like some cruel joke, it seemed completely out of place with the major's otherwise handsome appearance. As if on cue, another man entered the room with another file in his hand.

He was obviously working for the major and had entered the room on some kind of pre-arranged signal.

"Well, sir, I, uh, am responsible for the total administration of the entire prison." Constantine was a little flustered at the sight of the major's scar and at the unauthorized entry of the major's subordinate into his office. He tried not to show it, but a quizzical expression crossed his face. Where was this questioning leading? Why were they bothered with his job description?

"Good. Then you are just the man I need." Without turning around, the major raised his hand and his subordinate handed him the second file, which he opened. "Mr. D'Souza, you are to hand over one of your prisoners, No. 2377, Akbar Khan, to my custody. My associate will go and fetch him, and I am to interrogate him on a matter of the *utmost* national urgency. When we are done with him, you will be duly informed and can collect the prisoner, but on no account are you to tell anyone about this. Kindly call one of your wardens so that we can start the procedure, I'm a little rushed for time."

Constantine was totally taken aback. He realized when Colonel Tarkeen had called him last night that whatever task this was was something big, but he did not realize the enormity of it till this moment. It was true that the Agencies kept talking to various prisoners in the jail, but they had never asked for custody of a prisoner. To take him out without any court order, no paperwork? And for interrogation? He understood very well what an "interrogation" entailed. But who was responsible if something happened to the prisoner? This bloody two-bit major was ordering these things as if he was the ultimate authority in these matters. But Constantine's biggest shock was the identity of the prisoner. It *was* him. After all this time, they were still after him.

It took all of Constantine's experience and training to not register the shock on his face. "Are you aware, sir, that the prisoner you refer to is still a serving police officer?"

"Yes, DSP D'Souza, I am aware of that. So what? He is not above us. We are from the Agencies. We can interrogate whomever we like."

Constantine looked up at the major's aide and gestured towards the door. "Excuse us for a minute, please." The aide scowled at Constantine and refused to leave. The major made no attempt to intervene.

Very well, if that's the way you want to play it, you pompous son of a bitch, thought Constantine. "Well sir, I will certainly try and assist you, but I'm afraid everything that you have asked for is not possible." Constantine's voice took on its most dispassionate, bureaucratic tone as he started listing his objections. "First, sir, it is against the prison rules to physically remove the prisoner from the jail premises without a court order. If any questions are to be asked, they must be done on the premises. Second, the prisoner's cooperation during any questioning while serving in prison is entirely voluntary. We cannot interrogate him like we do in a police station, nor can you force him to assist you. The fact that he is classified as an A-class prisoner and is a serving police officer makes the issue of forcing his cooperation even more difficult. And third, sir, I cannot permit you or your associate to interview the prisoner alone. The presence of a member of the jail staff is compulsory. Since I understand the sensitivity of your enquiries, I will *personally* be present." The last condition was not, strictly speaking, necessary, but Constantine had decided that the major would have to deal with him if he wanted any cooperation. Besides that, his curiosity was piqued about what they wanted out of Akbar Khan.

Constantine expected that the major's reaction would be apoplectic, seeing how he had flatly refused the major in front of his snotty assistant. The thought brought a thin smile of satisfaction to his face, as he sat back and waited for the inevitable.

The major finally dismissed his aide with an embarrassed nod of the head, before turning to address Constantine. "Look here, you bloody civilian, who do you think you're dealing with? I'm not some village idiot off the street. I know exactly what's going on here. All of you bloody police people are corrupt!" An accusing finger stabbed the air as his face flushed crimson. "Let me tell you, if I don't get some cooperation from you, I will call Colonel Saleem in the Accountability Bureau to investigate you. I have heard all the stories about corruption in the jail. Taking money from people just to have their home-cooked food delivered to them, or for them to have an extra five-minute meeting with their families. I'm sure the Accountability chaps will be interested in knowing how you can afford to wear that expensive Rolex wristwatch on your government salary."

The thin smile remained fixed on Constantine's face. He waited for a moment before responding, noticing the major's smug grin. "It's not a Rolex, it's a Tissot, and as for where it came from, why don't you ask General Ibadat's wife, who considers me like a son and gave it to me as a present." That wiped the grin off the major's face. "I'm afraid you're missing the point here, Major. If you have an issue with my integrity, please feel free to take it up with Colonel Tarkeen." Yes, after all the "favors" he had done for Tarkeen over the years, that would be an interesting discussion. "But the problem over here isn't corruption. I am willing to assist you, but within reason. I cannot change the prison rules for you. If you feel you don't have the experience to deal with this problem, please contact Colonel Tarkeen for guidance. In fact, I'll call him myself."

As he spoke, Constantine grabbed his mobile phone off the table and started punching in the digits. He observed with some satisfaction that the major was speechless. Snotty little shit. What did he think—that he was the first self-important young major that he had dealt with? Or was he still naïve enough to think that only cops were on the take?

He got through to Colonel Tarkeen and explained the situation to him. After a brief pause, he handed the phone to the major. "The colonel wants to have a word with you." Constantine was now positively enjoying the major's uncomfortable expression.

"Sir!" The major came to attention in his chair. For the next three minutes, Constantine listened in on a pretty one-sided conversation which consisted of plenty of notes of "Sir" and "Yes, sir" on the part of the major. At the end of it, he silently handed the phone back.

"He's new and doesn't understand how things work. Help him, Constantine. Do it your way, but I need you to help us out. It's very important. Rommel will explain everything to you."

"Thank you, sir. I'll try my best."

There was an uncomfortable silence after the phone went dead. Constantine was impassive, while the major seemed to be composing himself.

"Well, Major sahib?"

The major exhaled. "As you probably know, seven days ago, an American journalist was kidnapped. His name was Jon Friedland. He was a reporter for the *San Francisco Chronicle*. The media have been covering nothing else." Indeed, as Constantine glanced at the morning's newspaper that had been lying on his desk, it was all about the kidnapping. The independent media channels had been running special broadcasts dedicated to just this event. "Two days after his abduction, a group calling itself Lashkar-e-Jihad Waziristan posted a picture of him on the Internet. They said he was a Jew. They made no demands but claimed that they would make a horrible example of him, in retribution for the government operation in the tribal areas." He hesitated. "And they have said that they would do it on 25th December."

"Christmas."

"Yes. There have been no further communiqués from the group since then. So far the police have had no breakthrough in the investigation, and we, or our sister agencies, have also not been able to turn up anything. We have been looking at all the regular channels, but Colonel Tarkeen thought that we should also look at some unorthodox methods. He suggested the name of Akbar Khan. I don't know much about his past, but apparently his information sources in the city were unrivalled, before he got himself in trouble over some murder. We have to try everything. Right now we're not even sure if the American is still being held in Karachi or whether he's been transported somewhere else. To be honest, other than their word, we can't even confirm if he's still alive or not. I'm sure you realize the international significance of this kidnapping, on top of the insurgency in the tribal areas and the proposed visit of the American president. The image of the country is at stake. And of course, the deadline of 25th December means we have very little time to work. And we have to keep it completely confidential. Do you understand now? Can you help?"

"Yes sir, I do understand. And of course I will help. We can go see Akbar immediately. But sir, to be honest, I don't think he can be of much help."

"What do you mean?"

"Well sir, Akbar has been here for two years now. At the time of his arrest he was heading a special task force fighting organized crime. He was arrested, along with his entire team, for killing a suspect in a fake police encounter. At first he tried very hard to secure his release, hiring the best lawyers, trying to talk to all the high-ups of the police and the Agencies. But everyone abandoned him. After one year in jail, his fellow team members all but gave up on trying to secure a joint release. Some of them changed their statements, distanced themselves, and asked for deals. He didn't. But he didn't stop any of the others either. The end result was that they all got out, one by one, and he was left alone, burdened with the entire responsibility for the case. It was almost as if he didn't care anymore. He had been a powerful and influential police officer, but when the world forgot him, he forgot the world. The last of his colleagues got out about a year ago. Since then he stopped pursuing the case, stopped meeting his lawyers, even sent his family to his village. Broke off all contact with his team members or any police officers, for that matter. The case continues in the courts but with no one really following it up, and the courts being as slow and overworked as they are, it'll probably continue for years to come."

"He meets with no one?"

"For the past six months, the only visitors that he has met with are the tableeghis. They are a religious social organization who keep sending their maulvis into the prison to teach some of the inmates to read the Quran. He meets with them regularly and spends the whole day praying and reciting the Quran. But he takes interest in nothing else. Usually, A-class prisoners have access to outside material such as newspapers and books, but he hasn't asked for anything in six months. So you see, sir, that's why I doubt whether he may be of any use. He probably doesn't even know that an American has been kidnapped."

The major pondered this for a moment. Then he shrugged. "Well, Colonel Tarkeen seems to think he could be helpful, so even if nothing comes out of it, I am here already and should give it a try."

"Well, in that case, sir, let's go meet him."

2

They exited the office into the passageway. The major's aide stood sulking in a corner. The major told him to go stand outside by the car. Both men left their mobile phones with the warden at the gate and turned towards the second black gate that led to the prison courtyard. In front of them was a brightly painted wall, its cheeriness in complete contrast to the general air of despondency of the place. Behind the wall, in the main jail kitchen, some prisoners were cleaning up after breakfast. The giant vats in which breakfast had been made were being washed so that they could be reused for lunch. Another group of prisoners was busy painting plant pots. The convicts worked silently and no one looked up at the two men, but Constantine could feel that everyone was watching them. There were no wardens around. The major seemed surprised and looked questioningly at Constantine.

"Not what you expected, is it, sir? No rows of cells like in Hollywood movies. No one in handcuffs or chains."

"No wardens either. What do you do if something happens?"

"Yes, we are extremely short-staffed. But the jail has its own system of discipline, so the wardens don't usually have to intervene. Most of these men are harmless. Just look at their eyes. There is nothing there but hopelessness."

They turned right from the kitchen and started walking along the prison wall. In the distance they saw a solitary barrack with an air-conditioning unit protruding out of it. It had a neat walking track constructed around it, and there were fresh flower beds that had recently been planted outside it. Constantine pointed out the building to the major.

"That is Akbar's barrack. It is the only A-class barrack, and he is the only A-class prisoner that we have. They were originally set up for the husband of the ex–prime minister. He had the walking track laid, and installed the air conditioners. The rule that we have here is that any improvements that a prisoner makes to the jail are gifted to the prison after the prisoner leaves. But after he was released, the jail never received another A-class prisoner till Akbar came."

"Why was Akbar classified as A-class?"

"Quite frankly, that was the only thing that they could classify him as. The jail had never had a prisoner like him. They couldn't put him with anybody else. First, since he is a senior police officer, of course, but more importantly, because he had so many enemies there would have been a serious threat to his life. He had put away hundreds of the inmates. United Front activists, kidnappers, drug lords. They had to isolate him. If the others got half a chance, they'd have tried to kill him. Anyway, he prefers to be on his own."

"So none of the other inmates have any access to him? They can't approach him anywhere?"

"No. The area around that barrack is off-limits to everyone. None of the other prisoners are allowed to even wander nearby. One of the regular C-class prisoners attends to him, cleans up the barrack, plants the flowers, and brings him his food. He doesn't even come out that much. Occasionally you see him walking on the track in the evenings. The tableeghis are the only ones who go to that barrack, and with whom he meets. They are simple souls—just interested in promoting the reading of the Quran, handing out free religious texts and exhorting all the inmates to lead better lives. They do their rounds of the jail nearly every day, trying to win over some of the poor souls."

"Do they get a lot of converts?"

"Some. They have certainly succeeded with him."

They were now outside the door to the barrack. The prisoner who had been tending to the flower beds greeted them silently and held open the door for them. Inside, the barrack was a revelation. The room was long and rectangular in shape. The walls were bare and painted spotlessly white. The floor tiles were also a glistening white color. The room had a faint antiseptic odor, like a hospital room. Immediately to the left of the door, in a corner, lay some unused exercise equipment, treadmills and some weights, left over by the previous occupant. In the far right corner of the room was a large wardrobe. In the center of the room was a big mattress with a red blanket. It was the only item of color in the otherwise sterile room. There were three low wooden stools facing the mattress. On one of them, with his back towards the door, a man sat hunched over, reciting from a copy of the Quran. He was dressed in a crumpled white cotton shalwar-kameez. He wore a white skullcap, and long, salt-and-pepper shoulder-length locks flowed from under the cap. The man had a shaggy, unkempt beard which had turned prematurely white. He looked as if he had lost a lot of weight, but his sinewy muscles remained taut under the fabric of his clothes. Although he was only middle-aged, his gaunt appearance made him look much older than he was.

The manservant who had ushered them in approached the seated man and whispered in his ear as Constantine and the major stood by the door. The man made no sign of acknowledgement and continued his recitation. The two officers shuffled uncomfortably, not knowing what to do next. Both of the room's split air-conditioning units were working at full blast, so the room was freezing cold. Constantine cleared his throat loudly a couple of times to catch the prisoner's attention, but it was a full five minutes till the man finished his recitation and turned to them. He beckoned them towards the empty stools and nodded his head in recognition to Constantine.

"Aur Consendine, how are you keeping these days?" His voice was raspy, as if rusty from lack of use.

"How are you, Akbar? You've become very fit, eh? On some new magic diet, are you?"

"Heh heh. Jail is the magic diet. Try it, and you'll also lose that belly of yours."

"I'll take your word for it." Constantine took one of the stools and beckoned the major to sit on the other. He was nervous, not sure how to begin, so he cleared his throat. "Do you have any problems in the jail that I can help you with?"

"Arre, Consendine, you and I know this isn't a social call. The real question is, how can I help you?" Akbar turned to the major. "Kyun, Major sahib, looks like you've lost your American songbird?" He cackled again, revealing a set of blackened, broken teeth.

Constantine raised his brow in surprise. The major, totally stunned, sputtered. "How the hell did you know my rank?"

"Relax, Major sahib. You are too young to be a colonel, and too old to be a mere captain. From the looks of you, you too have had some rough lovers, like me." He pushed his hair aside from the right side of his neck to reveal a nasty scar that had been caused by a jagged piece of metal.

For the second time that day, the major had to take a moment to compose himself. He took out a packet of cigarettes from his pocket and offered one to Akbar.

Akbar stared at the cigarette for a moment before taking it. "Heh. I haven't smoked one of these in six months." The major lit it for him, and he took a deep and appreciative puff.

"Well, uh, Akbar, I am here on behalf of Colonel Tarkeen to ask for your help in a matter of national emergency. You are correct in assuming that my query does concern the recent kidnapping of the American journalist. Any information that you may have, any way that you think you can help us, would be appreciated and the assistance that you provide will of course be looked upon favorably in any court proceeding."

Akbar seemed to reflect on the major's words. Then he smiled. "I'll say this for you, Major sahib, at least you're polite, compared to some of the other bastards in your department. No, thank you. I don't wish to help you."

"What do you mean you don't wish to help us? It's not a matter of wishing. If you have any information about this matter, you cannot withhold it. It's a matter of supreme *national importance*! *The nation's honor is at stake*!" The major's voice rose as his self-righteous indignation came to the surface.

"Fuck the nation's honor." The words were spoken softly but with such viciousness that the major looked as if he had been physically struck. Constantine's body tensed, preparing to step in to tackle in case either of the men became physical.

The major was on his feet. "Look here! You can't talk like that. I have served in this army for eleven years. I will not let anyone speak about the country in that fashion!"

Akbar waved him away. "Please, save it for some stupid chutiya straight out of the Training College, Major sahib. I'm not some child still suckling at his mother's breast! I know how your people work and how long they've been raping the 'nation's honor' as if it were some two-bit randi standing at the street corner. You people use words like 'honor' and 'country' to get people to do what you want them to do, then throw them away like a used condom! I'm one of your condoms too! Tell Tarkeen I haven't forgotten that!"

"I . . . I don't understand," stuttered the major.

"What don't you understand? What did you expect? That you would walk in here and give me your bullshit sermon, and I would roll over and kiss your boots and thank you and say that just getting the opportunity to serve my country was enough for me? What do you have to offer me in return, Major sahib? You'll have to barter with me if you want my help because, I'm sorry, but I have just about exhausted my stock of patriotism."

"But I'm not authorized to negotiate any terms."

"If you're not authorized to negotiate, you're not authorized to do anything, Major sahib. What can you do? 'Interrogate' me? I don't think so. I'm already in prison. I'm afraid we must conclude this meeting, Major sahib. I have to return to my recitations, and you must go back and pray that they don't find the body of a dead American in some gutter on Christmas day. Khuda Hafiz." With that, he turned around, picked up his book and started to read from it.

The major looked at Constantine for help. "Akbar, I know how you feel, but please think about it. Maybe Major Rommel can come back tomorrow after you've had some time to think it over?"

"I look forward to future visits from Major sahib, Consendine, but it is they who must do the thinking."

The major and Constantine got up and started walking towards the door. Just as they were about to open the door, Akbar called out to them.

"By the way, thank you for the cigarette, Major sahib. Because you are a nice man, I will tell you one thing. You needn't worry about sending search parties all over the country. Your songbird is still in Karachi, and he is still alive. Tell Colonel sahib he can confirm it from his special source, the one I introduced him to in the lobby of the Sheraton Hotel eight years ago."

Constantine guided the major back to his office. The younger man was quiet, as if suffering from shell shock. Constantine had also been astonished by Akbar's disclosure and was curious about how he had obtained his information, but he preferred to keep his own counsel till he found out more.

"Come sir, you've had a difficult morning, let's have a cup of tea." Constantine rang a bell on his desk to call his orderly. The tea arrived five minutes later, but the major didn't say a single word in the intervening time, absentmindedly staring at Akbar's file in his hand. *Just like Tarkeen to send this poor green bastard for this kind of assignment*, thought Constantine.

"He seemed to know you. From before, I mean."

"Yes, sir. We started out together, on the force. We were junior assistant sub-inspectors in Preedy Police Station. We served together for a number of years, in some tough times."

The major cupped his hands in front of his face and leaned forward in his chair. "Who is this man? I have never met anyone like him. Why does Colonel Tarkeen think he is so important?"

"He is perhaps the best police officer in the Karachi Police. At least in my years of service, I haven't seen a better one. You see, sir, to be a good police officer in this city, you need to have two qualities. First, very good sources of information, so that you can work out crimes, trace cases, catch the big criminals. And second, you need to have a lot of courage—courage to do what others are unwilling or unable to do. You need a very big heart, sir. Akbar had both qualities in abundance. At the height of his power, he had a steady stream of informants from all over the city, and from all walks of life. And courage? I have never seen a more courageous man than Akbar. Colonel sahib is not a fool. He knows the value of men very well, sir. And he certainly knows how valuable Akbar is."

"What did he do that was so valuable?"

"You are new in Karachi, sahib. It's your first posting here? Yes, you wouldn't know the times we went through. Back when Akbar and I started out, policing was very simple. Burglars, pickpockets, the odd phadda at the university. Simple criminals for a simple time. We were junior officers, and when our station in-charge sent us out into the field, we would round up a few miscreants, slap them around, and that was the end of it. The only weapons they had were knives and knuckledusters. The kid who had a revolver was considered a real terror. No one challenged the authority of the police. All the big badmashes of Karachi were tough guys in front of ordinary people, but when the lowliest head constable summoned them to the thana, they meekly obeyed. Things changed when the United Front came onto the scene and brought a new brand of goonda politics. Their leader, the Don, had started out as a student activist at the university. He created the system of the UF's wards and ward bosses. The wards were crews of young men who were supposed to create a party structure at the very basic neighborhood level. But in reality they created a parallel government where they had the power of taxation, dispute resolution, punishment, even life and death, over the citizens of the city. That's when the terror began. Kalashnikovs started coming into the city from Afghanistan, brought by Pathan truck drivers who sold them to their own people as well as their enemies. Then the campus violence began between the UF boys and everyone else. Things got nastier after that—massacres on buses, firing between rival groups, targeted killings. We didn't know how to confront these new criminals. That's when all our lives got truly fucked up, sahib." Constantine slowly shook his head, as if troubled by bitter memories. "Such a terrible time."

"How? I mean, how did things go wrong?" Rommel looked mesmerized by Constantine's account.

"Arre, sahib, we were so backward back then. We didn't know anything about weapons or tactics. I remember, the only rifles we had in the police station were World War II surplus rifles. I still remember their name—.303 Lee Enfield. Heh. But none of us was prepared for the wave of violence that swept this city over the next few years. When the UF first came to power, it was as if a mafia had taken over the city. Their rule was absolute. They crushed anyone who stood in their way. They made fake cases against their opponents and had them locked up. But all politicians do that. The UF went further than anyone else. They had hit squads to bump off their rivals. No case could be registered against their workers in any police station. If a station in-charge even talked to one of their ward bosses in a wrong tone, he would find himself demoted and posted to some godforsaken police station in the middle of the desert. Stopping their excesses was out of the question. The ward bosses extorted money, ran gambling dens, carried weapons openly, kidnapped people's daughters . . . and we would sit in our police stations and do nothing." His voice trailed off as if even the memory was painful. "I remember, one day I was the duty officer at Preedy Police Station and an old man came into the station, crying that his daughter had been kidnapped by the local UF ward boss because he fancied her. The old man sat in front of me on the station floor all day, crying and begging us to go with him, to try and save his daughter from getting gang-raped. We even knew which room of which building they were fucking her in. But none of us did anything because they were in power. Except for Akbar. He was the only one who stood up against them."

The major had grown more and more absorbed by the conversation and was about to ask how all of this related to Akbar, when his mobile phone rang. From the major's stirring it was obviously Tarkeen, and when the call finished, he got up.

"That was Colonel Tarkeen. I have to return to my office immediately. I will call and tell you if we need to conduct another interview with Akbar." He had walked to the door when he turned towards Constantine again. "I, uh, I would like to talk with you some more. Perhaps later, but I would like to listen. Thank you." He hesitated for a moment and looked awkwardly at the floor, perhaps wanting to say more, and then walked out.

Constantine, seemingly lost in the past, half rose from his chair and absentmindedly grunted his goodbyes. He sat back down and picked up his teacup. He stared intently at the swirling brown liquid within the cup, as if it would give him some sign of salvation. But it did not.

3

May 1996, ten years ago

Constantine was in a shitty mood. This seemed to be a continuous state for him these days. He walked out of his quarters, leaving behind the shrill voice of his wife, hoping that being outdoors would make him feel better. But it didn't. He felt a revulsion towards himself. He didn't understand why, but it had been this way for months now. A glance in the mirror as he walked out had only served to worsen his mood. He could see that his waist, while by no means fat, was beginning to slip; the hockey player's washboard stomach was no longer there. It had been ages since he had last exercised.

He had fought with his wife again: over what, he honestly couldn't tell. He seemed to pick fights with her for no real reason. Later, he would spend the rest of the day feeling bad about it, but he couldn't help himself. His father had forced him to get married to a nice Christian girl a year ago. Mary was a perfectly decent woman, pretty enough and dutiful to a fault. She took great pains to fit in with his family. A real homemaker. But he had never mentally adjusted to married life.

He had started to hide himself in his work. Long hours and late nights at the police station became an excuse for staying away from home. Constantine was the longest serving officer at Preedy Police Station. That in itself was quite an achievement, because Preedy was considered to be the most lucrative police station in the city and people would give an arm and a leg to be posted there even for a few months. A smart station in-charge could easily become a millionaire if he managed to eke out a half-decent tenure at Preedy. Constantine knew he would never become station in-charge because he had no influential political connections. But in his own way, because of his experience and contacts within the area, he was indispensable to those who did have the requisite contacts. After all, someone needed to actually run the station while the station in-charge conducted his business deals.

He had made some decent money over the years, nothing that would justify an early retirement but enough to support a young family's expenses. His daughter was now two months old, and he had to think about their future. Increasingly, though, even money held no charm for him anymore. There was a sense of lost purpose that gnawed at him, the impending fear of wasted youth and the onset of dreary middle age. The job no longer held any challenges for Constantine. And after what had happened two days ago, there was no honor either.

He decided to walk the short distance from his quarters in the police lines to the station. It was hot and sticky. A sea of humanity engulfed the streets of Karachi's city center. He walked past the electronics market where prosperous shop owners, who had just refurbished their stalls with new air conditioners and shiny tiles, tried to shoo away passersby who spat out betel juice on the freshly painted walls. Street hawkers, weighed down by their carry trays, offered every conceivable model of mobile phone accessory to passing customers. Past the electronics market, he crossed the junction where the old booksellers bazaar intersected the tire market. Metallic radial Bridgestone tires sold alongside dog-eared copies of the complete works of Jane Austen. The vibrancy of the city at this hour never failed to amaze Constantine, and he would usually take a minute out of his walk to stand there and smell the ozone fumes. It was the smell of progress, his mentor station officer used to say. Today he didn't linger, and, as he strode into the thana to report for his shift, the officer he was about to relieve greeted him with a warm smile.

"Arre, Consendine sahib, thirty minutes early? I was expecting you to come late today. Didn't the naika arrange a hot date for you?"

"I never went. I wasn't in the mood for it, Ali Hasan."

Sub-inspector Ali Hasan frowned. "Arre, sahib, this is what the English mean when they say it is looking a gift horse in the mouth. First, the naika, the chief madam and the most powerful figure in the locality, arranges the girl for you, free of cost. And then you don't even bother going because you say you didn't feel like it? Sahib, I have been here six months, and I am still waiting for the day the naika offers me a girl for free. I can't even complain openly lest she gets annoyed and slams shut our monthly payment. After all, she is the guarantor of our economic prosperity. When she comes to the station to negotiate the monthly rate for the brothels, we mere mortals have to lower our eyes and say 'Adab' to her like Mughal courtiers. But you? You are her favorite sub-inspector. You're exempt from all the arse-kissing. I bet she's offered you more pussy than she has to the station in-charge."

"That's just because I've been here so long that I knew her before she even became the naika. I am sure she only does it out of pity for my pathetic career prospects."

"Arre, sahib, leave it. Do you know how many times I had to go sit outside the ward office to get my posting here? While the rest of us run after one sifarish or the other, you have been enjoying yourself in this thana for years because everyone knows that the station in-charge won't be able to run the area without you. Arre, sahib, the senior officers think well of you, even the party has a good impression of you. The other night I had gone to pay my respects at the ward office, and the ward boss was telling one of the UF ministers that you are a very fair man. If you would just heed my advice and come with me one day to meet him, he'll have you posted as the SHO within the week."

"I told you, I'm not going to go down that path. I don't want to have anything to do with the UF or any of their ward bosses. I'm fine where I am, Ali Hasan. Now tell me, where is in-charge sahib?"

"Suit yourself, sahib. But I'll tell you one thing. The boss is on his way out. A smart man would take advantage of that. He was called in to the ward office. Apparently the party didn't like the disturbance that was caused when the old man came looking for his daughter a couple of days ago. Yesterday the girl committed suicide, and it's caused a bit of a scandal. The father was screaming and abusing the Don at the funeral. I think one of the newspapers also got hold of the story and wrote about it. That's why the ward boys were out on the streets early today, to confiscate all the copies of the paper. Anyway, they aren't happy with the way in-charge sahib handled the situation."

Constantine stared blankly at Ali Hasan and then broke into a cynical smile. "Why, what the hell did they expect us to do? They raped the girl to their heart's content, we didn't stop them. We sat here like a bunch of cockless hijras! How else would they like in-charge sahib to further improve the quality of his service? Did they want us to join in?"

"Consendine sahib, how could we intervene? They had taken her to the ward office. You know their boys are off-limits for us. Anyway, the wardias say that in-charge sahib shouldn't have allowed the father to loiter at the station for the whole day. It just attracted attention to the situation. He should have thrown out the old man well before the evening. They say that is precisely why they had in-charge sahib posted here, to handle situations like these."

"Oh, I see. So it was inconvenient to have the old man beg for his daughter's life, was it? What about our job as police officers?"

"Consendine sahib, now you're acting like a child. Power is in their hands, and we have to listen to those who are in power. You think I didn't feel bad for that old man that day? Of course I did. We all have daughters, sisters, and wives. But we stay quiet because we don't want what happened to his daughter to happen to our loved ones. Our duty is to obey the ruling party, not the law. And the Don and his wardias rule this city. Who are we to say anything to them?"

"Yes, the great Don controls this city from America but doesn't have the balls to step inside it."

Ali Hasan's tone dipped to a whisper, and he looked around to ensure that he was not overheard. "I am trying to advise you for your own good, but then you keep making such loose talk. If you want to make a mess of your own career, that's fine, but don't drag the rest of us down. The Don doesn't need to come back to order the killing of a stupid sub-inspector with a big mouth, or a hundred others who don't know when to keep quiet. Now stop being foolish and take over the desk. I want to get home."

Ali Hasan shoved the station register towards Constantine with some irritation. For the briefest moment, it occurred to Constantine that Ali Hasan would report their conversation to the ward office, but he was past caring anymore. It had brought back all the disgust and the deep sense of impotence he had been experiencing since the day the girl was abducted. He could taste the bile rising in his stomach. He looked again at Ali Hasan and saw in his face the smug self-assuredness of a man who was content in the knowledge that he was going places in life. Just as Constantine sat down, he saw the station in-charge, Inspector Deedar, cross the outgoing Ali Hasan at the station gate. The SHO had the look of a condemned man, and Constantine saw the subtle snub that Ali Hasan directed at him by not saluting him properly. He decided that, no matter what he thought of his boss, he would give him due respect even if his authority was slipping away.

"Ah good, Consendine, you're already here. Ensure that all the pickets and patrols are sent out. I can't deal with that right now, I've got too much on my plate. Oh, and send the patrolling vehicle to the house of the ward boss. His family needs to attend a wedding, and they need the escort." He tossed a brown envelope onto the table. "Oh, and the beater has just delivered the weekly collection. Take out the station expenses and bring the rest of it in to my retiring room."

Constantine took out the thin wad of bills from the brown envelope. "Sir, the beater has given you less than the fixed amount today. And sir, we only have one pickup today because the other two are in the workshop. If we send this one away on escort duty, the area will be empty."

Inspector Deedar's frustration boiled over at Constantine's response. "Look, dammit, I've had enough of you, you bloody Christian! Do you have any idea of the problems I have to face? I am in trouble with the ward boss because you let that old fool sit in front of you all day long! Why did you even listen to his complaint? You should have thrown him out of the station or, even better, arrested him! I had to pay the ward boss half of this month's collection to get them to clear us! I have no desire to end my days arresting sheepfuckers on the edge of the desert or worse, being taken into a ward office and being tortured! Maybe you do. If so, you can call up the ward boss and inform him yourself that you find it inconvenient to send an escort for his family. I have tolerated you enough! You may be a good manager but if you don't learn your place in this police station, you might as well just fuck off from here!"

Constantine's face reddened and his body tensed, as if to strike the SHO. But Ashraf, who was the duty constable alongside him, restrained him. Inspector Deedar turned around and walked towards his room. Constantine glared after him, as Ashraf whispered in his ear to calm him down. He needed to get out of there, so he stormed out of the station. He was still fuming when he got to the main gate and didn't notice the man in the starched white shalwar-kameez who came up to him and tapped him on the shoulder. He was very fair, with a shock of brown hair and a bristling handlebar moustache that had been finely waxed.

"Kya, Consendine. So much anger at me? Just because I still owe you a little money?"

"Akbar!" For the first time that day, Constantine's face lit up. "What are you doing here? And it isn't a little amount you owe me, it's quite a lot! But I am so happy to see you. I'm having a really bad day. The in-charge is probably going to have me booted out of here. Come, let's get out of here and get something to eat."

Akbar grew concerned. He put his hand on Constantine's shoulder as they walked out of the station gates towards a nearby roadside restaurant. "What's wrong? What happened? Anything I can do to help?"

"It's nothing, yaar. Normal work phaddas—political interference, all that kind of stuff. You know how it is. Fact is, these past few days I just haven't been myself. But tell me about yourself. Are you still holed up in that Special Investigation Cell of yours? Don't you ever want to do a real job?"

They had seated themselves in a booth of a restaurant across the street from the police station. The restaurant had an old, faded sign that proclaimed it as IRANI CAFÉ, with SPONSORED BY PEPSI hand-painted in small print below the name. Nobody knew why it was called Irani Café, as there was nothing remotely Iranian about it, from the food (which consisted mostly of variations of the same basic curry, with mutton, prawn, and chicken, and the Special, which was also the same curry with a hard-boiled egg thrown in for good measure) to the staff, whose hooked noses and fair skin earmarked them as men from the Swat Valley. Indeed, even the owner, a fat Punjabi who sat at the counter overseeing the various vats of curry bubble away, couldn't have told you why the name was what it was, except to say that this had been the name when he had bought the joint from its previous owner thirty years ago.

A raised hand from Constantine to the owner brought them instant service. After all, the owner was on excellent terms with all the police wallahs at the station. He allowed the constables to eat for free and gave a hefty discount to the officers. In return, no one ever bothered to ask him for extortion money and, in the evenings, his waiters could extend the restaurant's seating area from the curbside, encroaching right onto half of the main road. Communicating with his staff only through very slight movements of his head, he ensured that four waiters, laden with several plates of curry representing more or less everything on the menu, soft drinks, and naan hot from the tandoor descended upon Constantine and Akbar even before they had settled down.

Akbar tore off a piece of naan and dipped it into a plate of curry swimming in oil. "Arre, chutiya, this is your misconception. That is our real work. Catching criminals, not this clerical work and political ass-kissing that you do in Preedy. But I'm not in the Cell anymore."

"Have you gone back to a thana? Which one?"

"Not exactly. I got suspended last week."

"What for?"

"I got this complaint, that someone was kidnapping young boys from their neighborhood in New Karachi and demanding ransom from the parents. I haven't worked in that area before, but my informer gave me a hint of who it was. Turned out it was a group of madarchod ward boys who were making some money for themselves on the side. The children they were abducting were barely four or five years old. I raided the apartment and recovered one of them. You know me, I became a meter. I took the madarchod ward boss and dragged him by his hair down to the street. The whole neighborhood saw it. He tried to threaten me, so I told him I'd fuck his mother in front of his eyes, and then I thrashed him in front of everyone. That shut him up for good. Heh. I took him back to the cell and locked him up. My own DSP shat a brick when he found out, but I told him: 'Sahib, these haramkhors were abducting children. If I hadn't caught them red-handed it would be a different thing, but now that I've got them, I'm not going to let them off. So I booked them.'" Akbar narrated all of this with his particular brand of nonchalance, stuffing his mouth with raw onion and radish from a plate of salad and downing almost an entire can of Pepsi, before belching in satisfaction.

"You booked them, and the party allowed you to book their boys? Simple as that?"

"Well, they told the DSP to suspend me. He was more than happy to do it because he didn't want this film around his neck. But the fact is that once the case is registered, it's a matter for the judge. Nothing they do to me is going to help them out in that respect."

"What will you do now? I'm sure they aren't going to stop with just your suspension, and at this moment in time you're not going to be able to find anyone to do sifarish for you."

"Arre, Consendine, I'm not going to beg them for a job. Besides, I'm glad to be rid of that DSP. Saala, his fatigues were never-ending. Do you know, before this incident happened, I was getting screwed with him because of my friendship with you."

"Who is your DSP?"

"Maqsood Mahr."

"But I don't even know him. Why would he screw you because of me?"

"Heh. I know you don't know him, but he knows you are Christian. Somehow he got it in his head that being a Christian, you'd have easy access to foreign booze because so many of the bootleggers in the city are Christian. So he started making demands on me. First it was a bottle of whisky every other day. Then it became a couple of bottles a day. Then a whole case of Black Label every week. A whole fucking case! Do you know how much that costs? Bhenchod, I nearly went broke! I started having nightmares about cases of Black Label. And every time I had to fulfil the *fatigue*, I would curse you. I wanted to tell him that my chutiya Christian friend wouldn't know the difference between whisky and a bottle of piss. But kya karoon, that bastard Mahr just doesn't take no for an answer. He's so bloody greedy. No matter how much money he makes, his stomach asks for more. Never satisfied. Good riddance."

Constantine smiled. It was a typical Akbar Khan story. "But seriously, what are you going to do about the UF? You know they aren't going to let you go like this."

"Look Consendine, I did what I had to do. Now they can do whatever the fuck they want. You can't live your life always scared of the fact that someone is going to take a shit on you from above. These UF madarchods aren't the final authority on life and death in this city. There are forces more powerful than them also."

"Look Akbar, this is hardly the time to start becoming religious. God isn't going to come down and help you when a ward boss is holding a gun to your head."

"Arre, chutiya, I'm not talking about God. I'm talking about the Agencies. No one is more powerful than them in this country." He lowered his tone and spoke in a conspiratorial whisper. "They called me, you know. The day after I booked the ward boss. Very nice fellow, a major called Tarkeen. I told him the whole story, and he told me not to worry. They are taking up my case. You see, both the Agencies—the Kaaley Gate wallahs and the Bleak House wallahs—are not very happy with the UF government. And you know what that means."

"What does that mean? Aren't the Agencies part of the same government that the United Front heads? What can they possibly do?"

"Arre, Consendine, are you actually that thick or is this an act that you're putting on? Arre, baba, the Agencies are never under any party or government. They are above the government. They decide who gets to rule and who doesn't. And if they've decided that they aren't happy with the UF, then it means these ward thugs are on their way out. The Agencies have started their work. Major Tarkeen told me that they were taking notice of all these stories about the UF ward bosses and soon they were going to set up a special unit to deal with these bastards. They are going to put me in charge of the unit. It's all top-secret right now."

Constantine heard himself respond to Akbar in a whisper. "Are you serious?"

"Yes. There are many people in the corridors of power who are sick of the UF's gangsterism. Major sahib has told me that I can bring anyone I want with me into the unit. That's why I came to see you—to ask if you want to be in this with me. Don't worry about a thing. You don't have to do anything right now. When the time is right, the Agencies will call for us and then we will be working solely for them. No bloody interference from anybody. And I'm telling you, the time isn't far. I know you've been having a tough time over here. But this will be work that matters. We will have a mission, a purpose."

"But Akbar, all of this sounds too fantastic—special units, working without any interference. No one even dare raise their eyes to anything the UF does, leave alone taking them on. How will all these things come to pass? This major of yours has just fed you a tall tale."

"These are the Agencies, Consendine. Anything is possible for them. Besides, what is the alternative? Do you want to continue to work like you are right now? I overheard your argument with your SHO. Is this the kind of bullshit that you want to put up with? Is this the way you want to live? I don't know about you, but I took up this job to be a police officer, not a bloody clerk. I came to you because I have always thought that you felt the same way. So come on, are you with me?"

Constantine took a sharp intake of breath and stared at Akbar, who was holding out his hand across the small table. He looked around for an instant, to check if anyone had overheard them, and then gazed out from the window of the little restaurant onto the crush of traffic outside. All he could hear was the cacophony of bus horns, blown by drivers desperate to get home. He bit his lower lip, as if deliberating over a particularly difficult decision. But the truth was, his decision was never really that hard. He had reached the same conclusion and it was fate, or the Lord's will, as his father would have put it, that Akbar had come to visit him this day. His face cracked into a smile, and he finally took Akbar's hand in his.

"Akbar Khan, you are my oldest friend in the force. I would follow you anywhere. Count me in."

Akbar's eyes sparkled. "Heh. That's more like it. Now I wish I had saved some of that Black Label."

4

The stench was overpowering. Constantine could smell it over the carbon dioxide fumes of the rickshaw. What was worse, the monsoon rain had reduced the garbage into a kind of slushy mixture that flowed ankle-deep onto the road. The rain had been beating down hard for the past three hours. Constantine cursed as the rickshaw driver pulled up just short of the police station compound. It meant he would have to wade through the slush just to get to the gate of the station. But the driver had flatly refused to go right up to the gate, because he feared that he might be taken for a police sympathizer. Constantine shook his head in disgust. Orangi was a long way from the bright lights of Preedy.

The sentry at the gate was a frightened rookie, barely out of his teens. He wore a uniform three sizes too large and viewed Constantine with great suspicion, unbelieving that a police officer would actually want to come to this place. Finally, having satisfied himself that Constantine was indeed a sub-inspector, he took him inside. On one side of the station wall, there was a gaping hole with blast marks on the edges. A pair of shirtless laborers continued to repair the wall despite the rain.

The sentry took Constantine into a room which had a signboard outside proclaiming it to be the station in-charge's office. To call it an office would be stretching imagination considerably, as it was little more than a shack walled with unplastered bricks. There were several buckets in the room to collect water from the innumerable leaks in the ceiling, and a dangerously exposed electric wire was connected to the solitary light bulb.

At the desk sat Akbar Khan, looking out of place in this hovel with his smart new uniform and freshly waxed moustache.

"Well, you took your bloody time getting here, didn't you?" The young sentry was surprised that it was the new sub-inspector who mouthed those words, rather than in-charge sahib.

"Consendine! Thank God you're here. It's so good to see you! Come, sit. Bachay, go tell the munshi to send some tea. And some samosas, if you get any in this godforsaken locality. So Consendine, remember what I told you last time we met? These UF bastards were on their way out. I told you the Agencies would come through."

"Yeah, you told me that over a year ago. When we last spoke, I thought it was going to happen in a matter of days. I picked a fight with my SHO and, as a result, got posted to Orangi Extension, the worst thana in the city. I have been stuck in that shithole for the past year and a half, hoping for deliverance from your Agencies."

"Arre, baba, they don't work on exact schedules. Sometimes events come in the way of their planning. When I spoke to you that day in Preedy, they had already begun working on getting rid of the UF. But then these things can take time, yaar. The Agencies have to also look at the big picture in the country."

"You and your damn Agencies, Akbar. They are also badshah log. First they created this monster of a party, and then when that party started getting too big for its boots, they tired of it and decided that it was being run by a bunch of anti-state criminals. They should never have given these UF bastards so much leeway. Now it's impossible to control them. No one is willing to move against the ward bosses. So what have they sent you here for, after so long? This operation has been on for the past three months, but no sign of you."

"They got my suspension reversed as soon as the UF left the coalition, but they had me posted to the interior, because there was still a possibility of the government cutting a deal with the UF. I told Major Tarkeen that it was foolish to think the party would change its ways, but there were those in the government who still wanted the United Front's political support at any price."

"Well, it's a price we've been paying in blood here in the streets."

"I had heard it had gotten worse, but I didn't realize how bad. When I came to take charge yesterday, no one was wearing uniform in this station. Then last night, they fired a rocket at the station wall."

"The rocket is the local ward's way of greeting the new SHO. They did the same thing to the fellow you replaced. He didn't step out of this compound after that for three months. No one wears a uniform because no one wants to be identified as a police officer outside. The rickshaw driver who dropped me here wasn't willing to pull up in front of the station gates. In some cases some officers still go out in the area, like my SHO, for instance. But that's because he has an understanding with the ward boss. It's the same all over. Either our people have been frightened off, or they've become collaborators. If I were you, I'd be very careful about my own staff. Half of them are linked to the party."

"Yes, I got that impression from their reluctance to disclose any information on the whereabouts of the local ward office. They're more scared of those bhenchods than they are of me. Heh. But that will soon change."

"You can't blame them, Akbar. The few who did try and conduct some raids were killed the next day by UF death squads. Everyone else chickened out after that. Myself included."

Akbar stared out of the tiny slit between concrete blocks that served as a window. "You see those laborers working in the rain? Last night they weren't willing to come and fix the wall. I even offered to double their wages. They still said no. Like your rickshaw driver, they were wary of being identified with the police. Then I held a pistol to the foreman's head and told him to get to work, so now you see they are still working despite the downpour. You have to show everybody that you are the bigger badmash."

"So what do you want me to do?"

"You are going to be my eyes and ears. You are the only one I can trust here. That's why I arranged your posting here as my No. 2. You are going to run things on my behalf over here. Whatever you say goes. If there's anyone else you want to bring with you from Orangi Extension, tell me and I'll get their orders done. Anyone whom you feel is mixed up with the wardias, we'll have them transferred out. By the way, who's the SP?"

"You mean you haven't met Hanuman yet?"

"No. Our orders came straight from corps headquarters. They didn't want the information to leak out before we had taken charge, so Major Tarkeen ordered me to go straight to the police station. I haven't been to the SP office yet. Hanuman. Is he a Hindu?"

Constantine chuckled. "No, that's his nickname. You know the story about the Hindu God Hanuman having two faces? That's our SP sahib. One minute he says one thing, the next minute he will do the exact opposite. Somehow he manages to get along with whoever is in power. Before the operation started, everyone used to say he was the khas-o-khas of the UF. Now the new government has come in, and he is the only SP in Karachi who hasn't been replaced. Competent fellow, though. Knows every nook and cranny of the area, knows exactly what's going on where. Always keeps us on our toes. And he's not averse to calling up the thana in the middle of the night and speaking to the duty sentry, to find out what's going on."

"Is he into money?"

"A little bit here and there. Nothing like Maqsood Mahr."

"Sounds like an interesting fellow. I'll have to meet him. But first, tell me about the area."

"In one word, it's a tinderbox waiting to explode. The Pathans live on Pirabad Hill, the Bengalis and the Biharis live at the base of the hill. The communities have been at each other's throats for years. On top of that the UF goondas moved in, and now they run the place like a feudal fiefdom."

"So where do I find these feudal lords?"

"Their ward office is in an abandoned school halfway up the hill. They call it the Hajji Camp."

"What sort of a name is that?"

"Because they say that going there is almost as good as going for Hajj. If you survive what they put you through, then God will surely absolve you of all your sins."

"Heh. Witty bastards, aren't they? How's the money in this thana?"

"It used to be very good. There were a number of gambling and prostitution dens running in the area, but now they all pay the ward instead of the thana because they recognize that the real power lies there. The officers before you were afraid of offending the ward boss, so they never challenged that claim. They resorted to doing all the things that our mentor Chaudhry Latif used to warn us against, when we were probationary ASIs in Preedy."

"You mean they were taking drug money?"

"Not just that. They also took money from cop killers to look the other way. And whatever other crumbs the ward boss chose to give to them."

"Madarchods. Heh. Old Chaudhry Latif was a wise man. He had his own moral code and never compromised on it through a lifetime of cleaning up the shit in this city."

"Yes, he was a good man."

"So, since all our problems stem from the ward office, let's raid it."

"Akbar, are you serious? It's virtually a fortress. They have a massive arms dump there, living quarters for their men and torture chambers in the basement. No SHO has ever raided the Hajji Camp."

"Good. All the better if we can recover some weapons from them." Akbar saw the look of awe and horror on Constantine's face and smiled. "Look Consendine, I didn't come here to sit in this shitty little room for three months and be scared of my own fucking shadow. Either I'm going to stay in this area or these madarchods will. Now make me plans for the raid. I want to do it tonight. We'll catch the bastards off-guard."

By nightfall the rain had finally let up, but the sky was pitch-black. Constantine had spent the time since his meeting with Akbar making preparations for the raid. The staff at the station, not accustomed to doing their jobs, were responding with a mixture of shock and awe as Constantine supervised them. They stared at him with wide-eyed bewilderment even when he gave the simplest of orders. A few hours and many curses later, Constantine was confident that he had restored a semblance of discipline to the station.

He hadn't seen Akbar since morning, but as there was a steady stream of visitors of varying backgrounds to and from his office, he assumed that Akbar had been inside all day long, getting some feedback on the area. It was approaching midnight, and he walked to the SHO's room to apprise Akbar of the station's state of near readiness. As he entered the room, he saw a figure dressed in tattered clothes with his back turned towards the door, taking off a filthy head cloth and placing it on the table. Constantine shook his head. It was shocking that a street beggar could walk into the SHO's office like this without being challenged.

He grabbed the man by the back of his neck. "Oye saale, where do you think you are? Is this your bloody bedroom that you feel you can comfortably undress here?"

A smiling Akbar Khan turned around to face him. His normally immaculate moustache was smeared with mud and boot polish. "Well, maybe not my bedroom, but certainly my office."

"Akbar! I thought you were in your office the whole day! What have you been up to?"

"I thought I'd go for a stroll in the area to get a feel of it. I called in one of my old trusted informants from the Cell, and he took me around. He gave me this costume as well. Like it?"

"If you were walking around Orangi all day long and the wardias didn't fill your body with holes, I'd say it's a pretty good disguise. I came in to tell you that I've got the staff in some kind of order. I had actually called one of my informers to get the layout of the Hajji Camp. You can meet him if you want."

"No need. I've been right up to the gate. The guards even gave me ten rupees to get some bread. Don't call your man. The fewer people who know, the better it is. By the way, I saw your efforts with the men: very impressive. I didn't think this lot could be kicked into shape. So, if you're ready, let's load them up in the jeeps. You haven't told them anything, right?"

"No, of course not. We still don't know how many of them are the UF's people. They just know that they're preparing for a raid, they don't know where it's going to be. But Akbar, that's the point I wanted to make to you: let's delay this for a couple of days until we have a chance to weed out the informers from our ranks. We'll have a better understanding of the area and more confidence in the men. If we go in blindly like this, they are likely to ambush us. Also, let's not go at this time. Look, all these wardia bastards are ayaash. They are all up drinking, gambling, and whoring late into the night. If we go now, they'll be alert. If we delay the raid till just before dawn, there's a chance we'll catch most of them sleeping."

"I'll grant you the point about the timing of the raid. But I'm not going to delay. We will go today. These wardia bastards must see that there's a new SHO in here, and they should get to know that I'm not afraid to go after them. Otherwise we'll never get rid of them."

A few hours later, the rickety old police pickup climbed up the single dirt path that led up to Pirabad Hill. The monsoon clouds still hadn't lifted, so the night was moonless and dark. With the racket that the old engine was making, it wouldn't be surprising if people a mile away heard them coming.

But that was exactly the plan. From where he was, climbing up on foot from the other side of the hill, Constantine could see the mobile with its solitary flashing police light. He and Akbar were at the head of the bulk of their force, some twenty to thirty men, making their way to the Hajji Camp. The mobile was meant to be a decoy, and was under instructions to turn tail and run the minute the first shot was heard from the camp. In his reconnaissance, Akbar had found out that the rear side of the camp bordered an old, abandoned graveyard. That was going to be their entry point. The ward boys didn't bother to post sentries at the back because they had assumed that it was virtually inaccessible. The path led through thick, thorny kikar bushes and all the garbage the locality generated was strewn about the broken graves, throwing up an awful stench. The graveyard was believed to be haunted, so locals kept away from it. The police too had never ventured so far, and Constantine smiled to himself as he turned around and saw his men struggling under the weight of their heavy Kalashnikov rifles, cursing under their breath. They must have thought that the new SHO and his deputy were a pair of madmen to make them march through the graveyard.

The ward boys had cleared the last fifty meters of brush from their wall to have a clear line of sight, and it was this exposed patch of land that the police party now approached. Akbar turned around and gave a signal for the group to spread out, as he took the safety latch off his automatic rifle. He and Constantine started edging closer to the wall of the compound.

It was then that all hell broke loose.

To Constantine, the sky seemed lit up with bright red tracer bullets, and the sound was deafening as multiple gun positions opened fire at the same time. Before anyone could figure out what was happening, Constantine realized that he and Akbar were the only ones left exposed in the no-man's land between the wall and the bushes. The rest of the force hadn't bothered to advance with them. Constantine hugged the ground and turned towards the wall, trying to pinpoint a position at which he could fire back. Just then he felt a sensation in his leg and shoulder, as if someone had thrust a white-hot knife into him. After that instant, Constantine felt no more immediate pain, but everything seemed to slow down. He could see, in slow motion, another couple of bullets hit the dirt inches from his face. He saw Akbar, who had scrambled to cover under the wall, screaming at him and gesturing frantically, but his voice seemed to come from a million miles away. He could hear, in the background, the incessant tuk-tuk of the machine guns. Then he felt the dampness on his trousers and was surprised to see the dark crimson patch spreading on his leg. The shock kicked in at the sight of blood, but just before he passed out one of the last things he heard was a bloodcurdling scream. And then the tuk-tuk of the guns stopped.

5

Maqsood Mahr was getting impatient. After trying unsuccessfully for the past hour to read the file in front of him, he finally pushed his chair back and took off his thick reading glasses. His thinning hair, jet-black from coloring and shiny from being oiled, was slicked back. His lips were dark blue from his non-stop smoking and almost matched the pallor of his skin. Unlike other police officers, he never bothered to wear his uniform, which hung on a rack behind him. Instead, he wore an off-white safari suit, with a bright gold watch on his wrist. The entire get-up gave him the look of an insurance salesman from the 1970s.

His work had suffered greatly over the past week. There were stacks of case files on his desk and on the floor. The American Jon Friedland seemed to be dominating all his waking hours and most of his sleeping hours too. He couldn't remember the last time he had gotten a good night's rest. The fate of Friedland was of more significance to him than to anyone else. For Maqsood Mahr was the deputy inspector general of investigations for the Karachi Police, and in that capacity, he was the man directly responsible for recovering the American.

Maqsood Mahr was one of the most powerful men in the city. He was connected to everyone—the government, the opposition and all the Agencies. Some said his influence stretched all the way to the presidency in Islamabad. Others claimed he was in direct contact with the Don, the shadowy head of the United Front who lived in self-imposed exile in New York. Not all of these rumors were strictly true, but Maqsood Mahr subtly encouraged such talk. He had learned over the course of a very long career that the illusion of power was often more important than the reality.

He had risen to his present exalted position from the lowliest of ranks, and the rise had been meteoric. Maqsood Mahr knew where a lot of bodies were buried. That was the secret of his success. That, and the fact that he knew how to make money—for himself, and for his patrons. To say that Maqsood Mahr was corrupt would be an understatement. He had turned extortion into an art, and his greed was insatiable.

Of course, he didn't see things that way. Coming from where he started, to get to where he had reached was an incredible achievement and would have been well nigh impossible had he followed a more orthodox or honest path. It was easy for the directly appointed police officers to call him corrupt. Maqsood called these officers the "competition wallahs" because they entered the police service after passing a competitive exam and went straight to cushy jobs as supervisory officers. They were all members of the elite, from good families and prosperous backgrounds. He had nothing but contempt for these men. They could never imagine what it was like to sleep hungry even for a night. What it was to have been born without any advantages, the son of a dirt-poor laborer in a village in the middle of nowhere, with no prospects of ever being able to get out of there. He had grabbed the one chance he got when the local landowner, on whose lands his father had worked all his life, nominated him to be recruited as a constable. The provincial Chief Minister had given the landowner a certain quota for recruitment, as political payback. And the landowner had selected Mahr because he considered him a simple fellow. Besides, the old wadero thought that it would be useful to have one of his personal retainers in the local police. Little did he realize how far that boy would travel!

Maqsood Mahr had never looked back after that. He had grabbed the chance with both hands and used every opportunity, every edge he got, to consolidate his position. He had taught himself how to read and write and got himself assigned as an assistant to the police-station clerk, voraciously learning everything about police procedure. From there he had steadily moved up the ladder, becoming an officer first, then in-charge of the police station, then head of the district police, eventually moving to the provincial capital, Karachi. Along every step of the way, he filled the pockets of his superiors and never said no to any order, legal or illegal. If he wasn't the most professional investigator in the police, he was definitely the most pliable. He delivered the results that the people in power wanted. When those people wanted to punish their political opponents, Maqsood would forge false cases against them. And when those same victimized opponents came to power, he would provide the same services for them. He had never bothered to catch a jihadi before, but when catching them became a priority for the government, Maqsood miraculously ensured that everyone he arrested, whether they were simple pickpockets or bank robbers, would be classified as jihadis. He had moved from being a big fish in the rural backwaters of the province to the big city, and had very quickly adjusted himself to the new realities that confronted him. He always told those close to him that adapting to different circumstances wasn't difficult. The nature of power, and of those who wielded it, did not change, whether it was a village or a cosmopolitan city like Karachi. Those who wielded power always wanted things done their way. It didn't matter if it was an illiterate feudal wadero or a highly educated, seemingly sophisticated army general. Sure, everyone paid lip service to such concepts as rule of law, human rights, and public duty. But Maqsood Mahr's thirty-five years in the circles of power had taught him that no one really gave a shit about what the people wanted.

He not only catered to the professional wishes of his superiors but also satisfied their personal whims. He strove to provide them with whatever they desired. He tried to ensure that his was the first number they called if anything went wrong. Whether it was the inspector general, who wanted to hush things up after his spoilt son shot someone at a party, the city police chief who wanted him to pick up the bill for his wife's shopping excursions to Dubai, or the industrialist who had been caught with an underage girl. All of these matters had been handled with discretion and, over the years, these services had made him indispensable to those in power. The measure of Maqsood Mahr's success was that the incumbency board that hung behind his desk carried only one name on it. For the past twelve years, he had been the sole occupant of this office.

His ability to provide these services depended upon his ability to have large sums of money continuously at his disposal. Maqsood Mahr had always been very honest about his dishonesty. He couldn't abide by those competition wallahs who made a hue and cry about his corruption, while at the same time drinking from the same well themselves. In his eyes, that was the worst kind of hypocrisy. Many of them came from wealthy backgrounds and had no need for more money but took it anyway, out of sheer greed. He believed they singled him out because he wasn't one of them. He hadn't sat behind a desk and given orders all his life like they had. He had gotten his hands dirty. Who were they to call him greedy? He wasn't just lining his own pockets. He also had to provide the money for various operational expenses, as well as maintaining his bosses in the luxurious lifestyle they had become accustomed to.

But ever since this American had been kidnapped, Maqsood Mahr's carefully crafted world had become endangered. All of a sudden his bosses, while still appreciative of his services, were no longer ignoring his professional shortcomings. The only thing that mattered to any of them now was the recovery of this American.

The problem was that there was literally no trace of this accursed Jon Friedland. The earth seemed to have swallowed him up. Maqsood had been spending cash like water from an open faucet on this case, throwing money at informers for even the most worthless scraps of information. But to no avail. And he could see, with each passing day that the American remained missing, his own aura of indispensability slipping away. He was desperate.

This was why he had placed a call to Constantine's office exactly thirty minutes after Major Rommel had left from there. One of Constantine's wardens, who was on Mahr's payroll, had promptly informed him of the major's visit. Maqsood Mahr invested good money for information just like this. He hadn't said much to Constantine on the phone, but then he seldom did because he always suspected that his phones might be tapped. He had simply ordered Constantine to come to his office. He knew Rommel was working on this case with Tarkeen. And his informant had also told him that Rommel and Constantine had gone to visit Akbar Khan. That was a matter of great concern for him. He had half expected them to do something along those lines, but he hadn't expected them to get that desperate so soon. Mahr's greatest fear was that the Agencies might decide to bring back his greatest rival, Akbar, to replace him.

Maqsood Mahr was petrified of Akbar Khan. He knew that Akbar was better than him in every way—more resourceful, more courageous, and more professional. Maqsood freely acknowledged that. He had never overestimated his own abilities. He knew that his durability was the outcome of his ability to eliminate his rivals rather than professional efficiency. Once upon a time, he and Akbar had worked together, but then Akbar's subsequent fall from grace had allowed Mahr to develop a monopoly on "delivering results" for the bosses, and he did not want them to have any alternative option other than himself in this area. Especially an alternative like Akbar.

And so he waited impatiently for Constantine to arrive. He wanted to find out why the major had met with Akbar, and he wanted to nip any prospects of Akbar's resurrection in the bud. Constantine was in a position to help him with this task. Constantine had served under him for a while, in his Special Investigation Cell. The Cell had some of the best officers in the Karachi Police. It was a good place to work because it gave the officers the opportunity to work independently, unhindered by the daily problems and issues of a typical police station. Here they could go after the big criminals, who were also always the most lucrative ones to catch. Not only did these criminals have large bounties affixed on them, but, when caught, they were more than willing to pay the officers handsomely for "softening" the charges against them. Naturally, with so much money to be made, the Cell presented a highly competitive environment. But even there, Constantine had stood out because of his impeccable professionalism. In fact, Constantine had been working there under Mahr's supervision when he had traced out the case of the murdered Shi'a doctors a few years ago. That had been the most important case for the police at the time. Maqsood Mahr knew and liked Constantine. But he also knew that the Christian was always vulnerable. He had no heavyweight political connections, so he could easily be browbeaten into doing Maqsood's bidding. Constantine had left the prison immediately after his phone call. The warden on his payroll had confirmed that. That was a good sign. It showed that Constantine didn't want to run the risk of pissing him off.

He coughed as he lit yet another cigarette. The room smelt of stale smoke, and the ashtray on his desk was overflowing with stubs. As the minutes ticked by, Maqsood's anxiety was getting the better of him. Just when he thought he couldn't wait any longer, his assistant announced Constantine's arrival. Maqsood brusquely ordered him to be sent in, and as Constantine came in, Maqsood waved away his salute and offered him a seat.

"Arre, baba Consendine, come, come sit. So now you're conspiring with the Bleak House boys to screw me over?" Mahr's tone was sharp.

One thing you could always say about Maqsood Mahr—he never wasted time in getting to the point. His directness was deliberate, to throw people off, and it succeeded with Constantine. "Sir? Sir, I have done no such thing. You can ask anyone at the prison. If they come and ask to see a prisoner, I can't stop them. These are the Agencies after all, sir. But I didn't say anything against you. Please talk to Colonel Tarkeen to verify what I am saying, sir." A bead of sweat dripped from Constantine's brow.

Maqsood Mahr chuckled. "I know, Consendine, I know. I know you wouldn't dare do such a thing. Why would you, anyway? You owe me so much. After all, I got you your last promotion in the Shi'a doctors' case. I know you won't be that ungrateful. But what did they want with him?"

Mahr smiled inwardly while Constantine tried to compose himself. His deliberate mention of the debt Constantine owed him for his promotion had achieved its purpose of reminding the Christian of his place in the world, should he have any delusions. It was inconsequential to Mahr that the detection of the Shi'a case at the time had saved his own neck too. Or that Constantine still had to pay him an arm and a leg just to get him to sign the promotion citation.

"They asked him if he had any information about the American journalist's kidnapping. He didn't, sir."

Maqsood Mahr's beady black eyes stared intently at Constantine as if trying to look into his soul. His brow furrowed as he debated whether Constantine was lying to him. It was a police officer's look, trying to decipher whether a suspect was guilty or not. "Do you think he may have information?"

"No, sir. He has isolated himself for the past six months, sir. He has no knowledge of the world. He doesn't even get newspapers anymore. He has committed himself to praying for betterment in the afterlife."

"Why did they think he might have known something?"

"They must be pretty desperate, sir, to get a breakthrough. You can just imagine, for Colonel Tarkeen to have sent the major to see Akbar. They are chasing all possible sources, even long shots." Constantine paused before going on. "They don't seem to be satisfied with the police investigation."

Mahr exhaled sharply and reached for another cigarette, apparently satisfied that Constantine was telling the truth. "Bastards." He lit the cigarette and took a puff. His earlier brash, bullying tone was replaced by an unsure whine. "What the hell do they expect me to do? I am doing all I can! What do they think—that I can just pluck him from the stars and he'll be here tomorrow?"

"Who is out to get you, sir?"

"All of them! Everyone! The IG, whose household expenses come out of my pocket, doesn't talk to me with a straight face anymore! My own boss, Hanuman, is increasingly sarcastic with me! All the bosses sit around in the air-conditioned conference room at the head office, sipping tea and criticizing me. And Tarkeen? I start my day by doing a round of their offices, asking if they need anything. My investigation in-charge at Preedy Station has standing orders to provide them with ten new mobile phones and SIMs from the electronics market every day! But it's never enough. When it comes to this case, no one wants to listen to my problems. They have all made me personally responsible for whatever happens to this American! The way all of them have ganged up against me, you'd think I had fornicated with their mothers!"

In his animated state, Mahr knocked over his stuffed ashtray. He rang a bell and asked his orderly to clean up and bring them some tea. He welcomed Constantine's presence as an opportunity to vent his own frustration.

"If you don't mind my asking, sir, what is the problem in the case? I haven't really been following it in the press. What exactly happened?"

"Arre, baba, this American was a journalist for some newspaper—the *San Francisco Chronicle*, I think. He had been up north, in Islamabad for a while, and then in the tribal areas, covering the fighting over there. He came here alone, just two days before the kidnapping. No one even knew he was in the city. He didn't check into a hotel, but was staying with some friends who he had gone to university with. They live in a huge, posh bungalow in Defence. Big shots, industrialists, very well connected. But perfectly normal. Very modern, liberal. They drink, and the girls in the house were wearing jeans even when we went to interview them. Nothing remotely extremist about them."

"Was he working on some kind of controversial story, sir, or had he met or interviewed some shady characters?"

"No, that's the thing. He didn't seem to be working on a story. He was just here on a break from his assignments. He spent all the time shopping, eating out, and going to parties. No meetings, no interviews. The Americans checked his laptop. He hadn't filed a story since coming to Karachi."

"How did they grab him?"

"That's the other worry. In the evening, around 10:00 p.m., he was with some friends at the Okra restaurant in Zamzama. Three men in a brand-new Honda Civic pulled up in front of the restaurant as the American was walking out with his friends and took him at gunpoint. Nothing like this has ever happened in that area. All the restaurants and shops are buzzing at that time. In fact, usually there's a traffic jam on that street. And you know the crowd over there—Clifton Defence wallahs, rich people looking for a good time. Now, as if we haven't got enough to worry about, the big shots are complaining to the IG that they can't send their sons and daughters out of the house even to Zamzama anymore. For this also he blames me and demands an official explanation, as if it's my fault!"

"The car?"

"Stolen three days before the incident. It was brand-new. It was snatched from the owner as he drove it home from the dealership outlet near Tariq Road."

"No ransom calls or leads of any sort?"

"Just that picture on the Internet. And leads? Not a peep. We have teams scouring every madrasa in the city, every empty farmhouse on the outskirts, but nothing so far."

"Well sir, it appears to me that it's hardly your fault. You're doing the best you can."

"That's what I keep telling them, Consendine. But no one is willing to listen. I tell you, Consendine, it's becoming too much. I can't fulfil everyone's wishes and keep them all happy. Our bosses, the Bleak House wallahs, the Kaaley Gate wallahs, the minister . . ." Just as he said it, his mobile phone rang. He took the call, jotting down some instructions on a notepad. When the call ended, he looked up at Constantine and rolled his eyes. "See, this is exactly what I'm talking about. That was the Home Minister. He wants two of the priciest girls and a suite at a five-star hotel tonight. I just paid 25,000 rupees for that model two days ago. But the man's dick can't get enough. They all think I'm a goddamn bank or something. Say, you don't happen to have any connections to get two girls, do you?"

"Uh, no sir, sorry. I just have the jail now, sir. I don't think Minister sahib would be content with what's in there."

Mahr smiled as he picked up his phone and asked his operator to put him through to the investigation in-charge at Napier Road Police Station. It had been worth a shot, trying to put the fatigue on Constantine. After all, hadn't he been one of the naika's favorites once upon a time? Maqsood Mahr knew that the girls would be expensive. Not that the amount was going to come out of his pocket. He would just pass the fatigue on to another subordinate. After all, he was an accomplished champion at that. "Yes, you're right. I don't think he's into that. Yet. Who knows? He's a complete degenerate. I keep fearing that one day he might ask for dogs. The man's a moron. The only reason he's Home Minister is because the Don trusts him. And the Don's word is law in this city."

As he spoke, his call came through and he relayed the necessary instructions to his subordinate while puffing away at yet another cigarette. There was some apparent protestation at the other end of the line, because Mahr's voice once again became suddenly sharp. "Arre, baba, don't give me your fucking sob story. I don't care if you're going broke. I made you the investigation in-charge for Napier. If you can't get two girls for the night, what good are you? The whole goddamn red-light district is in your area! And mind you, don't be cheap. The girls better be good looking. I don't want a complaint from Minister sahib."

As he put the phone down, Constantine got up to leave. "Sir, I must beg your leave. If you'd like, I can take a look at the case file and check with some informants inside the prison, see if they have any information. If I find something, I'll tell you straightaway."

"Arre, baba Consendine, do something. Find someone on the inside. Take a copy of the file from my reader on your way out." He thought for a moment then added, "You think they'll come back to see him again?"

"Who, sir? Akbar? I don't think so, but even if they do, like I said, it will be a waste of their time."

"Consendine, you have to make sure that snake Akbar doesn't do a setting with them. Then he will be back in the game. It will ruin me. Ensure this doesn't happen. Do this for your old boss. After all, you don't want to be on the wrong side of me, do you?"

"No, sir. Of course not. Don't worry, sir. It won't happen."

"Good. Very good." Nevertheless, as Constantine saluted and left the room, Maqsood Mahr couldn't shake off his feeling of uneasiness. Which was why he decided to place a call to an old acquaintance in the UF central ward office.

6

The blue Toyota pickup tried to navigate through the choked traffic on I.I Chundrigar Road, the city's business district. The vehicle looked identical to the hundreds of police patrol vehicles all over the city; the only difference was that the word PRISONS was stencilled on the side door. Despite the driver's adroit efforts to cut from one lane to another, the traffic had come to a standstill. Workmen were digging up half the road to lay underground cables. The number of cables that were laid under Karachi's streets seemed countless to Constantine. Every week some road or the other was dug up. The dust from the digging had forced pedestrians and drivers in non-air-conditioned cars to cover their mouths. Constantine too covered his mouth with a handkerchief, cursing himself.

He was pissed off. Pissed that he was stuck in this god-awful traffic, travelling to a place he didn't want to go to, pissed that Maqsood Mahr had known about the visit from Major Rommel within thirty minutes of the major's leaving the jail, and pissed overall at why he had allowed himself to do what he had done at Mahr's office. He had just gambled his whole career by lying to Maqsood Mahr, and he wasn't even sure why he had done it. He cursed his stupid ego that had made him resent Mahr's condescending attitude towards him. To add to his woes, as soon as he had walked out of Mahr's office, he had received a call from Colonel Tarkeen. Tarkeen seemed to know of his visit to Maqsood already and, in that silky-smooth tone of his, had summoned Constantine to Bleak House.

This was exactly the kind of situation that Constantine had spent years trying to avoid. He was stuck in the middle of a game in which all the other players were more powerful than him and could destroy him. If he angered any one person, they wouldn't forget it. Mahr had certainly made his intentions perfectly clear. At the same time, he still didn't know what game the Agencies were playing, and he certainly didn't know what game Akbar was playing. He had been shocked to learn that Akbar knew about the kidnapping in the first place. He wondered how Akbar had that information, but what puzzled him even more was that, despite living in isolation for so long, Akbar was still interested in the game.

The fact that the case was about the kidnapping of an American by the jihadis was another aspect that made him uncomfortable. Constantine's Christianity had always been an asset for him. Since he was considered an outsider, a member of a minority community and therefore unobtrusive, nobody had anything to fear from him. Since he was also good at his job, he was liked and trusted by all. At one point he had been posted in an area of the city where there was a history of Sunni-Shi'a violence. At a time of heightened sectarian tension, the leaders of both groups would submit to his arbitration because he was a Christian and, therefore, not partial to either sect.

But these jihadis were different. They scared him. Their faith was frightening. They came from the poorest segment of society. A man with no hope was a man with no fear. You couldn't reason with them. This kind of people couldn't care less if Constantine was fair or unfair. To them, he would be just another non-believer, a kafir, and a kafir police wallah on top of that. What was it that one jihadi prisoner had called him the first week he had joined? George Bush ka chamcha, Bush's lackey. It'd all be over if someone got a whiff that he was in some way linked to the investigation of this case. They would send one of their suiciders to blow him up along with his family.

And what would happen then? You don't even have to be pursuing them. You just needed to be at the wrong place at the wrong time, and they'd be scraping parts of your body out of the trees for weeks. Who would take care of your family then? Certainly not the department. The bosses would show up at your funeral, pat your son or brother on the head, and then forget about you. Your wife could spend the next five years running from one clerk to another in the head office, just trying to get your pension.

The pickup moved past the modern-looking glass towers, Karachi's version of skyscrapers, that adorned Chundrigar Road. The vehicle swept onto the peculiarly named Love Lane Bridge, leaving behind the rail yards of the City Station, and the classic sandstone façade and rotunda of the PortTrust building. The bridge was peculiarly named, for there wasn't a hint of romance in it, situated as it was at the hub of the city's main traffic routes, leading from the port to the industrial zones. The air was thick with soot, and the stench of fish from the port and the tanneries nearby was overpowering. In spite of all this, the panoramic vista on view was quite spectacular. On one side the buildings of Chundrigar Road, especially the Stock Exchange, the MCB building, and the Habib Bank Plaza, lunged at the sky like daggers. On the other side was the port, with ships docking at the quays and unloading their wares from around the world. The vehicle turned off the bridge in the direction of Mai Kolachi bypass, a tiny strip of reclaimed land that connected the city center to the upscale suburbs of Defence and Clifton. Driving past the Boating Basin, a popular rendezvous point with rows of restaurants, the pickup entered a swanky residential area dotted with smart whitewashed mansions. It pulled up in front of a typically official-looking bungalow with a big black gate. The only thing that distinguished this particular bungalow from the dozens of others that looked just like it was the pair of CCTV cameras perched above the gate. Constantine got out and knocked on the gate. The door opened, and a man with a clipboard came out, ticked his name off wordlessly, and escorted him into the building. The building itself, once a palatial mansion, had been converted into offices. Large rooms were partitioned into cubicles where men huddled over their desks and pored over confidential files. Constantine was led to a first-floor office with a glass door and partition, which seemed to be a little more private than the rest. A bald man with a trim silver beard, dressed in a smart suit, looked up and rose from his swivel chair to greet Constantine like a long-lost comrade.

"Constantine, how nice to see you! Now there's no need for that sort of formality between us." He brushed aside Constantine's attempt to salute and grabbed him with both hands and hugged him. "Come, let's have some of that special Bleak House coffee." He gestured to the usher, "Tell the mess to send up two whipped coffees, and I don't want to be disturbed for the next hour."

That was the thing with Colonel Tarkeen. In complete contrast to Maqsood Mahr, who was blunt to the point of rudeness with his subordinates, Tarkeen would always kill you with kindness no matter what your rank. Getting up to receive you, making you feel important, going to inordinate lengths to put you at ease. All the better to strike you when your guard was down.

"How is Maqsood? Going crazy about us meeting Akbar, I expect."

"He is worried, sir. He seems to be under a lot of pressure."

"Well, he should be. This investigation is now monitored at the very highest level. The Americans are looking into it as well. And quite frankly, his work so far has just not been up to the mark. No one is satisfied. And as for pressure, well, all of us are under pressure. The president is under pressure. Our friend Maqsood doesn't have a problem with pressure when he's running any one of his numerous money-making schemes. We ignore his little 'projects' because we want him around for times like these. *When results have to be delivered.* I'm afraid poor Maqsood has completely misread the situation. He started treating this case like any other. He never understood the *gravity* of it. And he overestimated his own usefulness. Now, there may be serious consequences for him."

Constantine hadn't realized that things had gone so far. If Tarkeen was speaking this way, then very soon, worrying about Akbar would be the least of Maqsood Mahr's problems. The way the intelligence boys worked, they would crawl over him with a microscope, if they felt he hadn't been cooperative with them. The thought of the mighty Maqsood Mahr having to face the full wrath of the Agencies gave Constantine a warm, tingly feeling inside.

"Did you tell him about the information Akbar gave?"

"No, sir. I didn't think it was appropriate for me to say anything about that to anyone else."

"Good, Constantine, good. That's why I've always liked you. Always the soul of discretion. I don't want him finding out and fucking anything up just because he's concerned about his own position. If he tries to cause trouble for you, just tell me and I'll sort him out."

"Sir, if you don't mind my asking, how come your people are looking into this matter? Aren't these jihadi-related matters usually dealt with by your sister agency, the Kaaley Gate wallahs?"

"Yes, usually this is their portfolio, but this case has been specially turned over to us. You see, Constantine, the very fact that the case was transferred to us signifies the seriousness of it. Do you know at what level a decision like that is made? No less than the president himself and the intelligence chiefs. That's what Maqsood never understood."

"But why, sir? What's so special about this man? I mean I know he's an American, but still, Americans have been kidnapped in the past. It's not a new phenomenon."

"You're right, it's not, but the timing couldn't have been worse. And I suspect that the kidnappers deliberately planned it that way. This journalist, Jon Friedland, had been covering the fighting in the tribal areas, as you must know by now. What you probably don't know is that he was ejected from the tribal areas ten days ago, on the instructions of our sister agency."

"But why was he thrown out, sir?"

"Apparently, they weren't happy with what he had been reporting. He had some very good contacts, and he gave widespread coverage to some of the excesses committed there—villages that were accidentally bombed, civilians killed by government forces, things like that. Didn't really go along with what was given in the official press pack. In his recent articles, he had portrayed the tribals as some sort of romantic freedom fighters. Our sister agency's local representatives decided that he was being too critical of the government. So they sent in a confidential memo saying that his presence was compromising national security and had him expelled. That's how he was in Karachi. He had decided to visit some old friends before heading back to the United States. The family he was staying with, their son had gone to college with him in America."

"So who knew he was coming to Karachi?"

"No one. It was only when he got kidnapped that these facts came out. It became very embarrassing for the government, because the Kaaley

Gate wallahs hadn't even told their number one in Islamabad. The whole thing had been handled at a local level. When the Americans found out, they were naturally very concerned. And very upset with our sister agency. There are still some doubts about their role in that previous American kidnapping. The American secretary of state made a specific request to the president that they shouldn't have anything to do with the investigation. She also made it clear to the president that the Americans expect the government to make all possible efforts to recover this man. Their president was supposed to come to Pakistan on a state visit in the New Year. That trip has been put on hold, depending on how this case ends up. That's why this matter was passed on to us. Their whole organization is under a cloud."

"Sir, do you think that they had anything to do with it?"

"That's an interesting question, Constantine. What do you think?"

Constantine paused and thought about it for a moment. "They would be very silly to orchestrate his kidnapping so soon after they had him ejected from the tribal areas. That would have been rather obvious. Fingers would be pointed towards them. Besides, I would think that their interest in him would be over once they had him removed. They know what the stakes are. My instinct says that they are not involved. They wouldn't be that stupid, would they?"

"Yes, I am inclined to agree with your assessment. That's what our enquiries have also found. So far. Not to say that it couldn't be one of the discarded skeletons from their closet. I know the kind of horror shows that they have patronized in the past. At this moment, I think that is their main fear in this matter: that the remotest link could be found between them and the kidnappers, without their having even been aware of it. If a random jihadi, who had worked with an operative of theirs years ago, is found to be behind this kidnapping, it would just consolidate everyone's suspicions. That would then become very problematic for them. However, as I said at the start, all of this couldn't have come at a worse time, and now with the release of that video on the Internet, we are racing against the clock. We have very few days left and today, for the first time, we got a break thanks to Akbar's information."

"Did you manage to verify Akbar's information? He had mentioned a source whom you know, who would be able to confirm it."

"Yes, it checked out. The source is a bookie Akbar had introduced me to years ago. It is not just him who verified the information. One of our own sources, whom we have been squeezing very hard, came up with the same today. So it's legitimate. How do you think Akbar came by the information?"

"To be honest, sir, I myself was completely astounded that he had information. I didn't think Akbar could be of any help in any matter, leave alone this one. He must still have some network of informers hidden somewhere that no one else in the jail knows about."

"I didn't expect it either. I had just sent Rommel on a hunch. But now, this has given us our first glimmer of hope in trying to solve this case. Constantine, I need your help in this. You have to convince him that helping us will be good for him too. It has to be you, because Rommel is too new to be able to handle any of this. Of course he will be there formally, but you have to take the lead. I would come, but from the report I got, Akbar is still a little upset with me."

"Well sir, he believes that you abandoned him and contributed to his downfall."

"I didn't abandon him, Constantine. You know how it works. Yes, he worked with me when I was with the Kaaley Gate wallahs. And yes, he worked with the people here at Bleak House as well. But my boss back then wasn't happy with him because he was doing more work for the people in this office. So when the encounter episode occurred, we just withdrew our support. As it was, everybody in your department was out to get him. You know how Akbar is—very good at what he does but rude, headstrong. No one likes that. Plus, Maqsood had all your bosses in his pocket. And of course, the United Front leadership had just been waiting for a chance for something to go wrong so they could nail him and settle old scores. It was a perfect storm for him. It was they, along with Maqsood, who initiated the entire investigation. Akbar had become radioactive by then. I don't think any of us are naïve enough to still believe in childish concepts like loyalty, Constantine."

Constantine sipped his coffee and shrugged his shoulders. "That's the way he feels, sir. He's very bitter. Understandably. What about an incentive for him? I don't think you can get him to cooperate without offering some benefit to him."

"Well, now *that* is a different matter. It all depends on how good his information is. If he really does have something, then we can negotiate. At this moment, *everything* is under discussion. But we must get him to the bargaining table first. And that's where you have to play your part. You know him, Constantine, you see him in the prison every day. Apart from that, you two go back a long way, don't you? I recall that the two of you served together several times."

"Yes, sir. We were first posted together as probationary officers at Preedy Police Station. We had the same mentor. After that, Akbar started working more in the special investigation units, while I kept shuttling from one police station to another. Then, when the troubles with the United Front began, he was posted as station house officer of Orangi and I was posted with him as his deputy."

"Yes, I remember that. Isn't that where you got wounded?"

"Yes, sir. Akbar saved my life."

"That was around the time I first met you. You traced that case and arrested the terrorist, what was his name, something Tension?"

"Ateeq Tension, sir. That was the case that got me my promotion to inspector."

"Of course. Ateeq Tension. Yes, all of them had these aliases which they used to attach to their names. Aslam Dada, Khurrum Klashinkov, Adnan Sexy. Some of them were hilarious. I remember when you arrested him, Akbar came to complain about you and said that Tension was such a dangerous criminal that you should have killed him when you caught him. Perhaps he was right. But this is exactly what I mean, Constantine. The two of you have such a long history together. You know him, you know what to say to him. You must speak to him often now."

"Actually, sir, since I took over as superintendent of the prison, today was the first day I went to see him. You see sir, I . . . it didn't feel right for me to meet him in these conditions. We had been so close, been through so much together, I didn't want to meet him in the role of his jailer. I mean, I kept tabs on him through my wardens and ensured that he was comfortable, but I didn't look in on him myself. And as for him, by the time I came to the prison, he had already retreated into himself. He didn't try to contact me. He didn't want anything from anybody."

"But he still has a bond with you, Constantine. You are the only hope we have. We need your help. I need your help. He knows something. I can't figure out how, but he does. You must help Rommel to draw him out. I know you're not comfortable working with us anymore. And I know that you came to the prison to hide. But fate has brought us together again. It is very fortunate that you are in a position to help us. Don't worry about anything else—Maqsood, the UF, your superiors. This case is the only thing that matters. None of them will create any problems for you, I guarantee it. And I won't forget what you do for us."

"What do you wish me to do, sir?"

"We are working on a couple of other leads with the FBI investigators today. I will send Rommel again tomorrow morning. He will have the power to negotiate on my behalf. Akbar's immediate release, reinstatement—everything is on the agenda if his information is accurate. Use the time between now and then to communicate with him. Get him into a more helpful frame of mind. Make him realize that this could be his last chance at redemption."

"Very well sir, I will try my best."

"That's why I have faith in you, Constantine. Thank you."

And with that, the meeting concluded.

7

December 1998

The cold hurt his arm. He had been noticing it for the past two weeks, whenever the cool winds came in from Quetta and made the temperature drop. But luckily, that, and the tingly feeling he sometimes felt where the bullet was still lodged in his leg, seemed to be the only long-term effects of Constantine's injuries. When Akbar had taken him to the hospital on the night of the attack on the Hajji Camp, the doctors had not thought he would survive because he had lost so much blood. They had dug three bullets out of his leg and four more from his arms and stomach. It was a miracle that his vital organs had been spared.

He was surprised that his recovery had been fairly quick. The doctors praised his iron constitution and attributed it to his physical fitness. He had almost fully recovered now. Initially, when he returned to Orangi, Akbar kept finding excuses to keep him in the station instead of sending him out on patrol. Though they never spoke about it, Constantine knew it was because Akbar felt guilty about the raid, for not having heeded his warnings. He felt responsible for what had happened at the Hajji Camp. That was all fine, but Constantine needed to go out again for his own sake. Otherwise the men would think he had lost his nerve. So he had taken the opportunity of Akbar's absence today. For a couple of weeks now, they had been working on catching a group of UF arsonists. Whenever the party gave a strike call, these boys would set fire to vehicles on the main road. That would ensure that everyone else stayed at home, and the strike would be successful. Now Constantine had good information on them, and so he had planned and led a raiding party personally to arrest the men.

It was good to be back out on the streets. Constantine had once again felt the rush of adrenaline when he entered the suspect's house. The thrill of being so close to danger. And finally, when he caught the boys, the unadulterated joy of the hunter who had secured his prey. The house that they raided had been close to the Hajji Camp. It was Constantine's first time back here since the night of the raid. He had passed the camp on the way to and from the raid, but a lot had changed in this neighborhood since that night. The once impregnable ward office was a shell of its former self. The building itself now lay empty. Akbar's raid had been bold and unexpected, and it made an impression on the ward boys. They had abandoned their headquarters. The big party banners that had adorned the building and the walls had all been torn down. The iron gates and barricades that the ward boys had erected had been smashed open, and children were now playing cricket in the yard where prisoners used to be chained. A solitary police constable sat lazily in the ward boss's office, reading the newspaper and occasionally berating the children.

As Constantine drove back into the station compound, changes were evident there as well. For a change, the station was bustling with activity. A steady flow of visitors had started coming in to report their daily complaints. Akbar's workmen had now started work on a gun turret on top of the station gate. Alongside the wall, there was a line of shackled prisoners stretching from the duty officer's room right round the corner. Most of them were UF activists waiting to be taken to court. Since there were so many mouths to feed in the station, Akbar had gotten a local caterer to set up an open-air kitchen in the yard. A man stood there now over a huge vat of biryani, doling out the rice in plastic bags to the prisoners and their guards alike.

Constantine dragged the young boy he had just arrested by the collar and shoved him into Akbar's office. The boy, barely eighteen or nineteen, was shivering with fear. Akbar sat at his desk, in deep conversation with a smartly dressed, slightly balding man, and seemed surprised to see him enter.

"Consendine, where have you been?"

"I got some information about the arsonist boys, so I decided to take a party to pick them up. You didn't expect to keep me confined here forever, did you? Here, I got you a present." Constantine whipped the blindfold off his suspect and gave him a thump on the back of his neck. "Meet Wajahat, a.k.a. Wajju Bhai. Used to be the tea boy at the ward office. Then he decided to get into more serious things. He's the one who came up with the idea to burn cars on the road to make the wardia strikes more effective."

A sly smile crept across Akbar's face as he sized the boy up. "Kyun re, bhenchod. You think you're a real smartass, don't you? Think your fucking party will protect you now? Do you know who I am?"

The boy, who was by now shaking violently, started to cry. "Yes, sahib. You are Akbar Khan, SHO of Orangi."

"Yes. And you know what I do to little cockroaches like you, don't you?" Akbar crooked his two fingers in the shape of a gun. "Tuk-tuk. Where are your ward bosses now?"

The boy nodded his head in some trepidation. "They are all dead or have run away from the area."

"Then are you more intelligent than them that you decided to remain behind to fuck around in my area? Do you know what a headache I've had because of your car burnings, madarchod?" Akbar picked up the pistol that had been lying on his desk and pointed it menacingly at the boy.

"Sahib, please, sahib, please. I am my mother's only son. I got involved in all of this by mistake, sahib. I didn't want to burn any cars, the party made me do it. They would tell us to steal cars the night before a strike and set them on fire in the early morning. Please, sahib, don't kill me. I'll do anything you say. I'll help you out in any way I can."

"Saala bharwa, I think I'll sort you out along with that other bastard I've just caught." Akbar rose from his chair and went into the little chamber that served as his retiring room. He came out holding a prisoner whose arms and legs were shackled, and whose head was covered with a dirty sackcloth. In all this time Constantine had observed that the distinguished, balding gentleman had listened to the conversation with interest. Being ever cautious, he didn't like the way Akbar had spoken so freely in front of a stranger. He looked at him inquisitively until Akbar caught his eye.

"Arre, Consendine, no need to worry. Sorry, in my excitement, I forgot to introduce you. Consendine, this is Major Tarkeen. He's our friend from the Agencies."

"Constantine. Akbar consistently keeps mispronouncing your name, but he's told me a lot about you. It's a pleasure to finally meet with you."

Constantine wasn't sure whether to salute or shake hands, what with Wajahat still clinging to him. Clumsily, he wiped his hand, clammy from Wajahat's sweat, on his trouser pants and saluted Tarkeen awkwardly.

"Arre, Tarkeen sahib, didn't I tell you Consendine was efficient? His first patrol after recovering from his injuries, and he catches a big fish. Sahib, this is perfect. I'll take both of them out together."

On hearing that, Wajahat started weeping uncontrollably. "Sahib, I'm no big fish, sahib, please, I am my mother's only son."

Akbar paid him no further attention. "Arre, Consendine, I have a surprise for you too. Remember the bastards who opened fire on us at the Hajji Camp? Well, I've caught the head madarchod." He pulled the sack-cloth off his prisoner's head, revealing a frightened middle-aged man who, had it not been for his present surroundings and the smell of shit that ema-nated from his soiled trousers, could have easily passed for an IT technician.

"But Akbar, I don't understand. I thought you killed the ward boss that night. Who is this then?"

"I did. After you went down, I jumped the wall of the compound and put my Klashin on full auto. I shot five of them at point-blank range, including Saad Dittoo, who was the ward boss at the time. But a whole bunch of them got away, including this pig. Meet Adnan Doodhwala. He was in charge of all their weapons. He was the prick who gave the order to open fire on us that night. He doesn't look like much, but he's a real slip-pery son of a whore. Even now, I caught him with a bloody light machine gun. Army issue. Kyun, Tarkeen sahib?"

"Yes. A very dangerous weapon. It could probably level this thana. Our soldiers go through a six-week course before they use this gun. I'd be very interested to know how he was trained to use it."

"Arre, sahib, he'll tell you everything. When I'm done with him, he'll sing ghazals for you. Kyun re, who gave you the training to use a light machine gun?"

Adnan Doodhwala hesitated in answering, not really due to any effort to conceal information, but more due to the fact that he was paralysed with fear. He kept staring at the prominent brown stain that was spreading downwards from the seat of his pants. It was Wajahat who first broke the silence.

"Sahib, please sahib, I'll tell you. I'll tell you anything you want to know. It was a man from our central headquarters, sahib. They sent him to Orangi to teach two of the boys how to use the big gun. The boys at the ward office kept saying he had served in the army for a while."

"Go on. What was his name, and where is he now?"

"His name was Ateeq, sahib. Everyone called him Tension bhai, but one time I overheard him talking on the phone, and he was talking to a girl, and she called him Ateeq. Ateeq Tension, yes, that's right. I don't know where he is now, sahib, but if you let me go, I promise you, I'll trace him out for you."

Akbar eyed Wajahat with renewed interest. "Saale, you think just because you give me one piece of information which may or may not be true, I'll let you go? You think I'm running a charity house over here? All this does is that it makes you a somewhat interesting person, and that means I won't thoko you with this other bastard."

Wajahat drew a sharp breath, while Constantine patted him on the back. "Arre, chutiya, don't try and be over smart. Be thankful that you're getting away with your life. We'll check your information, and if it's correct, we'll still book you, but in a minor case. You'll get out in a few months. Even this is a huge favor for you, because the government orders are to book you UF bastards in the heaviest cases. At least this way, your mother will still have a son."

As Wajahat nodded his assent, Constantine called out for the duty officer to take him away and book him. He sat down on the chair next to Tarkeen and took a sip from the cup of tea that the major graciously pushed towards him.

"Good work, Constantine."

"Thank you, sir. We'll book the boy in a small arms case. He'll get out in a couple of months, and I'll make sure he's so grateful to us that we'll have a good informer on our hands. He's sharp. We can get good work out of him. What about the other one, Akbar? How many cases are we putting on him? Definitely show the recovery of the machine gun from him."

Akbar and Tarkeen shared a look and smiled. "We're not making any cases on him. Not even the machine gun. I'm mounting the gun on the gate, as a warning to any other wardia bastards who think of attacking this station again."

"What? Then what the hell are we doing with him?"

Akbar shrugged his shoulders and then crooked two fingers and a thumb. "Tuk-tuk."

"Akbar, are you crazy? Listen, it's one thing having a shootout and killing a couple of their bastards. That's natural. But we can't arrest him and then take him out and shoot him. There are fifty people in this thana who must have seen you bring him in. There must have been a hundred who saw you arrest him. Why do you want to make all of them potential witnesses against yourself?"

"I don't see any witnesses. All of these people saw me arrest *someone*. Who's to say who that was? Maybe you and I just ran across this Doodhwala when we were out on patrol later tonight. Maybe he pulled a Klashin on us, and maybe we shot him in self-defence. That's the case I foresee."

"Akbar, for God's sake don't do this. It's not worth it. It will become a big phadda that we won't be able to cover. If you're worried about him getting out, then just don't worry. I will make the cases myself, and I'll bring such solid evidence against this bhenchod that his great-grandchildren will be married by the time he gets out of jail."

"I don't care about whether he gets out of jail or not. I don't care if it becomes a phadda. I'll face it. You don't get it, Consendine, I want him dead. This madarchod opened fire on us. You almost died! I won't ever forget that, and I'll never let these bastards forget. When I'm done with them, they'll never dare open fire on another police officer ever again!"

"Akbar, we're police officers, not butchers."

"And what are they, Consendine? Don't be so naïve. You think this son of a whore, who's standing here shitting his pants, you think if the tables were turned, he would be as forgiving as you? Am I right, Major sahib?"

"Absolutely, Akbar. These thugs represent a grave threat to our national security. They have to be dealt with, Constantine. We can't afford to be squeamish."

"Come on, Consendine, we are wasting time. I'll have my orderly clean this bastard up, and then we'll take him to the alley behind the thana and we'll just do him there." Akbar bent to pick up the prisoner from the floor, where he had collapsed.

"No, Akbar. I'm sorry. I can't do this. Look, I told you I don't have a problem killing them in an encounter, when they fire on us and we fire on them. But I can't do it like this, taking him out of the lockup and shooting him in cold blood. I . . . I'm sorry, I just can't do it. I understand if that's what you feel you need to do, but I can't be a part of it."

There was silence for a moment. Major Tarkeen stared at the floor uncomfortably, while Akbar looked at Constantine contemplatively. For the slightest moment, there seemed to be a look of disappointment in his eyes. Then he grunted and shrugged his shoulders. "Heh. Suit yourself. If you don't want to be part of this, then I suggest you make yourself scarce over here. I have to start working on him. Go to the duty officer's room and start doing the paperwork that you seem to love so much."

The next day

Akbar and Constantine drove silently in the police pickup, on the way to the SP's office. Akbar hadn't spoken with Constantine since his refusal to take part in the shooting. There was a certain coldness to his manner. No rudeness, nothing that anyone else would have been able to pick up, but a reserve. Constantine felt like a child who had failed to live up to his father's expectations. It was a strange realization that Akbar's validation mattered so much to him.

And yet, as their pickup passed the burnt-out hulks of two buses and a normally bustling bazaar that had the look of a ghost town, Constantine couldn't help but think that he had been right. Akbar's killing of Adnan Doodhwala had created a firestorm. On hearing the news of his death, the UF party leadership had called a press conference and alleged that Akbar had tortured Doodhwala and killed him in cold blood. The party had called a general strike, and their activists had shut down half the city by force.

Akbar and Constantine had spent most of their day helping out in other police stations because Orangi itself remained strikingly calm. It showed that Akbar's tactics had certainly left a mark on the ward bosses. They were loath to try anything in his area.

Around noon, they had received an urgent wireless message to report to the SP's office immediately. The message was for both of them, so Constantine surmised that Hanuman had called to enquire into the death of Adnan Doodhwala. He knew that Hanuman had already done his homework. The night duty officer had told him that SP sahib had called at 3:00 a.m., and had spoken to the duty sentry and asked him what was going on. Hanuman was crafty like that. He never stood on protocol and didn't depend solely on what his subordinates told him. His summons, in the middle of a riot, didn't bode well. Constantine's own conscientious objection was unlikely to work in his favor. Only he and Akbar were aware of it, and, besides that, everyone knew that the two of them were inseparable.

Akbar seemed unmoved by the urgency of Hanuman's call. He yawned lazily and stretched in the passenger seat of the pickup. "It's good Hanuman called. I haven't slept all night, and I needed a break from inhaling all that fucking tear gas."

"Why do you think he's called? It's almost certainly got to do with Doodhwala."

"Who cares why he's called. So what if it does? Fuck him."

They entered Hanuman's office compound to find a small crowd had gathered outside the gate and was being held back by a platoon of nervous-looking riot police. They were waving UF flags and chanting anti-police slogans. The two men disembarked from the vehicle and put on their berets before entering the office. The smell of burning rubber wafted across. Inside, Hanuman sat behind an enormous desk in a cavernous room. He had a lean, sharp, clean-shaven face with close-cropped, receding hair. His dark eyes betrayed an uncommon intelligence. Akbar and Constantine saluted in unison and took up a couple of seats just opposite Hanuman.

Hanuman looked up from his desk and spoke in a calm, nasal voice, as if he was discussing the sports pages rather than the grave law and order situation. "What is this problem you've created for me? I have protesters outside my office shouting for your head. Their boys have blocked all the main routes to the city."

"Heh. There is no problem in Orangi. The fault is with our own SHOs, sahib. They are too scared. Give me a free hand, and your roads will be open in five minutes."

"I just spoke with one of their former ministers. This boy who was killed was his nephew. He says he had no criminal record."

"He opened fire on a police party with a light machine gun. I think that counts as a criminal act."

"Hmm. They say he never fired on the police. They say that you arrested him beforehand from his house, and kept him at the police station for several hours before you killed him."

"Of course they will say that. They are lying. Why are you giving so much weight to what they say, sahib? He was a bloody criminal who got killed because of his own actions. These UF bastards just need an excuse to call a strike."

"Hmm. I give their version weight because I tend to agree with it."

The two men stared at each other from across the table. Constantine could see the blood rushing to Akbar's eyes, and he intervened in the conversation just as Akbar was about to speak out. "Uh, excuse me, sir, but we know for a fact that he was involved in criminal activities before this as well. My sources tell me that he was also present at the Hajji Camp the night we raided it, sir."

Hanuman turned to him. "You're Consendine, right?"

"Yes, sir."

"Hmm. And you've been in this district longer than Akbar, haven't you?"

"Yes, sir. Almost two years now."

"You recently came back after getting wounded, isn't it?"

"Yes, sir."

"Tell me truthfully what happened, Consendine. I have heard from my sources that you were opposed to the killing of this Doodhwala character, and in fact there was another prisoner whom Akbar wanted to kill, but you insisted on booking him in a case instead. That's good. I like your instincts. You have nothing to fear. This has become a very serious political issue, and I doubt if your friend Akbar can survive in this post for long. The UF is naming him specifically and is demanding that the inspector general take action against him. It is their price for stopping the rioting. Tell me the truth, and I will appoint you as SHO in his place."

Constantine looked at Akbar, who was staring out the window, apparently unfazed by Hanuman's revelations. Then he looked back across at Hanuman. "No sir, your informers must have been mistaken, sir. Everything happened just as it's written in the report, sir. He came out of an alley and started firing at our police patrol. Akbar fired back and managed to hit him, sir. It was a 200 per cent legitimate encounter, sir."

"Hmm. Suit yourself. If that's your story, you'll share his fate. I had called the two of you in to give you a last chance. As it stands, the matter is out of my hands. The new inspector general took over yesterday, and he has decided to deal with this issue personally. He has called us and representatives of the UF for a durbar at Police Headquarters tomorrow. Be there at 9:00 a.m. sharp."

The next morning dawned bright. Constantine hadn't slept the whole night. He took particular care with his uniform and decided to walk the short distance from his house to Police Headquarters. He had heard that the new inspector general was a real stickler for how an officer was turned out.

The durbar was an old police tradition. The inspector general would call all ranks and address them directly. The durbar was meant to ensure that the commander of the force maintained a direct link with his men. It was often a grand affair, and the staff at the headquarters, eager to impress the new boss, were putting up an impressive show. A bright canopy had been placed over the reviewing stand to provide shade for the IG and his entourage. Chalk lines had been drawn on the ground to ensure that everyone knew exactly where to stand. Constantine noticed that the burnt-out hulks of old police vehicles that usually littered the parade ground had been removed overnight. The headquarters staff could manage miracles, given the right motivation. He grunted and cursed under his breath as he saw Akbar lining up on the parade ground.

"Don't know why the damn IG had to call an entire durbar."

"He's new. He must like all this pomp and ceremony. What difference does it make to you, Consendine?"

"I wouldn't appreciate it if the boss fired us in public, in front of five hundred people." He nodded his head towards the gate, where a cavalcade of cars was entering the parade ground, flying UF party flags. "Especially if he does it in front of those bastards."

"You worry too much. I think it's good. The whole point of the durbar is that the IG hears our side as well. Much better than if the entire matter had been left in Hanuman's hands. God knows what that devious bastard would have done. Besides, I hear this IG's a good man. When he was in Balochistan, they used to call him Dr. Death, because he had given the police a shoot-to-kill policy for all criminals. A man after my own heart."

"You idiot, that's not the reason why he's called Dr. Death. They call him that because he's death to serve under. He's so strict on discipline, that it's your death if he finds you've violated the rules. He's been known to have publicly handcuffed full inspectors in their own police stations and had them sent to jail. And forget about your Major Tarkeen intervening to save us. If anyone tries to do sifarish with this one, he'll just double your punishment."

"Oh. Really?"

"Yes. You've really fucked us this time, Akbar."

"Thanks for standing with me in front of Hanuman. Look, if you want, I'll take the whole thing on my own head. You didn't have anything to do with it, anyway."

"No. I'm not looking for a way out. We're in this together, good or bad. Besides, who knows? You might turn out to be right about Dr. Death."

Just then, the bugler sounded the arrival of the inspector general. To their surprise, they saw Major Tarkeen emerge from the same car. The major, still in his civvies, stood unobtrusively to one side while Hanuman introduced the UF representatives to the inspector general. Dr. Death was a tall man with a ramrod-straight back. He had the demeanor of a man used to command. The UF representative, a short, fat man who had been a minister in the last regime, looked like a midget standing next to him. Constantine noted that Dr. Death didn't greet the ex-minister with the same obsequiousness that other police officers had.

Akbar and Constantine stood stiffly at attention, and they could see the UF representatives engaged in animated discussions with Hanuman and Dr. Death. They couldn't hear much of what was being said, but in the few snippets of conversation that did reach them, Akbar's name was mentioned several times and the UF representatives gesticulated frantically towards them. Finally, Dr. Death turned to address the police officers.

"Who is Akbar Khan?" His voice was like a cannon shot booming across the parade ground.

Akbar came forward from the line and saluted sharply.

"What is this tamasha, Akbar Khan? These people say their party activists will stop rioting on the sole condition that you are placed under arrest."

"Permission to speak freely, sir!" Dr. Death granted it with a nod. "There is another way to stop their rioting, sir. Give me three hours and then ask me again if these people have stopped rioting or not. These people"—he pointed accusingly at the UF minister—"want to hold this city hostage. They want senior officers like you to grovel before them, begging them to restrain their boys. Your SHOs are afraid of going out on the streets and doing their job. How dare these bastards bargain with the police? Ask them, why don't they do anything in my area? Because they know that if they try it, I'll teach them such a lesson that they would rather fornicate with their grandmothers than try to break the law again. Ask these men standing next to you, sahib, how they can dare to try and negotiate with us about breaking the law. We are the law!"

The outburst did not seem to have any impact on Dr. Death's equilibrium, though the UF minister seemed to cringe when Akbar stared at him. "They say that their activist was killed extrajudicially. He was the nephew of one of their MPs."

"Call it what you will, sahib. These are legal terms, made up by judges and magistrates and senior police officers sitting in air-conditioned offices. All I know is that the people who use these words don't live on the streets of this city. They don't have to pick up the tortured bodies of their colleagues that the UF gangsters dumped by the side of the road. They have never had to explain to a constable's son that all that's left of his father is in a filthy canvas sack. These big shots have never heard the threats that were made to anyone who made the mistake of standing up against these madarchods. We go to work every day not knowing if we will come back in the evening. It's the law of the jungle out there. Either we survive, or they survive. So yes, sahib, if you want to know, yes, I killed him. He opened fire on my men, and he would have done it again had he gotten the chance. I got my chance, and I killed him. Ask this snivelling bastard standing next to you if he believes in his heart that his nephew wasn't a criminal. So what if the bloody MP was his uncle. No one grieves when we die, because everyone says we do it in the line of duty, and none of us have any uncles who are MPs."

The UF representative spluttered with surprise and anger, but one look at the ferocity in Akbar's eyes made him think better than speak out. The mood at the parade seemed to have changed after the outburst. The delegation from the UF, who had been so sure of securing Akbar's head on a platter, had lost some of its swagger. There was silence for several moments, until, finally, the UF minister, having regained some composure, attempted to speak to Dr. Death but was cut short by his raised hand.

"Is this true? Did your man fire on police officers?"

"Well, no, it's not that simple. You see, these are false allegations laid by this murderer—"

"Yes, sahib! Everything that Akbar Khan has said is true!" The voice belonged to an aged inspector who had been standing in line behind Akbar and Constantine. The old man was so frail that his entire body shook as he shouted out. "What can we do, sahib? When they kill us, nobody cares, but if one of them is killed, they burn down half the city. I have forty years of service, and I have never seen anybody slaughter policemen like they do. Every Friday, we line up on this same ground to say funeral prayers for our colleagues. I have borne the weight of too many coffins to remain silent now. Nobody hears our plight, sahib."

"I am here to listen to you, barey mian. I am your commander. I do not know what the commanders before me did or didn't do, but I have a very simple policy. From now onwards, if any criminal, belonging to any party, attacks a police officer, he is to be hunted down and killed. If I hear of a police officer's body being found on the road, I want the body of a ward boss lying on the exact same spot within twenty-four hours. And I will hang the SHO who fails to do this. This is how I deal with criminals. I suggest, Mr. Minister, that you take your delegation off my parade ground before I decide to order your arrest as an accomplice to the murder of a police officer." The horrified UF delegation beat a hasty retreat and sped off in their cavalcade. Dr. Death saw them go, then turned to Hanuman, who was at his side. "This Akbar Khan fellow. Promote him."

Akbar chuckled as the parade was dismissed. "See, what did I tell you, Consendine? Nothing to worry. They call this one Dr. Death for a reason."

8

October was the worst month in the city. The cool sea breeze stopped, and the humidity rose to unbearable levels. By the time he got out of his car, Constantine's heavily starched uniform was already wilting in the heat. His pickup had stopped outside a nondescript-looking video shop on a dusty street. Every building on the street had a low-hanging balcony draped with flowers strung together. In the evening, ladies of the night would come onto the balconies and parade their wares to the gawking customers on the street. Most of the shops masqueraded as music stores but were actually the entrances to the brothels. Constantine smiled. It had been a while since he had been back here on Napier Road.

Constantine was amazed to notice that the red-light area remained oblivious to the growing violence in the city. The local residents stared as his escort jumped off the pickup, wearing bulletproof vests with their assault rifles cocked, and formed a security perimeter around him. To the locals, they may as well have come from another planet.

The months since the IG's durbar had been eventful. The ward bosses had started a full-fledged insurgency, and, under Dr. Death, the police weren't taking any prisoners anymore. Soon after the IG's durbar, Constantine had been given command of his own police station in north Karachi. It was hardly a plum assignment, being the second-worst police station in the city after Orangi, but as Akbar often joked with him, they had gotten so used to difficult areas by now that they wouldn't know what to do with themselves if they ever got a peaceful police station. By all accounts, Napier Road remained one of those cushy, peaceful areas. No matter what the level of violence in the city, everyone still needed to fuck, whether they were policemen or ward bosses. In the meantime, the pimps and tarts raked in the profits.

This was what had brought Constantine here in the first place. He had arrested many criminals in north Karachi, and the crime situation had been transformed since he had been posted there. But he had maintained his principled stance and restricted his operations against the UF to arresting their ward boys, rather than killing them in police encounters. However, he had not yet been able to capture the person who was number one on his most-wanted list—the ward boss called Ateeq Tension.

Ateeq Tension had become a big man in UF circles since Constantine had first heard of him that day in Akbar's office. He was one of the most dangerous men in the city, a trained, cold-blooded killer. He had become the leader of the UF's most vicious hit squad. It was rumored that he received his orders directly from the Don himself. If the Don called Ateeq Tension and gave him a name, it was the equivalent of a death warrant. He had such a bloodthirsty reputation that he even scared the more moderate members of his own party. He killed men on the slightest excuse. If he thought even for the briefest instant that a party member had been disloyal or a businessman was about to complain to the police about the extortion calls he was getting from the ward, their lives would be forfeit. He was absolutely ruthless, a high priest of murder, the chief enforcer of the reign of terror the Don had unleashed on the city. He had gained the sobriquet "Tension" because it was said that once you met him, there would be nothing but tension in your life.

Constantine had become particularly obsessed with Ateeq Tension. When he took over his new charge in north Karachi, he heard dozens of stories about how Tension and his men had terrorized the local residents and how the police had been powerless to stop it. But the one story that really rankled at him was how Tension had paid regular visits to the house of a slain police officer and repeatedly raped his young daughter, while the mother was forced to watch. The police officer's quarters were at the back of the thana and, every time Constantine drove into the station, it assailed his conscience. He spent many hours planning, scheming, dreaming about how he would catch Tension. He often fantasized about what he would do when he did catch him. If there was one man for whom Constantine was willing to violate his own rule about not killing criminals, it was Tension.

Then one day his luck changed. Wajahat had just been released after a short stint in prison, and he had contacted Constantine on his release and thanked him for his kindness. He also brought with him information about Tension. Apparently, he had fallen in love with a girl from the red-light area. He fawned over her, and was a frequent visitor to her kotha on Napier Road. The brothels were one place where even criminals lowered their guard. Like all men, they had urges, and when they came to fulfil them they were vulnerable. Wajahat had told Constantine that Tension could be picked up from there. The only problem was the naika. As chief madam of all the prostitutes, she had declared the red-light area as neutral territory. All men, irrespective of which side of the law they were on, were welcome to spend their money there. As a result, the police were not allowed to conduct raids on the brothels. The price for breaking the naika's rules was hefty. If she grew angry, she would stop the local police station's rather lucrative monthly payments. Law and order in the area would break down, and "sympathetic" journalists would start publishing unflattering stories about the local station in-charge in the tabloids. Sooner or later, a senior bureaucrat or police officer whom the naika had entertained would react to all the reports of "police brutality against women in the area" and sack the in-charge. After all, the naika had contacts everywhere, and it was a very brave or a very foolhardy SHO who'd choose to tangle with her.

It was no wonder then that the local police had never dared to cross her. And Constantine was aware that if he wanted to catch Tension, he would have to ask a huge favor of her, something she would not normally grant to anybody. But then, he had never been just anybody to her. Constantine's first posting had been as picket in-charge of the Napier Road police post. He had been full of himself in those days—smart, young, energetic, an athlete with a body that girls swooned over. One such girl had been a young prostitute who, in spite of being new to the profession herself, had become famous for her dazzling beauty.

Salma Begum was the talk of all the kothas, and grown men would fight like boys just for the right to pay her any price she demanded. She was a smart businesswoman and made a small fortune in a very short time, but she had eyes only for the young Christian assistant sub-inspector. The feeling was mutual, and the two soon started seeing each other. He was like none of the men who frequented her kotha. Constantine was remarkably shy and old-fashioned around women, but she could see that he had an inner confidence, a sense of moral purpose that none of her very rich and powerful clients had. And he loved her zest for life and acerbic sense of humor. He fell madly in love with her. But the space she inhabited was far removed from his world and his puritanical upbringing. When he looked at her, he entertained thoughts of making a life with her. It wasn't unheard of for policemen to marry prostitutes. In fact, many who were posted in the locality did. But Constantine knew how the others sniggered at these men in the station. It was whispered that they pimped their wives and prayed for the birth of daughters instead of sons, so that when their wives grew old and lost their looks, the daughters could enter into the business and fund their old age. No one took these men seriously anymore. They had no career prospects of their own, but remained in the force just to facilitate their business activities. Constantine didn't want to become one of them. He couldn't swallow his pride and ignore the snide comments made in the station, no matter how much money was on offer. If Salma had left her profession, it may have been a different story, still not an easy one but perhaps manageable. But she was a rising star of the area, and many were already looking to her as a future naika. Besides, she had never been ashamed of what she was.

He knew that their relationship was a fleeting one, but it was hard to reconcile. Neither of them wanted to accept the harsh reality of their situation. Finally, he decided to get himself posted away from Napier to make a clean break. He volunteered for a commando course that would take him away from the city for at least a year. The night before he left, they finally made love for the first time. Salma Begum had had hundreds of lovers before Constantine; she had performed this act on a daily basis. But never had it hurt so much as it did this one time.

Constantine's feelings for her never died out completely, but he did his best to suppress them. When he returned from his training, he met her formally. When he was posted to Preedy, she would send messages to him, even after she became the all-powerful naika, but he would make excuses for not meeting her. She understood his reasons and accepted them, but she never got over him. She fawned over him, sending him expensive gifts, money, anything that he wanted. He refused to let her employ the considerable resources at her disposal to help him in his career. The only thing he would accept, from time to time, when his weakness overcame him, was her girls. To Salma Begum, in a strange way, it was as if he made love to her through her girls.

All of that had ended when Constantine left for Orangi. He hadn't even spoken to her in over two years. But the desire to catch Ateeq Tension was so great that he had overcome his inhibitions and arrived at her doorstep. He entered the video store; an efficient-looking man sat behind the counter, poring over a thick, dusty ledger. He looked up at Constantine from glasses perched on the edge of his nose, and then, apparently not thinking much of a mere sub-inspector, went right back to his ledger.

"What do you want?" he asked in a rude tone.

"Tell the naika that the SHO of north Karachi has come to see her regarding an important official matter."

"The naika doesn't have the time or inclination to see every bloody police officer who comes by. You must have an appointment. If you don't, then leave your name and number with me and, if she feels like it, she will contact you."

Constantine stepped up to the counter and, gently but firmly, shut the man's ledger. When the man looked up at him with some annoyance, he smiled. "My name is Constantine D'Souza, and I'm pretty sure she'll want to see me. So I suggest you go upstairs and announce me."

The man looked at Constantine for a moment, as if evaluating the seriousness of his purpose. Then he wordlessly turned and climbed the stairs to the kotha. From the sound of rushing feet, clattering silverware and hushed but excited tones, Constantine could make out that his arrival seemed to have electrified the household. The man rushed back down, almost tripping himself on the stairs, and wordlessly bowed his head and gestured for him to go up. As Constantine walked upstairs, he could see the opulently decorated private apartments of the naika. The room smelt of faded jasmine flowers. Plump velvet cushions lay on the floor, surrounding a low table made of solid silver. Richly brocaded silk curtains filtered the bright light from outside, and a couple of huge, hand-woven tapestries adorned the walls. In front of the silver table was a single, beautifully hand-carved mahogany rocking chair. The servant girl hurriedly brought a solid gold hookah and placed it next to the chair. Another maid came scurrying out of the kitchen carrying a tray laden with tea and an array of sweet and savory snacks. But despite the opulence of the room, there was a melancholy to it. The furniture felt like it had been placed without a personal touch. The Salma he remembered would have hated the décor. She always used to talk about how tacky all the naikas were, more interested in giving the impression of grandeur rather than investing in anything truly classy. At that time, she was still a small-town girl with limited exposure to the big city, but Constantine always thought she had an amazing sense of style in everything she did. As he looked around this room, he didn't see any sign of the Salma he had known.

He had just taken his first sip of tea, when she walked in. Time had been kind to her. She remained a strikingly attractive woman, even in advancing middle age. Her skin was fair and flawless, her hair still trailed to the small of her back, even though Constantine was surprised to see her head covered demurely in a dupatta. The Salma he remembered never used to cover her head. She was still a fit woman, perhaps not the classic hourglass figure of her youth, but not too far from it either. But her eyes, those gray-green eyes, were still as bewitching as when Constantine had first stared into them fifteen years ago.

She bowed her head slightly and lifted her hand to her temple to greet him, in the style of courtesans of old. He rose from the cushions out of deference for her position, and, only when she had seated herself on the chair and he was back on the cushions, did he understand why there were no other chairs in the room. Everyone who came here came as a humble supplicant, and thus had to sit at the naika's feet.

"You look tired, Consendine."

"It's the long hours, Naika Begum."

"You don't have to call me that."

"Oh, but I do. That is your title. Let's not be naïve. It's been a long time since you were merely Salma Begum."

"Maybe. But have a care. The favor you come to ask can only be granted by Salma Begum, because the naika would not do such a thing for you."

"How do you know what I come to ask for?"

She smiled at him. "Now who is being naïve? Everyone knows that you are looking for Ateeq Tension, and everybody knows that he sleeps regularly with one of my girls, Rukshanda."

"Any number of criminals frequent your kothas. Why would you think I want Ateeq Tension in particular?"

"Because you are obsessed with catching him. He makes your blood boil because of what he did to that dead policeman's daughter. Besides, he's the only one left. Your friend Akbar Khan has killed nearly all the other ward bosses in the city."

Constantine smiled. "And how do you come to all these conclusions about me? You must have some very good sources in my thana."

"I don't need sources in your thana, Consendine. I know you. He boasts about the policeman's daughter openly. And I know that was something you would never forgive or forget."

"Well, since you know why I'm here, we don't have to beat around the bush. Will you help me?"

"How is your wife? And your little girl?"

"They are fine. I have another baby girl now, but Salma, you're changing the topic . . ."

"Please, Consendine. Allow me for five minutes to live in my fantasy of what could have been."

Constantine fell silent and stared at Salma. "Okay. What would you like to know?"

"Your little one. How old is she?"

"She'll be a year old in February. She's very naughty. She knows her mother cannot control her when I'm in the house. She can barely walk, but the minute I get home, she comes scurrying to me."

"What's her name?"

"Katherina. But we all call her Choti."

"Choti. That sounds nice." Salma got up from her chair all of a sudden and walked over to a large closet near the door. She took a key from a bunch that was tied to the end of her dupatta and opened a small safety box inside the closet. She took out a silver bracelet and handed it to Constantine. "Please give this to her when she's old enough. Tell her it's from an old aunt. And tell both the girls that if they ever need anything they should ask their father to call their aunt."

"I can't accept this."

"Please. It will make me happy." She thrust her hand out towards him, and he took the bracelet. Her voice cracked a little as she said the words. But she regained her composure and continued. "As for your other matter, Tension comes to see Rukshanda every Wednesday night, without fail. She has a little flat, in one of the gullies just off the main road. He is madly in love with her, but he is a sadist. He beats her when he is with her. Normally, I would have thrown him out for such behavior, but everyone is terrified of his name. And he pays the girl well, so she doesn't mind it. My man will provide you a key to the back entrance of the flat. He comes alone, but his men park their car a little distance away. If you come from the back, no one will even know that the police was there. If you get him inside, there will be no problem."

"Won't they suspect your girl?"

"I'll send her away with a good dowry, to find a nice husband in her village."

"What about you?"

"What will they do to me? I'm the naika. They might protest a bit, but I'll say it was probably one of their own men who informed on him. They'll grumble, but no one wants to disrupt the flow of business on this street. Not even the UF."

"Thank you." Constantine nodded his head and rose from the cushions.

"Won't you stay for a bit, or do you have to rush off now that you've got what you wanted."

"No, it's not that. I . . . I have to get back to my thana." He turned towards the door then hesitated for a moment. "Listen, you don't have to . . . I mean if you don't want to . . . I don't want to put you in an awkward position because of me."

"That doesn't matter to me. I . . . you . . . you got shot. I heard about how you would have died, had Akbar Khan not got you out of there. I . . .

I didn't know if you would survive. I thought of coming to the hospital, but I wasn't sure I could bear to see you lying there helpless. Besides, I didn't want to cause a problem between you and your wife. So I used to send one of my girls every day. She befriended the nurses and got me daily updates on your condition. The point is that I didn't think I would ever see you again. Your reason for being here doesn't matter to me. It's enough for me that you're standing here in front of me once again."

Five days later, Constantine and a small police party were lying in wait in the alley behind the building. The naika's man had tied up all the details for them. He had provided Constantine a key and pointed to the flat where a light could be seen. Tension had been there for an hour, which meant he would be suitably drunk by now not to be able to resist arrest. His men were parked on the front side of the building and similarly preoccupied with alcohol and passing women.

Constantine counted the seconds go by. When he was sure that sufficient time had passed, he signalled five of his men to follow him up the narrow spiral staircase. As he put the key into the latch, he could hear the screams of a woman from inside. The flat was tiny, with a small sitting area with an attached kitchen leading into a bedroom. The door of the bedroom was partially ajar, and Constantine could just about make out the shape of a man on a woman. The man had left his pants in the outer room, and a .357 Magnum lay on the table next to a half-empty bottle of locally made Murree vodka.

Constantine signalled his men to hold back as he silently cocked his pistol and approached the door. The woman's screams had changed into a soft moan, while the man emitted loud grunts. Constantine was so close he could smell the man's rancid sweat. Although he still couldn't see the face, something within him told him that this was Ateeq Tension. He stood there for an instant, a mixture of fear and excitement enveloping him, and then he decided that it was now or never.

He kicked the door in and rushed inside the room, his pistol extended in front of him. The gun had reached the back of Tension's head before he had a chance to react to what was going on. Ashraf, Constantine's bodyguard, rushed inside a second later, his Kalashnikov poking into Tension's ribs. A wave of relief swept over Constantine before he realized that Tension was still inside the woman. She was screaming hysterically now. He grabbed him by the hair and yanked him off the prostitute's body. Tension was not a man used to the embarrassment of being arrested or having his wilting manhood exposed to a group of police officers. He tried to thrash about, until a sharp poke from Ashraf's rifle butt knocked him on the floor.

Constantine stared at him long and hard. There was nothing remarkable about him. He had long, shoulder-length hair and a lean body. "So this is the mighty Ateeq Tension."

The effects of alcohol and lust quickly drained from Tension's eyes as he took stock of his predicament. When he finally spoke, it was a squeaky voice, trembling with rage and fear. "You don't know what you're doing, you bloody thulla. You don't know who I am. Let me go, and I'll forget that you came here. It'll be easier on your life."

Such threats were standard from UF ward bosses who were used to exercising unchallenged authority. When Constantine and Akbar had been together in Orangi, Constantine was always the calmer of the two in situations like these. He would laugh off the impotent threats, whereas Akbar would endeavor ever harder to make plain to the offender the reality of his situation. Here, too, Constantine smiled and was about to walk away when he saw the bruises on the girl's ribs as she hurriedly tried to cover herself. Something snapped inside him.

He grabbed Tension by his long hair and started raining punches on his still naked body. He raised his gun again and pointed it at Tension's chest. Tension went white with fear at the realization that Constantine was about to pull the trigger. He closed his eyes.

For many years subsequently, Constantine would relive this moment in his mind. He could never quite put his finger on why he hadn't pulled the trigger in that instant. Maybe it was the pathetic sight of a naked man's rapidly shrinking cock as he saw his life ebb in front of his eyes. Or maybe Consntantine just lost his nerve for an instant. Whatever it was, instead of pulling the trigger, he lowered his weapon and dragged Tension down the stairs and into the street outside. The plan had been to sneak him out by the back door, but Constantine didn't care anymore. He continued to drag a now pleading Ateeq Tension, in front of dozens of stunned onlookers, right up to where his car was parked. Tension's gunmen were totally overcome with the shock of seeing their boss being so publicly humiliated. They hadn't even reached for their weapons before Constantine's team closed in and disarmed them.

Constantine still didn't know what to do with his rage. He couldn't kill him, but he still needed to do something. He grabbed Tension again and whacked the side of his head with his pistol butt. Tension was wailing like a school girl, still trying to hide his manhood between his legs. He was still under the impression that Constantine would kill him. He begged for his life, promising to confess to all of his crimes. Constantine was taken aback by the sight of it. Here was the terrible Ateeq Tension, whom he had built up in his mind to be some kind of ghoul. But Constantine had ripped off the layers on top of the man, and the person who was now soiling himself in front of dozens of people on a public street had no resemblance to the Ateeq Tension of legend. The man in front of Constantine was pathetic. And with that realization, Constantine's obsession with Tension came to an abrupt end.

Major (now Colonel) Tarkeen's office, one week later

"Constantine, my *dear* fellow, welcome! Come on in. Well done on finally catching Ateeq Tension. Excellent job you did."

"Thank you, sir. I hear congratulations are in order. I went by your old office, and they told me you had moved to the bigger room upstairs, Colonel sahib."

"Yes, my promotion came through. I was hoping to be back in uniform, but they decided the situation was too sensitive to bring in a new hand. So they kicked me upstairs here. But I believe I am not the only one who got promoted this week, *Inspector*. I take it this is for the Tension case?"

"Yes, sir. The IG has announced it, but it hasn't come through formally yet. But I don't know now, with the new military government set-up . . ."

"Don't worry about it. I will ensure that the new authorities don't delay it in any way."

"Thank you, sir. I would greatly appreciate that. It's just that, you know, the takeover happened totally unexpectedly. Everyone is a little unsettled. There are new masters, new orders. Some captain came to the thana the other day at eight in the morning and told me that he was going to report me for being late. I was trying to explain to him that I went home at seven in the morning."

Colonel Tarkeen laughed. "Yes, the regular army officers aren't used to your style of working like we are. The next time he says something to you, tell him you're working with me. He won't bother you again. By the way, Akbar came to see me the day after you caught Tension. He was very angry with you. He kept saying you had gone soft, and that you should have killed Tension. But I'm very happy you didn't."

"Why, sir?"

"Well, with the new government, there's a new scenario. We are evaluating the ongoing operation against the UF. It is possible that the government may require the services of the party sometime in the future. An accommodation may be needed. You know how it is in politics. There's also a feeling in some quarters that the last government went too far in this operation. Therefore we are suspending the shoot-to-kill policy for a while, though we will continue to monitor the situation. Had you killed Tension, it would have complicated things for you."

"But sir! What about all the people the ward bosses have killed? If the operation is stopped, they will come back worse than before. Come on, sir, you know all the details. You have been with us in this from the beginning. I thought you said they represented a national security threat?"

"Threat perceptions change, Constantine. As I said, politics makes the strangest of bedfellows. Oh, I'm not saying I agree with all this. Not at all. My view of the UF remains what it always was. But that's just the way things are."

"So, sir, what will happen to all of us who were in the operation? The UF will be out for our blood."

"Well, yes. It's true that they are urging the new government to take action against certain police officers, but we have made it clear that we will not allow that, as we consider those people our assets. Their main target is Akbar. Our intelligence has indicated that they are planning to assassinate him. I had a word with him and with your superiors, and I thought it was best for him to be posted to the interior for a while. At least until things calm down a bit. That's why I'm glad you didn't kill Tension. If you had, they might have made an issue about you as well. But you don't have anything to worry about."

"Did he agree? I mean Akbar, sir."

"Not at first, but he really didn't have a choice in the matter. A spell outside the city will do him some good. Calm him down a bit. Give him some time for reflection. He was starting to run a little too fast anyway."

"What do you mean, sir?"

"Well, you know he had become Dr. Death's bright-eyed boy. We were starting to receive a lot of complaints from your own officers about him overreaching himself. He also started to do a lot of work for our sister agency. We don't have an issue with that, but one mustn't forget who one's original friends are."

"So what happens to me now, sir? Where do I go, and what do I do with Tension?"

"You're fine, Constantine. You will continue to work as before. Yes, the operation is halted, so don't go after any more ward bosses, but manage the regular crime in your area. And since Tension was caught before the operation ended, no one will question you about him. Prosecute him like any normal criminal."

"Yes, sir." Constantine's voice lacked its usual surety.

"Don't worry, Constantine. I have my eye on you. You are a valuable officer. We will have a need for you in the future as well. There will be other operations, maybe not against the UF, but other targets. This Nawaz Chandio fellow, for instance. The brother of the opposition leader Yousaf Chandio. He's been in exile for many years, but we know he's been in contact with anti-state forces. His brother aspires to become the next Chief Minister, but he's got some very dubious friends in the underworld."

"But sir, I thought Nawaz Chandio was just a politician—and not a very good one. No one ever took him seriously. His brother was the one who did all the hard work politically, by staying in the country while he was having a good time in Switzerland or wherever he was."

"No, it's more serious than that. He had excellent contacts with the Russians and the Indians. We believe he's secretly building an underworld army that may ultimately even rival the UF's wards. His aim is to provide his brother with muscle in the streets. His point man over here is a Pathan called Shashlik Khan. Have you ever heard of him?"

"He's a medium-level operator, sir. Runs a couple of books and a gambling den in Sohrab Goth. But do you think he's that big a player?"

"He may become big if Chandio's brother becomes Chief Minister. So, you see, Constantine, believe me when I say that I will need you in the near future."

9

Day 1, 4:01 p.m.

Walking out of Tarkeen's office, Constantine knew that he didn't have a way out. His involvement in this case was unavoidable. Therefore, he decided to go to the scene of the crime to see it for himself. Zamzama, the chic shopping and restaurant district where Friedland had been abducted, wasn't too far from Bleak House. Whenever Constantine passed by there, he always felt that he had been transported out of Pakistan to some glamorous foreign location. Zamzama was a haunt of the wealthy and well-heeled. Rows of shops sold everything from iPods to Armani jeans. Designer boutiques displayed lavish, 100,000-rupee wedding dresses. A range of cafés and trattorias offered superb international cuisine from every corner of the world to the privileged. There was a price for all of this, of course. A meal at one of the trendy restaurants cost what an average person earned in a month. In short, the city's elite had created a little oasis for themselves, a place where they could shut out the problems of this chaotic metropolis. Constantine balked as he passed by a billboard showing a scantily clad woman advertising lingerie. He knew that the changing attitudes of the last few years had led to the liberalization of a lot of things. After all, a billboard like this one would have been unthinkable just five years ago. But Constantine remained a prudish man at heart. These things were fine for the barey log, the rich people who frequented Zamzama and bought such things, but he still believed that there needed to be some limits set to the growing licentiousness. People often assumed that because he was a Christian, he would be a more liberal person.

He resented that presumption. As an Anglican preacher's son who had spent all his life in Karachi, both his faith and background ensured that he remained staunchly conservative in his views.

His pickup pulled up in a small lane off Zamzama, where the Okra restaurant was located. This was the place where Jon Friedland had been kidnapped. It was mid-afternoon, and the narrow street was virtually deserted. A private security guard dozed in a chair outside the restaurant. Inside, the waiters, dressed in bow ties and waistcoats, were getting the place ready for the evening dinner rush. They had all been questioned by Maqsood Mahr's men several times already. Constantine asked them a few questions, but they had nothing new to add. Friedland had finished his meal and had stepped out with his friends, when a group of men had approached him. They brandished their weapons, so that passersby would be frightened off. Then, one of the men had held a gun to his head and pushed him towards a waiting car. Everyone had been shell-shocked and did not react. The security guard, an old, half-blind man who had been on duty that day, had thought that the men were initially coming to rob the restaurant. He had panicked and did not even attempt to stop them with his ancient shotgun. He hadn't noticed the car with the engine running. He had assumed that it belonged to one of the patrons who was looking for a parking space, like several other cars on the block. Once the kidnappers shoved Friedland into the vehicle, they had sped away. The descriptions that Constantine got were not helpful either. The kidnappers' faces had been covered with scarves, but they had been dressed normally, in shirts and jeans.

The incident had shaken up the area. Things like this just didn't happen in Zamzama. Kidnappings, car snatchings, and armed holdups were bad anecdotes that happened in faraway corners of the city. People in Zamzama were immune to these things, cocooned behind their high-walled mansions and legions of servants, watching satellite TV and dreaming of shopping excursions to Dubai. They were more attuned to what went on in London than in Lahore. Their principal cause of concern since this war on terror had started were the problems they had in securing US visas. So when the American was kidnapped from their midst, everyone here had gotten spooked. The restaurants and boutiques, usually overflowing with customers, had been deserted for the past few days. The city's reality had hit just a little too close to home.

They weren't even used to the questioning of the police. The barey log, the big shots, had buffered themselves from the droll problems of everyday life. If the water board didn't provide water, they would just buy private tankers. If there were power outages, they bought generators. And if they had a problem with the police, they wouldn't deign to go to the local police station. They would just call someone up to sort things out, the higher the person in the chain of command, the better. A man like Maqsood Mahr flourished in the company of such people. He was like a plumber to them, putting his hands in their shit and cleaning up after them. He was their "one man in low places," the connection that everyone needed to have, to get around the silly impositions of the law. Constantine had always dreaded being posted in this area and had avoided it so far. He had heard the stories of those officers who had spent time here. Crime fighting was low on their list of priorities, if indeed they ever got around to it. No, the biggest component of the job was VIP ego massaging. Everyone was a big shot, and thus everyone had a "source" they could call up. The most inconsequential fender bender could become an issue, because the rival parties would start pressurizing the local station in-charge to adhere to their point of view, each side using its own heavyweight to prevail over the local constabulary. Constantine remembered how his mentor, Chaudhry Latif, used to always warn them of the pitfalls of duty in posh areas. "It may look very glamorous from afar, making connections with these barey log all the time, but remember one thing. It is always better to be the SHO of a poor neighborhood rather than a rich one. In a poor mohalla, even if a hundred people get killed on your watch, no one will be too bothered. In a rich mohalla, if someone's cat goes missing, they'll hang you by your balls."

Therefore, the recent incursions of the police regarding this case had not been welcome. Individuals who were not accustomed to speaking to any police officer below the city police chief now had to give statements to lowly inspectors and sub-inspectors. Everyone understood, of course, the importance of the case. After all, if the Americans were to be killed by a bunch of nut jobs, it would become even harder to get a five-year, multiple-entry US visa. Nevertheless, the local population was losing patience. Constantine sensed from the furtive looks the waiters and managers were giving him that a complaint about him was imminent. It was a good time for him to leave.

There was nothing else to do here. The answers, if there were any to be found, would not be found in Zamzama. Constantine decided to go meet an old informer of his on the other side of the town. The drive to Boulton Market, in the center of the old city, was like entering another world. Gone were the sights and scents of immaculately groomed begum sahibs and choti memsahibs, flitting from one boutique to another, doing some late afternoon shopping or sipping a latte in a coffee shop. These were replaced by the odors of working men's sweat, and the stink of the carbon fumes that choked the air. Instead of the glossy and spacious boutiques stood cabins, barely ten by ten, selling all sorts of wares, from car tires to open spices heaped in little mounds in front of the customers. The traffic, too, changed. It grew far more congested as one travelled deeper into the heart of the city, coming to an almost complete stop in the alleys, where more than half the road had been encroached by shopkeepers stacking their wares. Auto rickshaws spouting black smoke, beat-up old Suzuki wagons, camels, and donkeys clogged the roads. There was no sign of the Mercedes saloons and Toyota SUVs that flocked to Zamzama.

Constantine had come to see Wajahat. The former ward tea boy and professional arsonist had come a long way since the day Akbar Khan had spared his life in Orangi. He had done only a short stint in prison, as Constantine had promised, and as soon as he got out, he became one of Constantine's most trusted informers, often alerting him to crucial snippets of information that came his way. He had drifted from the UF towards sectarian politics, joining a militant Sunni organization. There, he started specializing in orchestrating hostile takeovers of mosques that belonged to rival sects. He remained loyal to Constantine, though, and kept providing him with useful information. Ultimately, he was arrested again and, after serving a second, longer spell in prison, he had gone straight. But there were few men in this city who could match his knowledge of the city's underworld.

Boulton Market, where Constantine alighted from his pickup, was the city's traditional cloth market. In many ways it resembled a Moroccan kasbah—a massive covered market holding hundreds of stalls with narrow, winding passageways for customers to navigate. Constantine drew a few stares as he tried to push his way through the rush to the particular spot he was looking for, where the shop where Wajahat now worked was located. The shop itself was identical to dozens of others in the market. It was literally nothing more than a deep alcove in the wall, with four or five chairs placed in a narrow space in front of a raised platform. The shop owners and their assistants sat on the floor of the platform and displayed gigantic folds of cloth to the customers. An assistant would use a stick with a hook at its end to pull down the particular design requested by the customer from the wall. As Constantine approached the shop, he saw a young man with a prematurely gray beard opening a roll of cloth and speaking to a customer. He wore a prayer cap, and a pair of unfashionable, thick, horn-rimmed spectacles rested on his nose. He was dressed in a modest, sky-blue shalwar-kameez, and no one could have imagined, looking at him now, that he had once been one of the most feared goondas in the city. As he saw Constantine enter the shop, his eyes widened in shock and surprise. Before anyone else could react, he moved towards Constantine and grasped both his hands.

"Arre, Consendine sahib, how nice to see you! I know you had said you wanted a nice saree for your wife, but I didn't know you would come down here yourself. Why did you bother? I would have brought it home for you! But now you are here, please, have a cup of tea with me. Come this way, sahib, there is a chai wallah just round the corner. We have so much to catch up on, let's go and sit there, where we won't be disturbed."

Wajahat nervously ushered a slightly bemused Constantine out of the shop and towards the tea stall. The two men occupied a small table with two chairs in one corner of the stall and ordered tea.

Constantine smiled as Wajahat looked around anxiously. "Worried that I'd open my mouth about your past in front of your employers?"

"Arre, no sahib, it's not you I'm worried about. I just generally don't like to answer too many questions about my past around here. It's just better to maintain a low profile."

"Would they fire you if they found out you once burned twenty cars in a single day, not too far away from here? I'm sure some of those cars must have belonged to the merchants here."

"No sahib, they can't fire me. I have a part ownership share in the shop."

"Now I am impressed, Wajahat. Where did a tapori like you get the money to buy a share of a shop in Boulton Market? Are you freelancing for your religious friends again? And since when did you start wearing glasses?"

"I'm not working for the mullahs anymore, sahib. You know that. I quit when I went to jail last time. But the problem is, the last masjid I took over, you know that Makki Masjid in Gurumandir? Where we held the Pesh Imam at gunpoint and told him to go back to his village? Well, I, uh, kept some of the funds from the masjid collection. I didn't hand them back. It was quite a sizeable collection because the previous occupants had an aggressive fundraising program. It was about ten lakh, sahib. I hid it and told the mullahs that the police had confiscated it when they arrested me. I did my stint in jail, and then, when I got out, I decided to use the money to buy a share in this shop. As for the glasses, these are just there to soften the image. My old look wouldn't have gone down well in these parts." When he had been a UF activist, Wajahat was prone to wearing a dirty old leather jacket on top of a vest in the fashion of Bollywood heroes from a decade ago. When he turned to the religious parties, the look remained the same but he had sprouted a beard, and taken to wearing a checked scarf around his neck and a prayer cap on his head.

Constantine laughed heartily. "I had heard that there was no honor among thieves anymore, but no honor among mullahs? My, my, what a world we live in if we cannot have faith in the men of God."

"Arre, sahib, what God and what honor? It's all about the money. If I hadn't taken the money, those bloody mullahs would have pocketed it. It was exactly the same in the UF. The ward in-charges always thought that the only way to uphold the party's interests was by lining their own pockets. Besides, these mullahs are hardly God's chosen ones. When I was in jail the first time, I got sucked in by their rhetoric about defending Islam and all that. But when I started working for them, all they were interested in was trying to capture the rich mosques from their rival sects so that they had a better cash flow. It's all business at the end of the day. I saw an opportunity and decided to cash out. My mother is too old now to come and see me rotting in a police lockup."

"I am sorry for the intrusion. It wasn't my intention to alert your employers to your sordid past, but I urgently needed some information."

"That's okay, sahib, no harm done. They don't know everything about my past, but they know enough to know that I could be a dangerous man if they tried to cheat me. And your visit does no harm, because it shows that I have good contacts in the police. They will be a little more deferential to me now. But what is it that you wish to know?"

"Do you still have your contacts with the religious groups?"

"Yes, I still maintain some informal contacts. I told them I was leaving because I was the only support for my old mother. Which is true enough. The only bit I left out was that I was earning my bread with their money."

"What do you know about the kidnapping of this American journalist?"

At the mention of the American, Wajahat's mood suddenly changed. His smile disappeared, and he glared at Constantine. "Consendine sahib, what kind of things are you getting into? Stay away from that case. Don't even mention that name again in public, sahib. Besides, you are in the Prisons, why are you interested in this matter?"

"I'm just professionally curious, I'm not investigating the case. What do you know about it?"

"Nothing much, sahib. Any time somebody mentions the American, everyone shuts up. No one wants to know about it."

"Why is everyone afraid? Are they being threatened by someone?"

"No one has come forward, but the word is that there is some kind of ruthless new organization behind the kidnapping. No one has ever heard of this group before, but the fact that they picked him up so successfully the way they did, on their first mission, has given them a lot of credibility. I have heard that even the Agencies didn't know this American was in the city, but somehow this group found out. That shows that they have some very powerful sources and connections. That's why everyone is scared. Who knows what might happen to someone who was found to be digging for information about them."

"There must be a name on the street?"

"Qari Saif. That's the only name I've heard."

"Who is he? I've never really come across that name before."

"Neither have I, sahib. He wasn't really known in our circles. Apparently, he used to run a madrasa somewhere in the tribal areas. But I don't even know if he's actually involved in this. I heard his name once, when someone mentioned that if anyone knew about the American's whereabouts, it would be him."

"Are you sure that's all you know, Wajahat, or do I need to have a chat with your partners in the shop?"

"Arre, sahib, how long have you known me? Would I lie to you? I haven't heard anything else, and neither do I want to know more about this case. I suggest you do the same, Consendine sahib, and forget your professional curiosity. You have enough to worry about as it is."

"What's that supposed to mean?"

"Sahib, I was going to call you anyway today, before you came. You need to be very careful. You remember Ateeq Tension? You know the UF got him out of jail when they joined the government. It was one of their conditions for joining the coalition. Well, not only is he out of jail, but he's also back in the good books of the party. They've given him a position of authority. And he's got his old ward boys working with him again."

"So what? I know he got out months ago."

"An old friend of mine who's still a ward member overheard him talking to some others. He wants revenge. They were talking about you and trying to work out how to hit you. Tension said that he wanted 'the Christian dog' at any price. Apparently, they put out a fielding for you twice in Nazimabad, before you were transferred to the jail."

"What sort of a fielding?"

"A strong one, sahib. Ten boys, at least three motorcycle pairs. They had it all set in Nazimabad, but for some reason they couldn't carry it out. They would have tried again for you, but the jail is harder for them to ambush you in."

Constantine was stunned. He blinked several times and sipped his by now ice-cold cup of tea to regain control of himself as Wajahat continued.

"Sahib, just be careful. I remember Tension from the old days. He was always a crazy madarchod. And he hasn't forgotten how you publicly humiliated him when you arrested him. He's going to come after you. Watch out." He glanced up once again to check if anyone had overheard them, and then he got up from the chair. "I have to go back to the shop now, sahib, but take care and please, whatever you do, don't come back here again."

The prison, later that evening

Constantine had been sitting at his desk studying the sheaf of papers in front of him. It had been dark for a while. He could hear the muezzin's azan, calling for the Ish'a prayer, the last of the day. Very soon the jail would start shutting down for the night. The guards and wardens of the night shift would take over from the morning-shift staff, the barracks would be locked, and silence would descend upon the whole compound. Constantine stretched his arms and rubbed his eyes. He realized he hadn't eaten all day. His only sustenance had been the numerous cups of tea he had consumed. He smiled as he called his orderly to get him some food. Endless cups of tea were an important component of a police officer's life. His first station in-charge always told them that one of the most important tasks for a police officer was to have excellent relations with the best chai wallah in his jurisdiction so that tea could easily be procured at any time of the day or night. In a job that often involved long periods of waiting and irregular hours, it was a necessity.

Tarkeen's last sentence had been delivered as a very subtle hint, Constantine realized. Whether Tarkeen remembered his role in helping them or not, he would certainly not forget if he *didn't* help. Like it or not, his fate was now linked with Akbar's.

He turned to the papers scattered on his desk. There were the intelligence reports that Tarkeen had given him, the papers from Maqsood's case file and various newspaper clippings from the past few days. The hours since his return to the jail had been busy ones. He had to deal with the daily administrative tasks that had piled up, but for the past two hours he had devoted himself to learning all he could about the kidnapping. His orderly brought in his dinner—dal, lentil stew cooked in the prison kitchen, and freshly baked naan. Constantine broke off a piece of naan and hungrily dug into the dal. The prison's dal was famous all over the city for being delicious.

Constantine glanced once again at the newspaper clippings. Most of the stories carried Jon Friedland's life story. He was a young man, only twenty-seven. Unmarried, which was probably a good thing in his profession. In the short time that he had been a reporter, he seemed to have gotten around quite a bit. He had worked in Iraq, Beirut, and Egypt before coming to Pakistan. The press had gotten wind of the fact that he had been expelled from the tribal areas a couple of days ago and had absolutely crucified the government. Journalists had virtually accused the intelligence chiefs of being complicit in the kidnapping. The press was convinced that the government had a role in it. In an unlikely role reversal, the Agencies, who usually used the press for their own purposes—to plant false information or to attack their own critics—were being ripped to shreds in the popular papers and, at this point in time, had no way to respond. Free press was a good thing until it came and bit you in the ass, reflected Constantine.

The local papers had carried a few excerpts from the stories Friedland had filed from the tribal areas. It was obvious that his sources were excellent. He had not followed the standard government-prescribed sources, but gone off and made contacts on his own, which in itself was an achievement for an American in the tribal areas. Constantine wondered for a second if perhaps he was working undercover for the CIA. In Pakistan, most Western reporters were assumed to be working for the CIA, Mossad, or MI6. Friedland's stories were almost gushing over the tribals and were entirely anti-government. If he was indeed so favorably inclined towards the jihadis, why would they abduct him? Well, presumably to create an international incident, but still, if they wanted to nab him, it seemed to Constantine that it would have been far easier to do it in the tribal areas. Yet he had moved around freely over there, often without any kind of government escort, going to remote villages under protection of the tribals, and nothing had happened to him. He arrived in Karachi, and within forty-eight hours he was kidnapped from Zamzama, the most modern, liberal, and prosperous enclave in the city, where one was more likely to see a miniskirt than a madrasa. It just didn't make sense. It was as if someone was trying to frame the Agencies.

Maqsood Mahr's case file was not particularly enlightening either. It had the initial report, the FIR, which described how a brand-new white Honda Civic had pulled up outside the restaurant just as Friedland was exiting with a group of friends. They had shown the group their weapons and grabbed Friedland, tossed him in the back seat of the car, and driven off. The account tallied with what Constantine had learnt from the scene of the crime. The statements from the family that Friedland had been staying with were also pretty similar—that he had been on holiday, he had not undertaken any work-related meetings. Their servants, and the chauffeur who had been driving him around, confirmed all of this. The family itself, as Mahr had said, was extremely well off. They had a business—a factory in SITE, the industrial zone. The children had all gone to college abroad. There were several servants in the house, all of whom had been questioned but only in the presence of the family members. No one had been taken to the police station. Apparently, the family patriarch was a good friend of Hanuman, and he had requested the chief that his servants not be subjected to any form of torture or harassment.

Now, that was unfortunate because Constantine thought that questioning them separately might have been worth it. Someone must have told the kidnappers about Friedland's whereabouts, quite likely someone from inside. Taking the servants to the police station did not necessarily imply beating them up to confess something, but the mere atmosphere of a thana was often quite intimidating to the common man, and their reactions and answers may have been different in that environment as opposed to when they were questioned in their employer's home. Certainly, it seemed that one of the servants, the houseboy, was worth probing some more because he had recently come to Karachi from Azad Kashmir. Since there were a large number of training camps and jihadi organizations operating in Kashmir, it was a logical assumption that he may have been in contact with those sorts of individuals. It looked like Maqsood Mahr had missed a trick there. True, the head of the family had intervened on behalf of the servants, but one would assume that in a case of this magnitude, such considerations would have been overlooked. Mahr's people had not really pushed the point.

Constantine tried to think hard. His best bet had been Wajahat, but other than a vague reference to a name, he had nothing. Further telephonic enquiries with other possible sources about Qari Saif had also proved fruitless. He pushed aside his half-eaten plate in frustration. What did he think he was doing? This was exactly what he hadn't wanted. These were the kind of intrigues he was running away from, and now he was bang in the middle of them again. He was looking at the case papers as if he was the investigating officer. His detective instincts had been awakened by the challenge of an unusual case. Here he was, stuck in the middle of this great game between Tarkeen, Mahr, and Akbar, and he seemed to be the ping-pong ball in the middle. And did he think that he could somehow solve the kidnapping of Jon Friedland on his own, like some modern-day Sherlock Holmes, just by staring at the case papers?

Brought crashing down to earth by that last thought, Constantine hurriedly gathered all the documents and shoved them into a manila folder. He then wrote down his own findings and whatever he had learned from his informers and added this to the folder as well. Wajahat's warning rang in his ears and led him to a practical conclusion. He decided that he was definitely not going to go down that path again.

He called his reader into his office. His reader was the only one that he could absolutely trust from amongst his staff. "Are you sure that Akbar hasn't met with anyone recently?"

"Absolutely, sir. He hasn't had any visitors for six months."

"And he hasn't communicated with any of the other prisoners?"

"No one, sir. You know his barrack is completely out of bounds. The only one who goes there is that C-class prisoner who takes his food to his cell and cleans up the place for him. Bilal, his name is, but he's a simple-minded fellow. A little slow in the head."

"Does this boy have any political connections?"

"No sir, not at all. He is just a normal prisoner. He's not even from the city. He's from a village in the interior. He was locked up for murdering some relative in a family dispute. That's why he was assigned to

Akbar. He isn't connected with anyone. He hardly meets anyone else. He's very content just doing chores for Akbar. Neither of them meets anybody. Well, except the hari-pagri wallahs who come for tableegh every day."

"All right. Take this folder, don't let anybody see what's in it and don't talk to any of the wardens or guards. Go to Akbar's barrack and hand him the folder. Then come back and report to me. I'm waiting here." The reader took the folder and left.

Constantine had decided he would act as Tarkeen's facilitator, but nothing more. He did not want anything to do with this case directly, although he would try and help Akbar indirectly. He hadn't figured out how Akbar knew what he knew, but he wanted to see what Akbar made of the case file. He still had to be careful. Akbar's detractors were far from finished. He could not risk someone finding out that he was helping Akbar even a bit. As Wajahat had categorically warned him, he had bigger things to worry about. If Ateeq Tension were really after him, he shouldn't do anything conspicuous to attract attention. He would have to find someone within the UF who would act as a mediator between him and Tension. Any such mediation would probably involve some level of grovelling on his part. Constantine was a proud man and certainly not ashamed of having done his job, but in these times, with a United Front government in power and Akbar locked up, he could see no other alternative. In the past, Akbar's fearsome reputation in UF circles always ensured that they stayed clear from Constantine as well. But that was not the case anymore.

The reader returned ten minutes later. He reported that he had handed over the folder to Akbar.

"No one saw you?"

"No, sir."

"What did he say when you handed it to him?"

"Nothing, sir. He had been saying his prayers. I told him that you had sent him the folder. He took the papers out, looked at them, and then told me to go."

"He didn't say anything?"

"No, sir."

"Very well. Thank you." He couldn't discern whether Akbar's silence had been a good sign or bad. There was little else he could do at this stage. Constantine got up from the chair, stretched again, and decided to go home. It had been a long day, and tomorrow promised to be even longer.

10

Rommel was in the habit of waking early. The military academy had inculcated the habit in him. He loved the crispness and the quiet of the early morning. He had served in many parts of the country, and in every place he always found something different to savor about the morning. The only exception was here in Karachi. The hustle and bustle of commerce and industry that was the bedrock of the city would start intruding upon the peace and quiet from daybreak. The tropical heat and humidity would begin to swallow the early morning coolness far too quickly. It was only the recent inclement weather that had made things more tolerable for Rommel.

He got out of bed and strolled out to the lawn for his daily exercise. That was another habit that he had maintained since the academy days. It was a cold and misty day, although, for Rommel, "cold" was a relative term. The locals may have shivered with their teeth chattering, but, to a man whose last posting had been the frozen wastes of the Siachen Glacier, the city's cold snap was like a summer breeze. Rommel was amused by the complaints about the "biting cold." He had been hardened by the fury of the glacial winds that used to cut through skin like a knife. He recalled the term "wind rape," which the soldiers had given to the manner in which the icy-cold winds ravaged the exposed part of the body when someone went out in the open to take a leak. Now that had been biting cold. The weather here was a joke. As he stepped onto the grass, he wore only a vest and a pair of shorts. He enjoyed the cool air on his back as he went ahead with his stretches. For a change, he enjoyed his workout because it was actually quiet, with everyone staying indoors to avoid the cold of the early morning. The staff around him, covered in layers of sweaters and jackets, thought he was crazy. He, in turn, thought that they had all gone soft. None of his fellow officers was present either. Rommel was living alone in a guest room on the Bleak House premises. The room he was staying in had been built to house VIP prisoners. It was strictly functional, comfortable but without any character. And, of course, it was lonely. Rommel missed the camaraderie of a regimental mess.

He finished exercising and returned to his room for breakfast. The bearer had laid out hard-boiled eggs, toast, and a cup of tea for him. He took a sip from the cup and almost spat it out. The teabag tea tasted vile. Rommel much preferred the traditionally brewed tea, brought to a boil together with milk. Doodhpatti, they called it. Ever since he had arrived there, all he had been able to get was this weak, Anglicized version of tea. All the officers at Bleak House either preferred it that way or drank coffee. The only decent cup of tea that Rommel had drunk had been in Constantine's office the previous day. It was yet another reason for him to despise the place. Everything over here was different to what he was used to in the army. The thing Rommel always found reassuring about army life was the regimentation. No matter what part of the country you were in, you got the same routine in every mess. There was an automatic familiarity and predictability, right down to the snacks that were served at midday "tea break," which was as much a part of army life as a tank or rifle.

Rommel loved life in the army. Mornings spent training with the men, pushing them and oneself to the limits of physical endurance; the camaraderie and bond that developed between officers and their men; and the raucous company of one's brother officers in the mess at night. But in his current assignment, this routine was nowhere to be found. Everyone seemed to work rather secretively. It was quite possible that one had no knowledge of what the man sitting at the desk opposite was working on. And to Rommel's eternal consternation, the most useful tool in this business was that accursed invention, the mobile phone. Rommel, an avid hater of modern technology, detested mobile phones. And since the work here involved intelligence gathering, or managing informers, the working hours were irregular. The staff at Bleak House often worked late into the night. All of these things were anathema to Rommel.

He was not happy to have been sent here in the first place. He never wanted to be posted to Karachi, and he certainly hadn't wanted a posting in intelligence. Rommel knew that there were many young men who would love to be in his position. Junior officers loved being associated with the Agencies. It gave them some clout, opened doors for them that would otherwise be closed and gave them a sense of power. And, of course, where better to exercise that power and influence than in a city like this? But the charms of life in the Agencies, as well as life in the city, were wasted on Rommel. He had always served in the border areas and remote outposts, and he had preferred it that way. Others termed these as hard postings and tried to stay away from them. To Rommel, they were the essence of what the army represented to him. There was no greater thrill than to be on the frontier, whether in the wilds of Waziristan or on the icy peaks of the Karakoram Mountains.

The army was in Rommel's blood. His father and grandfather had both served in the army. His grandfather had fought and been decorated for valor in World War II, while his father had made his bones in the 1965 war with India. The army that Rommel was used to, that he wanted to be a part of, was the traditional army of uniforms, regiments, and pretty cantonment towns. Of course, it wasn't always fun and games. Rommel had seen his fair share of action. He had been wounded in the line of duty. But he loved the action, the element of danger that he had experienced on the front lines. He had never aspired to be mixed up with the cloak-and-dagger life of the Agencies. Rommel was beginning to learn that the differences between regular army duty and intelligence duty ran far deeper than just the requirement of not wearing a uniform. Here, nothing was as it appeared. There were wheels within wheels, hidden agendas in all activities, and everyone had a smug, superior "know-it-all, we are the masters of the universe" mentality. Rommel hated his job.

There was something about this city, completely different to anything he had experienced before. Young officers enjoyed being in Karachi because social life here was far more vibrant than in any of the small, sleepy cantonment towns. One could dine out in fancy restaurants, meet pretty girls, and spend time on the beaches. All of these things naturally held the highest priority for virile young men with a lot of time on their hands. Rommel was not immune to these attractions. He might have enjoyed the solitude of the mountains, but it wasn't as if he was averse to enjoying the temptations of the big city. Indeed, as a young lieutenant he had been known to be quite a Casanova. After his injury, though, he had become a little self-conscious about his appearance. He had been lucky that he had not lost his eye. The surgeons had done an excellent job, and, after the army sent him to Germany for reconstructive surgery, all that remained was his distinct scar. His friends told him that it was quite appealing, that it gave him an air of mystery and danger, another weapon to use in his amorous arsenal. But so far he hadn't worked up the confidence again to get back in the wooing game. Besides, he hadn't had much of a chance to explore the beautiful side of the city yet. So far, he had only been exposed to its ugly underbelly.

He was on a steep learning curve, and everything he was learning, about Akbar, Constantine, the police, or the United Front, completely challenged all the assumptions he'd had before he came here. He had been brought up with a healthy contempt for the corruption and incompetence of the police, especially when compared with the integrity and the organizational effectiveness of the army. But when he began to get into it, it wasn't quite as simple as that. The police had its good and bad points, like any other organization. And from what he was beginning to see, the police of this city had made great sacrifices, in the most trying conditions. Rommel could not understand how the president could tolerate such fascists like the UF to be his partners. In his mind, there was no difference between them and the jihadis. Both parties hid their criminal actions behind the veil of political ideology. There were so many things that Rommel was only beginning to understand now. Rather than being repelled by all that he had heard from Akbar and Constantine, his curiosity was piqued. He wanted to know more. Colonel Tarkeen had deputed him to go and see Akbar again today. Whether or not they were able to get any useful information out of him about this case, on a personal level Akbar fascinated him. Everyone was out to destroy this now powerless man sitting in a solitary cell, who was still unwilling to compromise with the world. Rommel saw a certain nobility in that.

As he finished dressing and walked out towards his jeep, he reflected upon the kidnapping. This case, of course, was complicated further because of the presence of the Americans. As Friedland was an American citizen, an FBI team had been working with them on the investigation. Rommel struggled to understand why his boss, Colonel Tarkeen, was reluctant to cooperate with them. Tarkeen was innately suspicious of the Americans, reluctant to share too much information with them or to appear too cooperative in general. To Rommel, the problem was simple. Friedland had been kidnapped, it had become an international embarrassment for the country and their task was to do whatever they could to get him back. If that meant working side by side with the Americans, then that was what had to be done. He had tried to argue this point with Tarkeen one day.

"Sir, if we have to get rid of them, don't you think the best way to do that is to cooperate with them? I can understand their point of view, sir. When we don't appear to be forthcoming, they start suspecting us. Let's try to be transparent. One of their citizens is missing. Our reluctance sends the wrong signal and creates more pressure for us from above."

"No, Rommel. We just can't trust them. They betrayed us in the past, and they'll do it again, once they cease to have a need for us. We open the store up for them, and they'll take everything. They don't understand how we work. They never can."

The Americans themselves did not help things with their attitude. They were understandably anxious about the fate of Friedland, especially after the release of the video on the Internet. They could not afford another global media event, a high-profile execution of one of their citizens by jihadis, performed live on YouTube for all to see—something that would become a "recruiting poster" for every mullah from Marrakech to Macau. The War on Terror had turned into one long no-hitter for them, and they badly needed a win.

But they were arrogant and overly cocky. Rommel had tried to befriend them, but they were contemptuous and patronizing towards the Pakistanis. He had become friendly with the team leader, a man named Jim, a streetwise ex-cop from Brooklyn who was extremely confident that his computers and electronic gadgets would solve the case for them. "Criminals always slip up somewhere," he said to Rommel by way of explanation one day. "They always make one transaction, a phone call, a credit card, something that puts them on our net, and that's what we wait for. Then we go in for the kill."

"Jim, these men are different from the regular criminals. They are jihadis."

"Hey, please, Rommel, don't tell me you buy their crap about waging a legitimate holy war."

"No, not at all. All I'm trying to explain to you is that their training and indoctrination give them a very different worldview from ours. They don't do things the way we do."

"A perp's a perp. Doesn't matter if they keep saying Allahu Akbar while committing the crime. Our technology is too good for these cave-dwelling sons of bitches. They aren't that smart."

"You have too much faith in your technology. Let me tell you one thing. I have been in a lot of tough situations, and the one thing I've learned is that the greatest weapon that you can use is the human spirit. These men, however misguided they may be, believe that they are on a divine mission. And they are willing to die for it. I'm a soldier, and I live to fight. But this war we are fighting isn't going to be won by your technology or your smart bombs. It's going to be won by the side whose spirit is the strongest. Remember that."

The Americans' desperation to solve the case was made worse by their patent distrust of their Pakistani counterparts. To the Americans, every move the Agencies made appeared to be a part of some grand conspiracy designed to make fools out of them. The more they voiced their suspicions to their superiors, the more pressure Bleak House received from the top to ensure a positive conclusion to the case. Frankly, at this point, achieving that conclusion would require a feat of alchemy more impressive than turning copper into gold, and a conjurer greater than any of the medieval charlatans who had practised those dark and dubious arts.

But perhaps, Rommel pondered, they had found such a conjurer in Akbar Khan. His revelations had produced a clue that had been beyond the scope of the not inconsiderable resources of the FBI, Bleak House, and

Maqsood Mahr. Rommel chided himself for having acted the way he had with Akbar and Constantine the day before. It was the typical knee-jerk reaction of a brash officer, a rather stupid and immature outburst. He had realized that Akbar was the key to cracking the puzzle and Constantine was a vital cog in unravelling Akbar. As he got into his jeep to begin his drive to the prison, he decided that he would have to develop a more intelligent strategy if he wanted to get what he needed out of Akbar. Today he would not go as the arrogant young army officer. Instead he would be the humble supplicant, lending a sympathetic ear to the prisoner.

11

Constantine loved waking up in the morning to see his daughters off to school. When he had been an SHO, or even a deputy superintendent, the routine of the thana was so hectic that the girls usually went to bed before he came home and left for school while he was still asleep. Now, the more regular hours of the jail enabled him to have breakfast with his daughters every day. He considered this to be the biggest perk of his current posting. His eldest daughter was almost ten years old, a precocious child who was always poring over her schoolbooks. Constantine was very proud of the fact that she was so studious. Despite her young age, he was already dreaming of her becoming a doctor. His younger daughter was just seven, but far more street-smart and playful. Her mother always said she took after her father.

Constantine would take great pains over the girls' breakfast, eating with them, helping them recite their lessons, and then sending them to school with his trusted driver and bodyguard, Ashraf. This morning, he got up twenty minutes late. The girls were already dressed, and his elder daughter was at the table, digging into her buttered toast, a textbook held inches from her nose. Constantine walked into the kitchen wearing a vest and rumpled shalwar, the sleep not yet gone from his eyes. His wife, who taught the morning shift at a nearby girls' college, had left a steaming cup of tea for him on the counter. He playfully tousled his daughter's hair as he sipped from his cup.

"Your mother's gone to work, Malia?"

"Yes, Papaji."

"And where's Choti?"

"She is outside, Papaji."

"And you let your younger sister just go off on her own?"

"She's just gone down to the gully, Papaji. She plays there every day."

Just then Choti came skipping through the front door, holding a lollipop. The smile on her face was enough to vanquish the darkest thoughts from Constantine's mind. "Papaji!" she shouted and leapt into his arms.

"Where did you go so early in the morning, Choti? And why are you having this before your breakfast?"

"I was in the gully, Papaji. A man gave it to me."

"What man?"

"The man in the gully, Papaji. He called me by my name and said he was your friend, and asked me what time you come home from work. I told him you were at home now."

Constantine put the teacup down because he did not want the girls to see his hand shaking. He struggled to keep his voice calm. "What else did he ask you?"

"He asked me which school I was in, and told me if I needed a lift to school, he would drop me. But I told him that in our house Ashraf Chacha drops us to school. I asked him if he wanted to see you, but he said he was in a hurry and would come another day."

Constantine set his daughter down on the table and then hurried to his bedroom. He took out his Beretta pistol from his bedside drawer and walked towards the open door.

"Papaji?"

"Malia, take Choti into your room and don't come out of there until I come back, do you understand?"

"Yes, Papaji."

Constantine's house was one of the larger quarters in the Preedy Station police lines. Most of Karachi's old police stations had been built with residential police lines next to them. The quarters had originally been spacious and comfortable, but, over the years, with an expanding force and no concurrent expansion in the housing facilities, the same quarters kept getting subdivided, and most had now become little better than hovels. Constantine had been lucky. He had managed to secure a large quarter when he had first been posted at Preedy Police Station many years ago, and he had been able to resist his neighbors' attempts at encroachment. He stepped out of the compound into the adjoining alley, his gun raised and cocked. He scanned the area for any sign of anyone suspicious, evoking nervous stares from passersby who just saw a half-dressed man with a gun in his hand. His bodyguard, Ashraf, who had been washing the pickup, sensed the seriousness of the situation from the crazed look in Constantine's eyes and came running from behind with his Kalashnikov cocked and loaded.

"Sahib! Sahib, what's wrong?"

"Ashraf, go call the duty officer at the thana and tell him to send a motorcycle patrol into these alleys. Tell them to pick up anyone remotely suspicious, I don't care who they are! Tell them that! And tell Saeedullah to stand guard at the front door and not to let anyone near the house. Not anyone, do you hear?"

"Yes, sahib."

His heart was pounding. It was still early enough in the morning for there to be a chill in the air, but Constantine couldn't feel the cold. Beads of sweat dripped from his forehead into his eyes. He couldn't believe they had come to his house. He had been alarmed when Wajahat had told him Ateeq Tension's plans, but he always figured they would target him directly. Not like this. They had approached his daughter. That was a line they had never crossed before.

As Rommel drove into the prison courtyard, he noticed that Constantine was not waiting for him outside, as he had done the previous day. It must have been a calculated snub, probably in response to his behavior yesterday. It didn't bother Rommel. In all fairness, he felt he probably deserved it. But he was surprised when an orderly received him and told him that Constantine hadn't reached the jail yet. Rommel had deliberately come later than he would have, in deference to the fact that police officers did not follow the same timetable as the army.

Constantine arrived in his office, clearly preoccupied, just as Rommel had sat down in his chair. The last hour had been a nightmare for him.

He had first debated keeping the girls home from school and then decided it would probably be safer if they were in school. But he had gone to drop them off himself, and had requested one of the Sisters at the convent not to allow them to talk to any stranger. Just as insurance he had left Ashraf at the school gate, with orders to shoot anyone who tried to approach the girls. But, like any worried parent, he was not satisfied. He would have stood outside the school himself all day, but he knew he could not now rest easy until he traced out the men who were after his family; to do that, he couldn't sit at home. With his mind focused elsewhere, the rude major from yesterday was an irritant for him. After having deposited his beret and stick on his desk, he impatiently got up and pointed towards the door.

"Shall we proceed, sir?"

"We'll get to that soon enough. If you don't mind, I'd like to sit and have a word with you. And, of course, a cup of that strong tea that you serve here. I am beginning to learn that a good cup of tea is very important in this job."

"What? Oh, uh yes, but of course, sir." The two men sat down again and Constantine ordered the tea.

"Consendine, I uh, I'm sorry, Constantine. I'm sorry I still haven't gotten your name right."

"That's all right, sir. I've gotten so used to people mispronouncing it that it's all the same to me."

"I wanted to apologize for yesterday. It was stupid of me to have barged in the way I did. I'm very new to all this. Where I come from, I am used to things being very definite—black or white. Now that I've come here, it seems as if I'm serving in a different world. I don't understand a lot of things. But I was fascinated by what you started telling me yesterday and I would like to learn a lot more about you, Akbar, everything really. I think it will help me. You know how busy Colonel Tarkeen has been; he hasn't really had the time to brief me. And besides that, a briefing or a file only conveys what happened, not the how or why. I cannot comprehend the feelings of the men who were there, from words written in a file. I want to know things from your point of view."

As the orderly came back into the room with the tea, there was a pause, as Constantine looked at the major in a new light. "If you don't mind my saying, Major sahib, this kind of intelligence work doesn't seem to suit you. You aren't really like the other officers. What are you doing here?"

The major smiled. "Yes, you're not the first one to tell me that. And quite frankly, I'm not sure what they were thinking when they sent me here. You're absolutely right. I've never worked in intelligence before. I have spent my entire career in the regular army. I was in Siachen, Kargil, Landi Kotal near the Khyber Pass, then Kashmir. I was in Bosnia as well, with the UN peacekeepers. The army kept sending me to these godforsaken outposts, and I liked them so much that when my tenure ended, I would volunteer to stay on. I think they ran out of frontiers to send me to, so they pushed me here."

"All the places you mentioned were hard postings. You must have seen a lot of action. Is that how you got your injury?" Constantine pointed to the major's eye.

"Yes, they were hard areas, but I enjoyed the life there. It was a proper soldiering life. As for this," he pointed to his eye, "this I picked up in Kargil."

"You're a brave man, sir."

"I never really thought of it that way. You know, that kind of job is much easier. You do what you have to, you know which side the enemy is on. There's a clearly defined mission. Since I came to this job, I always seem to be chasing shadows." The major pondered the thought. "But enough about me. What about you? Why did you join the police? I'm sure it wasn't a very normal career path for a Christian."

"No, it wasn't, sir. My father never wanted me to do this. I had to lie to him when I went to take the physical test. He wanted me to join the church, like him. He felt it would give me a lot of opportunities to travel, maybe even settle abroad. He believed that the church could isolate me from the problems of this world, keep me out of trouble. But I was a natural troublemaker. I was never a reading-writing type of boy. We had this police constable, Ghafoor Chacha, who used to patrol our mohalla. When we boys got up to some mischief while playing in the street, harassing the shopkeepers, he used to tick us off. But from time to time he used to tell us these magical stories about life at the police station, about catching crooks, and the big afsars, the officers who were so respected and powerful. I suppose for him, as a constable, even a sub-inspector was a big shot, but we didn't know that at the time. He would keep us spellbound with his stories. And I saw how the people of the mohalla treated him with respect. The shopkeepers would provide him with a stool to sit on while he was on duty, they would give him tea and food. Everyone who passed him salaamed him. I always loved looking at his uniform. It fascinated me. It was intoxicating for me, as a young boy."

The major laughed. "Wardi ka shouk. Love of the uniform. I think it's the same everywhere for young men. I used to love seeing my father dressed in his uniform. That's where I caught the army bug. And what does your father think of you now?"

"He passed away a few years ago, God bless his soul. I think he came to terms with it. My father always believed in hard work, merit. He believed in having compassion, he believed that virtue should be its own reward. But the world doesn't necessarily run on those principles, sir. He never understood that. I have seen that you can be the most hard-working, virtuous chutiya in the world and still get nowhere. The thing with our society, sir, is that if you are not a rich or powerful person, if you are a small person like myself, you need to have access to power just to survive—access to a little bit of influence, so that your existence can be bearable. Otherwise life can be very difficult in this city. You see these poor police constables in the stations, sir. Their lives are pathetic. They work long hours, twelve-hour shifts most of the time, no leave and dangerous duty. Our department doesn't take care of its men like your army does, sir. We have to do everything for ourselves. You might think why would anyone want this miserable job? Yet the number of people who want to be recruited is never-ending. You need big sifarishes just to get your name on the selection list. It's because all those people standing in line want to have a slight touch of being close to the circles of power and influence. Because even if they are mere constables, they are somebody. This job enables me to survive in this city. It means no one will be rude to my wife and daughters, that my family will not have to pay extortion to the UF thugs or the police. It means I can get an electricity meter and phone line much quicker than an ordinary person. My daughters will get admission into a good school because the principal will always have some problem or the other for which he will need to know a police officer. I will be able to make some money and secure my children's future. That is enough for me."

"You paint a very bleak picture of life."

"Sahib, it is not bleak. It is realistic. This is what life is for us. You army people live in a cozy cocoon. From the minute you enter the military academy, everything is taken care of for the rest of your life. You live in safe cantonment areas where schools, hospitals, parks are all provided for. At the end of your career you get a nice plot of land and enough money to secure your retirement. It's a good life."

"Do you resent us? Colonel Tarkeen said you were reluctant to work with the Agencies. Is this why?"

"No, sahib. I don't begrudge you your life. My only issue is when people like you come and make assumptions about our lives without understanding our compulsions, like you did yesterday. You accused me of being corrupt. Yes, I cannot deny that I have taken money from people. But I do it because I want to survive in this world, I want to try and give my children a slightly better life than I had, and I cannot do that if I do not become a part of this system. In our country, sahib, it is the system that makes the individual bad. But what you think of me doesn't really matter. You have your ways, and we have ours. I don't have some kind of principled stand that I will not work with the Agencies. As Colonel Tarkeen must have told you, I have done so in the past. And very successfully too. But sir, when you have spent as much time in the police as I have, you see a lot of ups and downs. When you are younger, the thrill of being at the center of events keeps you going; it's like a drug. You are dealing with the big cases, talking directly to your superiors, the Agencies calling you, wanting you to work with them. You are willing to get through the bad times because the good times are so good. But when you get to my age, you don't have the nerve to face up to the bad times. The truth is, sir, that I . . . I don't want to end up like Akbar."

There was silence as both men finished their tea.

"What happened with Akbar, Constantine? I still don't understand."

"Ask him yourself, sir. I think we should go and see him now."

The two men left the office and once again entered the jail courtyard. As they approached Akbar's barrack, they saw that the door of the barrack was slightly ajar; inside, Akbar was holding court with four bearded tableeghis. They were all holding copies of the Quran and reciting from it. Akbar was wearing the same crumpled white shalwar-kameez of the previous day. As Constantine and the major stepped in, the group quickly broke up, and the four men got up and left the room as if on cue. Akbar grinned widely as he put away his Quran. Constantine noticed that the folder that he had sent the previous night was lying open on the side of the mattress. It had obviously been read.

"Arre, Major sahib, welcome back! Didn't I tell you, Consendine, that Major sahib would find my company so stimulating that he would come back? What can I do for you today, sahib?"

"I just wanted to chat with you today, Akbar sahib. As I was telling Constantine earlier, I am new to Karachi and I don't know much about what happened in the past. I do know that you are a fascinating man. I would like to learn more about you. If you have the time, of course."

Constantine looked at the major admiringly as they both sat down on the stools. He had appealed to Akbar's vanity, inviting him to air his grievances, without so much as referring to the kidnapping. He was not the impatient young man of yesterday but a rather shrewd judge of a situation. Smart.

"One thing you have plenty of in jail, Major sahib, is time. What would you like to know about me?"

The major took out his pack of cigarettes and offered one to Akbar. "Is this your brand?"

Akbar smiled. "Gold Leaf. Yes, it was my brand, Major sahib. Thank you."

"I am beginning to learn that being a police officer in Karachi is not as straightforward a business as I thought. Constantine has been tutoring me on the subject."

"Haha. Yes, Consendine and I can tell you a few stories." He nodded towards Constantine. "He's a good man."

"So are you. That's what everyone says. Colonel Tarkeen certainly holds you in very high regard."

"Tarkeen. Hah. He of all people should."

"I would like to know what happened to you. I know you were a good police officer because everyone says so. You blame Colonel Tarkeen for what happened to you, yet other than some very basic details, none of my reports explain what happened with you. Apparently it's classified above my level. I have tried asking him, but he is evasive about it."

"I killed a man."

"From what Constantine tells me, it wasn't the first for you. You killed many men, many criminals."

"It was the wrong man."

"I don't follow."

Akbar sighed and let out a long trail of cigarette smoke from his lungs. "What can I tell you, sahib? This is the way the system works. If you're good at the job, then everyone wants you every time there's a crisis. When things go back to normal, you get discarded. I worked with everyone, all the Agencies, your people as well as the Kaaley Gate wallahs. I made all the enemies. I took everyone on. Ninety-eight kills. That's my record."

The major nodded approvingly. "But all these people were criminals. They got what they deserved. Justice was served. That's a good thing, isn't it?"

Akbar snorted. "That's what you say now, sahib, but when things go wrong then no one is willing to listen. That's what happened five years ago. I did something at the behest of my bosses and the Agencies, but things didn't go the way they were planned. Mistakes were made. Then I got double-crossed."

"So it must have been an operational mistake. It happens to us in the army as well. It's understandable. What was the problem in that?"

"Hehe. Big problem, sahib. The story doesn't end there. You see, the Don and his UF dogs had been waiting for me to make a mistake. Up till then they had not been able to harm me, personally or professionally, even though they had been trying for years. They tried to get me killed a couple of times, but I was always protected by the Agencies because I was working for them. That and the fact that the police bosses found me useful every time they wanted a mess cleaned up. You see, every time the crime rate goes up, it's a big issue with the press. The reporters taunt the bosses with crime statistics. *IG sahib, this many kidnappings have occurred this month, IG sahib, that many cars have been snatched, and you are doing nothing about it.* The bosses start panicking when this happens, because it means some politician might read the newspapers one day and decide that the IG is incompetent and needs to be replaced. Big headache for them. I was always their aspirin for this headache. That's why I survived. But this incident presented the UF with a golden opportunity to finally get rid of me."

"But why didn't the Agencies protect you this time?"

"Ah, that's the real rub of the matter. You see, Major sahib, at the time Colonel Tarkeen was with the Kaaley Gate wallahs. He and his boss had not been happy when I started working with your people. So the same Colonel sahib, who, as you say, has such high regard for me, decided to punish me. Kya sahib, we small people get crushed in the battles of the big shots and the barey log. Colonel sahib was unhappy with me for working with his rivals. What could I do? If I didn't work with them, the others would have been unhappy. I was like a man with four wives. How could I possibly keep everyone happy at the same time?"

"So they threw you in jail?"

"No. They didn't. *That* was done by that madarchod Maqsood Mahr. Ever since my stock was rising, his market had gone down. He's only good for pimping, anyway. He's never done a day's professional police work in his life. A poor fellow comes into his office to make a complaint about an investigation, and he has him arrested and says he is responsible for bombing the US embassy. Those are the kinds of 'jihadis' he catches. Son of a whore. He concocted a false case against me. And in all the time I have been here, he has kept spinning his false stories to try and keep me in here. And the Agencies have stood by and accepted his stories because it suited them to do so, even when they knew the truth."

The major sat silently, staring at the floor. At length, he looked up again and looked Akbar in the eye. "Akbar, I am a soldier and have always been very proud to be one. I was almost killed in Kargil, and I would have happily given my life for my country. I remember it was a very cold night. My men and I were dug into our positions on the side of a mountain. We were caught up in a blizzard, just trying to keep warm somehow, when the attack came. The bullet grazed my cheek before I knew what had happened, and two of my men dropped dead in front of my eyes. We were in a forward post, isolated from the rest of our company, so it was not easy for them to reinforce us. There were just two of us left and, although we couldn't see the enemy, we could hear them approaching. We both realized that they would not take us alive. I was losing a lot of blood from my wound, as was my comrade. The situation seemed hopeless, but we kept fighting. I was so tired that I didn't really even care whether I survived or not. The only thing that kept me going was that I knew my comrade was in worse shape than me, and I knew that I could not abandon him. That's the fundamental principle that is drilled into us. Fight for the man next to you and never abandon him. You are a warrior too. You may wear a different uniform but you put your life on the line, same as I did. Our people should have protected you. They should never have abandoned you. It's shameful that they did. I know nothing I say can make up for what you have lost. But all I will say is this: the smartest people are those who grab the opportunities staring at them. In your case, out of nowhere, this opportunity has presented itself. All of your enemies are desperate now. Colonel Tarkeen, who left you at the mercy of Maqsood Mahr, is now initiating a corruption enquiry against the same man. None of us even had a clue where this American was until you spoke yesterday. Right now they are willing to offer you anything. If you have any knowledge of this case, use it to your advantage. Don't do it for your country. Do it for yourself."

Akbar had descended into a trance-like state, and then, as if struck by a sudden epiphany, he burst out laughing. "Arre, Consendine, Major sahib is a superb fellow, but totally unsuited to intelligence work! I don't mean that in a bad way, Major sahib, but the fellows who usually get posted here are sneaky little shits. Your posting orders must have gotten swapped or something. I'm sure there's a little bastard stuck in Waziristan somewhere, pissing his pants trying to figure out how the fuck he ended up there instead of sitting behind a cushy desk in Karachi. You are a man of honor. Thank you for saying what you said. It may not mean much to you, but it does to me."

Constantine smiled and found himself liking the major more and more. An honorable man was hard to find in their world.

"Very well, Major sahib. Let's see what I can do to help you. Because one thing is for sure. If Maqsood Mahr keeps investigating this case, then President sahib is definitely going to have to explain to his mai-baap, the American president, how he allowed an American to get killed in Pakistan. Maqsood Mahr couldn't find this Friedland fellow if the jihadis had hidden him up his arse! The thing is, sahib, Karachi is a huge city. You haven't travelled around much in Karachi, have you, sahib?"

"No, I'm afraid I haven't."

"If you want to find someone in Karachi, it is important that you know where to start looking. This idiot Mahr is sending his men all over the city, checking every madrasa. They won't find anything. Does he think these jihadis are so stupid?"

"And you know where he is?"

"No. Not yet. But I know where to start looking. He was picked up from outside a restaurant in Zamzama, where only he and his friends who were with him knew they were going. Either he was being followed round the clock, or someone informed the kidnappers of his movements. Now, he was living in a big bungalow in Defence, with a rich family. It would be hard for any group to put surveillance on him there, because all the houses have private security guards who would notice a suspicious car or motorcycle standing on the street. They would call the police, and because all the people who live in Defence are barey log, the police does regular patrolling and promptly responds to emergency calls. So that option is unlikely. The second option, therefore, starts looking more plausible—that someone from within the house gave him away. Now, on the face of it, the family members are all very modern and liberal. The servants were also checked out. But there was one discrepancy— a houseboy who had been employed recently. He was from Kashmir, and my information tells me that in the past he had links with some of the jihadi organizations based there. The boy worked inside the house and could easily have overheard a conversation in which the American was discussing his dinner plans. My information is that the boy gave the jihadis the touch."

"But we never really considered that as a serious possibility. How did you come up with that theory?"

"Sahib, you didn't consider it because you are being led by whatever Maqsood says. And forgive me, but your people's investigating skills are totally nil. It is like the blind leading the blind. And this is not my theory. This is what really happened. My sources have checked it and confirmed it to me."

"But that is fantastic. All we need to do is pick up the boy and he will lead us to the American!"

"No, sahib. The last thing you want to do is pick up the boy. You go near the boy, and before you bring him from his house to the police station, they will know and the American will be dead. Besides, the boy doesn't know where the American is. He doesn't even know who his contact is. He just knows the number he has to call to give the information. They gave him a mobile phone recently. What we have to do is to get the call record of that mobile number for the days that Friedland was in their house. That shouldn't be too difficult. Mahr probably already has the number written on a file somewhere. Single out those mobile numbers that have been called only once. And then triangulate them through their booster towers to see which area the person who received the calls was in. You can narrow it down to the numbers which were based in two areas: Nazimabad and Orangi. Your kidnappers are based in these two areas."

"Why do we look at only the mobile numbers and why these two areas?"

"Because the jihadis find it more secure to communicate through mobile phones rather than on a landline. Harder to tap, and also they can keep changing their mobile number frequently. They wouldn't have received a call on one number more than once. If they were to use a land-line, they would have to leave their hideout to go make a call from a public call office in another area. This way, they can stay close to home and keep communicating." It was Constantine who answered.

"Exactly. And we only have to look in these two areas because my informers tell me that the boys who did this job are from these two localities. I should have more precise information by tomorrow."

Although Akbar tried to hide it, Constantine could see from his body language the exhilaration he was feeling at once again being involved in a case. It was the thrill of the chase. His voice had remained even, but his hand gestures had grown more animated as the conversation progressed.

"How did you know that he was alive?" the major asked.

"There are two groups involved in this kidnapping. Both are newly formed groups, which are splinters of older groups. The thing with the jihadis is that after a little while, the firebrands in any group start thinking that the others have gone soft just because they are not blowing something up every day. So they split and form their own, more violent splinter group. And so the cycle continues. In this case, there was actually a falling out between the two groups. One group wanted to kill him immediately, but the other did not because he had praised the Taliban in the tribal areas. The compromise was this date of 25 December. Their feuding will keep him alive. At least until the 25th."

The major was almost beside himself with joy. "Akbar, this is miraculous. How do you know so much? Who are your sources?"

Akbar shook his head playfully. "Now, now, Major sahib. If I reveal everything to you, what will I then bargain with? I can't tell you who my sources are."

"Akbar, if this information is accurate, I am confident that you won't be here for long. I will personally ensure it."

"Not so fast, Major sahib. Things won't be as simple as you think. Do what I have told you, and see where the trail leads. We may be on the right track, but we are still far away from recovering the American. As for me, if my information turns out to be correct, then come to me tomorrow. But bring Colonel Tarkeen with you. He is the one who will have to settle accounts with me. Nobody else can do it."

The meeting ended. Constantine and the major rushed back to Constantine's office. As they left, Constantine noticed the group of tableeghis who were with Akbar when they entered and had been waiting outside patiently file back into the room. The major was clearly excited at the prospect of a break in the case.

"How is he doing it, Constantine? How is he getting such precise details while sitting in here?"

Constantine considered discussing his suspicions with Rommel but decided to stay quiet. After all, he may have started liking Rommel, but he still knew nothing about him. "I . . . I don't know, sir."

"Well, however he's doing it, I wish him well. I am personally amazed by him."

Both men walked past Constantine's office, through the outer gate of the prison, to where the major's jeep was parked.

"Well, I must go and report what Akbar said to Colonel sahib." He shook Constantine's hand and climbed into the jeep. "By the way, out of curiosity, how do you know General Ibadat? You mentioned him when I made a stupid accusation yesterday. He was my commanding officer in Kargil. He was very kind and took a personal interest in my recovery when I was wounded. I owe him a great deal."

"It's something like that with me as well, sir. When he was a brigadier, he was posted in Karachi and his nephew was kidnapped from near the airport. I worked on the case and was able to recover his nephew. We even managed to arrest and convict the kidnappers. Since then, his entire family has always treated me like one of their own. He became my sifarshi—whenever I needed a good word in somebody's ear to get a posting, he would oblige. I owe my current post to his kindness as well. I am sorry if I offended you by mentioning him yesterday."

"Not at all. The fault was all mine. I was being crass. Take care, Constantine."

12

The house was festooned with fairy lights. Constantine found a parking spot some distance away, but he could see a bright red tent top protruding over the high walls. The house itself was brand-new, so new that the white-washed walls still looked damp and some of the fixtures still had their plastic covers on. Caterers and guests tiptoed over the construction debris that lay uncleared by the main gate. As Constantine walked in, he could see a motley mix of people gathered inside. Bearded and robed religious leaders sipped juice and chatted with bankers in pinstriped suits. Clean-cut young army officers looked distinctly uncomfortable standing next to street toughs with gelled-back hair and leather jackets. Constantine could not help but smile. These people would never have associated with each other in the normal course of their lives, yet here they were compelled to do so under the same roof. None of them could afford to miss out on this occasion. After all, Akbar Khan was throwing a party.

Constantine was amazed at how Akbar always managed such a diverse group of friends. But that had always been the secret of his success. Contacts at all levels of the social spectrum enabled him to squeeze out those golden nuggets of information that no one else could get. Most of the time, it was that information which made the difference between success and failure in this town. Constantine circulated between the various groups for a bit, but there was no sign of Akbar. He hadn't spoken with Akbar since his return to the city, but he had heard of his exploits. A year and a half in the boonies had not dampened Akbar's resolve or his skill.

He had been brought back to deal with the growing menace of organized crime, and, within a week of his return, he had shot dead the head of the city's biggest kidnapping gang.

This party was a celebration of his return to the big leagues. Akbar's personal bodyguard, Aziz, had specially called him in the afternoon and relayed Akbar's message, that he must come because there was something urgent to be discussed. Yet, despite his having searched every room in the house, there wasn't a trace of Akbar. At present, he heard voices coming from the roof, so he found a stairwell that led there. The roof was dark. There were no fairy lights here. The only illumination came from the starry sky and a small clay lamp that had been set on a low table, surrounded by four charpoys. A bucket of ice lay on the table, next to a half-empty bottle of Chivas Regal. Four men lounged on the charpoys, sipping their whisky and nibbling from a tray of samosa and chicken tikka. Akbar was the only one sitting on a chair, not drinking or eating, just watching the others while smoking.

The men hushed up immediately when they saw Constantine. Like schoolboys who had been caught sipping their fathers' hooch, they pushed their glasses as far away as possible from themselves. Akbar rose to greet him. He had grown a little chubbier since Constantine had last seen him.

"Arre, Consendine! Where are you? I haven't seen you since I got back into town."

"You get around so fast, Akbar, I can't keep up with you! One minute you're stuck in the wilderness, the next minute you're back in action, nabbing the biggest kidnapper in the city. And promoted again, with this lovely new house to boot!"

"Heh. Thanks. I reckon I deserved the promotion after two years sifting through cow shit in the boonies. And the house, well, I figured it was time to put down some roots somewhere. But I'm glad to see you. I heard you're working with Maqsood Mahr now. Is he still the greedy bastard he was when I worked with him?"

"Worse, now that he's become an SP. There's not a single paisa that he can bear to see go anywhere but his own pocket. What happened to your neck?"

"When they heard I got back, some wardia madarchods attempted to send me a welcome-home present. But they'll have to work a lot harder

if they want to kill me. Come, I want you to meet some friends." The
men had still not resumed their drinking and eyed Constantine with considerable suspicion. They all had flowing beards, and their shalwars were
hitched up above their ankles. Sensing their hesitation, Akbar waved to
them. "Don't worry, Consendine's one of my oldest friends. You don't
have to hide anything from him."

Visibly relieved, the men immediately reached for their glasses and
downed them in unison. Constantine recognized one of them, the fattest
one of the lot. He had been a small-time cheater whom Akbar had once
arrested in Orangi.

"Nomi?"

The man broke into a sheepish grin. Droplets of whisky ran down his
matted beard. Before he could answer, Akbar thumped him on his back.
"Not Nomi anymore. It's Sheikh Noman now. Our friend is going into a
new business—the business of religious education. He has just come back
from a pilgrimage. Pilgrimage to where, I don't know, but he brought
back a madrasa certificate proving that he is a religious scholar equivalent
to an English Masters level. And he miraculously got all this education in
two weeks. Heh heh."

The fat sheikh's grin became even more sheepish. "Akbar bhai, come
now. You know I've always been a spiritual sort of person. I want to help
the impoverished youth of this country follow the true path of God.
Inshallah, by God's Grace, Consendine sahib, we are close to concluding
a deal that will establish a madrasa for boys, where everything will be free
for them."

Akbar laughed raucously. "*Concluding a deal.* Nomi? You've even
begun to talk like some respectable white-collar person. What he means,
Consendine, is that they have almost completed the successful illegal occu-
pation of the land where this madrasa will be built. And it's conveniently
located right next door to Nomi's, sorry, the *sheikh's* gambling den. That
works out well, doesn't it? That's the beauty of this city. Respectability is
just one step removed from outright criminality. A bookie who makes a
little money transforms himself into a 'stockbroker.' And a street-smart
fraudster who used to cheat people by creating fake religious charities now
calls himself a sheikh. He wears fine clothes, dabs his body with expensive

perfume when just a few years ago he didn't know the difference between a bar of soap and a biscuit, and is now acknowledged as a scholar of Islam. And all of this in such a short span of time! Now that's what I call a genuine Karachi success story."

The sheikh smiled benevolently at Akbar's ribbing and cast a spiritual glance towards the heavens. Then he interlocked the fingers of both hands, as if explaining some profound metaphysical concept. "Din and duniya, Akbar Khan. Din and duniya. The material world and the spiritual world must exist side by side. Does not the Quran teach us not to neglect matters of trade and business? Why, the Holy Prophet himself was a trader, and a successful one at that." The three other mullahs nodded enthusiastically at the sheikh's mantra.

"Perhaps, sheikh, but I'm pretty sure the Quran's definition of business didn't include land grabbing and gambling. Anyway, to each his own, as long as you don't stop sending me my cut."

"But of course, Akbar bhai. This project of ours could not have taken off if it hadn't been for your support. And I pray that Allah should always keep you protected from those that wish to harm you, like these United Front haramkhors."

All the men said amen and then another one of them, a short, stout fellow, piped up. "Waise, Akbar Khan, you should take extra precaution now, especially after this last attack on you. These UF bastards will never let you go. You really gave it to them back in the day. I have some boys who fought along with Mullah Omar in Afghanistan. They are tough, trained commandos. They can do anything. If you want to cut somebody's line, I can arrange it. Very precise, very professional. Just two of them are enough to take on an entire ward. At the very least, you should keep them with you for your personal protection."

"I appreciate your offer, but after this thing that just happened in New York, if anyone were to find out about your boys, they would probably hand us all over to the Americans. I suggest you hide them somewhere for the time being."

A third mullah, obviously sufficiently inebriated by now, roused himself up from his reclining position. "The Americans will run when they see us coming, ji! They will become petrified just by hearing my name! Maulvi Ali! We saw off the Russians in battle, what are these Americans?"

The man was trying very hard to balance himself and the overflowing glass in his hand on the narrow charpoy, but, with his last vigorous gesture, he tipped over and fell off the bed to hoots of derision from his fellow drinkers.

"The only battle that one will be fighting will be the battle to get sober in time for the dawn prayers." Akbar gestured to Constantine to follow him to a dark corner of the roof. The volume of the gathering around the table increased as the quantity of the Chivas decreased, with each individual fighting his own imaginary battles in the Panjshir Valley and Kandahar. Akbar lit another cigarette and offered one to Constantine.

"What's the matter, Akbar? Is the problem with the UF really serious? I thought things would have gotten sorted out, with you returning to the city and Dr. Death being made the IG again. He got you your promotion in a big hurry, didn't he?"

"He felt bad that I got screwed when the operation against the UF ended abruptly. The kidnapper was a one-off. Dr. Death has been posted back here with a specific agenda. They want to start an operation against the jihadis. That's all anyone is interested in these days. I had information about the boys who put a hit on me, but nobody wanted to hear about the UF. The party is now a partner in this War on Terror, and so all their sins are forgiven and forgotten. Colonel Tarkeen also wants me to start working on the jihadis."

"So what's the problem?"

"I don't want to get involved in that. These people do God's work. Besides, I already have an enmity with the UF, I can't afford to create one with these jihadis. If they manage to defeat the Americans, they'll hang us."

"You've got to be joking, Akbar. You think they can defeat the Americans? Have you seen CNN? The Americans have a bomb called the bunker buster that can destroy an entire mountain, and you think these whisky-guzzling idiots can defeat them? You think these morons are doing God's work?"

"Not these chutiyas. Of course not. But there are others who are genuinely committed to their cause. The truth is, Consendine, I'm scared. How do you intimidate someone who is willing to give his life up for God? How do you fight that? It's like setting yourself up for failure."

"Okay, so you don't want to work on the jihadis, and you can't work on the UF. So what are you going to do?"

"The Bleak House wallahs are doing some work on this Nawaz Chandio fellow. He returned from his exile when his brother became Chief Minister last year. The government dropped all the criminal cases against him as part of an amnesty, but the Agencies suspect that he has been setting up an underworld organization in the city to use as an independent power base."

"I heard something about that. In fact, Colonel Tarkeen mentioned him as a potential threat a while back."

"Yes. But Tarkeen is singing a different tune now. He wants to use Chandio's thugs against the jihadis because they are all old leftist sorts. The Bleak House wallahs aren't willing to compromise, because they say he committed treason when he was in exile."

"He was never serious. He ran a half-baked 'insurgency' from a hotel suite in Geneva. How could he be a threat to the state? And now his brother is Chief Minister, so what's the big deal? They can't touch him anyway. They should forgive and forget; otherwise they will make him into something bigger than he is."

"They say treason is treason and that's unpardonable. They don't want him to become another Don. And if they can't touch him yet, at least his friends can be neutralized. Chandio's front man is Shashlik Khan, the drug dealer and gunrunner. They've asked me to bring him in. That's where I need your help."

"I don't know Shashlik, nor do I have any information on him."

"But you are friendly with that fellow Rodrigues. You introduced me to him once, remember? He's a clearing agent at the port."

"Yes, I know Rodrigues, but what does he have to do with this?"

"Rodrigues is Shashlik's liquor supplier. When the Agencies started making a fuss over Chandio's associates, Shashlik went underground. Disappeared completely. He hasn't been in contact with any of his people. But the thing about Shashlik is, he can't live without his booze. And Rodrigues is an extremely resourceful fellow. He has a small but very elite client list, and they say he can get any kind of liquor, from anywhere in the world, at twenty-four hours' notice. So I'm pretty sure that if Shashlik is talking to anybody, he's talking to Rodrigues. He must know where Shashlik is, and that's how we can get to him."

"Akbar, there's no 'we' in this. I don't want to get involved. Do you actually think that we'll be able to arrest the CM's brother's best friend, who is himself connected to half the officials in this city, without having a ton of shit land on our heads? No way. I don't want to hear any more."

"Arre, yaar, you have to help me. I'm desperate. I have to find a target. If I manage to do this, the UF won't be able to have me thrown out of the city again because I'll be too useful. I need this, Consendine. Please."

"Why don't you try being a normal cop? Look, you got promoted again, you've bought yourself this lovely house, this is the perfect opportunity for you. Find a nice side posting and enjoy the rest of your career, rather than running around at the behest of Dr. Death and the Agencies."

"I have to do this. Dr. Death says he brought me back from the boonies to do big work, not just to sit around. I'm only useful to the Agencies and our bosses if I keep hitting the big targets. If I stop doing that, they'll have no more utility for me and then I'll be at the mercy of the UF."

Constantine stared hard at Akbar. "You're lying. That's not the only reason you keep doing this. It's an ego thing for you. You tell yourself that you're Akbar Khan, and no target is impossible for you. The harder the challenge, the more you enjoy it, because it gives you a chance to prove to everyone once again how tough you are."

Akbar was silent for so long that Constantine thought he may have gone too far. Then, without warning, he broke into a childish grin. "Okay, okay, so what if I do enjoy it? I can't work like a normal cop. So kill me. But please, please, help me to get to Rodrigues. Who else can I turn to but you? You are the only one I can trust, Consendine."

Constantine sighed, but he knew in his heart he could not say no to Akbar. "All right. I'll go with you to see Rodrigues."

"Thanks."

Constantine arranged a meeting with Rodrigues near the docks the following evening. Rodrigues was a regular churchgoer, present every Sunday at St. Andrews Church in Saddar, and Constantine had contacted him through their common pastor to arrange this meeting. Akbar and

Constantine waited in a police pickup on the side of the road that led to the main docks. The spot where they were standing reeked of that peculiar smell of the dockyards—a mixture of sea salt, rotting fish, and gasoline, a bizarre blend of nature and industry. It was close to quitting time, and a long train of trucks and tankers crawled past them, carrying their wares out of the port towards the city. The vehicles emerged out of a massive gate, which had several levels of checks to ensure that no contraband items got out of the port area. Dozens of security guards in shiny new uniforms were deployed all over the place, all of them attempting to look useful. In addition to the gate, a high wall with barbed wire and corner turrets had been constructed to completely seal off the port.

The sight of these elaborate security measures brought a smile to Constantine's face. A long time ago, when Akbar and he had joined the force, there never used to be any walls around the port area. The SHO of the Docks Police Station was the richest police officer in the city, because he had direct access to every ship that used to dock at the port. Every time a ship docked, he would be informed, and he would walk over, take his pick of whatever contraband there was on offer, and then trudge off. After years of this practice, some bright individual got the idea that this was facilitating corruption, and that the problem could be solved if only the police were shut out. As if the police were the problem. The corruption hadn't stopped, only the rates went up. The number of palms to be greased increased. As for the local SHO, he didn't mind. For, as he put it, it didn't matter if they put up a wall around the docks area. He just set up a police check post five meters up the road from the main gate. All those trucks laden with goods had to come out onto the main road eventually. And the road was still in the police station's jurisdiction.

"You know, these dockyards are the heart of this city. They keep the city alive and vibrant. And these tankers and trucks are like arteries, taking the supply of blood to wherever the body requires." Akbar, who had been serenely smoking his cigarette and staring out towards the sea, seemed to have awakened from a trance.

"It sure keeps the blood circulating in the local police's bodies. Tell me—is the story about Maqsood Mahr and his wife true? You know, the one about how, when he was posted at Docks, he left her funeral when he heard a new ship had docked?"

"Yes. He told the mourners that he could get a new wife any time he wanted, but ships laden with luxury goods didn't roll into the port every day of the week. He told me the story himself when I used to work with him."

Constantine chuckled. Just then his mobile phone started ringing. "It's him. He must be getting out. I'll call him over."

Constantine spoke into his phone, and presently they saw a short, dark man cross the busy road, hopping to and fro to avoid the heavy traffic, and walking towards their pickup. The man wore several gold chains around his neck and had a paunch that signalled a significant level of prosperity. Constantine and Akbar got out of the pickup to meet him.

"Hey man, Constantine man, how are you and ya'lls' family?" The man spoke in the sing-song accent common in Goanese Christians.

"I'm good, Rodrigues. Meet my friend, DSP Akbar Khan."

"Man, I have heard of this fellow. Didn't you kill a whole lot of ward bosses a few years back? Man, you must be a dangerous fellow."

"Trust me, Rodrigues, he's as meek as a kitten. But I called you here because Akbar and I have a proposition for you."

Rodrigues looked at them suspiciously. "What kind of proposition, man? Look, Constantine, I'm running a little late and I have a delivery for a very important client, so maybe we could meet up another time. Maybe we can have brunch together with our families after church this Sunday?"

"Why are you in such a hurry, Rodrigues? Who's your very important client? Not Shashlik Khan, by any chance?"

Beads of nervous sweat started streaming down Rodrigues' face. "Look man, Constantine, tell your friend I don't know about any such matters, okay? I don't know any Shashlik Khan."

Akbar put a gentle hand on the bootlegger's shoulder. "Look Rodrigues, we know that you're Shashlik's supplier. He uses you because you're the best, and I also know for a fact that he's still using your services. They say you can deliver any brand or type at very short notice. That's very impressive. We're not interested in your booze clients or where you get your stash from. But, as Consendine said, we have a proposition for you that might be mutually beneficial to us all."

"What's that?"

"Tell me where he is. Don't try and deny it. I know that you know the location. After all, you go personally to deliver his booze to him. I'm willing to remunerate you handsomely for your information. I have one peti for you lying in the dashboard. You can have it right now, if you want."

That got Rodrigues' attention, and he stared at the car's dashboard like a hungry dog after a bone. But he was still hesitant. "Look, it's not that simple. His and Chandio's people are everywhere. If they find out I talked to you, they'll kill me."

Akbar sighed. "All right Rodrigues, how much do you want?"

"Five petis. Up front."

"Five lakh! Are you joking? For information that isn't even verified? No way! Come Consendine, we'll get Shashlik some other way."

"I can give him to you right now. I'll take the one peti you have as an advance, so long as the rest is paid no later than tomorrow. Constantine can stand as a guarantor for me."

"How will you give him to us right now?"

"I have to make a delivery to him at 7:00 p.m. It's 5:30 now. He had asked for a rare liqueur, something they call absinthe. Very expensive, one bottle worth 75,000 rupees, very hard to get as well. I'll deliver it personally. He's living in a rented villa in Defence. There'll be no one there at this time, because he's planning to have a party later in the evening. That's why he told me to come at this time, because he said we would be able to talk and settle accounts without any interruptions. But my price is non-negotiable, man. And the deal is that you have to do it now. They have people everywhere, and if it leaks out that I was talking to you people, then man, I'll be in serious trouble. If you come with me now, I will slip away and it will look spontaneous, like you found his place on your own information."

Akbar looked quizzically at Constantine, as if looking for his approval. Constantine nodded his head slowly. "He's reliable, Akbar. He wouldn't cross me. I don't think he would set a trap for us. And he's got a fair point. You know how the department is. No one can keep a secret. If it got out that we were meeting with him, he would get burned. But we will have to pick up some additional force."

"No man, you don't need any additional force, man. He's all on his own, keeping a very low profile. Don't go for any extra men. Just come with me now. The two of you will be enough, man. Trust me, I'm not lying."

Akbar twirled his moustache for a moment, again looking out towards the sea. Then he turned to the car, took out a brown envelope from the glove compartment, and tossed it to Rodrigues. "Okay, let's go. I'll trust you. But I find that you've fucked with us, and you'll end up like all those ward bosses that you've heard about: six feet under."

The fat man thumbed the notes inside the envelope. His eyes lit up, and a contented smile broke out across his face. The three men got into the front cabin of the pickup together, and Constantine got behind the wheel while Akbar continued to question Rodrigues.

"How many times a week do you make a drop to him?"

"Since he's been underground, about once a week. But if there's something special he wants, I'll go in whenever he calls, man."

"How many people know about this place?"

"None of his own people. He couldn't trust that the police wouldn't weasel it out of them. That why I say, man, you won't have to worry. No security. When do I get the rest of my money?"

"When the job gets done. Don't worry, you'll get paid. Why does he trust you so much?"

"No man, it's not about trust. I give him the thing he needs. He can't live without his alcohol, and he needs a variety of the best stuff. Every Friday night he calls some close friends for a party, and I always get a call that day. That's why I was going to see him tonight."

"For a man who is in hiding, he sure leads a very public life. Who are these friends?"

"I don't know all of them, man, but they're all very powerful people. They would never inform on him, man. Listen man, his people can't find out I spoke to you, or else they'll come after my whole family. Please, Constantine, tell your friend it'll become a big problem for me, no?"

By this time, the sights and smells of the port had been replaced with rows of whitewashed and pink-tiled villas and quiet suburban streets. In contrast to the chaotic hustle and bustle of the port, everything seemed so orderly in this part of town. At Rodrigues' directions, they turned onto a side street and were greeted by a vast array of different architectural styles. The first house was all marble and columns, like a latter-day Greco-Roman temple. Right next to it was a Spanish hacienda and, next to that, a mock Tudor mansion.

Akbar whistled. "People in this neighborhood sure have the money to blow on styling their houses. Look at all this marble. Must be imported."

"You're hardly one to talk, Akbar. After all, your new place isn't too far away from here. You've also joined the ranks of the respectable people."

Rodrigues pointed to a house at the end of the street. It was a single-storey bungalow, modest in its pretensions compared to the palaces surrounding it. The structure itself took up little space on the plot, leaving plenty of land for a large garden area. But an overgrowth of untended weeds and creepers had climbed over the low walls, giving the place a dilapidated look.

"Is this it? This place looks like a dump."

Rodrigues nodded. "This is it, man. Trust me, the outside is mis-leading. It's mind-blowing from the inside, man. Look, I'll get off here. I don't want to be spotted by anyone. You can enter easily enough. If you ring the bell, an old chowkidar will answer the door. Normally there's one other maid in the house who does the cooking and cleaning."

Constantine slowed the vehicle down, and Rodrigues jumped out. He looked at Akbar, who shrugged his shoulders. They stopped the car a couple of houses away from the bungalow and got out. Akbar had two bodyguards in the back of his pickup, and he told them to circle round the back of the house on foot. He and Constantine drew their weapons and gingerly approached the gate. The gate had no house number or name fixed upon it. There was a button on one side, presumably for a bell, but it had been completely covered by creepers.

"What do you think? Should we ring it?"

"No. Let's just go over the wall. The bushes will give us some cover as well."

Both men tucked their pistols in their belts, and, while Constantine managed to scale the wall quite easily, it took Akbar three attempts before he could climb over. The inside of the compound was a complete con-trast to the decrepit condition outside. A gleaming black Mercedes-Benz

S-Class sat in the driveway, while an olive green Land Rover, equally new, was parked next to it. At the side of the house was a huge sunken swimming pool with an attached hot tub. Two marble lions poured water into the pool from spouts. The front door was solid oak, with a big brass handle.

But there was an eerie, ghostly feel to the place. No one had yet challenged their entry, which made Constantine more suspicious. How could such a prominent underworld figure be living without any kind of protection? They approached the front door. It was unlocked. As they entered, they could hear a record playing an old Bollywood film song from the 1950s. The scratchy, imperfect recording had an ethereal quality to it. *Chaudhvin Ka Chand.* Constantine remembered the movie. It had been one of his father's favorites.

Rodrigues had been correct. The interior of the house was certainly mind-blowing. Wall-to-wall marble flooring and a huge cut-glass chandelier dominated the lobby. A glass door led from the lobby into a den. The den had been set up as a retro discotheque. A giant strobe light hung from the ceiling, and there were mirrors everywhere. Pornographic art was displayed on the walls and in every nook and cranny of the room. The décor may not have been particularly classy, but it did seem expensive. But the *pièce de résistance* of the entire house was the bar. It dominated half the room, and the top was magnificent carved mahogany. Behind it, Constantine guessed that there were probably close to a thousand bottles, in every imaginable shape, size, and color, containing virtually every brand known to man. Shashlik Khan may not have been a connoisseur of fine art, but he did take his drink seriously.

Suddenly, a naked woman emerged from a side door that led to a toilet. She was obviously on something, because it took her a second to comprehend their presence. Constantine guessed, from her looks and grooming, that she was probably a servant girl. He also figured out why they had managed to enter the house unchallenged. The big man probably didn't want anyone else around when he was banging the maid. It was at that point that she started screaming hysterically.

Akbar moved fast. He cleared the distance between the woman and himself in half a second and struck her hard on her cheek. She buckled and fell while he moved into the toilet. Inside, a man was bent over the washbasin top, snorting white powder. An Uzi machine pistol lay next to the line of powder. Before the man had a chance to grasp the gun, Akbar was on top of him, dragging him out of the toilet and into the den. In the meantime, Constantine had managed to bind and gag the woman with her own clothes that had been lying discarded on the floor.

"Shashlik Khan." Akbar said the name with deliberateness. The man bent over on the ground in front of him was heavyset, built like a rugby player. Remnants of the white powder were still stuck on his nose. The buttons on his silk shirt were open, revealing a milky-white complexion. But there was no fear in his eyes as he looked up expectantly at Akbar, not saying a word. The girl, however, still whimpered and shook uncontrollably. Her wide-eyed stare indicated that she was in a state of shock. Constantine stepped into the next room to find something to cover her with. The room was a bedroom, decorated in the same gaudy style, with a huge ceiling mirror hanging over a heart-shaped bed. He found a satin bed sheet and draped it over the woman.

"Akbar Khan sahib, please, let us talk." His voice was calm, unfazed by this unexpected turn of events.

"Oh, don't worry, Shashlik Khan. We'll have all the time in the world to talk in the thana."

"Akbar Khan, just hear me out. We don't have to go to the thana. We can settle this amongst ourselves. Just forget you ever saw me. I'll give you one khokha."

"Get up."

"Two khokhas."

"Bhenchod, do you think this is a fish market where I will negotiate a price for you?"

"Three."

Akbar hit him hard with the back of his hand, drawing a trickle of blood from his forehead. "I told you, I'm not for sale. I'm not one of your pimps."

"Khan sahib, I mean no disrespect. I have heard of your name and your reputation. We all admire what you did to those UF bastards. I would not offer you such a large amount if I did not have regard for your skills. But we are both men of the world. What is the point of arresting me? We both know that this is a game being played by others to trap Nawaz Chandio. You and I are just pawns."

"Bhenchod, you're building a private army of criminals in this city, and you say you're a mere pawn?"

"Khan sahib, I can promise you, my activities will never harm your interests. We are just trying to protect ourselves from the UF and the other forces in this city. I can be very useful to you. Just do me a favor. Ask your friend to go behind the bar, there's a secret compartment just under the top. Please ask him to open it. I swear on my mother's life, it is not a trap."

Akbar looked warily at Shashlik Khan and then signalled Constantine to check behind the bar. Under the bar top Constantine found a button and pressed it, to find a compartment that he could never have guessed was even there slide open. The little drawer was packed with 1,000-rupee notes. On top of the bundles lay a gold-plated World War II vintage German Mauser. Constantine had never seen so much cash before in his life.

"What is it, Consendine?"

"It's, uh, it's money. More than I've ever seen. I don't know how much. It would probably take an hour to count it."

"It's 5 crore, in untraceable cash. The two of you can take it and walk out of here, and no one will ever know. I can help you in other ways as well, Khan sahib. I will ask Nawaz to speak to his brother, and we will get you another promotion. I read in the papers recently that you have become a DSP, right? How would you like to be an SP next week? Just tell the people who sent you after me the same thing that all the other police officers told them. That no matter how hard you tried, you couldn't find me. Nawaz will sort this mess out soon enough."

Akbar walked over to the bar and stared into the compartment, lifting the Mauser and examining it closely. He nodded appreciatively at Shashlik, then put the gun back in the drawer.

"Very impressive, Shashlik. Very impressive indeed. So that's what five khokhas look like in real life? You're right—we can walk away with the money and pretend we never found you. After all, no one knows we're here.

I was almost tempted to accept your offer. But you said all the other cops took your money and forgot where you were. I'm not like other cops. I'm Akbar Khan, and I'm taking you in. So get up off your fat ass and start walking towards the door."

13

Nawaz Chandio was going insane. At least that's what his retainers thought. They were sure somebody had performed black magic on Sayeen Baba so that he would become incapacitated like this, unable to talk except for some unintelligible muttering under his breath. He had been pacing the room for three straight hours, ignoring all entreaties for food, drink, or conversation. The retainers stood around, not sure how to deal with the situation because they had never seen the master in such a state. The only thing he would do was smoke one cigarette after the other without a break, carelessly throwing the stubs on to the tiger-skin rug.

Worry did not come easily to Sayeen Baba. His elder brother had been the worrier in the family. Nawaz Chandio had always glided through life, using his immense charm and charisma to get through. While people respected his elder brother Yousaf's capacity for hard work and his grasp of realpolitik, men gave their hearts to Nawaz. It helped that he was a strikingly handsome man. The older retainers among the family claimed he was the spitting image of the old sardar's father, his grandfather. Even if he hadn't been the younger scion of the oldest and most powerful tribal family in the country, his chiselled features and muscular six-foot frame would have made him stand out. But his familiar manner, which he somehow managed to intersperse with an imperious bearing, ensured that he was a natural leader.

Leadership was the Chandios' lot in life. Many said it was their curse as well. They had been an established political force even before the British arrived in these parts, tribal sardars who ruled as absolute monarchs and depended upon banditry to feed their people. They had fought the British at first, ultimately accepting their suzerainty after a prolonged struggle. It had been the British who first made the Chandios truly rich, when, in return for laying down their weapons, they gave them large tracts of the most fertile land along the banks of the Indus. Thus, in addition to their tribal lineage, the family also became one of the largest landowners in the province. But the streak of rebellion had not totally evaporated from the family's genes. Nawaz's look-alike, his grandfather, had joined Gandhi's Quit India movement during World War II, at a time when no other landowner in the region was willing to risk taking on the Imperium. He had been hung for that, but the sardar's devotees had been so incensed that the lands of the lower Indus became aflame with revolt. Unable to deal with such a rebellion in the middle of a global war, the colonial masters did not dare confiscate any of the family's lands. Instead, they decided to whisk away the new sardar, then barely a boy in his teens, to boarding school at Winchester, to be properly anglicized.

The young sardar had returned and grew into an even abler politician than his father, ultimately rising to become the country's first populist prime minister, until deposed by a military junta. He too shared his father's fate, being taken to the gallows by an illegitimate government who thought that the mystique of the Chandios could be snuffed out with the death of a single man. Once again, the powers that be were proved wrong. But this time round, there was a slight twist in the tale. The young sardar left behind him two sons—Nawaz and his elder brother Yousaf. Both men had very different ideas about keeping the flame of their father's legacy alive.

Yousaf opted for the cut and thrust of politics, spending a dozen years alternately braving periods of house arrest and more formal incarceration, making a thousand deals to survive but never advocating a violent struggle against the State. Nawaz, on the other hand, was a firebrand. He would not abide by the injustice of his father's execution. Like his grandfather a generation before, he raised the red flag of revolt, escaping into the tribal hinterland to wage a guerilla war. His followers did not see the point of another martyr from the family, so they eventually convinced him to flee via Afghanistan to Switzerland, where a young wife and infant daughter awaited him. Frustrated by his predicament, he bowed to the logic of his fellow rebels and left. But throughout his years in exile, he kept in touch with his tribal fighters, inquiring after them and sharing in their smallest joys, and griefs from a thousand miles away.

The rule of the junta came to an end a few years later, and Yousaf was absorbed into the political process, becoming a key figure in the politics of the province. But coming home was not so simple a task for Nawaz. His guerilla band had been responsible for several acts of terrorism during their self-styled insurgency, acts that had led to the deaths of police and paramilitary officers. These acts were not so easily forgiven by the State and, in particular, the military. It took another few years, and a second military dictator, for Yousaf to finally broker an amnesty that would allow his brother to return home.

These years in the wilderness had given Nawaz an almost mythical status among the Chandios' followers, and especially those of his "fidayeen" who had been with him in the barren hills during the insurgency. He returned the conquering hero and quickly took his place by the side of his brother, who was by now the Chief Minister of the province. But it was rumored that Yousaf had grown jealous of his younger brother's popularity, of the common touch that came so naturally to Nawaz and always eluded Yousaf. On the day he was sworn in as an MP at the assembly, Nawaz had publicly slapped a United Front member who had clashed with him on the floor of the House, drawing universal cheers from the gathered throng. These populist leanings had made some quarters think of him as a potential rival to his brother. Common people, and more than common people the media, liked his plainspokenness, his willingness to speak his mind about all matters, his insistence on following an unorthodox path, and his unashamed cultivation of those who were deemed "dangerous" friends. They seemed to like the fact that he generally avoided the skullduggery and backstabbing that was the mother's milk of politics.

But Yousaf also needed Nawaz. He had become Chief Minister for the second time as a result of a deal with the new military government, but it was evident from the beginning that neither party trusted the other. And so, despite his initial opposition to Nawaz's contacts with the criminal underworld of the city, he had come around to thinking that one day he might need such people.

And so the uneasy arrangement had worked, in spite of Nawaz's bluntness and Yousaf's politicking. Until now. Two weeks ago, Shashlik Khan had been arrested by some DSP called Akbar Khan, and things started coming unscrewed for Nawaz. What few understood was that Shashlik was the linchpin of the entire deal. Nawaz was a pretty face, a brand name to attract people. He could give the occasional fire-and-brimstone speech to rally the troops but, always having been handed everything on a plate, he was not an organizer. He didn't know how to get his hands dirty. It was Shashlik who had the underworld contacts; Shashlik who had welded them into some kind of coalition loyal to him and Nawaz; he who went and made peace between the brothers and explained to Yousaf the utility of being friends with his friends. He had even convinced Nawaz to meet with Tarkeen, despite the fact that intelligence officers were anathema to Nawaz. Tarkeen had wanted to use them as a force against the jihadis. Shashlik saw an opportunity to cement a relationship with the Agencies and a chance to undercut the UF. Nawaz just saw a man in khaki, a color he had learned to hate since his father's death. He had lived his life railing against the military, and he wasn't about to change his tune for some short-term political benefit. And so, just before the meeting was scheduled to happen, Nawaz changed his mind and refused to meet Tarkeen.

Shashlik's arrest, therefore, created a void in Nawaz's life. Suddenly stripped of his brain's trust, he became an impotent schoolboy, blind with rage but unable to articulate what he wanted to do. That's when the pacing had begun. He had been like this for several days. Initially, Nawaz had been confident that the arrest had been the result of some petty foolishness on the part of a particularly stubborn police officer. He expected that his brother would speak to the IG and have Shashlik released. But it hadn't worked out that way. It was only after several days that Nawaz started to realize that Shashlik's arrest had been more than just an attitude problem attributable to Akbar Khan. There were other forces behind this gambit, forces implacably opposed to him, and forces that Yousaf was not willing, or able, to cross.

Wracked by indecision, Nawaz Chandio had agonized over his next move. Would he stay quiet, biding his time, so as not to give anyone an excuse to overturn his brother's government? And then, when the time was right, cut just the right kind of deal to get Shashlik back? Or would he live up to his reputation as a man who never compromised with his enemies? The first option may have been the smart political move, but Nawaz Chandio had never made decisions based on what was politically exigent. What mattered more to him was how his legion of devotees looked at him. These were the men whom he always surrounded himself with, violent, untamed men who had fought for him in the mountains and had sworn their lives to his service. He looked at them now and saw in their eyes what they expected of their Sayeen Baba. The enemy had made their move and they needed to respond with equal strength. To do anything else would be unworthy of the great Nawaz Chandio.

Maqsood Mahr's office

Shashlik Khan lounged on the office sofa, scooping mouthfuls of kebab into his mouth, while Maqsood Mahr sat opposite him and lit his thirtieth cigarette of the day. It was only after Shashlik had ravenously devoured his third plate of kebabs and washed it down with a glass of sweet buttermilk that he noticed the worried expression on Mahr's face.

"Aren't you hungry, Maqsood?" Shashlik belched loudly as he spoke.

"That's all you can think of right now? Didn't you hear the call I just received from Dr. Death? Everything we've been working for is going to be destroyed. They're out to get you, and they'll screw me for having helped you."

"You're being a bit dramatic."

"How? You heard him. Dr. Death wants you transferred back to Akbar's custody. Do you know how difficult it was to have your investigation transferred to me in the first place? Arre, baba, the CM had to beg the IG even for this small favor. Dr. Death had refused him point-blank when he asked for your release. He told the CM that you were engaged in acts of treason. That's the bloody problem with posting honest officers. You can't depend on them to be pliable. I warned the CM about this when he was posting Dr. sahib. But at that time, all he was interested in was having a 'firm, reputable officer at the helm during these difficult times.'

Arre, baba, fuck reputable! You need people like me at times like this, to manage things for you."

"Look, the CM did what he had to do at the time. What's the big deal? Just convince Death to leave me in your tender care. Tell him you're on the verge of breaking me, and it's imperative that my custody remains with you because I have vital information to reveal."

"That's what I've been saying to him for the past ten days. But he's not listening anymore. Akbar Khan is the IG's pet. Death was pissed off enough when the CM got the case transferred to me, and, now that he hasn't seen any results from my investigation, he's out for my blood. He just told me Akbar's on his way down to take custody of you."

"What? Maqsood, you can't let him take me back. That madarchod hung me up by my balls. Me, Shashlik Khan! As if I was some common criminal!"

"That's not your only problem. If Akbar makes the case against you, you're going to go away for a very long time. He's not going to go easy like me. So you better start making some calls to those powerful friends of yours right now."

"Maqsood, I have been trying all these days, but that bastard Dr. Death doesn't listen to anybody's sifarish. Tarkeen hasn't answered my phone calls ever since he learned the Bleak House wallahs were after me, and now for the past couple of days, the CM hasn't called me back either. Death must have prevailed over him to cut me loose."

"So speak to Nawaz. Tell him to go to his brother. I don't understand why he hasn't done more. I sent him several messages on your behalf."

"He wouldn't. I . . . you don't understand, Nawaz. He's a very proud man. He's not practical like you or me. He would have expected the CM to help me without his having to ask for it. And he certainly won't go to any police officer or fauji to beg for my release. He'd rather die."

"Then what the hell do you want me to do?"

"Listen, Maqsood, I'm paying you very good money to manage all our affairs with the police. So start earning your keep and start figuring something . . ."

The color drained from Shashlik's face when he saw Akbar enter the room.

"Looks like you've fucked up yet another case, Maqsood. No wonder you haven't gotten any information out of him. This place isn't an inter-rogation room, it's a five-star hotel. Dr. Death is not going to be pleased when he hears about this. Come on, you fat fuck, you're coming with me to a real thana."

"Arre, baba Akbar, look, I was your boss for so many years. I did you so many good turns. Lets just keep this between ourselves, okay? We can work something out."

"I remember all the 'good turns' you did for me. Like when you suspended me when I caught that ward boss. This one already offered me three khokhas to let him go and I refused that, so what can you do to top that? As for the IG, I don't know what kind of chutiya you think he is. He's not like the other officers that you keep buying up. He's an honest man, and he knows exactly what you've been doing. Why do you think he sent me here?"

Akbar grabbed Shashlik Khan by the scruff of his neck, causing him to drop the glass of buttermilk in his hand.

"Arre, baba, you can't take him without any paperwork. Where's the warrant? The transfer order?"

"Maqsood, I don't have a lot of time to spend arguing with you, so I'm just going to go. I suggest you ask the IG for the paperwork, if you feel so strongly about it."

Maqsood Mahr could see his professional life flash by in front of his eyes. He had banked on the fact that Shashlik's connections with the CM would enable him to push his career forward. But those hopes had turned to dust three hours ago, when Akbar had taken Shashlik. The CM was power-less to help him, Nawaz Chandio wouldn't even answer his calls, and Dr. Death thought he was an incompetent buffoon at best and an associate of Shashlik Khan's at worst. If the Bleak House wallahs got word of the fact that he had taken money from Shashlik, that would really be it for him.

He tore his hair out as he tried to figure out how things had gone so wrong for him. Akbar Khan was sure to be given another promotion for this case. At this rate, one day he would end up as Maqsood's boss. The thought caused Maqsood so much anxiety that he accidentally lit his cigarette from the wrong end. He was not a sentimental man, but if ever there had been a time in his life when he felt like crying, it was now.

There was a commotion outside his door. Loud voices, the roar of 4x4 engines, and then a burst of automatic weapons' fire. Maqsood's first instinct was to duck behind his desk. Surely killing him was a bit of an extreme reaction, even for Dr. Death. But then his orderly rushed into the room and motioned him to come outside. Maqsood was loath to leave the safety of the solid walnut desk, and he emerged only when the orderly had assured him that there was no imminent threat.

The minute Maqsood Mahr stepped out of his office, he saw the reason for the commotion. Several Toyota pickups were parked in the yard of the office, with a squad of armed men. They all wore armbands affixed with a photo of Nawaz Chandio. They had fanned out from their pickups and taken positions all over the office compound. Right at the entrance of the office was parked a fire-engine red Mitsubishi Pajero, with the number plate NAWAZ 1.

Maqsood started slowly advancing towards the lockup area. Inside, Nawaz Chandio was bent over trying to scrutinize a register. He had a red-and-white chequered keffiyeh tied round his neck, Palestinian style. One of his fidayeen announced the arrival of Maqsood. Nawaz Chandio pulled himself up to his impressive six-foot-four height and stared down gravely at the diminutive Maqsood.

"And who is this turd?" Nawaz asked the question of no one in particular.

"Sayeen Baba, it's me, Maqsood Mahr. I'm the SP in charge of investigations. I have been trying to call you for several days. I am one of your father's oldest supporters. He was the one who was responsible for getting me my job . . ."

"So you're the bastard in charge of torturing my friend Shashlik?"

"No, no, you misunderstand. I haven't tortured him at all, that was that other haramkhor, Akbar Khan. I was trying to protect him."

"Where is he?!" There was violence behind Nawaz's tone. Maqsood gulped as he saw the anger and frustration in the taller man's eyes. These emotions had been festering inside Nawaz for the past few days, and it was clear that they were about to boil over.

Suddenly, he grabbed Maqsood by his lapel and shoved him against the wall. "Where is he?" he screamed the words, his mouth inches away from Maqsood's face.

"Uh, Sayeen Baba, I don't have him anymore. The IG ordered me to hand him back over to Akbar Khan, so I had to. That's why I have been trying to call you, but I never got a response from—"

"Shut up! You say you were trying to protect Shashlik, and then you hand him back to the same people who tortured him? And you dare to call yourself my father's loyalist?"

The blow felt like a jackhammer to Maqsood. He staggered against the wall like a drunk, too shocked to react in any other way. He could not believe that Nawaz Chandio had just struck him. Yet he still had enough presence of mind to see one of his constables stiffen and reach for his weapon. Immediately he held his hand up, signalling all of his officers to do nothing. Maqsood Mahr had been in this game too long to still have hang-ups about such quaint concepts as self-respect. He could always buy more self-respect, but he would never be able to manage things if the Chandio crown prince was injured or worse in his office.

One of the fidayeen came up to Nawaz and reported that the compound was indeed empty and there was no sign of Shashlik Khan. The news seemed to restrain Nawaz from further violence, but his anger had not yet abated.

"Listen, pig, if anything happens to Shashlik, I am going to hold you responsible. I will come back here and hang you from the streetlight, do you hear?"

Maqsood Mahr kept sitting on the cold lockup floor with his head in his hands, listening to the retreating footsteps of Nawaz Chandio and his men, and he had no doubt that if anything happened to Shashlik Khan, Chandio would fulfill his promise. He knew then that he would have to change the entire dynamics of the game, if he wanted to survive.

Constantine was intimidated. He shuffled nervously as he rode the elevator to the third floor of Police Headquarters. He had never been on the inspector general's floor before. You only went there if you were in a lot of trouble, or if you were a senior officer, and since Constantine had been happy to have never been in either predicament, he had never ventured that far.

A liveried attendant opened the door of the lift, looked contemptuously at the ranks on Constantine's shoulders, and then turned his disapproving glance towards the door of the conference room. Constantine had to steady himself to stop from slipping on the highly polished marble. The conference room itself had wood panelling and high-backed green leather chairs. Constantine was impressed. So this was where the development fund got spent.

Several others had already taken their seats in the room before him. Akbar was there, sitting alone on one side of the long conference table, lounging in the chair as if he sat in on these sorts of meetings every day. On the other side sat Hanuman, now the IG's principal staff officer; Colonel Tarkeen, his hair having considerably receded since the first time that Constantine had met him; and Maqsood Mahr, who was wearing what appeared to Constantine to be an absurdly oversized neck brace. Mahr glared at him as he took a seat next to Akbar. He had been so involved with Akbar in the past two weeks since Shashlik's arrest that he had forgotten that Maqsood was still technically his boss.

The twenty-four hours since Nawaz Chandio's visit to his office had not gone well for Maqsood. Word had spread very quickly via the departmental grapevine that the CM's brother had humiliated Maqsood. It seemed to him that his authority was slipping away. This morning he imagined that he had seen the sentry at his house snickering behind his back. Dr. Death had been predictably furious. What had made it worse was Akbar's performance in comparison to Maqsood. Upon hearing what had happened, Akbar had moved Shashlik to a secret location and dispersed the staff from his office, to ensure that there would be no further incident with Chandio's fidayeen. As a result, when Nawaz finally got there, there was nobody around. Maqsood had been reduced to resorting to cheap, sophomoric efforts, such as purchasing the neck brace, to try and garner some sliver of sympathy. He looked at the confident expression on Akbar's face and grimaced. Yes, Akbar was probably sizing up the drapes in his office.

A side door opened and all of them rose as Dr. Death entered the room. His jaw seemed to be perpetually clenched and, as he sat down, Constantine could see Maqsood's hand shaking and his lip quivering.

It was Hanuman who spoke first. "Sir, as you are aware, you called this meeting to discuss the situation arising from the visit of Mr. Nawaz Chandio to the offices of the Special Investigation Cell. The purpose of Mr. Chandio's visit was to snatch his associate Shashlik Khan from police custody. The update on this situation is that Akbar moved Shashlik to a secret location, and, as a result, Nawaz Chandio was not able to find him last night. But during his visit to the SIC, he and his men manhandled several officers, including the SP, Maqsood—"

"Arre, sahib, what manhandled? Manhandled is too light a word. He has humiliated me. He has stripped me of my honor. I was almost killed by those thugs. But my life is unimportant. What is more important is that those criminals impugned the honor of the police. Sir, you may not be happy with me, but I still am a member of your force. An insult to me is an insult to you. I lay my izzat at your feet, sir."

"You should have thought about that when he was tearing your office apart." Dr. Death glared at Maqsood.

"What could I do, sir? He is the CM's brother. I am a poor man from a village near their lands, sir. The Chandios would never forgive me if something happened to Nawaz. Punish me any way you want, sir, but this was beyond my capability. I am not the strong man you are, sir. See, you took on the UF, now you are fighting the jihadis. The men are demoralized. We all look up to you, sir. You are our commander. Please sir, you are the only one who can do anything." Constantine and Akbar exchanged a glance. This was not how they had expected Maqsood to react. Constantine didn't buy it, but something had obviously struck home with Dr. Death, who had restrained his anger and looked pensive. Hanuman's face was inscrutable as usual, but, perhaps sensing where things were going, he spoke up again.

"Well sir, it's true that the Nawaz Chandio situation is an irritant, but in fact, we haven't really lost anything. After all, Shashlik Khan is still in Akbar's custody. They haven't been able to free him. As long as that is the situation, we have nothing to worry about. I don't think morale has been affected that seriously. We should handle the matter tactfully. What do you say, Colonel Tarkeen?"

"Well sir, my organization had, as you know, opposed the arrest of Shashlik Khan in the first place. We felt that we could turn him into an asset to be used against jihadi groups. Akbar acted at the behest of our sister agency to apprehend him, and we feel he acted too quickly."

"He was a criminal, Colonel sahib. That's all there is to it as far as I understand."

"Well, be that as it may, Akbar, but in any case what's done is done. I also think we should proceed further in this matter with some tact, especially knowing Nawaz Chandio's mercurial temperament."

"No." There was a finality in the way Dr. Death spoke that one word. He picked up the phone and asked to speak with the Chief Minister. Everyone waited in silence for the call to be connected, with a growing sense of trepidation. The call came through, and the IG cradled the receiver in his hand. Without bothering with pleasantries, he got straight to the point.

"Sir, your brother has violated the sanctity of one of my police stations. Now I may not like the officer who was in charge there, but he is still my officer. I am the commander of this force, and I cannot hold my head high if they think that I am unable to control one man and his group of hoodlums, just because he is your brother. His men have to disarm themselves, and he has to submit to the law, otherwise I will not have the moral authority to act against the UF or even these jihadis. I am sorry, sir, but I have to arrest Nawaz. I am not asking you to make him surrender, but I am informing you that I will go after him. I understand that this may be a difficult choice for you, but this is why you appointed me. To make the tough choices. I would appreciate your support in this matter. If you cannot give me that support, then I am afraid I can no longer serve as your inspector general under these conditions."

There was what appeared to Constantine to be some sort of animated discussion on the other end of the line. The CM was obviously not used to receiving ultimatums like this. He was sure that the IG would be sacked on the spot, yet Dr. Death's face was like smooth granite, devoid of emotion. Constantine looked around the room. His father had always said that a moment of crisis revealed a lot on men's faces. Hanuman continued to scribble on his notepad, as if that were the most normal thing to do at a moment like this. Tarkeen stared out the window, as if resigned to the inevitable. Then he saw that two of the men in the room were smiling, but for different reasons. Akbar's smile was guileless, a gesture of pride for his commander. But Maqsood Mahr was smiling too, and one look at the expression on his face convinced Constantine that Dr. Death had been set up. It all made sense in that instant, the seemingly selfless act of acknowledging his failure and his impassioned call for the protection of the department's honor. Dr. Death had swallowed it up.

The IG put the receiver down. "It's done. I want Nawaz Chandio arrested within forty-eight hours. I want his fidayeen disarmed. And they are not to be treated as some sort of political personalities; they are to be dealt with like common criminals."

Maqsood spoke up gleefully. "Arre, sir, thank you, thank you. You have restored my faith as a police officer. Arre, sir, I have never heard any IG speak to the CM like that before. I wish I had always had a commander like you. And permit me to say, sir, that if you want this task accomplished correctly, there is only one officer in your entire department who has the heart to do it. You must give this task to Akbar."

Akbar glared at Maqsood, the realization of Maqsood's gambit hitting him at that moment. He felt the anger rising within him, but only part of it was for Maqsood. The greater part was aimed at himself, for not having spotted his motives earlier. A thousand things rushed to the tip of his tongue—curses, taunts about Maqsood's loss of manhood, threats to break his legs. But a reminder of his surroundings made him hold his tongue.

"For once, I agree with this buffoon. Akbar, you are the only one I can trust to do this right. My own honor is at stake on this. You are like a son to me, and you have never disappointed me. Don't fail me now, either. Bring me Nawaz Chandio's head."

"Yes, sir! Don't worry, sir, it will be done. Your honor is our honor."

Akbar rose, saluted smartly with some panache, and left the room, quickly followed by Constantine. As they waited for the elevator, Constantine saw a trickle of sweat crawl down Akbar's cheek.

"Akbar, what the hell did you just do? You know Maqsood was setting you up. No one wants to touch this case because of Nawaz Chandio. He is not like the UF. He is a political icon. Why didn't you tell the IG to give the case back to that madarchod Maqsood? It's his mess, he should sort it out himself. Look, let's go see Dr. Death privately after this meeting. You can tell him you don't want to get involved in cleaning up Maqsood's problems. Look, any way you look at it, this case is a loser. If you arrest him, his followers will never forgive you. You're already on the UF's hit list, I don't think you can afford to be on another group's as well. And let's not even talk about what the CM will do to you. Dr. Death isn't going to be the IG forever, you know. The CM will wait till he's gone, then he'll fuck you. And if you don't get Nawaz, or God forbid something else happens, all the good work you've done in the past will be forgotten. You heard Tarkeen in there. His tone has changed just because you did a job for the Bleak House wallahs. These people will crucify you if anything goes wrong."

Akbar looked contemplatively at the elevator door as they rode down. "You know, when we joined the force, I used to come to this same head-quarters and stare at this lift. It seemed to me to be the most marvellous piece of technology I had ever seen. Heh, I was such a simple chutiya. I never imagined that one day I would ride in it all the way to the IG's office. I never thought I would come face to face with the IG even once, leave alone on a daily basis. Akbar Khan has come a long way in a very short time, but he is at heart still a simple assistant sub-inspector. I know that going after Chandio is suicidal, that there is only a very slim chance that it will not all end in tears. But yaar Consendine, when Dr. Death stands in front of me wearing those crossed swords on his shoulders and all his decorations on his chest, and he calls me son and tells me that his honor is in my hands, how can I say no to him? Dr. sahib is our mai-baap, Consendine. He has done everything for me. I have to do this thing for him. As for how it turns out, I will leave that to God. If he has written some good for me in my kismet, then we will be fine, and if he has ordained something bad, then there is nothing we can do about it."

14

Just as Constantine tried to get his day into some sort of normal routine, he received a call from the Home Minister's office, asking him to immediately present himself there for a meeting. An urgent summons from the Home Minister could not be good news. Constantine had a sinking suspicion that Maqsood Mahr wasn't the only one who had started taking an interest in Akbar's rehabilitation.

The drive from the prison to the minister's office near the Provincial Assembly building took nearly an hour in the city's midday traffic. Constantine chuckled to himself as his pickup turned onto Shahra e Faisal, the city's main artery that connected the downtown area with the airport. The irony of it was inescapable. As usual, the Bleak House boys had made such a production about the supposed secrecy of their talks with Akbar. Rommel had wanted to exclude Constantine on the first day because the matter was supposed to be so "sensitive." And yet everyone in the city knew what was going on. It hadn't taken Maqsood Mahr long at all to figure it out, and the Home Minister and the UF weren't too far behind. At this rate, the jihadis probably knew by now about Akbar. There were no secrets in this city. It was a lesson one learned over the years here.

Constantine was not personally enthused at the prospect of meeting the Home Minister. Pakora, as he was nicknamed because of his bulbous nose and unattractive facial features, was a much despised figure within the police department. The levels of his avarice knew no bounds, and, even in a department where corruption flourished like crabgrass, Pakora had broken new records. Constantine had gotten firsthand experience of this when he had gone to pay him through an intermediary to secure his current posting. That had been his only previous personal contact with the minister.

Although Pakora's scruples were well known, no one had contemplated his removal from office because he was the chosen favorite of the Don. And, as Maqsood Mahr said, the Don's word was absolute law in this city. The party he created had evolved into much more than a simple political movement. It had an international network that mixed crime and politics and spread as far and wide as Thailand and Brazil. The Don himself sat at the apex of it, monitoring everything from his modest suburban New York town house, holding the city in a vice-like grip. Everybody had a theory about why the Don never came back to Karachi. He had gone for a medical checkup fifteen years ago and gone into self-imposed exile. Some said he stayed abroad to remain out of the clutches of the Agencies. Others claimed he was a CIA agent and that, by staying in New York yet continuing to control Karachi, he demonstrated his power to his American patrons. After all, it was far more impressive to be able to shut down a city of 16 million on the strength of a long-distance phone call. There was another story, that was only whispered in the darkest corners of the city, of a group of the Don's surviving victims who had sworn a blood oath to avenge themselves on him. No one knew who these people were, or where they were. Some were even reputed to be former ward bosses. And there was no way to confirm whether this mythical group had ever even committed any act of violence. But the Don believed in their existence. And the idea of a secret group of assassins plotting to kill him was terrifying. He had taken elaborate security arrangements, even in New York. It was said that a man from his retinue oversaw the preparation of all his meals, even when he ordered a pizza from the local Domino's, to ensure he wasn't poisoned. His party spent a fortune on the Don's security, paid for by the princely sums that were extorted by the ward bosses from the citizens of Karachi.

But in recent years, the Don's paranoia had come down a little. The party's years of fluctuating political fortune, when their ministers were as likely to go straight from their offices into jail cells, seemed to be over.

The president, in dire need of the Don's political support, had in return allowed the party a free hand to do what they pleased in the city.

As Constantine arrived in the office of the Home Minister, a dozen minions were at work in the antechamber, thrashing away at typewriters or computers, spewing out all sorts of directives. Orders for postings, transfers, promotions. And there was a price for every single one. The minister's secretaries scrutinized the various lists in their hands to put a value on every name, like a group of investment bankers working on an IPO. In one corner of the room, the minister's police escort detail lounged around on the sofas that were meant for the use of public visitors. Their appearance was slovenly, with the men sporting unshaved beards, dirty uniforms, and a variety of headgear, with their weapons slung untidily around their shoulders. Indeed, they looked less like policemen and more like street thugs, which is probably what some of them were anyway. Scores of former gun-toting United Front ward boys had been recruited into the police thanks to the largesse of Pakora.

He announced himself to one of the secretaries, who looked him up and down in a contemptuous manner, and then conferred with the telephone operator. Upon learning of the urgency of the demand for Constantine's presence, the secretary's attitude changed and he ushered Constantine into the minister's presence immediately. The smell of stale smoke and mouldy damp emanated from the office. Most of these government buildings were quite old and hadn't been renovated in a while. All the ministers wanted offices close to the Assembly building, and so were unwilling to move to newer buildings that were further away from the centers of power. New furniture had been moved into the room to please the minister, without any thought having been given to aesthetics. The pink leather couch and high-backed leather chairs clashed completely with everything else in the room. A giant plasma TV hung on a wall, framed by ugly damp stains and peeling paint. A table, far too large for the proportions of the room, had been dumped into the center of the room and covered with the standard green baize cloth. On one side of the table were stacked various awards, mementos, and a large framed picture of the Don. As if to further emphasize the point, a miniature UF party flag fluttered on the table next to a miniature national flag. On the other side was a bank of six hi-tech telephones with all sorts of flashing lights.

Behind the table sat Pakora. His face was dominated by a huge nose of almost cartoon-like proportions. Everything about the man seemed to be drawn from a caricature, from the jet-black French beard, thick Elvis side-burns to the Three Stooges' haircut. He wore an ill-fitting white polyester suit with an ugly pink tie. His fingers were adorned with several rings, far too many for a normal man but perhaps at par for a rap musician. He smoked his cigarette from a filter wedged between his lips in a rather effeminate manner.

Three men sat on chairs facing Pakora. The first man was the inspector general of Prisons, Constantine's immediate boss. He was a weak, snivel-ling toady of a man. For someone who had been a member of a uniformed service for so many years, his appearance was remarkably sloppy. His pants had lost their crease a long time ago, and the shirt was crumpled and hung loosely on his frame. Even his shoulder ranks had been fastened onto his shirt incorrectly, and one of the pips hung precariously, as if about to fall off. His beret was slouched towards the back of his head in a most unpro-fessional manner. He was a man willing to do anything to cling to his job. Constantine had found him to be panicky about the slightest of situ-ations because he feared that any remote eventuality would bring about his ouster. Overwhelmed by that fear, he fell at the feet of everyone and anyone who had the remotest influence and offered them his services like some sort of bureaucratic whore. He had raised spinelessness into an art form. Only when it came to demanding money from his subordinates did he seem to find his courage. He and Constantine despised each other. He had perceived Constantine's posting as superintendent of the prison as an attempt to take away a part of his little empire. But the only thing he could do was give Constantine a hard time. After a very heated initial meeting between the two men, they now barely spoke and generally avoided each other's company. Constantine had assigned one of his wardens to deliver to the IG his share of the weekly collection, which was just fine for the IG, as he was least interested in the day-to-day working of the prison.

The second man was Hanuman, and he was in complete contrast to Constantine's boss. His uniform was crisply starched and immaculate, with not a thread out of place. He had also moved up in the world since Constantine had last served with him, having now become the city's police chief. His posture was far more confident than Constantine's boss, but that was because Hanuman was the consummate insider. All of his bosses had always perceived him unfailingly to be "their man." His ultimate loyalty, though, was only to himself. His political malleability was not his only quality. Unlike Constantine's boss, Hanuman had always been an extraordinarily competent officer, with an encyclopedic knowledge of the city. His evaluation of his own subordinates' strengths and weaknesses was always on the mark. He was often found speaking softly into his mobile phone, defusing some crisis or other in some far-flung corner of the city. Even as Constantine entered he was speaking on the phone, and greeted him with a perfunctory nod.

But it was the third man, the only one who was not in uniform, who immediately caught Constantine's attention. He was dressed in jeans and a denim shirt, in contrast to the formal appearance of the other three people in the room. His hair was cut severely in a crew cut, or what the local barbers called a "fauji cut." His eyes were hidden behind a pair of sunglasses. The man kept flexing his knuckles and chewing on a toothpick, as if impatient to be sitting down. He had a rather sinister-looking appearance, which was heightened by a five o'clock shadow on his face and the self-evident bulge under his shirt. There was an air of malice about the man, who seemed more suited to the mean streets of the city than these hallowed ministerial chambers. Constantine recognized him instantly. The years had changed Ateeq Tension's appearance somewhat, but he still looked like a nasty son of a bitch.

When he had arrested him, Constantine had prepared a very solid case against Tension, despite great difficulties. It had been hard to get anyone to testify. Constantine persevered, and got Tension convicted for murder. But in the time that it took for his appeal to move through the judicial system, the UF returned to power and Tension was released from prison. Over the years, Constantine had heard fleeting rumors that Tension bore a grudge against him, but he had never given much credence to such talk. That was, until Wajahat's warning the previous day and the incident with his daughter that morning. And now it was just too much of a coincidence that Tension was sitting in this office at this particular moment. Perhaps this meeting had nothing to do with Akbar after all.

Constantine saluted the minister, with one eye still on Tension. He was not offered a seat. Pakora's bullying nature was well known in the police. Clearly, this would not be a social call.

"So this is Consendine D'Souza?" sneered the minister, turning towards Tension. "You seem to be a very troublesome chap, D'Souza."

"Yes sir, he's a big troublemaker. Good for nothing. Ever since you posted him to the central prison, he's been causing me problems." The reply came from Constantine's boss.

"Arre, I'm not talking about the jail, you idiot! You also have a one-track mind. Everything comes back to *your* problems running the Prisons! Sometimes I think *you* are the problem!"

"Of course, sir. Of course you aren't. I'm sorry, sir, I misunderstood." Constantine felt physically sick, watching his boss's snivelling demeanor.

"D'Souza, weren't you posted as DSP in charge of Nazimabad subdivision before your current posting as superintendent of the Prison?"

"Yes, sir. I was there for nine months."

"I have heard a lot of complaints about you from our party workers in that area, D'Souza. Isn't that so, Ateeq Bhai?"

Ateeq "Bhai" nodded. By the deference Pakora showed Tension, it was clear that in the party hierarchy, the street thug outranked the minister.

"Yes, our people complained that you had a bias against the party. You arrested some of the workers while they were on party business. Are you aware of my directive—that no party worker is to be arrested anywhere in the city without approval from this office?"

Constantine understood that any answer he gave would be treated as the wrong one. So he decided to be bold about it. "I am aware of your directive, sir, but I had no choice, given the situation at the time. Your party workers were molesting young girls in a shopping arcade in front of hundreds of people. The girls came to a police kiosk in the bazaar and pleaded with me for help. Had I not arrested your workers there and then, it would have become very humiliating for the police. Not to mention, for your party as well. My prompt action saved your party a great deal of embarrassment."

"Don't try and be smart. Okay, you may have been justified on this occasion, but this is not the first incident between you and our party. You have a history of being biased against us. Didn't you participate in the operation that the police undertook against us? It has come to my attention that you were involved in arresting and torturing hundreds of our poor, innocent workers!"

Constantine's body stiffened. There was no way out of this one. "Sir, as a police officer I am bound to obey the orders of my superiors and the government. Any operation I took part in was ordered by the government of the day. I have never discriminated on a personal basis between your party people and any others. The treatment they received at the police station was no different to any other arrested person. Although," and he turned his steely gaze towards Tension, "many of those arrested were proven to be hardened criminals, and were convicted by the courts. I was just doing my job as a police officer."

His answer made Tension scowl. Constantine's boss fidgeted uncomfortably in his seat. The minister stared at him malevolently. The only one who seemed completely unmoved was Hanuman.

The minister turned to Constantine's boss. "Are you seeing this? Are you witnessing this? Such insolence! Ateeq Bhai was absolutely right about this fellow. He is actually taking *pride* in having tortured our poor workers! I think we need to take serious action against this man."

"Yes, sir. Very serious. Very serious matter. Very serious action. There should be a case registered against him."

Tension and the minister both nodded gravely. Fear crept up Constantine's back. In his mind he tried to remember how many police guards had been sitting outside the office, and whether they were indolent enough for him to be able to get past them if the need arose to make a break for it. It was then that Hanuman spoke up in his lazy, nasal drawl.

"Well sir, we *could* register cases, but that could become *tricky* for us. If we do it that way, then there would be a case against every single officer who was in the Karachi Police at the time. *Technically*, even I was serving here back then. It would set a dangerous precedent. The opposition would then insist on the same treatment for those officers who had arrested their workers to help you out. They may not be able to do anything about it now, but they *could* implement such sanctions if they came to power. If this kind of tit-for-tat process started happening, it would hamper our ability to provide your party with *favorable* treatment. I think you should give the matter some more consideration."

"Hmm, yes perhaps. I think, Ateeq Bhai, you personally enquire into the matter of this officer in *some detail*, and liaise with the inspector general of Prisons as to what we should do with him."

Tension had the look of a predator whose prey had managed to run away at the last instant. He frowned but bowed his head in agreement.

Constantine, still standing stiffly at attention, imperceptibly breathed a sigh of relief. He was debating whether to go or stay when Pakora piped up again.

"One more matter. You have that police terrorist, Akbar Khan, in your custody. That man's hands are stained with our party workers' blood. I have heard he has had some irregular visits in the jail from *outside authorities* and that he is spinning some false story to them about being able to help in tracing the kidnapping of this American. He is just telling them lies! Lies, I tell you! Our party people have confirmed that whatever information he may have given out is completely false. He is just trying to get out of jail. You are to ensure that he does not meet with the representatives of the outside Agencies anymore. If they come to you, you are to discredit his information as being totally false, and you are to refuse them access to him. In fact, he is to be isolated completely. No one is allowed to meet him. Am I making myself very clear on this point? Your future prospects could depend on how well you carry out this task."

"Yes, sir." Constantine just wanted to get out of there at this moment, and he was in enough trouble as it was, so he did not contradict the minister.

The minister dismissed him, but Hanuman signalled him to wait outside. As he stepped out of the office into the courtyard, his mind was in a quandary.

Two things were clear. Ateeq Tension, formerly one of the chief militants of the UF, murderer of policemen, and convicted criminal, was now apparently the chief advisor to the minister directly responsible for the police. And he obviously had a bone to pick with Constantine. Such were the vagaries of politics in this city. The second thing was that, as

Constantine had predicted, the UF knew about Akbar's contacts, and they were clearly not happy about them. They were not going to give Akbar any chance to avail of this opportunity. It didn't matter to them that his information could save the American's life.

He was about to phone Tarkeen when Hanuman walked out. Still on his phone, which seemed to be surgically attached to his ear, he motioned to Constantine to ride with him in his official vehicle, a gleaming black Toyota Prado jeep. They set out from the minister's office in the government barracks next to the high court, towards the police head office. They drove past the Provincial Assembly building and the Hindu Gymkhana, and then onto Chundrigar Road with its concrete skyscrapers and plazas. The police head office, a building constructed in the boom of the early 1970s, stood out for its ugliness, even on a road renowned for ugly buildings. A mass of cables and wires spewed out from each office window and were draped across the front of the building. The sentry snapped to attention and saluted the vehicle as it pulled in to the porch. Hanuman and Constantine got out and took the lift to the fourth-floor office of the Karachi Police chief.

Hanuman had been talking incessantly on his phone, getting information from all parts of the city, giving orders to his officers, and talking to members of the public. His accessibility had always been his greatest virtue. In a culture where senior officers built a bubble of officialdom around themselves and took pride in being as inaccessible as possible, both to the public and to their subordinates, Hanuman had always bucked this trend. He always kept his channels of communication open with all rungs of society.

Hanuman took off his beret and collapsed in his chair, rubbing his tired eyes. Being the police chief of this city was a twenty-four-hours-a-day, seven-days-a-week job. Even if he were not in his office or in one of numerous meetings, he would be on the road, going to the scene of an incident or dealing with one of the dozen or more mini-crises that erupted every couple of hours in the city. It was an exhausting job, and Constantine wondered how Hanuman had managed to do it for four straight years.

He sipped from a mug of green tea that had been lying on his side table. "Why did you leave Nazimabad? You were doing well there.

You had been there less than a year, but the crime in the area was down, and both the Shi'a and Sunni leaders there liked you. They praised you all the time."

"They were not the issue, sir. It was Minister sahib's people. They expected me to turn a blind eye to everything. It was getting very uncomfortable for me. I couldn't be one of their loyalist officers. So I decided to get myself posted out. I was offered a post in CID, but their business is hunting jihadis. I didn't want to get involved in that game. I would have ended up on some group's hit list. As it is, I would have been a prime target because I'm a Christian. That's why I decided to go to the Prisons, sir."

Feigning ignorance, Hanuman asked in his usual drawl, "Who was that man in the minister's office?"

"Sir, you know everything about what happened back then. You were also posted here at that time. That was Ateeq Tension, the ward boss who I arrested when I was station in-charge in north Karachi."

"Hmm. And now he wants to get his revenge on you."

"It appears that way, sir. What do these people want, sir? We were government officials doing our jobs. And that man was hardly some innocent party activist. He was a murderer. Sir, it is unfair to penalize me for doing my job."

"Hmm. You know what these people are like. Anyone who did anything against their party is a sinner in their eyes. They are in power, so we can't do anything about it. What's the other issue with Akbar?"

"That's the other problem, sir. Now Colonel Tarkeen and his people want to meet Akbar for help in that American's case. How am I supposed to stop them, sir? It's a high-profile case, and they are the *Agencies*, sir. What am I supposed to do?"

"Hmm. And Akbar has obviously been of some help, otherwise they wouldn't have come back to see him today. You think he can help find the American?"

Constantine debated whether to tell Hanuman the truth, but then he figured he would find it out anyway, and besides, unlike Maqsood Mahr, Hanuman didn't have a vested interest in keeping Akbar locked up. "Yes, sir. I believe he can."

"Good. What does he want?"

"Obviously sir, he has been locked up for so long, he wants to drive a hard bargain with Colonel Tarkeen."

"Hmm. Obviously."

Constantine waited for a more in-depth answer, but none was forthcoming. "Uh, sir, so what should I do? About the minister's directive regarding Akbar?"

Hanuman sighed. "What can you do? We are always stuck in the middle between more powerful masters, having to do their bidding. You can't say no to the Agencies because the case is an important one; besides, they would never understand your reasons and would always hold it against you. You can't really say no to the UF because they are out for your blood anyway and, if it was discovered that you were assisting in securing the release of their mortal enemy, Akbar, *they* would never forgive you. I can't really advise you on what to do. You have been around long enough. Figure something out. But whatever you do, handle it *tactfully*." This was Hanuman's catchphrase for any and all situations. "Talk to Tarkeen. Tell him they are pressurizing you. I would think that in a case of this magnitude, the Agencies *may* prevail over the UF high command."

"Yes, sir."

"Maqsood is worried as well. He keeps calling me and asking me to intervene with Colonel Tarkeen. But I think it's good that they are talking to Akbar. There should be some competition in the market after all." A thin smile broke out across Hanuman's face.

"Yes, sir." For the first time that day, Constantine smiled too.

15

He woke with a start. His wife had been trying to rouse him for a couple of minutes. He could vaguely hear the phone ringing. Constantine was so used to communicating on his mobile that he hardly bothered about answering the landline anymore. It was usually Mary's relatives calling anyway. But now she was on top of him, telling him it was from work, and it was urgent. He stared at his mobile lying at his bedside. He had switched it off when he came home because he was exhausted and Maqsood Mahr had been trying to get in touch with him frantically. He cursed his office staff. One of Mahr's informers among them must have leaked his home number.

"Hello?"

"Superintendent D'Souza?"

"Yes. Who is this?"

"Please hold for the Home Minister." Constantine could hear a faint buzzing on the other end as the operator connected the call. A second later Pakora came on the line.

"D'Souza, are you in the jail?"

"No sir, I had come home to sleep. Is something wrong, sir?"

"Never mind that. Come over to my house. Immediately. But do not come in uniform and don't tell anyone where you are going. And come alone. Don't use your official vehicle. Come quickly. I'm waiting."

The line went dead.

The last remnants of drowsiness were swept out of Constantine's brain. Why was Pakora calling him to his residence in the dead of the night? And asking him to come alone? As he splashed some water onto his face, a feeling of dread crept over him. Perhaps it was no coincidence that he had received this summons on the same day that he saw Ateeq Tension again after so many years. It was evident from the morning's meeting that Constantine's sins of omission or commission had not been forgiven or forgotten. Pakora had made it clear that Tension and Constantine's boss would determine his final punishment. Hardly the two people who would ever be kindly disposed towards him. That afternoon, when Constantine had returned to the prison, his boss had made it very clear to him that the sanctions against him would be severe. But he had assumed that they would take the form of the normal, bureaucratic remedies— removal from his post, suspension, departmental enquiries. This summons was something else altogether. Did the sanctions against him include a higher punishment?

Was he being summoned to his own death? Tension certainly hated him enough. He had thought himself untouchable, until Constantine had gone after him. When no witnesses would come forward against him, it was Constantine who had gone to his old neighborhood and cajoled and convinced people to give statements against him. Tension would never forget his humiliation that night on Napier Road, when Constantine had beaten him like a dog. During his trial Constantine had planted evidence, conjured up false witnesses, done whatever he could to ensure that Tension wouldn't get off. He didn't. His first couple of years in jail had been difficult ones. For all his posturing, at heart Tension was a bully, capable of dishing out pain and hardship, but not quite so tough at receiving it. In the world of the prison it wasn't so easy being a tough guy, especially when your party was in opposition. In a way, Constantine could see why Tension hated him with such passion.

It wouldn't be the first time something like this had happened. The UF had murdered many cops. Constantine had heard that their hit squads were hunting down lower-level police officers who had been involved in the operation against them. Off-duty officers were killed in mafia-style hits by unidentified gunmen. No one even bothered investigating these cases properly. After a couple of days, the case file was flagged as unsolved. Everyone knew that the UF was behind the murders, but no one was brave enough to state that publicly. It would be very easy, in these circumstances, for Ateeq Tension to arrange an ambush for him. After all, who knew where he was going? Pakora had expressly told him not to tell anyone of the meeting. Even if he had informed someone, Pakora could just deny it. He was going to his house, after all, in a private vehicle, without his uniform or his bodyguards. The minister's residence was located in an area that was an absolute UF stronghold. Their activists roamed the streets openly brandishing automatic weapons. Anything could happen to him on the way. His body would be found lying in a jute sack on the side of some road in the morning, and his name would be added to the long list of the city's unsolved cases. Another statistic.

For a moment, just a brief moment, Constantine thought about not going. But he decided that it would not be possible to get out of a direct summons from the minister, especially as he had answered the phone himself. Besides, they could just as easily walk into his home and murder him in front of his wife and children. At least this way, his family would be spared. No, he would go, but he would take precautions. He took out his service pistol from the side table and stuck it in his pants. He went outside and called out to Ashraf. Two of Constantine's most trusted bodyguards remained with him at all times, even sleeping at his house. He told Ashraf and the other guard, Saeedullah, to arm themselves and follow him on a motorbike.

He looked in on his daughters in their room. Malia was busy studying for her exams, oblivious to the happenings around her, as children often are at exam time. Choti was already asleep. Mary was in the kitchen warming some milk for Malia. He walked up behind her and took the saucepan from her hand.

"Mary, quickly pack some things. And get the girls ready. We have to go right now."

In over ten years of marriage, she had grown accustomed to his irregular work hours and his having to rush off in the middle of the night. In all their time together, she had never asked him about his work. Constantine had always found that strange. He was, of course, glad not to have to rehash his professional life at home every day, but her complete and utter lack of interest in the subject also irked him at times. She had never asked him about his past, about the naika or the occasional whore over the years. He had stopped all of that years ago, but for all she knew, he could have continued his activities. A few years ago he had touched upon the subject, lightly suggesting that he could have been using work as an excuse for having a woman on the side. She had countered by saying that if the stink on his clothes when he came home from the police station was a woman's scent then she felt sorry for her, and for him.

But today was different. It was the first time he had ever told her to come with him. Though he tried to keep his tone even, she could sense the fear and anxiety in his voice, as only a wife could.

"What's wrong?"

He was in the girls' room, helping them get ready. He stared at her for a minute, not sure what to tell her. What could he tell her? That he was trying to figure out a safe place to move them to, while he himself was on his way to an appointment with death? And what was he basing these fears on? He had always tried to keep his family as far away from his professional life as possible, to protect them from the world he inhabited. There was no need to change that now. Even if this was the last time he ever saw them.

She sensed his hesitation and, not knowing what else to do, idiotically offered him the glass of milk that was in her hand. He smiled in spite of himself and took the milk.

"It's nothing that serious. There's just a rumor of a jailbreak at the prison. A couple of inmates might have gotten out, and they might want to come after the jail superintendent. Since everyone there knows where I live, I think it's a good idea to move you somewhere safer for a couple of days. You know, just until the prisoners are caught. Nothing to worry about. They're just normal prisoners, not jihadis or wardias."

"But where are you taking us? Should I just go to my parents' house?"

That was a good question, and Constantine had not given it much thought before this instant. He didn't want to send them to any of their relatives, because, if the UF were determined to come after them, they would already know where all of his relatives lived. A million thoughts kept shooting through his mind, until it hit him like a lightning bolt. There was only one place where he could guarantee their safety.

"I'll tell you about it on the way. Hurry up and get your things together."

He packed Mary and the girls into his battered old Toyota Corolla and, with Ashraf and Saeedullah following close behind on a motorcycle, started driving through Saddar, the city center. There were still plenty of signs of activity despite the late hour. Though most of the shops were closed, many roadside tea stalls and restaurants were open. The scent of chicken tikka and kebab grilling on skewers wafted through the car windows. Hermaphrodites in colorful outfits accosted pedestrians for a few rupees. As they approached Napier Road, Constantine could see the young girls on the balconies, their faces painted in garish makeup, waving at passersby, looking for potential customers for the night. Mary's eyes widened in shock and horror as she realized where they were, but she held her silence. The girls, happy for the midnight drive but also understanding, at some level, that all was not as it should be, kept unusually quiet and stared out the car windows.

There was a time when Napier Road was the acknowledged red-light district of the city, its boundaries clearly defined. But the distinction between decency and indecency had blurred in recent times. The brothels had moved to the upmarket locales of Defence and Clifton, where the "respectable" citizens of the city resided. After all, as in any other economic activity, the girls needed to be close to their client base. And the prostitution rackets had slowly been taken over by senior police officers like Maqsood Mahr, who themselves had links to organized crime. Nonetheless, most of the girls continued to live in this area, and the road remained the kingdom of the naika. All those who were under her protection were inviolable.

He drove up to the entrance of the naika's kotha. This time, he didn't bother stopping at the front desk downstairs. This drew no protest because, after all, it was peak business hours and the management was hardly going to start turning customers away, but the presence of Mary and the girls drew some questioning stares. At the top of the stairs they could hear the sound of musical instruments and a woman's singing, muffled by closed doors.

"Constantine, what do you think you're doing? Where in Christ's name have you brought us?"

He didn't bother to respond, and kept pushing everyone else out of their way like a man possessed. He entered the naika's audience chamber to find a line of petitioners sitting at her feet. They all grew silent at the sight of the girls.

"Salma Begum, I must speak with you privately."

Her gray-green eyes filled with panic, and then with concern. In all her fantasies, this was a scenario she would never have imagined. It took her a moment to regain her composure, but she got up from her chair and motioned them towards her private suite.

Constantine realized the need to calm the tension that was growing in his family. He set Choti, whom he had been carrying in his arms, on to the ground, and pointed to one of the naika's serving women.

"That lady over there will get you something to eat. I bet the two of you are hungry, aren't you, Choti? Do you remember the lovely smell of the kebabs on the street? Go with the lady and she will get you some."

Having dispatched his daughters, he finally turned to Mary once they were inside the naika's suite.

"Uh, Mary, Salma Begum is, uh, an old business acquaintance of mine." He hesitated. "Actually, she is more than that. At this point, she is the only person I can trust completely. Salma Begum, when I last came to you some years ago to ask you for a favor, you asked me to tell my daughters to think of you as an old aunt. Today I come to ask another favor from you. Men usually bring their wives and daughters to your doorstep asking for a good price for them. I come to you today to beg for their lives. I must go back and do certain things, but I need you to protect them. I do not have anywhere else to go in this city where I know they will be safe."

Both women stared at him, surprised by the emotion in his voice. Both knew that Constantine D'Souza had never been a demonstrative man, and neither woman had expected this.

"Consendine, what is wrong? What has happened?"

"Please, Naika. I beg of you. Protect them while I am gone." His voice quivered as he spoke.

Salma Begum stared at him, the glint of a teardrop collecting in her eye. And then, as if having remembered her position, she turned to a dumbstruck Mary and hugged her.

"Come, sister. You have nothing to fear. You will be safe with me. Do not worry, Consendine, I give you my word. As long as I am alive, no one will touch a hair on their heads."

He nodded slowly, with the overwhelming relief of a man who had managed to secure the safety of his family. He took out a brown paper bag from his trousers. It was filled with a thick bundle of notes, his weekly take from the prison, and handed it over to Mary.

"You might be here for a couple of days, so you will need this. Tell your parents that you and the girls are safe, but don't tell them where you are. As soon as my work is over, I will come back for you."

He thought of saying something else. He could see the questions in her eyes, about where they were, and about where he was going and why. But this was hardly the time to try and explain Salma to her. At a moment like this, anything he said would sound banal and bizarrely out of place. So he just nodded to her and walked towards the stairs.

"Consendine . . ." Salma Begum had followed him to the edge of the stairs, out of earshot of everyone. "What is it?"

"Salma Begum, Mary, she's . . . she's a good woman, but not wise in the ways of the world. If anything happens to me, she'll need help with the little things. Getting my pension out, getting permission to stay in my quarters for a while, things like that. Please help her out if you can."

The teardrop that had been perched precariously on the edge of her eyelid gushed down like a fast-flowing river. "Consendine, why are you talking like this? Nothing will happen to you. I know it in my heart."

She reached round her neck and took off an amulet that had been tied to a black piece of string. She held his arm and tied the string on to it. "This is an imam zamin. It will protect you from those who wish to harm you. And do not worry about your family. They are my responsibility now."

Constantine walked back to his car and drove off. He turned off Napier Road and onto the old Bunder Road. The big cinema houses were letting out the audience of the last shows. It was a chilly night, and the figures walking on the footpaths were wrapped in shawls or blankets as they tiptoed over the bodies of homeless beggars and heroin junkies shaking from the cold and their withdrawal symptoms. He drove past the sprawling mausoleum of the founder of the nation, the Quaide-Azam.

The marble of the tomb glowed ethereally in the reflection of the moon-light. He crossed the jail, which looked like some ancient fortress in the darkness, and entered Gulshan Iqbal, a middle-class residential area domi-nated by apartment complexes and shopping plazas. It was this middle class, which felt disenfranchised by the other political parties, that had given the United Front its core support in its formative years. As Constantine drove through the streets of Gulshan, he could still see the manifesta-tions of that support. The graffiti on the walls sang praises of the party. Slogans dedicated to flattering the Don were interspersed with drawings of airplanes, since the airplane was the election symbol of the party. There had also been some rudimentary attempts at English, with phrases such as "Don lifes" and the unfortunately worded "We want to make love to Don," which was a literal translation of an Urdu slogan (Hum Don se pyaar karna chahte hain) and which portrayed a very different sentiment.

Constantine drove very carefully, scanning the roads for any sign of the unusual, and keeping an eye on the rearview mirror to ensure that his guards were following him at a safe distance. He entered a street that had slightly larger houses than the rest of the neighborhood. The street was darkened, with just a solitary light shining at the far corner. From the police sentries posted at the gate of the house at the end of the street, Constantine guessed that that one was Pakora's.

Then, out of the shadows, four armed men emerged and hailed his car down with a flashlight. They were wearing bandanas with the red and black party colors of the UF. The local ward had set up an informal check-point near the minister's house. Of course, it occurred to Constantine that this would also be an excellent alibi for an ambush. Fully alert now, adrenaline pumping through his veins, he realized that he had a second to decide whether to slow down or push the accelerator. If he ran, he wouldn't be able to put enough distance between them and himself before they riddled his car with bullet holes from their Kalashnikov rifles. He could see the minister's sentries warming themselves in front of a brazier. For a moment, he felt safe. Tension wouldn't have him murdered in front of the police sentries, would he? Then again, if the UF boys did open fire, it was not like the policemen would rush to his rescue. Those sentries probably knew about these men but were under orders not to interfere with the ward's activities. These cops had learned a long time ago to look the other way when it came to things like this. The thought was not particularly comforting for Constantine. He reached for the gun on the passenger seat and cocked it even as he took his foot off the accelerator. It would be stupid to get killed in a case of mistaken identity if the men in front of him were indeed just part of a normal UF checkpoint. He would have to gamble on his motorcycle escort to save him if anything happened.

The man with the flashlight tapped the car window. Constantine gripped his pistol tightly as he rolled down his window. "Superintendent Constantine D'Souza, going to see the Home Minister."

The man looked at him suspiciously and flashed the light inside the car. "ID card."

Constantine let go of his gun and fished for his ID card inside his shirt pocket. It infuriated him to think of the fact that these street hoodlums had the gall to ask him, a senior police officer, for identification, when it should have been the other way around. But years of UF government had made these bastards brazen, and there was little Constantine could do about it in his present predicament.

The man peered at the ID card and then, apparently convinced, waved the car through. Constantine pointed to his gunmen on the motorcycle, who had stopped a few feet away. "They're with me. They're police officers too."

The man grunted, and Constantine drove on, his heart still in his throat. He pulled up at the end of the street in front of an ordinary-looking house. In contrast to the vigilance of the armed UF men, the police sentries at the house were quite laidback. They barely gave him a second look. Constantine gave his name to one of them and, soon, a servant emerged from inside the house and led him into a drawing room. The room reeked of nouveau-riche taste. Gaudy, overstuffed sofas had been placed in all four corners of the room. A fake gold chandelier hung from the ceiling, and plastic floral arrangements abounded everywhere. Like the minister's office, this room was also filled with plaques and mementos that Pakora had received over his political career.

Before entering politics, Pakora had been a poet. The walls were adorned with framed and calligraphed copies of his poems. Constantine had heard that Pakora's involvement with the party was fairly recent. It was rumored that when the Don first began his self-imposed exile in New York, he was a depressed man, stuck in a cold, alien land, so far away from the seat of his power. Pakora was a struggling poet who was just trying to get his works published at the time. He wrote several odes to the Don, and the Don, never wanting to be seen as an uncultured fellow and always partial to flattery, had revelled in Pakora's verses, especially as they only sang his praises. As a reward, the Don had elevated Pakora to the party's central committee. There was no looking back after that. Pakora had soon shed the garb of a struggling poet, and very quickly exchanged it for that of an ambitious politician. And his ministerial career didn't do much harm to his poetic aspirations either. For starters, it was no longer a problem for him to get published, especially when some party toughs personally called upon a few publishers and persuaded them to do a print run of a few thousand copies. Free of charge, of course. It was regarded as a privilege for the publishers to do such work. Besides, the publishers wanted to continue to be able to live and work in the city. Not only did his work get published, but soon it also became a bestseller as it became forced reading for party workers. And, of course, when Pakora took charge of the Home Ministry, it also became obligatory to stock his collected works in all of Karachi's police stations, right up with the police rules and the penal code. The Don would agree to all of Pakora's proposals, no matter how ludicrous they sounded, because whenever he got angry, Pakora would enchant him with a verse or two. And so the one-time poet and romantic, who had known little about politics and even less about the police, had come to be his party's preeminent and most powerful minister.

There was a massive poster-sized picture on the wall, depicting Pakora demurely sitting at the feet of the Don and receiving his blessings. It symbolized the relationship between the Don and all members of his party. The Don granted his blessings and favors like a medieval potentate, in return for absolute and unquestioning loyalty. Every command of his was obeyed, on pain of death. Subsequently, there were seldom any dissentions or defections from the party.

The servant returned and served Constantine a glass of flat Coke. Then another side door opened, and Pakora entered the room, looking flamboyant in a red silk dressing gown. Behind him Constantine could see a young lady in a state of undress, straightening herself up in a bedroom. Evidently, Maqsood Mahr's investigation in-charge had come through.

Pakora had a glass of whisky in his hands and was in a good mood, in contrast to his demeanor in the morning. "Ah, good you're here, D'Souza. Sit, sit. Do you want something else to drink?" He waved his glass in the air. "You people drink, don't you?"

"Yes, sir. I mean no, sir . . . I mean of course we Christians drink sir, but I don't. I mean I do, but I'm fine right now, sir."

"Relax, D'Souza, relax. I know you must be nervous because of this morning. Don't worry about it. That was a little drama that I had to put on. I wanted to have a serious talk with you, that's why I invited you here. Away from prying eyes and ears." He took a sip from his glass. "I have heard good things about you. General Ibadat strongly recommended you. He said you were a trustworthy fellow."

"Yes, sir. General sahib is too kind."

"The problem is that I don't know who to trust, D'Souza. The party has attached that idiot Ateeq Tension around my neck as my 'personal secretary.' The man is of no use to me and is only there to monitor me. I have to give him a share of every deal I do. I know you have a history with him. You arrested him. Good for you. He's an absolute scoundrel. You should have just killed him."

Constantine was completely bewildered. He had never expected such a response from the UF's almighty Home Minister. He began to think that this was another trap being set for him.

Pakora smiled at the expression on his face. "I know that what I'm saying is confusing you. But there are some of us who do not approve of the atrocities people commit in the name of the party." He looked at the Don's picture reflexively, as if worried that the demagogue would overhear his comments. "But we cannot say anything openly. Otherwise we would be next on the hit list. So we must tolerate men like Tension. But people like him do not understand the complexity of situations. Especially this situation. I have to maintain a constant effort to ensure that the Don doesn't listen to these fools. There is enormous pressure on all of us. I have sat in on the meetings. The Americans will have our heads if that journalist dies! Do you know that the president has to give the US ambassador a progress report twice a day? Arre, they are even questioning the Don! They are asking him how such a thing could happen, if he claims that nothing can move without his knowledge in this city!"

"Sir?"

Pakora lowered his voice to a conspiratorial whisper. "They have told us that they will hold the Don personally responsible if anything happens to the journalist. They told us this to my face. There is a good chance that they will throw him out of New York. No one in the police or the Agencies knows of this. Only a handful of us in the party know. It's a huge worry for us. He can't come back here, and he has nowhere else to go."

He allowed this last sentence to sink in with Constantine. For the Don to be thrown out of America would be huge. His mystique would be shattered.

"So you see my problem, D'Souza. I cannot reveal any of this to the rest of the party. Morale would collapse. But at the same time, I have these hardliner dogs like Tension who are just out for revenge and don't want the Don to cooperate or compromise with anyone. And the Don has been gone for so long that he doesn't understand the ground realities anymore. He listens to any rubbish that any idiot spews out. That's why I needed you to take such elaborate measures to come here. If it leaks out in the party that I was discussing these things, I would be dead before the American!" He laughed at the thought, and then sighed. "You know, sometimes I think I should have remained a poet!"

Constantine finally understood what the secrecy was all about. He also realized that he was now privy to the biggest secret in Karachi, with the exception, of course, of the location of Jon Friedland.

Pakora went on. "Colonel Tarkeen has been updating me on the progress he has made with Akbar. Apparently they have traced some six numbers from the phone he told them to trace. Colonel Tarkeen feels they are closing in on the kidnappers. But they need Akbar's continued assistance to recover the American. And Akbar naturally wants something in return. Presumably his freedom, a return of his status and position. I personally don't have a problem with him. I realize that he was doing his job. And between you and me, some of the ward bosses he killed deserved it. They were criminals. But you know that Akbar is number one on the party's hit list. The hardliners will not allow me to release him from prison."

"Then this scheme cannot work, sir. He won't cooperate unless he gets something in return. He made that very clear when Major Rommel first went to see him."

The minister wore a mischievous grin. "Take it easy. I said it would be difficult, not necessarily impossible. The circumstances of this case give me a lot of leverage. The recommendation of the Agencies will carry a lot of weight, and I think even the Don can be persuaded, because he is aware that his personal position in New York is precarious. But"—here he raised his hand and rubbed his thumb and forefinger together—"persuading is much easier with the help of the Quaid-e-Azam."

Constantine was silent, but the implication was clear. Pakora always came back to the one thing he loved the most, and the one thing that could solve all problems. Cold, hard cash. He nodded understandingly.

"Talk to him and explain my . . . point of view. You know, D'Souza, that your own department bosses are powerless in front of the party. Tell Akbar he may need a friend like me when he gets out. I can get him all the things he wants. A posting and immunity from the UF. I am very reasonable. I am sure he and I can come to an arrangement."

"I will convey your message, sir."

"Good. Colonel Tarkeen has told me that you have been invaluable in all of this. Don't worry. If we get the American back, I will ensure that you are suitably rewarded. And pay no heed to your boss. The man is a vegetable. I only keep him around because he pays well for the post."

"What about Tension, sir? I believe he wants to settle old scores with me."

"I'll deal with him in due course, but I can't move against him just yet. Until I can, you'll have to watch out for yourself. Just be very careful that none of this gets out. We have to do this very quickly, and very quietly. Go to the prison right now and give Akbar this SIM. My private mobile is already saved on it. Tell him to contact me on that number. But be sure no one suspects anything! If any of this gets out, it will ruin everything!"

"Sir."

A wave of relief swept over Constantine when he got back into his car. He had come back with his life intact. But the stakes in this case kept growing by the minute. Everyone was playing his own angle. The Agencies needed Akbar to break the case to prove their innocence to the Americans. Maqsood feared a draining of his power base if the case were solved by anyone but him, so he was hell bent on trying to stop Akbar. Hanuman would always ensure that, no matter what happened, he ended up on the winning side. The thing working in Maqsood's favor up till now had been the belief, shared by everyone, that the UF would never forgive Akbar. But now, that was no longer an absolute. Pakora's indication was clear. Old enmities could be buried, for the right price.

As he drove to the jail, he started thinking about how he would pass on Pakora's message to Akbar. There was no way he could walk into the prison in the middle of the night, go see Akbar, and not arouse suspicion. Constantine already knew that he could trust his own staff about as far as he could throw them. So he decided on an alternate plan. He pulled up at the prison and announced to an astonished night shift of wardens that he was here to conduct a snap inspection of the entire prison, to find and confiscate any contraband items being held by prisoners. They stared at him as if he had gone mad.

Virtually every item was considered contraband according to the prison rules, and therefore virtually every prisoner was in possession of some sort of contraband item. The jail staff already knew this and encouraged it because this was what their livelihood depended on. In most cases, they had supplied the items themselves. It was an exercise in futility, but at least it would give Constantine an excuse to wander around inside the prison at night.

Sirens and klaxons started ringing to alert the prisoners to the inspection. Constantine and the wardens fanned out through the prison compound. After casually inspecting a couple of barracks, Constantine took up a position near Akbar's barrack and instructed his staff to continue the search. All the lights of the prison had been turned on and the place became a hive of activity. Akbar, who had also woken up for the inspection, approached Constantine.

"Wah, Consendine. Midnight searches. You're growing well into this job. Becoming a big afsar."

Constantine passed Akbar an empty cigarette pack in which he had hidden his mobile phone, with Pakora's SIM fitted in it. "I just came from a very interesting meeting with Pakora."

"Oh really? And what did our beloved Home Minister ask about? Aren't you paying him enough of a monthly from the jail?"

"It wasn't about that. He was actually asking about you. He's quite keen to speak to you personally. He sent the SIM. His number's saved inside."

Akbar looked at Constantine quizzically. "Really? Must be getting close to the day of judgment if he wants to speak to me."

Constantine smiled. "Actually, it may be the day of judgment for their party. The Americans are threatening to throw the Don out of their country if the journalist is not recovered. Tarkeen has told them you are the only one who can help find Friedland."

"Really? That is fascinating. The old bastard kicked out of his little American empire. Heh."

"I never understood why he didn't come back after the last election. The party could easily have squared everything with the Agencies. It's not like someone was going to go up and arrest him while the police were in control of his party."

"It's not the police he worries about. It's the others. The ghosts who hunger for his blood."

"You think they really exist? Did you ever come across any of them?"

"I knew some people who knew some people. And yes, they do exist, these ghosts, but they are burrowed deep within his own party. No one has a clue. They could be part of his inner circle, they could be one of the bearers who make him his tea. That's what's driven the old bastard so crazy. He just doesn't know where and when these 'ghosts' will come for him, but they will come. The Don has caused so much pain to so many people in this city, you think their prayers don't reach God? I can guarantee you one thing. If that madarchod drags his ass back to this city, he will be dead within five days. No matter what precautions he takes. And he'll never see it coming. Why do you think he bumps off a couple of his ward bosses every few months? He can't be sure which one of them is loyal. That's what happens when you take so many lives. You learn to love your own. Heh."

"Well, anyway, Tarkeen has convinced Pakora that you can solve this mess, and he's willing to give you a clean sheet. Not just freedom but a posting as well. Complete reinstatement."

"What does he want in return? An apology for killing so many of their terrorist bastards? Hell will freeze over before that happens."

"Not at all. He's not so naïve. Pakora's a man of the world. He understands that these things happen in the line of duty. He only wants the one thing that he always wants."

Akbar let out a hearty laugh. "That's it? That's easy. This should be fun."

"Do you have the money? He won't come cheap. I had to pay five petis for this job. And that was a discount after I got General Ibadat and the Bishop of Karachi to call Pakora. Your matter is infinitely more complex."

Akbar slapped him on the back. "Ah, Consendine, didn't I always tell you back in Orangi that you approached problems the wrong way? Don't worry about the money. I'll sort that out. Their veto was the only thing I was worried about. By the way, you paid five petis for *this* posting? You could have gotten something much better for that amount."

"I wanted to come here. The job's really changed in the past few years. Everyone has become a mercenary, bartering services to the highest bidder. The Karachi Police isn't a disciplined force anymore; they're a rabble, with everyone trying to drag everyone else down. There's no professional pride left. I didn't want to become a member of a faction, so I opted out of the rat race."

"Still, you must be recouping your investment tenfold. After all, you're the head here. You can make a nice little nest egg for the family."

Constantine sighed. "I suppose I could. But the prison is different from a police station. Out there, you're like a hunter in the wild, living by your wits, looking for prey to sustain you. Here, making money is a captive sport. You just sit back and benefit from the misfortunes of these poor bastards in here. I'm not saying I don't take the money, but it doesn't sit well. There's no joy in it."

Akbar grunted understandingly. "Oh, thanks for sending me the case file. I couldn't have figured out the whole thing without it."

"I thought you were tapping the tableeghis."

"My informers had given me the overall picture, but the case file made me connect the dots."

"You really think he's still alive?"

"Are you asking, or Colonel Tarkeen?"

"Come on, Akbar. You know me well enough. Who do you think?"

Akbar scratched his beard. "The story I told the major was true. There are two groups involved. The funny thing is that in these reports everyone presumes that they marked him from the tribal areas. No such thing. It was just pure luck. One group was in touch with the informer, the houseboy. They had been waiting to do something big, but didn't have any resources. Then this American just fell into their lap when the boy called them. They couldn't really put together an operation in such a short time, so they contacted the other group for help. The second group was more professional. Hardcore jihadis. They agreed to help out, but they had connections in the tribal areas who knew the American and objected to him being targeted. Problem was that it was too good an opportunity to pass up. The operation itself was hurriedly planned. You can tell. The car they stole was brand-new, with no registration plates. They were very, very lucky not to get caught or stopped anywhere in the city. Completely amateur. The UF boys would never have done it like this. The name of this organization that they put up on the Internet. All made up. There is no such group. Just these two gangs, who continue to fight amongst themselves. That's the biggest guarantee of the American's survival."

"But if the crew is so amateurish, how come the Kaaley Gate wallahs haven't infiltrated them, or got a source on them?"

"Hah. They are so petrified that they will somehow be linked to this kidnapping, that some old contact of theirs will be found to be responsible, they aren't talking to any of their informers. They aren't even picking up their phones. I never thought I'd see the day when the Kaaley Gate wallahs would become as meek as kittens!"

"And the tableeghis's network is reliable enough?"

Akbar turned towards Constantine and grinned. "I never said it was the tableeghis. I always told you that I never share my sources. It's the only asset we have as police officers."

"Fair enough. What do you know about a man called Qari Saif? One of my informers mentioned him in relation to this case."

"Qari Saif? Never heard of him. His name hasn't come to my attention."

"Okay." Constantine shuddered involuntarily and rubbed his shoulders to warm himself. "I had a strange experience tonight. When I left for the minister's house, I thought I was going to be ambushed by Ateeq Tension. I didn't think I was going to make it home alive. I hadn't felt like this since that night in Orangi, when I was wounded. I didn't think I would come back from there either. I wasn't scared, just resigned to the fact. You saved my life that time. I wouldn't have made it out without you. It occurred to me that I never really thanked you for that."

"Ah, it was nothing. You were my friend. That's all that mattered. Life and death are in God's hands. All of us have a time of going that is written for us. I have always believed that. All of the Don's cocksuckers put together can't kill you if it isn't your time. Believe me, I know. They've tried with me."

Constantine was quiet, thinking back on a lifetime of shared experiences between the two of them. It was strange. They hadn't spoken for years, yet he couldn't think of another person in Karachi whom he would trust with his life.

"What happened with Tension? Why did you think he would try and kill you tonight?"

"Oh, nothing. He's out of prison, and the party has appointed him as Pakora's secretary. It's pretty obvious that he bears a grudge. But I'm not too worried anymore. What will happen will happen. The wardens are coming back. The inspection is coming to an end. I have to go. Talk to Pakora."

Akbar nodded. Constantine turned and walked back to his office.

16

Day 3, December 23, 12:00 p.m.
The prison

Constantine was surprised that the day began so normally. He had chosen to spend the night in his office, partially due to security reasons and also because he expected a flurry of activity in the morning. Besides, there was no one at home to go back to. He rose later than he normally did, closer to ten, and panicked for half a second when he saw the time. Only then did he remember that he didn't have to see the girls off to school today. He called the naika's kotha and was reassured when Salma's assistant informed him that the girls and Mary were safe and sound, but still asleep. The naika too had not yet woken, so he hung up.

He washed, and called for a barber to shave him. He glanced at his mobile phone as the man lathered his face. He hadn't received any further calls from Colonel Tarkeen or Major Rommel, or from Pakora. He did have a number of missed calls from Maqsood Mahr on both his office number and his mobile, which he chose to ignore. Maqsood Mahr had undoubtedly learned of the moves afoot to reinstate Akbar and would try to stall them if he could. He was also without a doubt aware of Constantine's role in all of this and would be furious at him for helping Akbar. But a strange serenity had come over Constantine in the past twenty-four hours. In the context of the threat to his family, a temper tantrum from Maqsood Mahr was an inconsequential thing. He would cross that bridge when he came to it. Besides, from the looks of things, Maqsood was currently in no position to harm him.

Constantine got through the routine paperwork and was just starting to worry about why there hadn't been any communication from anyone, when Colonel Tarkeen finally called at around two and said that he was on his way. Literally five minutes after he put the phone down, the sentry at the outer gate informed him that the colonel had arrived. Constantine quickly donned his beret and buckled his belt, and had just finished tucking in his shirt, when the colonel and Major Rommel walked into his office. They both seemed to be in a cheery mood. Constantine saluted Tarkeen and offered him his own seat.

Tarkeen firmly shook his head and sat down in the plastic chair opposite. "No, no, Constantine, not at all. We have come to your office, you are the boss. By the way, I was noticing the other day that you've put on a lot of weight. You were an athlete, weren't you? Captain of the police hockey team? Shame on you."

"Yes sir, I have been enjoying my wife's cooking a little too much of late. You look like you have good news, sir. I was getting concerned when I didn't hear from you in the morning."

"We were actually working with the FBI experts tracing down the numbers from the houseboy's phone. Akbar's clues seem to have put us on the right track. I feel we are closing in. Rommel tells me that Akbar insisted that I should come, personally, to . . . finalize things. But before we go in, Constantine, tell me, do you believe, 100 per cent, that he can lead us to the American? We have very little time left. This is basically the last throw of the dice."

"Yes sir, I do believe that. I spoke to him last night as well, and I think he is the only one who can recover the American."

"Good. Then let's get started."

The prison somehow seemed more crowded as they walked to Akbar's barrack. The inmates stared at them with an air of expectation. Constantine wondered how much they knew of what had been going on. Given the speed with which news travelled through the prison grapevine, it wouldn't be surprising if they were already aware of all the details. Akbar, having been informed of their arrival, was waiting at the door of his barrack to receive them. Colonel Tarkeen hugged him like a long-lost comrade. Akbar, immune to the irony of the situation, or perhaps revelling in it, reciprocated and welcomed them inside.

Before entering the barrack, the colonel turned and held up his hand to the major. "Uh, you wait for us here, Rommel. I'll deal with this one. We have some confidential matters to discuss. Come on in, Constantine."

The major's shock and humiliation at having been snubbed by his fellow officer was apparent on his face. Constantine felt for the major, but obviously there were matters that Tarkeen didn't want Rommel to know about. They may have shared a uniform, but the worlds they inhabited were completely different.

They entered and sat down on the low stools while Akbar sat down on the mattress opposite them and started stroking his beard, waiting for the colonel to begin.

"Akbar, first of all, thank you. I can see you haven't lost any of your zeal, or your talents. You can still pull a gem out of nowhere. You should have gotten into the jihadi hunting game a long time back. You have a natural flair for it. You might never have gotten stuck here."

"Oh, I don't know about that, Colonel sahib. I think I would have ended up in here irrespective. A lot of people would have made sure of that. But I never wanted to get into that game. I have moral objections. These people do God's work. They aren't criminal scum like the kidnappers or the UF. I don't think it's right for us to treat them in the same way."

"Oh please, Akbar! Don't tell me you're as deluded as the rest of these fools. I didn't expect this naïvety from you! God's work! How is killing innocent people God's work? They are exactly the same as any other criminal. You think they don't do it for money? All the charity funds they receive? You think that money doesn't end up lining their pockets? Why do you think they are always fighting over who gets to control which mosque? Why are they so willing to shed blood over such petty issues? It's the money. You know these things better than I do. You've worked on the streets. They're exactly the same as the UF, or the kidnappers. Jihad is just an excuse for them. They are just making a mockery of our religion and our country!"

"That's not what you used to say when they were working for you. People were getting killed back then as well. But you weren't willing to show the admirable concern that you do now. I seem to remember a conversation we once had, when your viewpoint was very different. You used to justify everything the jihadis did, just because you needed them. Now they turn their guns upon an American, and you suddenly awake to realize all their faults? At least these jihadis have some principles, Colonel sahib, unlike you. But that's my personal opinion. You can disagree with it if you want. You may be right. You are the *expert* on the subject, after all."

"That was a long time ago. Times change, situations change, policies change. We all have to look after our own self-interest. It is no longer in the national interest to support their activities. If you support these jihadis so much, why are you helping us?"

"Kya karoon, sahib? What to do? I guess it's part of my natural curiosity as a police officer. We can never let go of an interesting case. Or perhaps I'm also looking after my own self-interest. Besides, in spite of Consendine's hospitality, I am growing tired of my present luxurious surroundings."

"What do you want?"

"What are you offering, Colonel sahib?"

"I can get you out of here. Immediate release. Reinstatement, with full benefits. We'll have the police withdraw the charges. We can also recommend you for a good posting. We'll even have a word with the UF leadership not to veto your appointment. You'll work exclusively with us."

"Hmm. Not bad. What else?"

"What do you mean, what else? This is a sizeable package by any standard, Akbar."

"Come on, Colonel sahib, now it is you who is being naïve. These are all the things I had before I was put in here. You are just restoring to me what was mine by right. What about justice for what happened to me?"

Tarkeen examined his fingernails before answering. "You can't be serious. I think the time you have spent in here has detached you from reality. Justice from whom? I'm going to have a hard enough time convincing the UF to allow you to get out. You expect us to hold them accountable for what they did to you? The old days are gone, Akbar. The UF is here to stay. No one is interested in their criminality or their terrorism. The only thing that matters now is the jihadis. The United Front has declared that they are with the president in this fight. That means they have a blank cheque to do whatever they want. The president depends on them as his sole political support in this city. As far as we are concerned, as long as they remain on board with us, they can rape and pillage this city to their heart's content. I think I may have overestimated your intelligence, Akbar. This is your last chance to get back in the game. Take it."

Akbar stared Tarkeen straight in the eyes, and held his gaze. Constantine had a sense of déjà vu. He had seen the same fierce determination in Akbar's eyes once before: that day in Orangi, at the Hajji Camp.

"Colonel sahib, I understand the ground realities of the situation all too well. But you forget that it is you who came to me, and you still have an American journalist to find. If he dies, you, the UF, the Don won't be worth a pile of dog shit. I'm the only one who can get him back for you. You know that, too. So why don't you cut out your posturing, and don't pretend you're doing me a favor."

Tarkeen swallowed hard and pursed his lips. "Very well. What do you propose?"

Now Akbar smiled. "I'm not unreasonable, Colonel sahib. I never have been. I don't propose you overturn the system for me. I know all of the UF's sins have been washed away. I have far more modest demands. Don't worry about the party. I have my own back channel to them. They won't oppose me. In fact, they'll welcome me. But they weren't the only ones who screwed me over. I have a grudge against your pet, Maqsood Mahr. Look sahib, I know he kisses your ass ten times a day, but we are all practical men. If I come back out, there can't be two stallions in the same field. And well, honestly, if you ask yourself truly, Maqsood was never much of a stallion. More of a donkey, really. I always did better work than him. But now, his incompetence has become a liability. Otherwise you wouldn't have needed me. Now, I do feel that I should be, how shall I put it, compensated for the time I spent in here. After all, stupidity and incompetence should be punished, shouldn't it?"

All of a sudden there was a spark of interest on Tarkeen's face. "Yes, incompetence and stupidity cannot be tolerated." He repeated the words like an automaton. "How much?"

"Well sir, it has been two years of my life. I'm even willing to grant that he can be allowed to work in Karachi. After all, he is a good provider. But I will be completely independent, and you will keep him in check if he tries to come after me. As for how much, I want to put a fair price. Say, one khokha."

Constantine gasped out so loud that both men turned and looked at him. Colonel Tarkeen was amused and turned to bargain with Akbar as if this was an everyday trip to buy vegetables in the local bazaar. "Your price is too high, Akbar. Reduce it a little. Make it half that. Where will he get such a large amount?"

"Arre, Colonel sahib, why do you need to worry? You don't have to raise the money. He's a resourceful fellow. I have to make up for two years of unemployment. I have to pay my informers. Besides, this is just my demand. Seeing as how you are saving his skin, I think you are entitled to some compensation as well. Don't you?" Akbar grinned like the Cheshire cat. That was the ace up his sleeve.

The colonel nodded appreciatively and looked at Constantine. "Yes, I think you're right. Don't you agree, Constantine?"

"Absolutely, sir." Constantine couldn't keep the smile off his face.

"May I use your mobile, Constantine? You never know who's listening to mine."

"Certainly, sir."

Constantine dialled Mahr's number and handed the phone to Tarkeen, putting it on speaker. Mahr, thinking it was Constantine on the line, let loose a stream of abuse and threats in his trademark bullying tone.

"Bhenchod, who do you think you're fucking with? You think you can avoid my calls? You think you can do a setting with Akbar and that bald bastard Tarkeen, and I won't find out? I told you not to cross me! When I'm done with you, you'll wish you were directing traffic in the goddamn desert!"

Tarkeen allowed him to complete his tirade, and then spoke in a frosty tone. "Hello, Maqsood."

Maqsood started stuttering. "Sir! Sir, I'm so sorry, I thought it was Consendine! I didn't realize. I didn't mean any of what I said!"

"Shut up and listen for a change, you imbecile. You have fucked this case up enough as it is. Now I have to try and salvage the situation. Akbar needs to pay his informers and you owe him compensation anyway for what you did to him. Make arrangements for the immediate delivery of, oh, two crore."

"Sir, two khokhas! Where am I supposed to arrange that much money from? And why do I have to pay Akbar, sir? I will go broke!"

Please, Maqsood. I think we all know that you are in no danger of going broke. I know how much your weekly take is. After all, I'm the one preparing the corruption enquiry on you. I don't think this represents more than three or four weeks' takings for you. As for Akbar, well, you have to accept him as part of the equation. We cannot solve this case without his help, and if that's his price, then that's what you have to pay."

"But sir, if he gets out, he'll ruin me!"

"We all have to adapt to the ever-changing realities of this world, Maqsood. Besides, I don't think Akbar will be too concerned about you, just as long as you keep your nose out of his affairs. Now, have half the money sent to me, to distribute immediately, and the rest I'll tell you where to deliver."

There was a pause as Mahr debated what to do next. But there was never any real doubt about his answer. Maqsood Mahr was a defeated man. "Yes, sir."

"Oh, and Maqsood, one more thing. If this bald bastard finds that you have tried to harm Constantine in any way, you will be the one directing traffic in the desert. I hope I have made myself perfectly clear. You *know* I don't like to repeat myself."

Akbar, who had thoroughly enjoyed the entire exchange, chuckled and thrust his hand out for Tarkeen to shake. "Ah, Colonel sahib, you remain a maestro. It's good to be working with you again."

"I don't think Maqsood is an issue anymore. Even for you, Constantine. But we need to turn to our problem."

"Very well, Colonel sahib. Tell me, what do you have?"

"We got the boy's number. As you said, Maqsood's men had recorded it as part of standard procedure but hadn't investigated it any further. In the days that Friedland was living with the family, there were only six numbers that were called only once, and which were traced to the booster towers in Orangi or Nazimabad. Three in each area."

"No sahib, you can disregard the Nazimabad numbers. The boys involved in the kidnapping are definitely from Orangi. My informers confirmed that last night."

"All right. So now there are three numbers. Now what?"

"Sahib, tell me, are any of the numbers you have in a sequence? Similar to each other?"

Tarkeen looked at a list he had been carrying in his hand. "Why yes! There are two numbers, 03232435008 and 03232435009. But that's amazing! How did you know that?"

"My information is that one of the gang members works at a convenience store that sells prepaid SIM cards. He has been providing them SIM numbers in bulk, thirty or forty at a time. That's why they are in sequence. Because they were sold together. I don't know his real name, but he is known as 'Kana' in the locality, because he has only one eye. The other one is a glass eye. You can get the exact address of the shop from the mobile phone company who distributed this sequence of numbers to them. But from what my informers have described, the shop is located in the area on the far side of the Pirabad Hill, near the Pathan madrasas. Consendine knows it."

"Near the Hajji Camp? Yes, I know that area very well."

"Yes. Exactly there. Colonel sahib, if this Kana works in a shop there, I'm sure we can trace him easily in the locality, because he lives around there as well. If we manage to pick him up without the rest of the gang being alerted and then break him quickly, so that he reveals the American's location, we have a good chance. But it has to be done very carefully. One false step, and they will kill the American. I would suggest that you don't contact the local police station, because that will blow our cover. Ask Consendine whatever you need to know because he knows all the nooks and crannies."

Tarkeen thought about it for a moment. "Okay, let's do it. I will get the shop details from the mobile company. But Constantine, I am going to take you along with me, because I want someone reliable to guide me in the area. Akbar is right. I can't trust the local police. In fact, the only person I'm going to inform is Hanuman. Timing is everything. We must move tonight. We'll start interrogating him as soon as we pick him up. Akbar, let's hope this works out for all of us. I am going to strongly recommend to the Home Minister to give you a posting where you can work with us. I am sure he won't say no to us. As for the money, where do you want Maqsood to send it?"

"Sahib, I trust you. Ask Maqsood to give the money to Amir Sheikh for safekeeping. He's a bookie we both know and trust. Does a lot of sports betting, cricket match fixing, that sort of thing. If the American doesn't come back alive, the bookie will refund the money to Maqsood. After all, I wouldn't want poor old Maqsood to suffer a loss for no reason. Heh. And don't worry about the Home Minister. He and I are about to become very good friends."

Tarkeen raised his eyebrows and smiled. "I'm glad to see your pragmatism has returned. I always told you that the only reason Maqsood ever took the lead from you was because your 'idealism' held you back. I'm going to be looking forward to working with you again. Excellent. But I want to be able to contact you at any time, tonight, in case we run into any hitches. Has Constantine allowed you to smuggle in a mobile phone?"

Akbar picked up the phone that Constantine had given to him the previous night. "He did even better than that, sahib. He gave me his. Consendine, if you're with Colonel sahib, we'll be in touch. I will pray for all of you, and for the American, tonight."

Constantine nodded. The business concluded, the meeting broke up. Akbar saw them to the door, and they picked up Major Rommel from outside and started walking to Constantine's office. The major looked downcast, and Constantine's heart went out to him.

"Major sahib, there's something I've been wanting to ask you ever since I first met you. Why are you named after a German general?"

Rommel burst out laughing. "It was a practical joke on the part of my grandfather. He fought with the British forces in North Africa in World War II. He always used to tell me that the Indian army soldiers fighting in Africa hated their own British officers, who were mostly incompetent. But they all idolized the enemy general, Field Marshal Erwin Rommel, who was brilliant and ran circles around their commanders. My grandfather said that Rommel never let any of his opponents dominate him, and that's why he named me after him. I personally think my naming had as much to do with him wanting to piss off my grandmother, who wanted one of the more traditional Islamic names."

"But Rommel was ultimately defeated, sir." Constantine said this very solemnly. Rommel looked up and gave him a withering look, and then both men started laughing. "It's always like that with our elders, isn't it, sir? They name us thinking one thing, and we turn out completely different. I told you my father named me for some old West Indian cricketer and hoped I would become a man of the cloth. I never played a day of cricket in my life, always hockey, and I ran as far away from the church as possible. I ended up here."

The two men smiled. Over the past few days, a mutual respect had developed between them. In different ways, they were both victims of the same situation. The major turned and shook Constantine's hand. "Thank you, Constantine. You have really taught me a lot in these past few days. Good luck to you, and to Akbar. I wish we could have met under better circumstances. You're a good man. I would have been proud to have had you in my unit in Kargil."

"Major sahib, I keep telling you, you're in the wrong business. You are too nice a fellow to work in intelligence. And please, don't make a saint of me just yet. I revel in my sinful existence."

The major climbed into the driver's side of the jeep, put on his Aviators, waved one last time and then drove away, leaving behind a cloud of dust.

17

November 5, 2001

A cloud of dust rose as the police pickup sped along the single-track road. The barren landscape was occasionally punctuated with a few dry shrubs. There was no sign of any human habitation as far as the eye could see. The desert wind was dry and hot, like the devil whispering in one's ear. The policemen in the back of the pickup huddled together, trying to keep their faces low so as to avoid the blast of the wind and the dust.

Inside the pickup, things were not much better either. The windows of the cabin had been rolled up, ostensibly to facilitate the cooling of the air conditioner. But the AC unit had long ago given up the battle against the fierce desert heat, so that the inside of the cabin now felt like a furnace. Constantine tried to open the window, but the swirls of dust almost blinded both him and the driver. They took turns dipping their handkerchiefs in a bottle of water and dabbing their faces with it. It wasn't much, but it brought momentary respite from their hellish environment.

Constantine was wracked with guilt. It clung to him like a pungent odor. He imagined that his driver and the bodyguards at the back could also sense it. He imagined that they all knew what he had done and now felt nothing but contempt for him.

He tried to shut his eyes but got no relief. The bumpy road made it impossible to rest. Besides, every time his eyes closed, Akbar's image would appear in his mind, and he would replay the scene of their meeting the previous night. For two full days after the IG's meeting, Akbar had worked on every single informer and source that he had, to figure out a way to get Nawaz Chandio. The problem was not that Chandio had disappeared. Far from it, he kept popping up at various places, in the city and in various rural districts. The problem was to arrest him by playing according to the ludicrous rules that Dr. Death had devised.

Constantine was exasperated. "Blast it, Akbar, how the hell are we supposed to get him by sticking to these instructions? Arrest and disarm his guards, but not him. How are we supposed to do that? I thought Dr. sahib had cleared Nawaz's arrest with the CM that day at the meeting?"

"He did, but then the CM called him back privately, and requested certain conditions. Nawaz can't be humiliated in any way. For instance, if he were to be arrested by a lowly DSP like myself, that would be a humiliation. Plus, their tribal supporters would take it as an affront if their prince was arrested while his brother was the CM. They don't understand Dr. sahib's concepts of law and order. They only understand that it would be a stain on their honor. Besides, it would be politically suicidal for Yousaf. The fidayeen would suspect that Yousaf had done it deliberately, because he was afraid of Nawaz's popularity."

"Why did our IG accept them? He claims he never accepts any kind of political interference in his police work."

"The CM literally begged Dr. sahib. Yaar, Dr. sahib is also under a lot of pressure these days. He called me again after the meeting that day. He looked like hell. Thanks to Maqsood's shameless blubbering in front of the press, the UF is now making an issue out of this incident. They are saying that Dr. Death was very quick to sanction the police encounters of their ward bosses, even for the smallest of infractions. But now that the law is being broken by a powerful feudal, he is not so enthusiastic about pursuing the matter. That fucking Maqsood. He has no balls. Imagine, going to the press yourself and admitting that Chandio humiliated him in his own office. Khasi bhenchod."

"That's exactly my point. He is shameless and will go to any length. If it suited his purpose, Maqsood would have let Nawaz Chandio fuck him up the ass. He made it a public issue, knowing the UF would pounce on it because they have it in for Dr. sahib. And Maqsood knows that when Dr. sahib is pushed, he is only ever going to turn to you because you're the only one he can trust to do the job right. In this case, the UF and

Maqsood have the same objectives. If the slightest thing goes wrong, they are going to nail you to the wall."

Akbar sighed. "What can I do, Consendine? Dr. sahib is crawling up the walls. He calls me every two hours for an update. It's become a matter of prestige for him to at least have Nawaz's guards arrested, even if he can't get Nawaz himself. Dr. sahib is either shouting at me, or pleading with me to maintain his izzat. YaAllah, even in the worst days in Orangi, the pressure was never this terrible."

"Don't play their game. Don't get trapped in a situation where there is no escape hatch. They want you to disarm Nawaz Chandio's gunmen, but you cannot arrest him. You saw what he did to Maqsood when Shashlik was in his custody. You think he is going to stand around politely and allow you to disarm and detain his beloved fidayeen? Akbar, remember one thing—if anything goes wrong, and the chances of that happening are extremely high, none of these barey log are going to support you. Tarkeen, the Bleak House wallahs, all of them are going to refuse to acknowledge you even. Walk away now, while you can."

"Look, I know Tarkeen isn't going to help anymore. He's still sore about me working for the Bleak House wallahs. But Dr. sahib is another matter. He has never backed away from supporting me. Remember that time, back in Orangi, when Hanuman was willing to throw me to the wolves over the killing of Adnan Doodhwala? It was Dr. sahib who stood firm. He didn't even know me then, but he still supported me and even got me promoted. When he became IG for the second time, he was the one who brought me back from the wilderness and gave me another promotion. How can I say no to him when he needs me the most? As long as he is there, he will watch over our interests. I am sure he will never let any harm come to me."

"And what if he is no longer in a position to help you. What happens then?"

Akbar looked up at Constantine with a look of bewilderment, as if he had never considered this prospect. His brow furrowed; he took a deep breath and then exhaled. He went back to working on whatever he had been working on, while Constantine sat quietly across from him, more worried than ever. He had always thought Akbar was indestructible, the super policeman who had no weakness. But at that moment, he realized that at last he had finally seen the chink in Akbar's armor. It was that he had too much faith in the people he held dear. In an imperfect world, in a profession that taught one very early on to become an arch realist, Akbar, by some crazy quirk of fate, had remained an optimist. He wished, in that moment, that Akbar had had some other vice, like booze or women. Optimism was the ultimate sin, as far as Constantine was concerned.

"Look, Consendine, I've been thinking. We, uh, have a couple of leads to follow up on tomorrow. We won't be able to cover all of them unless we split up. See, one informer says he is almost certain to attend this political meeting in Garden. He's even prepared a speech for the occasion. But on the other hand, there's another report that he may go and visit the family of one of his old fidayeen. The family lives in a village near Jamshoro. Why don't you trace down the Jamshoro lead. If he's there, you can call me and we can set up a checkpoint to stop him on his way back into the city."

"Isn't that report out of date and unconfirmed? No one really thinks he's going to drive out to the middle of nowhere just to pay his respects to the family of one of his retainers."

"Well, it may be improbable, but we can't rule it out. I think you should go and check it out while I do a setting for the public meeting in Garden. You know, just in case. I really need you to go."

"Okay."

He had pretended to hesitate, pretended that he was trying to digest the logic of the trip to the village. He had thought that his momentary contemplation was a good act that Akbar wouldn't see through. But his consent had come just a nanosecond too quickly, the inflection in his voice, in spite of his efforts to deliberately make it sound reluctant, was a tad too enthusiastic. He knew that Akbar must have seen through him in an instant.

The truth was that Akbar had thrown him a lifeline out of this mess, and he hadn't been shy about accepting it. He also knew that if the situation had been reversed, Akbar would never have chosen to leave his side to go on a wild-goose chase in the middle of the desert. But even that wasn't the worst part of this. The worst part was that, even as he sat in the boiling cabin of the pickup, his guilt at having abandoned his friend eating him up from within like a cancer, he knew that if offered the same choice again, he would still choose the same way. This was not some momentary lapse of courage that overcame him. This was the fundamental difference between Akbar Khan and Constantine D'Souza.

The dust had limited the visibility from inside the pickup. It was hardly a problem though, because no other vehicle was expected to be on this lonely road. That was why both the driver and Constantine were slow in noticing the cloud of dust that was headed towards them from the opposite direction. The driver assumed it was a dust storm, and it was only when the motorcade was barely meters away that the driver realized his mistake. He reacted instinctively, jamming his brakes and swerving the pickup off the road at the same time. Constantine, who had been so lost in his thoughts that he had still not realized what was going on, cursed loudly as they swerved off the metal road onto the ditch, or bund, that ran parallel to the road.

Constantine hit his head on the roof of the car and was disorientated for a second. He looked around the cabin and saw that the windscreen was cracked where his driver had hit his head on it. A trickle of blood was flowing from his forehead. Now caked with dust, Constantine stepped out of the cabin. One of his guards had been thrown off the back of the pickup and had landed clear of the vehicle in the bund. The other was still in the back, clutching on to his rifle desperately. Thankfully, neither seemed to be seriously injured. The dust from the incoming motorcade still lingered on the road, but through it, Constantine could see that there were at least five cars travelling at very high speed. All the vehicles seemed to be filled with gun-toting men. Constantine cursed once again and wondered what sort of self-important son of a bitch was travelling here, in the absolute middle of nowhere, with such a convoy. There were no big landlords or feudals in this area. The only place that Constantine knew of at the end of this road was the small village where Akbar's informer had claimed that Nawaz was to make an appearance. But that report couldn't have been true. Nawaz Chandio would never come to such a godforsaken place. Would he?

Constantine turned to look at the motorcade. It was already a blur in the distance, so he couldn't make out the faces of the men, or the number plates on the cars. But he could see one thing quite clearly, in the distance. The middle car in the motorcade was a fire-engine red Pajero.

The realization of what had just happened struck Constantine at that moment. He rushed to the cabin of the pickup. The driver had gotten himself out and had managed to wipe off the blood from his forehead. But he and the two guards were now bent over the wheel, examining what appeared to be a broken axle. Constantine cursed again and asked them how long it would take to fix the axle. They assured him that they would try their best, but it was no small problem to fix, especially as they were stuck in the middle of nowhere. He took his mobile phone from his pocket and dialled Akbar's number, but there was no reception this far out in the desert. He tried frantically several times, each time his fingers jabbing the dial pad that much more violently, but to no avail. He was powerless to do anything at this moment. He cursed once again, and sat down in a pile of dirt.

Nawaz Chandio turned in his seat and stared behind at the distinctive blue police pickup now lying in the ditch by the side of the road. He was about to berate his driver for his rashness, but then he turned and looked more intently at the pickup. The vehicle's doors had "Karachi Police" sten-cilled on them. What was a Karachi Police pickup doing out here? Only then did it occur to him that the only possible reason for that car to be here was to get him.

The day after the storming of Maqsood Mahr's office, his brother Yousaf had warned him to go underground for a while. The inspector general had not taken kindly to one of his stations being attacked. But Nawaz had done the opposite. He was not some kind of fugitive, hiding in caves or nondescript apartments, constantly on the run. Besides, he was beginning to suspect that there was some truth behind the rumors that Yousaf had become jealous of his popularity and wanted him out of his way, at least for a while.

Every day, newspaper headlines screamed about how the inspector general had vowed to bring to justice those individuals who thought themselves to be above the law. The reference was pointedly at Nawaz, and the press faithfully reported how the police had set up a high-profile team to secure the arrest of his followers. Some of the tabloids had begun to keep day-by-day accounts of the progress of the so-called manhunt. But the funny thing was that, for all the hype created, no one had come to him directly, either to ask for his arrest or the surrender of his men. Nawaz found that more than a little odd, and that's where he suspected foul play on the part of his brother. For it was only on the CM's orders that the police would refrain from arresting him directly.

He didn't have a problem going to jail. That was the best possible thing for his political career. Jail was to subcontinental leaders what Oxbridge or the Ivy League were to their western counterparts—a finishing school where the true pedigree of a leader could be given its final touches. It was a rite of passage without which the public would never quite trust you. Nawaz's father had been revered for doing it. Even Yousaf, in his own way, had deemed it necessary for his political career to suffer prolonged periods of house arrest. So, in fact, Nawaz welcomed the opportunity.

One of Yousaf's aides had suggested to him that it would be expedient for him to hand over a couple of his fidayeen to the police. They would immediately secure bail, and it would assuage Dr. Death's ego. The man who delivered this message had been lucky to escape with all his body parts intact. Such a move was unconscionable to Nawaz. He would enter the prison gates before any of his men. His only condition was that he would not meekly offer himself up for arrest at the local police station. According to his own code, he did not think he had done anything wrong. If Dr. Death wanted him that bad, then he would have to show the balls to come and get him, to arrest him like a real man. Nawaz would not abide by one of those backroom deals that his brother was so fond of.

Therefore, Nawaz was even more surprised to see the police pickup, because it was the first tangible sign in four days that the police were even interested in arresting him. He thought it was a bit silly of Dr. Death to have sent this solitary vehicle with its four or five occupants, to arrest Nawaz Chandio. This battered old pickup could hardly be representative of the elite team of police professionals that the press claimed Dr. sahib had put together to capture him. Perhaps, he thought, it was his overactive imagination working overtime. It could just as well be a coincidence that the pickup was on the same road in the middle of the desert.

For a moment, he considered stopping and turning back to question the police constables. Then he remembered that he had promised his daughter Samar to be home in time for her birthday party. She was turning sixteen today, and she was his pride and joy. Nawaz had attained the joys of fatherhood relatively late in life. And many, including his Swiss wife, thought that a life lived exclusively in the company of violent young men in the wilds of Afghanistan, or worse, amidst the fleshpots of Geneva and Zurich, made him particularly ill-suited to be the father of a young girl. But his heart had melted the first time he saw his daughter's sparkling blue eyes. He had been a model father, and those who had known him for years felt that baby Samar had made her doting father a more temperate person. Several times, he had only half jokingly suggested to Shashlik Khan that he would give up politics if his daughter so commanded. Such statements always made Shashlik extremely nervous.

He took one more look back at the pickup, then stared at his watch. Karachi was still another couple of hours away, and the sun would have set by the time he got home. He wouldn't be able to keep his promise to Samar if he stopped now. Besides, as he kept saying, if the damned cops wanted him that badly, all they needed to do was to knock on his door.

"Hello? Hello? Consendine, what are you saying? I can't hear you, your voice is cutting out . . ."

The no-connection tone that came on was beginning to infuriate Akbar. The phones had been like this since Constantine's first garbled message two hours ago. Mobile phone signals were iffy that far out in the interior. Akbar had managed to catch bits of Constantine's conversation, just enough to understand that apparently Constantine had spotted Nawaz Chandio on his way back to the city. Meanwhile, Akbar had been present at the event where Chandio was supposed to have shown up at. He had never thought that Chandio would actually go to a nondescript village just to pay his respects to the kin of one of his old retainers.

Luckily, Constantine had been able to pass on the information. Akbar calculated that it would take Chandio at least two hours to get back to town. The best place to set up a check post was at the toll plaza, just outside the city. Chandio would have to cross from there. Akbar quickly moved his team into place. He stared at his watch. By his estimate they were in time, but the problem was he didn't know what he was up against. He had no clue how many people Nawaz was coming with, whether they were all armed or not, or whether they would resist arrest.

If Constantine had been around, he would never have let Akbar set up this checkpoint. He had argued that creating a confrontational situation like this would inevitably lead to a violent response from Chandio. Akbar couldn't deny Constantine's logic. Chandio was a raging bull. The slightest provocation set him off. And it wasn't like the old days with the ward bosses. In that case, the department bosses, the Agencies, and the politicians had all been on the same page. Now, no one was quite sure what to do about Nawaz Chandio. Sure, Dr. Death had made his arrest a point of prestige for the police, but Akbar suspected that even the good doctor didn't quite know how to sort out this mess. What was it Constantine had said last night—What if the Doctor himself isn't in a position to help us?

For the first time in his life, Akbar actually thought about pulling out of an operation. He was getting a bad feeling about this. He stood on the side of the highway, watching the cars and buses race by, the ash on his cigarette tipping over onto the ground. He was a creature of instinct, always had been. That had been the true secret of his success. He jumped forward where others feared to tread, because he didn't tie himself up in thinking about what might happen. But today, all his instincts were screaming at him not to go through with this operation.

He shook his head vigorously, as if to shake off the cobwebs of doubt from his mind. The cards had already been dealt. Akbar was a great believer in fate. He believed that fate had brought him to where he stood today. If things were going to go bad, then there was nothing he could do about it.

One of his bodyguards signalled to him. A motorcade was approaching. Even from this distance, the red Pajero was clearly visible. It was in the lead now, having left the other jeeps a little distance behind. The driver seemed to be in a hurry to get home. Akbar saw a glint of hope in that. Maybe this day wouldn't turn out to be so bad after all.

He ordered his men to allow the Pajero to pass through the checkpoint unmolested. They were to pay no heed at all to the Pajero. At the speed he was going, he would be yards ahead by the time the back-up vehicles found themselves blocked. That way, Akbar's men could quickly disarm Chandio's fidayeen. The highway had no U-turns, so Akbar planned to be long gone by the time Chandio's vehicle could make its way back to this point. Akbar smiled to himself. When he had just recited it to himself in his head, it had seemed like one of those plans that a kid worked out on the back of a matchbox. It left too many things to chance. But it was the best he could come up with in five minutes, so he would go with it.

As the red Pajero came closer, Akbar recognized the now familiar face of Nawaz Chandio sitting in the back seat. His heart started racing. This plan depended on inch-perfect timing, a quality that the Karachi Police was not famous for. Today, though, for about two minutes it seemed as if Akbar's men would truly surpass themselves. They dropped the barrier to block Chandio's backup vehicles with perfect precision. Their weapons were already trained on the cars by the time the fidayeen had figured out what was going on. Akbar cast a nervous glance towards Chandio's jeep. The driver had almost reached the toll barrier 400 yards ahead. In seconds he would cross the tolls, making it that much more difficult to turn the car around. Once the toll barrier was crossed, Akbar reckoned he had at least twenty minutes to wrap things up over here.

Just then, he heard a whistling sound. Something, a projectile of some sort, hit the pavement near his feet. As Akbar bent to see what the object was, he heard one of his guards shout, "They're firing at us!" He turned again to look towards the toll barrier. Just centimeters from it, the driver had noticed something was amiss, and Akbar could see the Pajero now hurtling towards him in reverse. He tried to scream, but he couldn't hear his own voice above the din of the automatic weapons fire. He was in the worst possible spot, stuck right in the middle of the cross-fire zone. He hugged the pavement, frantically waving his arms to get his men to stop firing. He looked towards the Pajero again, to see if it was going to run him over. Its velocity seemed to have slowed down. The fire-engine red body was now riddled with bullet holes, and there was nothing left of the back windscreen except shards of glass.

Akbar finally found his voice. Braving the bullets, half expecting to get shot at by his own men, he got up from the road by sheer force of will. This action of his had an impact, and the firing suddenly stopped. The inert bodies of several of Chandio's men who had been in the backup vehicles were strewn on the road. He rushed to the red Pajero, which had by now come to a complete halt. He peeked in the back seat, hoping against hope that Chandio had only been wounded, that the sturdy frame of the jeep had stopped the bullets from passing through. He looked in the back and saw Nawaz Chandio calmly sitting in the back seat. There was a serene expression on his face. For a second Akbar admired his courage. The man had not even bothered to duck. *The fellow was truly regal in character*, thought Akbar, all the while chanting a dozen prayers of thanks for having kept Nawaz alive. It was only when he opened the car door that Akbar realized that the back of Nawaz Chandio's head was no longer there.

18

November 5, 2001

Half an hour outside the city, Constantine's vehicle's wireless set had picked up the Karachi Police's band frequency. Dispatchers were urgently sending mobile units to the Super Highway, where, from what Constantine could make out, Akbar's unit had been involved in a shootout with Nawaz Chandio's men. Officers were also being deployed to Abbasi Shaheed Hospital, where the dead and injured had been taken. Every five minutes or so, the head dispatcher at Police Control would shout out, "All wait, all wait!" as he cut into the transmission and bellowed priority instructions to the local police about the imminent arrival of yet another senior officer at the hospital. After listening to the wireless chatter for about ten minutes, Constantine still couldn't figure out if Akbar had been injured or killed, but the movement of the top brass towards the hospital was not a good sign. Constantine crossed himself and told his driver to take a shortcut from a dirt road into the city. The scene of the crime could wait. He needed to know if Akbar was okay.

There was a sea of flashing lights outside Abbasi Shaheed. Police pickups, senior officers' staff cars, and ambulances were backed up three blocks away from the hospital building. Various uniformed officers, holding walkie-talkies and carrying their AK-47 rifles, flitted around here and there in a state of mass confusion. Constantine abandoned his pickup, the anxiety within him building by the second, and started running towards Emergency. He almost barrelled into Hanuman, who was whispering softly into his mobile phone.

"Where are you running?" asked Hanuman, as one of his bodyguards broke Constantine's run inches from the senior officer.

"Sir, I, uh . . . Akbar, the encounter, I was in Jamshoro . . . is Akbar dead?" The words almost choked in his throat.

"No, Akbar isn't dead. He isn't even injured . . ."

"Oh, thank Christ!"

". . . but Nawaz Chandio is."

Constantine's relief drained away, as the implication of what Hanuman had said sunk in.

"Sir, you mean, Nawaz Chandio, is actually . . . he must be seriously wounded or something?"

"No, he's dead." Hanuman said it with as much emotion as he would have mustered ordering a cup of tea. His gunman, a smart-looking fellow with his pants tucked into his boots commando style, approached with a chattering walkie-talkie in his hand.

"Sir, Eagle 1 is on his way."

Hanuman bobbed his head up and down. "Consendine, the Inspector General is inside somewhere. Go and inform him that the Chief Minister will be here in a moment."

"Sir, the CM is coming here? To the hospital?"

Hanuman looked at him irritably. "Yes, his brother has been killed. Of course he'll come to the hospital. Don't ask stupid questions, and find the IG. I will wait outside to receive the Chief Minister."

In a daze, Constantine saluted and headed to the entrance of the emergency ward. Inside, it seemed as if a war had broken out. Blood was spattered all over the floor of the ward, and doctors and nurses ran from one gurney to another, trying to tend to as many of the wounded as they could manage. At least a dozen men had been injured in the encounter, and Constantine noted that all of them seemed to be Chandio's fidayeen.

Towards one side of the casualty ward was a partially open door that marked the entrance to the mortuary. Inside, still as a statue, was Dr. Death, standing over the bloodied mess on the autopsy table. As Constantine shuffled into the room, he realized that the bloodied mess was, in fact, Nawaz Chandio. A man in a stained hospital smock was awkwardly cradling the back of Chandio's skull, trying to jam it back into place, as if fitting on the head of a store mannequin.

It took Constantine some effort to control his gagging reflex. So many years on the force had still not made him immune to such a sight. Having barely succeeded in keeping the contents of his stomach down, he approached Dr. Death and saluted, but the IG seemed oblivious to him. He was transfixed by the mortuary assistant's efforts to sew Chandio's head back on to his neck.

"Sir, the Chief Minister is on his way." Constantine said the words softly the first time and then a little louder when it was evident that they had had no impact on Dr. Death. He was about to repeat himself a third time when a firm hand grabbed hold of his shoulder, and a familiar balding figure pushed him back out of the mortuary doors.

Constantine had been so focused on Dr. Death, that he had not noticed Tarkeen in the room. He tried to speak, but Tarkeen held a finger to his lips and maneuvered him into a corner alcove of the casualty ward.

"Constantine, what the hell are you doing here? Are you mad? Get as far away from here as you can, before any of these fidayeen recognize you!"

"But sir, I was on my way back from Jamshoro when I heard about the encounter on the wireless . . . what happened, sir? Where is Akbar?"

"It's a damn mess. Akbar is still at the scene of the crime, thank God. If he were to show up while the Chief Minister was here, I don't know what would happen."

"But sir, why is the CM coming here? To the hospital? Wouldn't it be better for him to wait at the CM House, and get the IG and you to brief him there?"

"Yousaf Chandio is well and truly fucked in this one. Whatever the rumors may be that he was jealous of him, Nawaz was still his brother. Nawaz's loyal fidayeen have already started rioting, here in the city and in the Chandios' village. They are saying that Yousaf secretly ordered the police to kill Nawaz. And, you have to admit, it looks bad. The sitting Chief Minister, the head of the province, and his brother, who many considered his political rival, is killed in a ridiculous shootout with the police on the highway! And to top it all off, no policeman is even injured! The media is going to have a field day with this. Chandio has to show up, even if it's only to shed a few crocodile tears in front of the cameras. Otherwise, he might as well sign a confessional statement owning up to having killed Nawaz. God, what a fuck-up!"

Constantine had never heard Tarkeen swear before. His eyes swept the room repeatedly to ensure that they weren't being overheard or recognized, and a thin bead of sweat collected on his brow. These were signs that even the otherwise unflappable Tarkeen was flustered. The two men were positioned near a window that looked out into the porch of the hospital. They could see reporters and camera crews forming a scrum in front of the entrance, in anticipation of the arrival of somebody important. Just then, a wail of sirens drowned out the din of the casualty ward. Motorcycle outriders, with their blue lights flashing, sped into the porch and sent the gathered journalists scampering to one side. Police commandos dressed all in black disembarked from two moving open-topped jeeps and established a security perimeter. And behind them, driving at breakneck speed, a convoy of vehicles, led by two identical Mercedes cars with fluttering flags, came to a screeching halt.

Hanuman had managed to fight his way through the media scrum and awkwardly opened the heavy, bullet-proof door of the lead Mercedes. Constantine could see the figure that emerged from the car was quite dishevelled. The man's shoulders were hunched over, and he stooped while walking. The dark hair that was usually slicked back and held perfectly in place on the TV screen seemed to have turned gray and stood up from his head like antennae. The shalwar-kameez that he wore looked dirty and bedraggled. And as he stepped out of the car and stared vacantly at Hanuman, Constantine could see that the Chief Minister was barefoot. This was certainly not the deal-making, smooth-talking Yousaf Chandio that people were used to seeing.

Maqsood Mahr emerged from the other side of the Mercedes, took the doddering Yousaf by the hand, and led him into the hospital. As soon as the two men, followed by Hanuman and the Chief Minister's military aide, entered the mortuary, the police commandos barred the door, but from their vantage point, Constantine and Tarkeen could still hear what was going on inside. Constantine grimaced as Maqsood Mahr passed by. It was not a good sign if he had set himself up as the mourner-in-chief.

As if on cue, Maqsood started beating his breast and wailing. "Oh, Sayeen Baba! What have they done to you? You were the flower of our nation! What have these police wallahs done to you? Sir, this is why I always advocated restraint. I never wanted an accident like this to happen. Oh, Yousaf Sayeen, they have robbed you of your own brother!"

On hearing this, a guttural cry came from Yousaf Chandio. He started banging on Nawaz's inert body. "Wake up, Nawaz, wake up. I'm here, *Adda* Yousaf is here."

For several minutes, the only sound that Constantine and Tarkeen could hear was the muffled sobbing of Yousaf as he fell to the floor and buried his head in his brother's bloodied breast. Then, suddenly, he rose with an animal fury and stabbed a finger at a startled Dr. Death, his voice shrill with rage.

"You! I told you to go easy on my brother, didn't I? I told you! But you had too much pride. You had to go after him, you couldn't just let it go! Nawaz is dead, and what am I supposed to tell our mother? I will never forgive you for this. I will never forgive any of the people who were responsible for my brother's death. Never!"

Tarkeen and Constantine looked at each other. Nothing further needed to be said.

Four days later

Constantine awoke from another night of troubled sleep. He was alone in the house. Mary and the children were away on holiday in the north of the country. He had been scheduled to join them, until the Chandio mess had erupted. He cursed himself. Perhaps it would have been better if he had gone with Mary and the kids. He would have been thankful not to have been present in the city these past four days.

Ashraf had brought him his tea from the chai shop and had set all the newspapers on the table for him. Even after four days, the press was still not letting up. The papers were full of details of the shootout. Seventeen men had been killed, all of them Nawaz Chandio's fidayeen and including, of course, the young prince himself. Tarkeen had been right. The papers harped on about the fact that not a single police officer had been hurt and how this was evidence of the police having pre-planned the encounter.

The sharks were circling. The government was under intense pressure, and the media was all too eager to provide the final shove to topple it.

Constantine had always believed in the inherent strength of the State and its institutions. He was, after all, a police officer, a member of the coercive arm of that State. He always held that no one could overthrow the State, no matter how powerful they were, because the State would always be more powerful. So many had tried but, at the end of the day, the State prevailed. It was so strong in its foundations that all it had to do was send out minions like him and Akbar to deal with such pretenders. The UF had been a perfect example. For all the party's street power and its scores of ruthless militants, ultimately they were no match for the resources of the State. Therefore it had surprised him in these past four days how quickly that same usually self-confident State had begun to unravel.

In fact, it seemed as if the State had vanished altogether. Nawaz's death had brought about a backlash from his followers. Maddened by their grief, they had gone on the rampage. Fidayeen had been looting and burning with abandon on the streets, and the police didn't even bother to stop them. After the episode at the hospital, the CM, shaken physically and politically, had retreated to his village, officially in mourning for the death of his brother but more than a little frightened about what the fidayeen might do to him. Nawaz Chandio's killing had even shaken the usually resolute Dr. Death. And so, while the city had burned, the IG refused to order the police to intervene, for fear of further inciting the fidayeen.

The violence had stopped a day ago, but the recriminations had not. The media had already tried and convicted Akbar. Full-page editorials had condemned him and criticized Dr. Death for relying on such blood-thirsty officers. His record in Orangi, once a source of pride to everyone in the department, had been cited as evidence that Akbar was no better than a hired killer. Maqsood Mahr, with no IG to keep him in check any more, had given interviews in the press claiming that he had been taken off the case specifically because he had refused to kill Nawaz in cold blood. The United Front, never slow to exploit any opportunity, had started announcing that their ward bosses had been exterminated systematically by the same police officers who were responsible for Nawaz's death, and this was exactly what they had been saying all along: that the police department had become little better than a gang of criminals who were incapable of being controlled by the current political administration. In essence, they had made this case a referendum on Yousaf Chandio's government.

Constantine went through the papers, grimacing every time there was a reference to Akbar. His own name had not been mentioned anywhere. True, he hadn't been present at the shooting, but that had hardly stopped the media, the UF, and Maqsood Mahr from implicating dozens of officers against whom they had personal grudges in this case. Mahr had, in fact, become a kind of grand inquisitor, Torquemada in a safari suit. He had set up shop at his office. Every day he would call in dozens of officers and demand that they prove their non-involvement in this case. Most took the easy way out and paid him to clear them. Maqsood was running a roaring business these days.

Constantine had surprisingly not been summoned to these proceedings. He could not fathom a reason why Maqsood had gone easy on him, other than the fact that the ones who were summoned were all officers who Maqsood considered his rivals. Obviously, Maqsood did not think Constantine posed any threat.

Akbar, too, had not yet been summoned, but then Maqsood was probably saving him for last. Constantine found nothing new or alarming in Maqsood's tactics. That was the nature of the beast. Maqsood was a scavenger, and, sighting a weakened prey, he would always swoop in to feast on the carrion. But Maqsood could only go as far as the IG allowed him to go. And it was Dr. Death's silence that was the more worrying thing. Constantine could understand the Doctor's reluctance to use the police against the fidayeen, so soon after what had happened, for fear of an even more severe backlash. The bit he didn't get was why he was allowing Maqsood to flout every rule and convention that he had stood for so uprightly all these years. Maqsood's investigation had nothing to do with justice and everything to do with money. So then, why didn't Dr. Death speak up and put an end to it? Constantine had begun to have his doubts about the IG since he saw him that night at Abbasi Shaheed.

Akbar, however, remained steadfastly loyal to Dr. Death. He had been instructed to keep a low profile for a few days, for his own safety. Under normal circumstances Akbar would never have complied with such an order, but he had been in a very somber mood since the incident, and so he had made no argument. Constantine would go over to his place every day, and he and Akbar would sit together for hours, talking sparingly and mostly just staring into space. Akbar was in shock about what had happened, but his faith in Dr. Death was still unshakeable. He still believed that as soon as he was able to meet the IG and explain what had happened, Dr. sahib would take control of the situation.

Which was why today was all the more important. Up till now, the IG had himself been occupied dealing with the aftermath of the incident, so he hadn't had any time to meet Akbar, or so he claimed. Finally, Akbar had managed to get an appointment, and he had asked Constantine to come along. Constantine had reservations about going to see Dr. Death in the present circumstances, but he felt he had no choice but to go with Akbar even if, as he suspected, the trip would be a futile one.

Constantine put on his uniform and picked Akbar up from his house. Akbar looked cheerful and was in a chatty mood, the first time in days that he had been like this.

"Arre, Consendine, today Inshallah our problems will come to an end. Dr. sahib is back in the saddle."

"Akbar, he's been there all along. But he didn't stop Maqsood from registering a case against the police officers. Look, everybody knows it wasn't deliberate. Dr. sahib knows that more so than anybody else. Yet he allows the officers to be interrogated as if they were some bloody wardias."

"He's been under a lot of pressure. Apparently the CM hasn't spoken to him since that day. It's not easy for him. But the fact that he's agreed to see us proves that he's still standing with us. I keep telling you, he's not the sort of officer who'll cut and run. Trust me, Consendine."

Constantine did not answer but kept driving to Police Headquarters. They walked up to the IG's office as they had done a thousand times before, but this time round, everything seemed different. Even the orderly outside the IG's office greeted them more stiffly. He barred Akbar from entering immediately and instead asked them both to wait in a side room. The wait was not a short one. Several hours passed, and Constantine saw a stream of visitors who had arrived after them get ushered into the IG's office. All enquiries made to the staff were met with a stony silence. Akbar too seemed perplexed by this attitude, but said nothing.

Finally, near the end of the day, the orderly nodded towards the door to signal that Akbar had been summoned. Constantine rose from the couch with him, but the orderly shook his head, saying that the summons was only for Akbar. Akbar looked at Constantine, shrugged his shoulders, and walked in.

Inside, Dr. Death was sitting behind his large desk, a pile of paperwork on one side. He barely acknowledged Akbar's salute and did not offer him a seat. His attention seemed glued to a small TV screen in a corner of the room. The volume was turned low, but there was a cricket match on and the Doctor seemed totally engrossed in it. After a couple of minutes, the silence became uncomfortable, so Akbar asked if he could sit. Dr. Death grunted once in response. Taking that as a yes, he sat down.

Something had changed about Dr. sahib. The past few days had aged him. The posture, usually ramrod straight, was hunched in the chair. He seemed feeble and distracted. Akbar had never seen him like this before. Normally Dr. Death would waste no time in coming to the point, but today he kept staring at the television, not even attempting to start the conversation.

Akbar finally tentatively raised the issue himself. "Sir, uh, Maqsood registered a case against the officers who were present at the incident, and he's started to make arrests."

On the TV, Sachin Tendulkar hit a boundary. Dr. Death's gaze did not waver once from the six different replays of the shot.

"Uh, if he's allowed to do that, sir, it will be very demoralizing for the men. I mean, everyone knows that none of this was deliberate. It was an unfortunate accident, and they shouldn't be prosecuted for that."

There was still no response from the Doctor.

"Uh, sir, what do you want me to do with Shashlik? We need to start wrapping that case up as well. I'll start on that as soon as this matter is cleared up."

"You will hand Shashlik over to Maqsood immediately." The voice was cold, emotionless.

"Excuse me, sir? But you told me to take back Shashlik's custody because you suspected that Maqsood was on Shashlik's payroll. And you were right, sir. Maqsood is totally mixed up in this. The way he's trying to construct the case against the police proves this."

"What I said before is irrelevant now. You will hand Shashlik over to Maqsood because that's what the CM wants. And you will cooperate fully with Maqsood's investigation."

"But sir, Maqsood is concocting a false case against us. It would be crazy to go along with his—"

"I don't have the strength anymore to question the CM's orders." He said it matter-of-factly, as if this was something impersonal, detached from his self. But the impact of the statement was not lost on Akbar. Dr. Death had been the man who had refused to compromise with the UF's ward bosses, had traded body for body with them until they had run out of bullets. But Nawaz Chandio's death had humbled him. There was a haunted look in his eyes, and it was clear he didn't have the stomach for a fight anymore.

Still, Akbar made one last attempt. "Sir, whatever happened, we were following your orders. Your legitimate orders. We did nothing wrong. Maqsood is making it out as if we hatched a conspiracy to kill Nawaz Chandio."

"Not we. You."

Akbar felt physically sick. He could not believe that Dr. sahib had uttered such a sentence. He did not respond, but his pain was evident from his expression. Even Dr. sahib seemed to notice it, because he turned away from his TV screen for the first time and addressed Akbar directly. The crisp, commanding voice had been replaced with the doddering tone of an old man.

"Look Akbar, I can't afford to get involved in this. The CM is inconsolable at the moment. And the UF is putting a lot of pressure against you. They want you to be punished for what you did to their ward bosses. Maqsood has spoken with the CM and assured me that my name will not be associated with this case in any way. He has already secured that promise from the UF as well."

"Sir, I have always carried out your orders without question. You always told me I was like a son to you. I went after Chandio's guards because it had become a matter of personal prestige for you. How can you abandon me like this? Can't you see Maqsood is playing you?"

"I am sorry, Akbar. I truly am. It is true that I have always said you were like a son to me. But I have my own son, who I have a responsibility for. He is studying in college in America. What will happen to him if I go down for this? I have a year left before my retirement. I want to go home peacefully. I don't want my son to see me from behind iron bars."

"Arre, sahib, that's all well and good for you. But I have children too. What about them? What will they do? Who is responsible for their well-being? Can you give me an answer for that?"

But there was no answer. Dr. Death picked up the remote and turned up the volume to signal that this meeting was over.

Constantine had been sitting outside nervously. Though he had little hope of a positive response from the IG, Akbar's level of trust and confidence in Dr. Death had been so great that he thought that perhaps Akbar would be able to pull another rabbit out of his hat. One look at Akbar's face as he walked out of the IG's office brought all these burgeoning hopes crashing down. He seemed fine on the face of it, he still walked with his head held high, but it was his eyes that gave him away. There was a forlorn, faraway look in them, the look of a man who had come face to face with the reality of his illusions.

"Akbar! What happened?"

"Heh. Things didn't work out the way we wanted to, Constantine."

"What did Dr. sahib say to you?"

"It doesn't matter. I think you should go now, Constantine. You shouldn't be around for what's about to happen. No one has linked you to this case till now, and we need to keep it that way."

"But what happened, Akbar?"

"Everybody needs someone to blame for this mess. I'm the most convenient option. Move along, Consendine. I'm going to become toxic pretty soon."

"Akbar, we have to try and do something. Look, let's go see Colonel Tarkeen and ask for his help."

"There's no point. He's been angry with me since I started working with the Bleak House wallahs. He's hardly going to help me now. Besides,

I'm not going to debase myself by begging for his help. When Dr. sahib has given up, what can Tarkeen do? No Consendine, there's no point in fighting this anymore."

The Pizza Hut at Boat Basin was a good location for a low-profile meeting. Karachi's middle class flocked to it in droves, wanting their own little slice of globalization. The lines often stretched around the block, giving the fast-food chain the feel of a Michelin-star restaurant. Since the Americans had invaded Afghanistan, business had actually shot up. It seemed as if the denizens of the city, insecure about what the future held and worried that this new War on Terror would curtail their supply of deep-pan stuffed crusts, had decided to grab whatever they could while the going was still good.

Constantine sat at a discreet corner booth, close to the kitchen door. The smell of freshly baked pizza wafted towards him every time the door opened. Tarkeen had chosen to meet him here rather than in his office. Since Nawaz Chandio's death, the Agencies were keeping a low profile. The city's rumor mills had been full of stories suggesting their involvement in Chandio's death. The papers, which were filled with miraculously discovered new "facts" about the incident every day, all conveniently leaked by Maqsood Mahr's team, were now pursuing what they had termed as the "magic bullet" theory. It propounded that the first shot had been fired by a hidden shooter, who had obviously been in the employ of the Agencies.

Tarkeen had only consented to a meeting after Constantine had begged and pleaded with him. Akbar had been true to his word after his meeting with Dr. Death the day before. He had retreated to his home, to wait for whatever fate had in store for him. But in spite of Akbar's reservations about Tarkeen, Constantine had felt it was worth one last, desperate shot. After all, what was the alternative? Constantine was sure that it hadn't sunk into Akbar yet that if things continued the way they were going, Maqsood Mahr would throw him in jail. Constantine's pizza had just arrived when Tarkeen walked in, looking like a middle-aged bank executive in a dark suit and conservative tie.

"*Constantine*, my dear fellow, I'm glad you ordered already. I'm *famished*."

"Sir, thank you for coming. I wasn't sure you would. I know your people are getting quite a lot of flak from the Chandio thing, and I also know that you were angry with Akbar before this incident occurred."

"Not at all, *Constantine*. You know I would never refuse a request from you. As for our organization, well, we get used to the criticism. The opposition politicians will rant and rave for a while about how the government is using the Agencies to intimidate its enemies, but then they will all shut up and change their tune when they realize that they are about to form the next government. That's when everyone starts appreciating our utility. As for the rest, well, the chattering classes in this country will always chatter, but never really do anything. Deep down, they are quite happy to keep us around because the alternative is quite unpalatable for them. If we weren't there to keep everyone in check, the masses would tear apart these so-called elites."

"So you think the government is about to fall?"

"Oh, it's already been decided. The UF has concluded the deal with the president. He is going to cut Yousaf off and hand them this province in its entirety. No more power sharing or supporting from the fringes. He has agreed to all their demands, including complete control over the police. In return, they will support him wholeheartedly in this new campaign against the jihadis. And they have also promised to keep their new ward bosses within acceptable limits. It's quite a good arrangement all round, really."

"What about Akbar, sir? Please sir, I request you to help him. Put aside your personal feelings. He has two small children. This is his life we're talking about."

"My dear boy, I was never angry at Akbar. Yes, I was disappointed when he spurned us to go work for our rivals. After all, I was the one who made him what he is today. A man should never forget his place in life. But it was never personal against him."

"Then please, sir, help him in some way. He went to see the IG yesterday. I don't know what happened in the meeting, but before going in, Akbar had been very confident that Dr. sahib would stand up for him. That obviously didn't happen. He's become completely fatalistic now. He's just waiting for events to run their course. He's given up the fight."

Tarkeen chewed his pizza thoughtfully. "Yes, I didn't expect the good Doctor to have helped. You see, Constantine, the biggest casualty of this incident isn't Nawaz, or Akbar. It's the Doctor. For all his tough talk as a man of unflinching principles, he went to pieces when things went bad. Ironically, he's handed over all his authority to the man whom he despised. Maqsood is running the show now. He's become the honest broker in all of this. He saved the IG's neck, on the understanding that as soon as the government is formally dissolved, the good Doctor will be packed off to Islamabad, to serve out what little time is left in his career in some non-descript posting in a quiet corner of the federal government. But he is not to speak, or give any kind of evidence about this incident, ever. Hanuman is going to become the city police chief, because the United Front is comfortable with him, and Maqsood will become his second-in-command. Yousaf won't make too much of a fuss about being sacked as CM, so long as we turn a blind eye to all the ill-gotten gains he acquired in his tenure and we don't rock the boat as far as instigating his brother's fidayeen. He's got his hands full with them anyway, but an amnesty for their rioting after Nawaz's death and a little spreading of the Chandio wealth will hopefully placate them."

"But sir, the CM will give everything up as easily as that? And what about Shashlik? He's still in police custody. In fact, Maqsood's men took him from Akbar's office late last night."

"Well, there's not much Yousaf can do. Sometimes events overtake us all. I mean, we didn't feel this was an ideal situation, but you have to be flexible. You know, Maqsood has that quality. He really has been quite useful to us all. He brought Shashlik over to me last night and convinced him to throw in his lot with the government and the UF. Maqsood told him the alternative was that he would be indicted for planning the murder of his friend, Nawaz Chandio. Can you imagine, Shashlik and Akbar being charged for the same crime? Inventive fellow, that Maqsood. So Shashlik, predictably, agreed, and we'll even reward him by making him a minister for transport or labor or something like that."

"But sir, what about Akbar?"

Tarkeen sighed and took a sip from his Coke before answering. "As I said, Constantine, sometimes events overtake us. Maqsood's price for doing all of this was Akbar's head. Considering the circumstances, what could any of us do? I'm sorry, my boy. But you shouldn't worry on your own account. No one wants to pursue anything against you, not even Maqsood. He has never mentioned your name in connection with this case in all his discussions with us. Just continue working as usual, Constantine."

Constantine stared down at the cold slice of pizza on his plate. All around them, people unselfconsciously stuffed themselves, taking advantage of the latest meal deals, and piling their plates high at the salad bar. No one paid any attention to the pair of them. As far as everybody else in here was concerned, they were just two business associates. Who would have guessed that they were discussing the fate of a man's life? A bittersweet smile broke out across his face. So this was how the great Akbar Khan would come to his end. Not through a ward boss's bullet, but by the knife that his own officers had stuck in his back.

Tarkeen seemed to have sensed what he was thinking. "I can understand what you're feeling, Constantine. Just remember, it was never personal with Akbar, always business."

And with that, Colonel Tarkeen walked out of the Hut.

19

The big black Land Cruiser with tinted windows was parked on the side of the main road that led into Orangi from Banares Chowk. Two police pickups were parked next to it. Inside the Land Cruiser were four men. Colonel Tarkeen had traded his usual dapper suits for a combat fatigue jacket. Constantine too wore civilian clothes and was carrying his service pistol in his hand. In the driver's seat sat an inspector from Maqsood's investigation branch, who was officially liaising with Tarkeen on this case. There was one other person in the car, sitting in the back, quietly working on a laptop. He was a Caucasian with blond hair, cut very short, military style. He wore dark wraparound sunglasses even at night and a thick windbreaker with a bulge on the right side. Tarkeen had not formally told anyone where he was from. He had simply been introduced as "Jim," but it was evident that he was part of the FBI team that was helping out on this case.

Tarkeen stared at his watch for the fifth time in fifteen minutes. "Where's your man, Constantine?"

The colonel had contacted Constantine a couple of hours after leaving the prison. They had gotten the details of the shop from where the SIM numbers had been distributed. Constantine arranged to meet up with Tarkeen's team at Banares Chowk at about 9:00 p.m. This was the main route into Orangi. Constantine had already sent his man Ashraf ahead. He was to approach the shop in plainclothes, pretending to be a relative from Kana's village, asking after him. As soon as he got a location,

Ashraf would contact them and zero them in to where Kana was. The only problem was, Ashraf had been gone for almost an hour with no contact, and everyone was getting a little fidgety.

Constantine looked at his phone, willing it to ring. "He should be in contact soon, sir. He's very reliable."

"What if this guy doesn't live in the area? What's our plan B?" It was the American, who spoke in a thick Brooklyn accent.

The colonel and Constantine both looked at each other. The truth was, there was no plan B. The efforts of the police so far had been so utterly futile, that everyone had grasped at Akbar's information like drowning men holding on to a lifeboat.

"Don't worry, Jim. If this doesn't work out, then we have five or six other leads that we are pursuing." The colonel said this with a straight face and with as much confidence as he could muster.

Just as the American was about to ask a follow-up question, Constantine's phone rang. To everyone's relief, it was Ashraf. After speaking to him, Constantine turned to the group. "Ashraf found the shop. I had told him to go on the pretence of wanting to buy a SIM. He told the shop attendants that he was new in town, from Kana's village, and that someone in the village had told him to get in touch with Kana if he had any problems in the city." He looked at the American to explain. "You see, sir, in our culture, there is a great kinship among people from the same village. Often, when a person from the village moves to the big city, he is told by his elders to contact a fellow villager who moved earlier. It is quite a common practice and would not raise anyone's suspicions."

The FBI man nodded dubiously, suspicious as always of all the actions of the Pakistanis.

"Anyway, the shop attendant said he lived nearby and gave Ashraf directions."

"Excellent! Tell Ashraf to get to the address, and we will pick him up from there!" There was audible relief in Colonel Tarkeen's voice.

"Sir, I have a better idea. It will be more covert. The attendant told Ashraf that Kana would return around 11:00 p.m. to pick up his daily wages from the shop. We will ask Ashraf to stay put and sit in a nearby chai shop. He will leave word at the shop so that they inform Kana that he is sitting there, waiting for him. Meanwhile, we will move in closer to the spot. As soon as he comes into the chai shop and asks for Ashraf, we can jump him. By that time of night this area starts winding down, so there won't be that much activity and less chance of someone reporting Kana getting picked up immediately. If we pick him up from home, word will spread instantly. This way, we can gain a crucial couple of hours in which we can interrogate him and find out where the American is."

"Sounds good," said Jim. Everyone seemed to concur.

"We can drive till the crossing, a little further up, but then we should abandon the cars. Also Colonel sahib, if Mr. Jim comes along, we will lose our cover."

"Yes, we don't want to take that risk. Okay Jim, you stay here in the car. I'm also going to leave the inspector here with you. Constantine and I will take a couple of plainclothes officers from the other pickup." Tarkeen took out a pistol from his jacket and cocked it.

"Where is Major Rommel, sir? It would have been useful to have him with us." Constantine had noted that Rommel was conspicuous by his absence.

"I left Rommel at headquarters to coordinate things and to keep sending updates to our superiors. I wanted to supervise the field operation myself."

The two men stepped out of the SUV into the cool night air. Constantine liked the cold breeze on his face because it made him focus. He looked at his paunch and sighed. It was at times like these that he wished that he had maintained the fitness of his youth. One could never predict what might happen on a raid like this one, and it was always better to have a trained and tuned body. Constantine knew of policemen who had gotten injured in gunfights and bomb explosions for no other reason than that they were too fat to move fast enough to get out of the way. He selected his second gunman, Ashraf's partner Saeedullah, to go with them. The other constable they chose was a short, squat, middle-aged fellow, a complete contrast to Saeedullah, who was six feet tall, bearded, and looked extremely intimidating. The only reason the second man was chosen was that he was the only one who was not in uniform. It had been another cock-up from Maqsood Mahr to have sent such few plainclothes officers to assist in a case of such sensitivity. Constantine was not particularly enthused about the choice of the second constable. He was very choosy about the men he would take on raids with him. He usually never moved without having his own trusted men behind him. He had faith in their skill and training. Others, he couldn't vouch for. The biggest lesson he had learnt from Akbar in their years of working together had been that in these sorts of situations, the greatest danger came not from the enemy you faced but from the untrained exuberance of your own force. Ordinary constables did not have the level of training to execute such tricky operations flawlessly. Constantine's own men were different. They were from the anti-terrorist squad and were veterans of dozens of such operations. The second constable would be a bit of a gamble, but arranging a larger, better-trained team would have risked the operational secrecy of the mission. The movement of well-trained police commandos in shiny new police pickups would have been a dead giveaway in an area like Orangi.

Orangi was a maze. The road that the four men started walking on led past Banares Chowk into the massive slum. With a million human beings packed like sardines into a very small area, entering it was like entering another world. Such misery and destitution bred all sorts of problems. Orangi always remained a hotbed of vice, crime, and terrorist activity. The local population was also ethnically diverse, and that added to the Molotov cocktail of problems that plagued the locality. In the years since Akbar and Constantine had been posted here, the number of madrasas in the area had mushroomed. The madrasas represented an affordable means for the inhabitants to enable their children to gain some sort of basic education, even if it was just the rote learning of the Quran. Although the madrasas did not necessarily have any sinister agenda, the abject poverty and hopelessness of the area had made Orangi a rich recruiting ground for jihadis.

The small party walked off the wide main road, past the police station, into Orangi No. 6. The vehicles had been left outside the police station. It was just as well, because they could not have come any further. Past the station, the road disappeared and became a narrow, unpaved track, intersected by even narrower alleyways on either side, some just wide enough to allow one person to pass at a time. Raw sewage ran in ditches along the road. It had taken Constantine six months to get used to the odor of excrement that constantly hung in the air. The track itself was muddy and littered with black plastic bags and other refuse. It was pitch-dark, the absence of streetlights compounded by power cuts that enveloped the neighborhood in shadows. The party groped their way along, deeper into the labyrinth, and if Constantine had not known the area like the back of his hand, they would surely have gotten lost. The only illumination came from a shop that could be seen some distance away, and the hum of a small electric generator could be heard from the same direction.

Constantine checked his watch. It was almost eleven, the time at which Kana was supposed to make his rounds of the shop. Ashraf was sitting at a chai shop opposite, waiting for them. The cold weather had ensured that even fewer people than usual were out on the streets at this hour. That at least had worked in their favor, as everything depended on how quietly they picked up their target. If they could do it without raising too much alarm and keep their identities hidden, they would buy some time to interrogate Kana. In a rough neighborhood like this, it was not unusual for somebody to be picked up from the street, and it was not necessarily an automatic assumption that the police had done the picking up. UF wardias, various jihadi and religious parties, and the local land mafia all ran gangs in the area, and abduction, for whatever reasons, was standard practice for all of them.

The shop where Kana worked was across the street from the tea stall, and it was the same one that had been illuminated from a distance. The four men joined Ashraf at the table. The waiter, a young boy who couldn't have been older than twelve, brought them cups of wincingly sweet, Pathan-style green tea, served with a stick of cinnamon and a twist of lemon. The mobile phone shop was the only one in the area that had electricity. Ashraf told them that Kana was due any minute. Constantine noticed a rickety taxi cab parked next to the tea stall, with its driver snoozing inside.

The men sat in silence, nobody really wishing to speak, and all of them stared at the store. Adrenaline was pumping in their veins. After what seemed an interminable wait, a man approached the store just as the attendants were pulling the shutters down. He was dressed in a dirty gray shalwar-kameez. He sported a closely cropped beard and had a blue-colored glass eye in his right socket, where his eyeball should have been. As the store attendant pointed him in the direction of the tea stall, the men scattered from the table, leaving Ashraf sitting there alone. The man walked towards the stall and asked the handful of patrons still sitting there about who had been looking for him. Ashraf rose to ask him if he was Kana. As soon as he answered the question in the affirmative, Constantine and Saeedullah jumped him, one grabbing him by the hair and the other holding on to the elastic of his shalwar. Ashraf brandished a pistol to ward off any of the other occupants of the stall from attempting to help. Constantine and the others dragged the struggling Kana towards the taxi. They threw him hard into the back seat, injuring his head in the process. Then they piled in themselves. The taxi driver, abruptly awakened from his slumber, saw their weapons and thought his vehicle was being snatched. He jumped out without any protest and let Constantine in behind the wheel. He started the ignition and drove like a maniac, straight into narrow alleys that one would have thought would be impossible to drive a car through. Meanwhile, Kana continued to struggle with the two policemen crammed into the back seat.

Constantine's heart was racing. It had been some time since he had engaged in an exercise like this. The whole operation had taken under a minute. He turned to Colonel Tarkeen, who was sitting in the passenger seat beside him. "Sir, the best place to take him for interrogation is Orangi Police Station. It's our only choice. At this time of night, there will only be a skeleton staff there. I know the station munshi. We can occupy a back room and work on him there."

"All right. How much time do you think we have?"

"I reckon a couple of hours. The way we took the taxi, they probably all think we're local criminals settling scores with him. The taxi driver will come to the police station to report the theft of his vehicle in a bit, but they will keep giving him the runaround for a few hours until he produces some money for them to write up his report. Till the police declare whether it was a crime or not, his people might imagine that it was some village vendetta or something of that nature. That's good. If they keep thinking so for a while, the American will be safe."

As he spoke, they pulled up to the gate of Orangi Police Station, where they had left their vehicles. Constantine drove the taxi into the police station compound and told the sentry to close the gate. He walked into the duty officer's room, as Ashraf and the two others dragged Kana, now muffled with a cloth stuffed in his mouth, out of the car. The station munshi, an old man with a wizened face and small pince-nez glasses, was surprised to see Constantine step out from the driver's seat.

"*Arre,* Consendine sahib, what are you doing here?"

Constantine had always liked the munshi because he was an extremely discreet and efficient individual. "Abdul Rehman, I can't tell you much except that it's very important. We need an interrogation room, preferably not a very public one. Ensure that no one comes there. Oh, and if a taxi driver comes to file a report about a stolen taxi, tell the duty officer to give him the runaround and make him come back in the morning."

Without batting an eyelid, the old munshi went into action. He led them to a small room on the second floor of the police station. It had a table and a few chairs, and two hooks in the wall from which a suspect could be hung upside down. The walls were thick and the room windowless. The room was situated towards the rear of the station, so that a man's screams would not be heard in the front courtyard. It was perfect for their purposes.

As Ashraf and the other two guards secured the prisoner, Constantine turned to the colonel. "Sir, I think we should move our vehicles from the front of the station. There is a little space to park at the back. I will even have the taxi moved there for now. When the driver comes in the morning, they can tell him that it was found abandoned nearby. If you want to bring Mr. Jim, bring him in now, but please cover his face with a cloth so no one figures out that he's a foreigner. Let them think he is a secret informer and we are working on some major crime figure."

"Good idea. I'll get him and move the cars."

As Tarkeen left, Constantine turned to the munshi, who, seeing his shortness of breath, had brought him a glass of water.

"Is everything okay with you, Consendine sahib?"

"Yes, thank you, Abdul Rehman. I haven't done this in a while."

"I heard you were in the Prisons, sir. How is Akbar sahib? I pray for him. We all do. All of us still remember those difficult times. It was only when he became the in-charge that we actually started to feel like we were police officers. You two did so much for us, you were like our guardian angels."

"Keep praying. Your prayers may be answered sooner than you expect. Where's that drunkard boss of yours? I don't want him asking too many questions."

"Don't worry about him, sir. In-charge sahib is only interested in making points with the local ward boss and the wine shop owners. He goes off with his bottle at 8:00 p.m. every day and doesn't come in till ten, eleven in the morning. He doesn't even bother to check in by phone during the night."

"What if there's an emergency?"

"Consendine sahib, these days it's not like it used to be in your time, when you and Akbar sahib wouldn't go home for days. Now, everything runs on auto. The local gangs handle everything, whether it's the UF or the land mafia. The police are just a spare tire in the area."

"Well, in case anyone asks, just tell them the intelligence wallahs are doing something."

"Arre, sahib, is it something to do with that American's kidnapping?"

Constantine gave him a stern look. "Abdul Rehman, you wily old fool, you know better than to ask such questions."

Immediately chastened, the old man shook his head. "Never mind sahib, forgive me for asking. I will go and carry out your instructions. I'll tell the sentry not to let anyone up on this floor. If you need me for anything else, just call me."

"Thank you, Abdul Rehman."

The munshi passed Colonel Tarkeen and Jim coming up the stairs. Jim's face was completely covered with a dirty old shawl and he was indistinguishable as a foreigner. Constantine was worried. It would be a miracle if they got two hours to break Kana. He was unlikely to easily succumb to threats or torture. What made things worse for them was, they had such little background information on him. Akbar had just given them a name. They had no way of verifying if he was telling them the truth, even if he did start talking. The clock had begun to tick for the American.

"All set, Constantine. We've parked the cars at the back. No one can see them from the road."

"And I've spoken with the munshi, sahib. No one will disturb us here."

"Then let's begin. Each minute we waste is precious."

The three men entered the room, and Constantine took a good look at the subject for the first time. He was bleeding from a cut above his bad eye. The glass eye was still in place, though spattered with blood. His shirt was now torn, and his arms bruised from the struggle. He had a fair understanding by now of what was happening, so his earlier ferocity had been replaced with a quiet trepidation as he sat on his haunches on the floor in one corner of the room. But there was still a smouldering defiance in his one eye, which only increased when he saw Jim take the shawl off his face.

Constantine, Tarkeen, and Jim sat down on the three available plastic chairs, while Ashraf and the other two guards stood over Kana. The colonel began the interrogation.

"What is your name?"

Kana was silent.

"Are you the one whom they call Kana?"

Kana was silent, never for a moment taking his eyes off the American.

Constantine smiled at him. "Look, we already know you are Kana. We asked for you at the shop, and you responded to our man. So what's the harm in admitting that?"

No response.

"All right, where do you live? We should know where to inform your relatives that you have been picked up by the police."

He was silent, but his stare was so intense that it made Jim shift uncomfortably in his seat.

Tarkeen spoke up. "He's not going to cooperate this way. Strip him."

Ashraf struggled to take off his shirt, while the second guard pulled at his baggy shalwar. Kana thrashed about with increasing desperation. He was a strong man, and it took them a couple of minutes and several blows to undress him. He now stood in front of them, shivering slightly in the cold, trying to cover his nudity.

"Which camp did you receive your training at?"

Finally he spoke. "Why are you doing this to me? I haven't done anything to you. I don't even know who you are. I don't know anything about any camp."

"Ah. So you do have a voice. You are called Kana in the market. Yes or no? It's a simple question. You see the man standing behind you, with the bamboo stick? Every time you don't answer, he's going to hit you on your balls with the stick. Not hard, but just enough to make you writhe in pain. So, yes or no?"

"Yes, yes, I am called Kana. Can I put my clothes on?"

"In a minute. If you answer truthfully. How long have you worked at the store?"

"Six months."

"Where did you work before that?"

A slight hesitation in answering brought a short, sharp blow from the stick.

"Ah! Uh, I didn't work. I was unemployed."

"Where do you live?"

"Near the shop. Gully No. 34."

"Who lives with you?"

"My mother and my wife. And my little boy."

"How long have you lived at this address?"

"Six months."

"Where were you living before? How long have you been living in Karachi?"

"Before I lived in another house close by. I have lived in Karachi all my life."

"You're lying." A nod from Constantine brought another blow. "Was your father a fucking factory owner that you could afford to live in Karachi without a job? Don't try and be smart, madarchod. It will take us two minutes to drag your mother and wife into the thana and confirm what you are saying! You want to see them in here? You want them to see you like this? Or worse, for you to see them like this? We are police wallahs, madarchod, we are real harami. Now, where are you from?"

"I am from the Khyber Agency."

"Now we're getting somewhere. A jihadi from the tribal areas, huh? What have you been doing there? Were you involved in the fighting? Is that where you lost your eye?"

"No, sahib. I was in Karachi before. I moved back for a while to get married. Then I returned to the city six months ago and settled here. I'm not a jihadi, sahib. This eye, this was a childhood accident."

"It took you two years to get married? And you left the city and lived in the country in the middle of a war and you didn't do anything or see anything? I think you're lying to us again. Do you take us to be idiots? Ashraf, you're taking it too easy on him."

Two hard blows as Kana fell to the floor, screaming.

"You were fighting us like a trained professional when we picked you up. You must have been to a camp. Come on, make it easy for yourself. Which camp did you go to?"

"I just went for a few days. They came to my village and took us forcibly. Then I ran away, sahib. I swear. I didn't do any fighting anywhere. I just came back to Karachi, sahib. I am not involved in any jihadi business. I'm a family man."

Tarkeen looked at his watch anxiously and then gave a sideways glance at Constantine. They were working on a very short timetable. It usually took several hours to break a man like this. Constantine was conducting the interrogation expertly, slowly leading the suspect onto the matter that they were interested in. But he knew from Tarkeen's expression that he would have to rush it. And rushing things like this always led to mistakes.

"Okay, okay, Kana, good. You've been a good boy. I believe you. That's not what we're interested in anyway. Tell us about the store. Have you ever sold a large number of SIM cards to the same customer? Say thirty or forty of them?"

A look of alarm passed through Kana's good eye for an instant. "What? What do you mean, sahib? There has been no problem in my working at the store. I haven't given SIM cards to anybody."

"I didn't say you did. Why are you so worried at the mention of SIM cards? Which of your friends have you been giving them to?"

Kana reverted to his silent mode.

"Look, the houseboy already told us everything. About the SIMs, everything. Make it easy for yourself. Tell us who you gave the SIMs to and where they are."

Kana glanced sideways at Jim and then looked directly at Tarkeen and said, in a suddenly harder tone, "I don't know about any SIM cards. I don't know anything."

Ashraf rained blows upon him, but to no avail. They strung him up by his feet, using the hooks on the wall, and started repeatedly caning the soles of his feet until they were raw. A particularly painful exercise, yet one that left no permanent marks on the victim. But apart from his screams, Kana refused to utter a word. Constantine shook his head. He knew they were on to him, but he was buying time for his cohorts through his pain. Tarkeen's usually calm features were twisted into a grimace. The American, Jim, had a pained expression too, brought on either by witnessing a suspect being tortured or by the realization that the torture wasn't working. Constantine suspected it was probably the latter.

"Where have you kept the American? Where is he?!?" Tarkeen had suddenly gotten up from his chair and grabbed hold of Kana's head.

Kana, barely able to speak, just shook his head. The colonel's frustration had boiled over. A second later, so did Jim's. "Ah, goddammit, he ain't gonna tell us nothin'!"

Constantine signalled to both men to follow him out of the room. As they came out once again into the chill air, Tarkeen, having realized his mistake, immediately held his hand up in apology. The American, who hadn't, irritatedly asked, "Whadoyawant?"

"I apologize sir, but your outburst, and the colonel's handling of him, shows him that he is getting to us rather than the other way around. He knows he just has to last a few more hours, and then it will be too late to save Friedland. He knows that this is the worst we can do to him. We can't kill him, after all."

"You're right, Constantine, but what do we do? If we can't break him, we can't save Friedland."

"Colonel sahib, we don't have enough background information on him to interrogate him properly. I think we need to call Akbar. Maybe he can tell us how to unlock this bastard."

Constantine took out his mobile phone and called Akbar, who answered on the first ring.

"Akbar, we've got Kana, but we can't break him. We don't have time. Can you help us?"

Akbar briefly asked about the circumstances of the arrest. After Constantine had recounted the story, he told him to put Kana on the line. Constantine was a little skeptical. He didn't see how Akbar could speed up the process by just talking to the man. Still, he went back into the room, putting the phone on speaker. Kana had managed to get his breath back and was sitting on the floor, trying to cover himself.

"Here, someone wants to talk to you."

Surprised, Kana took the mobile phone in his hands. At the other end Akbar's distinct, raspy voice came across.

"Do you know who I am?"

"No . . . uh . . . I don't know." Constantine noticed that despite Kana's denial, there seemed to be some faint recognition of the voice. His eyes widened at the sound of it.

"Think again."

"Yes . . . you are Akbar, the police wallah." As he said it, Kana started trembling. It wasn't just from the cold.

"You know what I do, don't you?"

"Yes. You kill criminals."

"That's right. Pray you don't meet me; otherwise, your wife will end up a widow. But I don't want to kill you. I know you don't fear death. I know your faith is *strong*."

"Yes." The word came out barely above a whisper, and the look on Kana's face showed that he was anything but unafraid.

"If you recognize my voice and know my name, then you also know my other *friends*. So you will understand who I am speaking for when I say what I have to say to you. *Won't* you?"

"Yes." The man had begun to sweat despite the cold.

"Good. I salute your efforts. You have done very well. But your role in this is now finished. You don't have to worry about what happens to your friends, or to the American. You need not fear. You can tell these men what they want to know. Allah is witness to your deeds and will reward you as he sees fit. You *do* understand what I'm saying, don't you?"

"Yes."

Constantine took the phone back from him and went outside the room again, careful to be out of earshot of anyone else. "What have you said to him, Akbar?"

"Don't worry, Consendine. You shouldn't have any more problems. If there are, call me again."

"But Akbar—" Before he could finish the sentence, the phone went dead. Constantine looked at the incredulous expressions on Colonel Tarkeen's and Jim's faces. Just as Tarkeen was about to say something, Ashraf came out.

"Sahib, he says he wants to talk to you. But first he wants to cleanse himself and say his prayers."

"Let him do it. Give him his clothes back. And go with him to the washroom. But don't let him out of sight for a second. If he wants to take a piss, you hold his dick. When he's praying, stand next to him. Then bring him back here as soon as possible."

"Yes, sahib."

Ashraf went back into the room. He and the other two guards dressed Kana and took him downstairs to clean him up. Jim turned first to Tarkeen, then to Constantine, completely mystified by what was going on. "Now what?" he asked.

"I think we've gotten lucky, sir. Usually, these jihadis, when they want to make a confession, cleanse themselves and say their prayers to ask God's forgiveness. Then, with a clear conscience, they start talking."

"But what if he's lying?"

"I think he'll tell us the truth now. These people do not believe that their actions are criminal so they don't have a problem confessing, as long as it doesn't endanger their operational security."

"So what does that mean? You think they just abandoned the whole plan to kill Friedland? Just like that? Just 'cause your friend spoke with him on the phone?"

"To be honest, I don't know how he knew Akbar or what Akbar said that has triggered this response."

"Well," Tarkeen interjected, "recovering the journalist is all that matters. We can keep working on the whys and wherefores after we've gotten Friedland back."

In the meantime, Ashraf had brought Kana back. He had washed the cut above his eye, but was still limping from the blows to his testicles and feet. They sat him down on the floor, and Ashraf handed him a glass of water, which he gulped down. Before entering the room, Tarkeen signalled to Jim to stay outside.

"Hang on a minute, Jim. He seems to get aggravated by seeing you. Let us see what he says. Stay outside; I'll give you the entire debriefing when we're done."

The American was suspicious of Tarkeen's request. He suspected that the others were trying to trick him or hide something from him. But considering the circumstances and the gravity of the situation and, above all, his own uselessness in it, he nodded reluctantly and turned to go wait in the car.

Constantine and Tarkeen sat down in front of Kana once again, waiting for him to commence speaking. He seemed to be more relaxed.

"Sahib, it is good you didn't bring the damn gora in with you. It would have been wrong of me to talk in front of him."

"Of course. I understand that there are matters that should be discussed *only* between us countrymen." It was Tarkeen who spoke up.

"They are evil, sahib. Out to destroy us. They want to break up our country, and they want to enslave our religion."

"Well, we must tolerate them from time to time."

"No sahib, even then you shouldn't help them. These Americans are our sworn enemies. Especially you army people should definitely not collaborate with them."

"How did you know I was from the army?"

"Because you don't act like a police wallah. And you remind me of the major sahib who used to come to our training camp."

"When were you in your training camp?"

"I was in the camp seven years ago. At the time, they used to train fighters for jihad in Kashmir. Some went to Afghanistan. I stayed there for a while and became a trainer at the camp."

"But what were you doing there six months ago?"

"When the Americans attacked Afghanistan, the camp was shut down. I left and moved to Karachi to find work. Then six months ago, when the fighting in the tribal areas started, I wanted to go back. The government forces were bombing our villages and killing innocent women and children. I could not watch it on TV anymore. I wanted to fight."

"Did you?"

"No. I did not get the opportunity. When I got there, the local commanders told me I would be more useful in the city because I had lived here for so long. They told me to wait till they sent me a mission. So I came back and waited."

"Then what happened?"

"Their call never came. Then one day, this fellow that I had known in the camp came to see me at the shop. He told me that he had gotten involved with some Bengali boys who were running a small organization here. They were going to carry out a big operation, but they needed someone who had the experience of planning these types of operations. He took me to a meeting with them. Those boys were basically criminals. They weren't as committed to jihad as we had been. No discipline. But they had a source who was giving them information about an American."

"The houseboy?"

"Yes. That was, in fact, the only thing they had going for them. That, and their enthusiasm. They had no plan, just a few guns, and no place to keep the American once they got him. My friend had contacted me because I used to teach tactics in the camp. I planned the operation for them."

"So you went with them to steal the car, and then you were one of the men who picked him up from Zamzama?"

"No. I just gave them the plan. And then, because I worked in the shop, I sold them SIM cards in bulk, for their communications. I didn't go with them, sahib."

"So where did they arrange to keep him? You said these boys didn't have any place."

"Yes, sahib. They didn't. My friend contacted another group of people that we had known in the camps. They had a hiding place, and they agreed to go along with the plan. But then, when we got the American, some of their contacts from the tribal areas told them that they knew the American. He had been under their protection when he was up north. So the two factions started arguing with each other about what to do with him. The Bengali group wanted to make a video of his execution for the Internet because they didn't think they would get such an opportunity again. The tribal group felt they were still bound to protect him."

"So what did they decide?"

"They put the matter up for arbitration to a respected aalim. A learned man, a sheikh, a great man. He decided to keep the American in his custody till it was decided whether to execute him or not."

"If the decision was never taken, why did you people release that video on the Internet?"

"I had nothing to do with that, sahib. I'm an illiterate man. One of the Bengali boys was good at computers. So he made the video and put it on the Internet. That was just for publicity. Like a movie trailer."

"Who is the sheikh? Was he the mastermind of the operation? Did he tell you what to do?"

"No, no, sahib. He didn't order us at all. He is a truly pious man. He only got involved as an honest broker. He is holding the American for safekeeping. His name is Sheikh Noman."

Constantine had been observing the interview with a growing sense of unease and impatience and, with the mention of the sheikh's name, Constantine's unease increased. He had been silently mouthing the same question in his head again and again, wishing that Tarkeen would ask it, ever since he had seen Kana's response to Akbar. The question was, what was Akbar to this man? Now, with the reference to Sheikh Noman, there was a direct link to Akbar. The sheikh was the same Nomi, Akbar's one-time whisky-guzzling, land-grabbing business partner, who had really prospered since that night on Akbar's rooftop all those years ago. He was not only a very wealthy man, but was also considered an important religious leader in the city. His system of building his madrasas next to his gambling dens had worked brilliantly for him. Every time the police tried to raid one of his dens, the poor, unassuming madrasa students would be told that their seminary was being attacked, and they would rally vociferously to defend the premises. The police, facing a mob, would naturally back off. The sheikh's remote-control mobs had given him quite a bit of leverage over the city administration and the police, leverage that he would then use to garner further benefits for himself. A fine plot of land here, an extra bodyguard there.

But here was the puzzling bit. Although the sheikh had created a sufficient following to consider himself one of the city's movers and shakers, his name had never come up in relation to any sort of jihadi activities. His madrasas were not known to impart any kind of military training, nor had they sent any of their students to fight in Afghanistan or the tribal areas. In fact, the sheikh himself, in return for the government granting him various favors, expressed distinctly moderate political views. So Constantine could not figure out how he would have sanctioned the Friedland kidnapping. Also, the sheikh had remained a loyal friend to Akbar over the years. He had sent Akbar a cut from his gambling operations even when Akbar was languishing in a far-off village police station. The sheikh did all his posturing for the benefit of the department bosses and government ministers, but never in front of Akbar. If he were involved in this, it would have been impossible for Akbar not to have known.

"Where is the American now?"

"The sheikh has kept him somewhere. None of us know where. He was supposed to announce his decision sometime today. The entire group was supposed to have gone to see the sheikh today, to hear his judgment."

"Where are your other friends? Where do they live?"

"Most of the boys live in Orangi only. One or two live towards Pakistan Colony. They were all living in their own homes. Since the American wasn't with us, there was no need to take any elaborate security measures. That would have just raised suspicion. So everybody continued living just as they had been."

"You can lead us to their houses?"

Kana didn't answer immediately, as if struggling to reconcile Akbar's directives and his loyalty to his comrades. "Yes, sahib, I can. But even if they are all picked up, it will do you no good. The agreement was that if for some reason even one member of the group did not show up at the sheikh's madrasa on the twenty-fourth, the sheikh's men would immediately execute the American."

"You don't worry about that. You just lead us to them, and we'll figure out the rest."

Triumphant at last, Tarkeen rose from the chair, signalling the end of the interrogation. Unable to contain himself any longer, Constantine signalled to Ashraf to take all the other men outside as well, and he turned to ask the question that he had been dying to ask.

"By the way, how do you know Akbar?"

"Sheikh Akbar? We have heard many stories about him in the area, from when he was the SHO of Orangi. The sheikh speaks highly of him. He says he was a courageous man who fought against injustice."

"Yes, but how did you recognize his voice? Have you ever met him?"

"Oh no, sahib, but the sheikh told us that since he went to jail, he also became very pious. Once or twice, when we had gathered at the sheikh's for tableegh, he called up Akbar sahib and put the phone on speaker so that he could share his wisdom with us. He lectured us about the nature of jihad. The sheikh said that Akbar sahib was like a brother to him."

"Did Akbar ever talk to your group regarding the kidnapping of the American?" Constantine waited breathlessly for the answer.

"No, sahib. We last heard from him a few months ago, before the American even came into the picture. We haven't spoken to him since."

Constantine was visibly relieved but still perplexed. Tarkeen had been waiting for him at the door, and the two men walked out once more into the crisp night air. The electricity still hadn't been restored, and there was an eerie glow from the candles that had been lit in some of the rooms of the police station. The candle in the interrogation room had almost reached the end of its wick. Constantine told Ashraf to get another candle from the munshi. He and Tarkeen stood alone on the balcony of the station.

"I think I have heard of this sheikh. Isn't he in some sectarian peace committee that the IG set up recently?"

"Yes, sir. Akbar knows him very well. But if he is involved, it won't be easy to move against him. He has a decent following. They would see any direct raid on him as an affront. Besides, we don't know exactly where he's holding the American, so even if we were to go after him, there's a possibility that his followers would kill Friedland anyway."

"So what do you propose we do, Constantine? It's already well past two. According to this fellow, if his gang doesn't show up to see the sheikh later today, Friedland will be executed. Now we have to pick up the others tonight; otherwise, by sunrise, they will try and get word out to the sheikh to kill the American as quickly as possible."

"Sir, this part of the story doesn't make sense to me. This Sheikh Noman isn't a jihadi, he's a cheater. Why would he involve himself in something like this? Even arguing the fact that they brought him in to arbitrate, the minute he learnt about the American, he should have run a thousand miles from these boys. He speaks to Hanuman ten times a day, about the most mundane matters. Why didn't he say something?"

"What if his fraudster image was a cover, and he was always a jihadi deep down inside? Or he decided that taking part in this would win him a greater following, get his madrasas extra funding from radical groups? A man *can* change, Constantine."

"You are right, sir, but I don't think *this* man could change."

"Let me speak to Hanuman. He will be able to advise us better on how to go about this. No need to tell Jim until we've figured out what we need to do. He won't understand the *complexities* of the situation."

Hanuman answered Tarkeen's call on the first ring, even at this late hour. There was no panic or excitement in his voice as Tarkeen related the whole story. He just answered with his characteristic "Hmm," and asked to speak with Constantine. Constantine took the phone and walked off into a corner.

"Is what Tarkeen saying true?" Hanuman always liked to double-check his information with another source.

"Yes, sir."

"Do you trust this fellow you've picked up? You think he's telling the truth?"

"He wasn't earlier, sir, but he seems to have been pretty forthright after speaking with Akbar."

"Hmm. You think Sheikh Noman is involved in this?"

"I don't know, sir. My instinct tells me there's something wrong with this whole picture, but, on the other hand, we cannot ignore this information."

"Hmm. If you go to him directly, there will be trouble. The sheikh and his friends on the Sectarian Peace Committee have already been protesting against Maqsood's raids on their madrasas. I had to bribe them with an extra escort vehicle each, just to ensure that they kept their supporters off the streets. If we arrest the sheikh, they will shut the city down by tomorrow."

"Can you speak with him, sir? He calls you up daily."

"Hmm. No, if he wanted to tell me something, he would already have done it. If I approach him directly, all these Peace Committee people will perceive me to be biased against them, and that will hamper my ability to negotiate with them when I need to. Isn't there anyone else who knows him well?"

"Well, the only person who would be able to approach him would be Akbar."

"Yes, Akbar is perfect for this. Tell Tarkeen to get Akbar out. I'll speak to the Home Minister and explain the seriousness of the situation to him. That's the best way. But do it tactfully."

"Yes, sir."

Constantine finished the call and went back to Tarkeen.

"Sir, Hanuman says that if we move against the sheikh directly, there will be violence all over the city. He's probably right. Besides, there would be no guarantee that after taking such a gamble, we would get Friedland back. I think we need to get Akbar out, sir. We can't finish this without him. He is the only one who can approach the sheikh to get the American back. You can see from the behavior of this fellow that Akbar has some kind of hold on them. He will be able to sort out the level of the sheikh's involvement and tie up all of the loose strings of this case. I think that is our only option, sir."

"Talk to him."

Constantine dialled Akbar's number.

"Arre, Consendine, that was quick. Is your suspect giving you trouble again?"

"We have a problem. This man here says the American is with Sheikh Noman. How can we get him back? Do you think the sheikh will give him up? Is there any way we can get to him without creating a wider problem?"

Akbar was silent for a moment. "Hanuman is right. Sheikh Noman will raise hell if you try and pick him up. I'll have to go see him. I won't be able to do it over the phone."

"Akbar, the bottom line is, we are out of time. Do you think if you speak to him, you will be able to convince him to give up the American? Because you're our last chance. The sheikh will know once we've picked up these boys, and if they don't show up to meet him in the morning, he's supposed to kill the American. Can you get to him?" Tarkeen's normally composed voice was cracking.

"Sahib, I've known him since he was a two-bit con man. He may have become a big man in front of Hanuman and all those politicians, but for me he's still the street hustler who pissed in his pants when I locked him up the first time. I can get to him. Don't worry, Colonel sahib, I will get your American back. But I can't do it from in here."

The line went dead. Tarkeen put his hands on his hips, and then slowly nodded his head. "All right, it's settled then. The only way we can resolve this is to get Akbar out. Let's not waste any time. I'll call up my superiors and have them talk to Pakora about arranging for his immediate release. He can join us here, straight from the prison. In the meantime, we'll call for reinforcements. I'm sure Maqsood's inspector would have informed him that we were up to something in Orangi. Knowing Maqsood, he must already be on his way, to 'share' the credit of any breakthrough. That's fine. We'll use him to round up all of the other gang members. Since Kana said they all live in this area, it shouldn't be too much of a problem. The police can throw a big cordon around the entire locality, so it looks like some major operation is being launched. The confusion should buy us a few more hours until Akbar is able to contact the sheikh."

"Yes, sir. If you don't mind, sir, I will make my way back to the prison. Maqsood will be coming to assist you in any case, and, besides, I will need to be present to expedite the process of Akbar's release."

Tarkeen laughed. "Constantine, my boy, still worried about Maqsood? Don't be. He got my message loud and clear. You have been a tremendous asset to us in this matter. I will not forget that, nor will I let anyone else forget it. You really should come and work with us again, Constantine. You're too good at this. Now that Akbar will be back, the two of you can team up again."

"Thank you, sir, but I'm fine where I am. If things change, I will come knocking at your door."

The two men shook hands firmly, and then Constantine walked down the stairs. As he approached his pickup, he was distracted by the sound of wailing sirens. A motorcade of three police pickups, lights flashing, the men inside them dressed in full body armor like some crack unit, screeched to a halt outside the station gate. In the midst of the pickups was a black jeep with darkened windows, from which emerged Maqsood Mahr, but not until his bodyguards had secured a perimeter for him. Even then, he seemed a bit unsure of himself and stepped out gingerly, looking around repeatedly at the surrounding buildings. Constantine smiled bitterly. It had been a long time since Maqsood had been down to the dregs of the city. You couldn't really blame him for being a little nervous.

Constantine turned and was about to get into his car, when Maqsood called out to him. Constantine sighed. He had been trying to avoid this particular confrontation. It had been the reason for his haste in wanting to leave.

"Arre, Consendine, bhenchod, what the hell do you think you have been trying to pull? I know everything about how you've been actively helping that murderer Akbar Khan! Bhenchod, you think just because you've got Tarkeen on your side you are safe? Arre, baba, Tarkeen can only save you from departmental action. Wait till I share my information with the party! They will sort you out. And you know they don't bother with legal niceties. Your friend Ateeq Tension is fishing for you. They'll find you in a gunny sack by the side of the road. Your family too. I don't give you a week in this town, bhencho—"

Without even realizing what he was doing, Constantine grabbed Maqsood Mahr's lapel and shoved him hard against the car, momentarily knocking the wind out of him. He drew the pistol from his jacket pocket and held it to Mahr's head. Maqsood's storm troopers were too stunned to react, so they embarrassingly turned their backs and started searching for snipers on the rooftops.

"Get one thing very clear in your head, Maqsood. I don't care if you outrank me, or if you're the most powerful man in the department. I don't give a fuck about your politics anymore. You can go and report to whoever the fuck you want. Don't you ever mention my family again. Otherwise. the next time I hold a gun to your head, I'm going to pull the trigger."

The realization that Constantine was deadly serious brought a change in Maqsood's demeanor. For the first time, there was fear in his eyes. Constantine gave him another hard shove and walked away. At that moment in time, he wasn't sure what would happen to him but he did know one thing—he would never be afraid of Maqsood Mahr again.

20

Constantine left Maqsood Mahr in Orangi and went home. He figured that it would take Tarkeen a little time to get everything in place for Akbar's release. He found some food in the fridge, which he heated up, and settled down for a very late dinner or very early breakfast, depending on how one viewed it.

He showered and changed into a fresh uniform, but the sense of unease that he had felt during the interrogation seemed to continue. The links between Sheikh Noman and the kidnappers and Akbar and the sheikh were too convenient to be mere coincidence. A good police officer never believed in coincidence. Constantine had assumed that Akbar's information was coming from the tableeghis. What if his source was much closer to the kidnappers? After all, no other officer in the city had heard anything about the whereabouts of the American, and yet, every day, for the past three days, Akbar had been pulling a new rabbit out of his hat like a magician. He seemed to know the kidnappers' every move as if he was shadowing them himself. And what about the almost reverential reaction that Kana had when he spoke to Akbar? He had even called Akbar "Sheikh." Constantine knew that Akbar had grown religious in prison, but had he become radicalized enough to be an accomplice to the kidnapping of the American? Could Akbar ever do such a thing? Over the years that they worked together, there was nothing in Akbar's character or behavior that pointed to this conclusion. True, circumstances changed men, but this was Akbar. Akbar, the cop's cop, who had taken on the UF all by himself. How could he have anything to do with these second-rate jihadis? And yet, and yet.

No one else seemed to have picked up on these suspicions. Until the American was found, everything else was secondary. Tarkeen seemed to be least interested in the whole affair beyond the recovery of Friedland. He hadn't been bothered by these revelations, and neither had Hanuman. For them, it was a simple equation. They needed Akbar to get the American back. It didn't matter to them how he got him back. But Constantine had to know.

The false dawn was breaking as his pickup pulled up to the entrance to the prison. The place seemed to be buzzing with activity even at this early hour. Two cars were already standing outside the gate. The first one was a brand-new police jeep. The plastic covers hadn't even been taken off the seats. The driver stopped furiously polishing the hood of the car and saluted Constantine when he pulled up next to him.

"Aziz, what are you doing here? I haven't seen or heard from you in years."

Aziz couldn't keep the grin off his face as he tightly clasped Constantine's hand in both his hands. "Good to see you again, Consendine sahib. Didn't you hear? By God's Grace I am once again Akbar sahib's driver. We have come to pick him up. The gunmen are inside packing his things. The clerk at Police Headquarters called us up an hour ago and told us that we were to pick up this vehicle from the motor pool and bring it here for Akbar sahib. Look at the Almighty's workings, sahib. The same UF bastards who were after Akbar sahib's life have now authorized this brand-new jeep for him. Even the IG doesn't have a car this new! Inshallah sahib, we will be on top once again!"

It was hard not to be infected by Aziz's pure unadulterated joy. Many years ago this man had tied his fortunes with that of Akbar, shared his triumphs and disasters, and although recent times had seen far more disasters than triumphs, he could now see the light at the end of the tunnel.

The Lord did work in mysterious ways, thought Constantine. The driver was right. Who would have thought such a turn of events possible? Constantine remembered the last time he had seen Aziz. It had been the day Akbar had been arrested, five years ago.

It had happened the day after his meeting with Colonel Tarkeen. He had received a message to contact Maqsood Mahr. His first instinct was to suspect that Maqsood had finally decided to implicate him in the case as well. He had decided to go see Akbar one last time, before talking to Mahr.

It had been a chilly morning, much like the one today, and as he approached Akbar's house, he saw a line of police pickups stationed on his street. Akbar's bodyguards were lined up outside. Aziz was among them, tears streaming down his cheeks. Maqsood Mahr, on the other hand, stood to one side, looking even more smug and self-confident than usual.

"Arre, Consendine, baba where are you? I have been trying to get in touch with you since dawn. Arre, baba, you better start responding to my messages; after all, you are still under my command. Anyway, I'm glad you came here. I was calling you because I wanted you to lead the party that arrested Akbar Khan. You're late now, though. I've already sent someone else in."

"I'm sorry sir, that's not something I would have done. Akbar is my friend. But sir, I wish to make one request of you. Why are you arresting him? Sir, he is a police officer, and there is no conclusive evidence against him. Please sir, don't humiliate him like this."

"Arre, baba, you really haven't been following the news, have you? The conclusive evidence is there. Ballistics has matched the bullet that killed Sayeen Baba to Akbar's pistol. There now, what more evidence do you want?"

Constantine had looked at him disbelievingly. "Sir, you and I both know Akbar never fired his weapon. Besides, the bullet in Chandio's skull was from a Kalashnikov, not a pistol. How could Ballistics have matched the bullet?"

"Ballistics will do whatever I tell them to do. You would be well served to remember that whenever you discuss this case anywhere, Consendine." Maqsood's visage turned grim for a moment, as if to hammer the point home. Then, just as quickly, he flashed the fakest of smiles across his face. "Arre, baba, but you don't have to worry about a thing. You're on my team now. I have other important work for you."

"What do you want me to do, sir?"

"Shashlik Khan. True, he has agreed to join the new government, but we are going to keep the cases against him alive. The UF hasn't forgiven him completely. Since you helped to make the cases against him, you will maintain the case files, keep the evidence on record until such time as it is required in the future."

Constantine had nodded silently, hating himself for acquiescing to this deal. Akbar came out of his house at that very moment. Constantine could hear sobbing coming from inside the house, and several of Akbar's guards broke down when they saw their commander coming out of the house in handcuffs. But Constantine would never forget Akbar's nobility at that moment. He did not cry or beg or try to curry favor with his captors. There was the same look of resignation on his face that Constantine had glimpsed after his fateful last meeting with Dr. Death, but he still held his head high. As he had passed Constantine, the two men's eyes met. Neither man spoke, but Akbar acknowledged Constantine with a slight nod of his head, a gesture that signalled his understanding and forgiveness, for what Constantine was doing now, and what he would have to do in the future.

A lifetime seemed to have passed by since that day. Brought back to the present, he looked at Aziz and smiled again, revelling in the driver's exuberance. "Aziz, be careful. If you keep polishing that jeep so vigorously, you'll end up scratching it."

As Constantine walked towards the prison gate, he passed a second car. It was a sedan, not as new as the jeep but in good condition nonetheless. Constantine recognized it as his boss's car. Things were moving really fast if he was at the prison this early. His reader was waiting for him at the prison gate, wearing a worried expression. Before he could ask anything, the reader started.

"Sahib, what have you done? It's a madhouse today. Is everything okay?"

"Why, what's going on? And what's the IG doing here?"

"He's been here for the past half hour. We all received calls to come and open up your office. Just twenty minutes after we had all got here, he arrived. He's in a real huff. Told us to start the paperwork for the release of Akbar immediately. We told him, how could we start the paperwork if we didn't have any release order. Besides, it is against prison rules to release a prisoner in the middle of the night. He got very angry, started shouting at us, accusing us of deliberately obstructing government business. Sahib, he didn't spare even his favorite warden, the one who goes to deliver his money. We didn't know what to do, but just then the order was faxed from the Home Minister's office. Then, shortly after that, this jeep arrived. They said it was Akbar's sahib's new official vehicle. Sahib, IG sahib *even allowed* the armed guards *inside* the prison, to help Akbar sahib with his things. He's acting as if Akbar sahib has just become the prime minister!"

Constantine smiled. "Well, as far as we are concerned, Akbar might as well have. Has he asked for me?"

"No, sahib. That's the other thing. I was expecting that he would start calling for you, but when I asked him if we should contact you, he said there was no need to disturb you. Sahib, have you been posted out?"

"No. IG sahib just wants to ensure the prompt compliance of the Home Minister's orders. Come, let us see if we can help him out."

Constantine hadn't expected Colonel Tarkeen's instructions to take effect this quickly. But the haste behind the directives underlined how desperate everyone was. Pakora obviously recognized the urgency, which was why he had roused and dispatched Constantine's incompetent boss to supervise things personally. The desperation to get the American seemed to be getting a lot of people out of bed early this morning.

Inside his office, the inspector general of Prisons was sitting on Constantine's chair, looking very harassed. He was still wearing his night clothes. Constantine, in complete contrast in his newly creased and starched uniform, saluted crisply.

"Ah, you're here, D'Souza. There was no need for you to come. The minister told me he had sent you on an important task with Colonel Tarkeen. Of course, I understand. I hadn't realized you were that close to the minister, and to Colonel Tarkeen. You should have told me, D'Souza, I would have taken more care of you. You know, D'Souza, the first day you took charge here, I could see that you were a real mover. A star. Very dedicated."

Constantine was not quite sure how to deal with his boss's new fawning attitude. "I'm sorry I couldn't get here earlier, sir. But there was no need for you to disturb yourself personally over this matter. I would have taken care of it."

"No, no, D'Souza, I had to come. The Home Minister called me up in the middle of the night and ordered me to personally supervise this. Not only are they releasing this Akbar fellow, but the minister has also sent an accompanying order, giving him a posting and ordering him to report immediately to Colonel Tarkeen for special duty. God knows what this special duty is. And God knows how this Akbar has become so important all of a sudden. But Minister sahib has said it, so it must be done."

"You don't have to worry yourself about anything, sir. You can go home. If there are any problems, I'll sort them out."

There was visible relief on the IG's face. "Oh good, D'Souza. Yes. I can rely on you. Here is the fax copy of the release order. Are you sure I can leave? You'll handle it, won't you?"

"Of course, sir."

"If you ask my personal opinion, I don't think they should release him. He looks like trouble."

"Have you ever met Akbar, sir?"

"What? Oh no, no I haven't. I'm just not comfortable with these sudden directives that arrive in the middle of the night. After all, D'Souza, it is my neck at the end of the day. What if the next government starts asking questions about all of this?" Then, realizing that he might have said too much, he suddenly changed tack. "I mean, not to say that there will be another government for a long time. And I'm sure whatever the minister orders us to do is correct, because, after all, he is the minister."

Suddenly, a look of fear passed over his face. Before getting into the car, he seized Constantine's arm. "Look D'Souza, please don't repeat anything that I said. The minister will think I am being disloyal to him. I'm not in his good books these days. But you seem to know him. Please, put in a good word for me. I will give you anything you like. Consider yourself the de facto IG Prisons. Please, D'Souza. If he revokes my contract, I'll never get another job like this one. This job was supposed to secure the future of my children. Please help me."

"Sir, you don't have to worry like this. After all, you are a retired army officer."

"You know, D'Souza, when you're a retired officer, it's the 'retired' bit that people look at. We are the same as everyone else." His shoulders sagged as he said the words.

Seeing a senior officer reduced to begging, Constantine, for the first time, felt a pang of sympathy for this man. He may have been a sycophant, but he shared the same compulsions as the rest of them. Family. A slightly better life for their children. A little bit of power and influence. At the end of the day, they were all in the same boat. Swimming in the rough shoals of this city, trying to find a way to survive. The only difference was in the degree that each thought was necessary for survival.

"Sir, you don't need to say anything else. Please go home, and I will take care of everything."

"Oh, thank you. Thank you so much."

Constantine went back to his office and picked up the fax. The first sheet was a directive from the Home Department, ordering the withdrawal of all outstanding criminal cases against Deputy Superintendent of Police Akbar Khan. The inspector general of Prisons was ordered to release the prisoner immediately on parole. That much Constantine had obviously expected. The second fax sheet was a little more startling. It was another Home Office directive, ordering the reinstatement of Akbar and his posting to head a special police unit, which would probe kidnapping cases and other high-profile investigations. The order further stated that the unit would be completely independent and would be responsible for liaising with all external Agencies. Not only had Pakora managed to absolve Akbar in the eyes of the UF, he had also carved out a nice little empire for him.

He proceeded to walk towards Akbar's barrack. The cracks of first light were seeping through the dark sky. It was still bitterly cold. Outside Akbar's barrack, two armed gunmen and a warden were helping carry things out of the room. Constantine's own arrival went by unacknowledged, such was the hustle and bustle in the barrack. He entered the room, which looked even barer than it usually did. The only things left were the mattress and the stools. For a change, the air conditioning was turned off. Akbar was wrapping his Quran in an embroidered silk cloth. His appearance had changed too. The long hair had been cut to a neat regulation length. The beard had been trimmed and brushed. The wrinkled, crumpled shalwar-kameez had been replaced by a clean, heavily starched one. Even the wild look in his eyes had dimmed, replaced by a more calculating gaze. Gone was the wandering, spiritual holy man. In his place stood the image of middle-aged, middle-class respectability. Akbar could have passed as a factory boss or a small landowner. He looked up in surprise as Constantine entered the room.

"Arre, Consendine, what are you doing here? Aren't I supposed to be meeting you and Colonel Tarkeen in Orangi?"

"I came back to make sure things went smoothly over here. Maqsood's men are holding the fort with the colonel, so I'm not really needed there. Besides, haven't you heard? My boss is a stupid chutiya. If we left it in his hands, you'd end up on your way to Hyderabad Jail, instead of on your way out."

Akbar laughed heartily. "Well, in that case, I thank you for intervening on my behalf. You know, I must speak to Pakora about him some day. Money is one thing, but a man must have some basic intelligence to hold such an important post. I mean, being inspector general of the Prisons is no small thing."

"I see you and Pakora are getting along very well. You obviously made use of the SIM he sent. From the orders he's issued for you, you seem to have made quite an impression. Straight out of jail, and heading a new investigative unit. At this rate, Maqsood really should start worrying."

"Don't worry. This is just the beginning. I'm going to rip apart Maqsood's empire chunk by chunk. As for Pakora, well, let's say I made a sound investment out of some of Maqsood's money. Fifty petis goes a long way."

Constantine was incredulous. "Fifty petis? Akbar, if you pay him that much, you're going to run everyone out of the market. He'll want everybody to pay him that much. And where are you going to get such large sums of money from on a regular basis?"

"That was the price I had to pay Pakora to ensure that the party didn't create any hurdles for me. I also wanted to wean him off people like Maqsood. That's why I threw such a large bone at him. He hadn't even asked for it. I offered that much. Now, it's in his interest to protect me because I'm now his sone ki chidiya. On hearing the sum offered, he was all ready to do anything for me. He would have given me the clothes off Maqsood's back had I asked for them. The best bit is, I'm using Maqsood's own money to screw him."

"That's very impressive. All this, even without having first recovered the American."

"Consendine, Consendine. I told you, you worry too much. The American is as good as recovered."

"How do you know that, Akbar? How can you be so sure? What if your friend the sheikh has killed him? What if he doesn't listen to you?"

Akbar looked at Constantine and smiled. The two men were alone in the room. Akbar searched his breast pocket for a packet of cigarettes, took one out, and then lit it. He took a long puff and sighed. "I'll tell you something, if you promise not to repeat it."

"What?" Constantine's heart was racing, fearing the words that would come out of Akbar's mouth.

"The American is as safe as this packet of cigarettes in my pocket. He always has been."

"Akbar, are you involved in his kidnapping?"

"Don't be stupid, Consendine. Do you think I'm some kind of chutiya? I would never be involved in something like this. Where would you get a crazy idea like that? For that matter, neither is the sheikh."

"But Kana said the sheikh was holding him and that he had agreed to kill him if the two rival groups didn't show up for the arbitration today."

"Kana and the rest of them are simple-minded fools. The sheikh never had any intention of killing the American. You know the sheikh. Has he ever struck you as a militant sort? The only jihad he's ever contemplated is his personal jihad to make as much money as possible for himself. He has created a position for himself in the city. He has become one of the movers and shakers. The government negotiates with him, humors him because they think that he has the power to mobilize tens of thousands of his madrasa students and bring them out on to the streets. He blackmails Hanuman and the bosses every day for this sole reason, and for no other purpose than to increase his personal benefit. An extra bodyguard for his security, permission for one of his madrasas to encroach upon a little more public land, guarantees from the police that they won't raid one of his gambling operations. You think a man like that would jeopardize all of this for the sake of taking part in some half-baked plan to kill an American reporter? One of these poor, deluded fools who did the kidnapping was a disciple of the sheikh. When the two groups started fighting over what to do with the American, he suggested that they should get the fatwa of a holy man. Luckily for us, the only holy man he knew was our friend the sheikh."

"Why didn't the sheikh contact Hanuman?"

"Because he, God bless his soul, saw it as an opportunity to help me out. Initially, he was a bit worried when this problem got dumped in front of him. So he contacted me through these tableeghis who come every day, and asked me what he should do. I told him not to panic and to take custody of the American secretly. Once the American was out of the hands of those fools, he would be safe. And I realized that both of us could benefit from the situation. If the sheikh's followers thought he was willing to kill an American, that would improve his stock amongst his more radical supporters. The group who kidnapped him were such rank amateurs, it was almost too easy to dupe them. In the meantime, I would get my opportunity. I knew Tarkeen would have to come to me. The stakes were too high for everybody. Maqsood and his morons could never trace the case. The only thing I was worried about was that the UF would oppose me because of my past history with them. That's why your help was so beneficial. When you told me that the American government was applying pressure on the Don as well, it made my negotiating position even stronger. Finally, thank God that Pakora was Home Minister. It's so much easier to negotiate with a man who's willing to put a price on everything."

Constantine stared at Akbar, mouth wide open, as the shock registered on his face. "But Akbar, that makes you and the sheikh accomplices in kidnapping. How can you justify that? Tarkeen and Hanuman will figure it out. They aren't stupid."

Akbar's raspy voice grew harder. "How does it make anyone an accomplice? The sheikh saved the American's life by taking him away from the hands of those immature idiots. Only he couldn't tell anyone publicly because it would have undermined his own position with his supporters and potentially put his life in danger. So he turned to an old and trusted friend, me, who advised him on how to negotiate the situation tactfully. Isn't that what Hanuman always tells us to do? If I found myself at the core of this whole kidnapping business, well, it's just my luck, isn't it? After all these years in here, I deserve some. Besides, getting the American out safe and sound is the priority of Tarkeen and Hanuman. His recovery will save their neck. If that happens, I doubt if they'll bother about the details. Don't you agree?" Akbar cackled, thoroughly pleased with himself.

Constantine turned away, gazing at the corners of the now empty room. Akbar's logic was unassailable. That was exactly how it would play out. It suited Tarkeen and Hanuman not to examine the issue too closely. That left only him. Would he kick up a fuss? After all, what wrong had Akbar done? Had he committed a criminal act, or just taken advantage of a given situation and survived? Like his boss outside. Like Constantine himself. He turned around again and saw Akbar staring at him intently.

He cleared his throat. "Akbar, have you become a jihadi? Did you give lectures to the kidnappers? I'm not asking for Tarkeen or Hanuman or anybody else. I'm asking for myself. If you are a jihadi, then you consider me an unbeliever and would sanction my death. You supported them in front of Tarkeen. Would you do it?"

Akbar smiled. "Is that what worries you? Take a look at me. How long have you known me? Ever since our first day at Preedy Station all those years ago. Ever since Chaudhry Latif first sent us out on patrol together. Every day, for two years, we ate together, slept together, fucked girls together. We were inseparable. In Orangi, I spent the first six months thinking that I would be killed. The only man I trusted, the only man in whose hands I was willing to put my life, was you. It didn't matter to me then whether you were a Christian or a Muslim. It doesn't matter to me now. All that matters is that you are my friend. Jihad! What jihad? What do these misguided fools know about jihad? What we did was jihad. Fighting against the terrorists and gangsters who preyed upon innocent people who couldn't fight back. Risking our lives. We did it because it was our duty to do it! That was a real jihad! Not this! Kidnapping a silly American so that you can put a picture of him on the Internet with a gun to his head. How utterly stupid! You asked me if I gave religious lectures to those boys. Yes, I did. You told me I defended the jihadis in front of Tarkeen. Yes, I did. Five years ago, that bastard Maqsood screwed me only because he created this monopoly on hunting jihadis after 9/11. The Agencies embraced his efforts. I refused to do it so they discarded me, because no one wanted to go after the UF anymore. I had to get back in the game somehow, or I would have rotted in here for the rest of my life. I had to become an insider in the jihadi groups. That's why I turned to the religious organizations like the tableeghis and Sheikh Noman's people. That's why I pretended to become one of their 'sheikhs.' These people had the information that I wanted. And now, Inshallah, I will make my comeback thanks to them."

"So I guess turning to religion worked out well for you." The two men looked at each other intently for a moment and then burst out laughing.

"They say that if you look hard enough, those who really want to can even find God. So I figure finding a few jihadis should be a small matter then." This was the Akbar that Constantine always remembered and revered. Carefree, amusing, courageous, risk-taker, inveterate gambler, ready to put everything on the line for a long shot.

"You're crazy, you know."

They were not men given to signs of affection, else they would have hugged. They shook hands firmly, and Akbar patted Constantine on the back and they walked out of the room together. By now the sun had come out, but an early morning mist hung in the air. Akbar lit another cigarette and signalled to his gunman, who brought him a thick, stuffed envelope and a mobile phone.

"Here, thanks for lending me your phone. I'm returning it. And this," Akbar handed Constantine the envelope, "is for you. A little token of my appreciation. Thank you for helping me out. You didn't have to. You could have gone to Maqsood any time. You could have told Tarkeen that my information was useless. You didn't have to send me the case file. It's not enough to say that you did it because of our friendship. When a man is down, even his best friends walk away from him. You didn't."

Constantine peeked inside the partially open envelope. It was stuffed with wads of thousand-rupee notes. He looked at it, unsure what to do. "What's this?"

"It's five petis. Consider it a refund on your investment with Pakora. I would have given you more, but after giving half of my fortune to Pakora, I needed the rest of Maqsood's money for my own expenses."

"You got the money already?"

"Yes. Maqsood had dropped it off at the bookie's. I've tied up a weekly sum for you with the same bookie. His man will deliver it to you here every week."

"You didn't have to do this. I won't reveal your secret to anyone."

"I know. But why shouldn't you also profit from this situation? The rest of us surely will. Say, why don't you come with me? We could set up this new unit together. We would end up running the city. It'll be just like old times."

"I don't have your nerves of steel, Akbar. I wouldn't be able to survive the ups and downs that you thrive on. I don't want to reach for the stars. I'm happy walking in the middle of the road."

Akbar looked at him quizzically. "You know, I never understood this 'middle-of-the-road' philosophy of yours. What's the point of living your life like that? Always scared of the moves that other people may make. Never willing to do something for yourself. I enjoy the good times that much more, because I know how bad the bad times can be."

They had reached the gate of the prison. Akbar was presented with his release papers by one of the wardens, and he duly signed them. As the outer gates of the jail opened, revealing the world outside to Akbar for the first time in so many years, his eyes squinted at the soft sunlight. He hesitated for a moment, then looked over his shoulder to Constantine. "By the way, you don't have to worry about Ateeq Tension. He won't cause anyone trouble anymore."

"Akbar, what are you going to do?"

"What you should have done years ago. Don't worry about it. I cleared it with Pakora. In fact, he was quite happy to be rid of Tension."

"Akbar, are you sure you want to do this? I mean everything, not just Tension. They will all use you again. Tarkeen, Pakora, Hanuman. As soon as they have gotten what they want, they will ditch you."

Akbar shrugged his shoulders and sighed. "Arre, Consendine, what can I do? In our business we have to provide some sort of utility to our superiors, to the Agencies, to the politicians. I don't have a brother or father who is a big shot, a bureaucrat, or a member of parliament. I can't be a pimp like Maqsood. The only thing I have to offer is my personal ability. That is why when they have a problem, they call me. Yes, they will use me. If not them, then it will be someone else. What can I do? I can't quietly slip into the shadows like any other man. I am what I am. I cannot break out of this cycle. In the end, my friend, we are all prisoners of our own destiny."

The two men shook hands again. As Akbar went through, he turned to Constantine one last time.

"Are you sure you don't want to come? I could use you out there."

Constantine smiled and shook his head. Akbar shrugged his shoulders and walked out of the gates.

21

Day 4, December 24, 7:00 a.m.
The outskirts of the city

The jeep rolled along on the bumpy road, jumping from one pothole to another, until Akbar was convinced that Aziz was hitting each one deliberately, just to test the shocks on his new toy. The road was barely more than a half-paved track. Although they had not travelled very far since leaving the prison, the scene around them was a far cry from the metropolitan sprawl of the city. The road was a single track which wound round the side of a hill. The hill was barren, pockmarked with stone quarries that had been carved onto its side. Across the road was a line of shanties, where marble cutters were already at work, even at this early hour, cutting and shaping the blocks of stone that had been taken out of the hill. The sole concession to modernity was a shack at the corner that had a faded Coca-Cola advertisement on it. This was Mangopir, one of the last localities of the city before Karachi evaporated into the vast, arid landscape of the Baluch Desert. The area had the look of a frontier town in the American West, not quite part of the encroaching civilization of the city yet also not ready to be swallowed by the neighboring wilderness.

Akbar sat in the passenger seat of the jeep, preferring to keep the window down, despite the sharp gusts of wind that made the dust on the road swirl and dance like a dervish. Aziz kept looking at Akbar with some alarm, noting the dust coating the dashboard. But Akbar was enjoying the feel of the wind on his face and would have it no other way. He was experiencing the feeling after five years. He took a drag of his cigarette and then exhaled in a leisurely fashion, taking more of the crisp air into his lungs. He would not give up this feeling for all the new jeeps in the inspector general's motor pool. Freedom.

Even the settling dust on the dashboard could not dampen Aziz's spirits for long. "Sahib, which way do you want me to go? Are you taking charge in Mangopir? I would have thought you would have wanted to go back to Orangi, but I suppose this area isn't too bad either. There's good money to be made from the mining and reti bajri contracts in the area. There's so much dirt in the area, I'm sure the thana sells at least two dozen trucks a day. Don't you think so?"

"I think that you're getting ahead of yourself, Aziz. I have no earthly interest in how much the local SHO makes in selling trucks of dirt to the construction mafia in the city. I want you to go towards that madrasa, the one Sheikh Noman used to own. It's just a little further down the road. How's your family been?"

"They are all right, sahib, by the grace of God. It hasn't been easy since you were locked up. I was suspended for a while because everyone who had worked for you was under suspicion. Then, after a couple of months, I bribed the clerk at headquarters, so he quietly put me back on active duty in the motor pool. But it wasn't like when I was with you, sahib. It was normal duty, no excitement, no encounters, and no extra cash or rewards. Five years like that, sahib. My God, how do people work like that? I almost went crazy. I couldn't even afford to buy meat for my family. We have been eating dal for five years. Five bloody years, sahib. I had almost forgotten what chicken tasted like. I swear, sahib, I'm never going back to normal duty again. Now, Inshallah, you are here; things will be good again."

"Why didn't you go get yourself assigned to another officer? Things might have been easier for you."

"Arre, no, sahib. I can't work for any other officer. I have eaten your salt, I can't turn my back on that. I wouldn't betray you like that. Besides sahib, I'm too old now to get used to anybody else's style of working. I'm stuck with you, whether you like it or not. By the way, sahib, I kept your gun for you. I have been oiling it regularly. It's lying in the glove box."

Akbar grunted in amusement and lit another cigarette. The taste of the bitter tobacco felt good. He opened the glove box and felt the cold steel of the weapon. It was a Soviet-made Makarov pistol that he had once expropriated from a dead UF ward boss. His mind went back to when he had first met Aziz. He had been called into headquarters and told of his posting to Orangi. He had gotten the worst thana in the city, and he felt as if the sky had fallen on his head. As he walked out of the chief's office, the staff standing outside had commiserated with him as if he were a condemned man on death row. That's what Orangi had been at the time: a death sentence, certainly not a promotion. Only one constable had come forward and begged to go with him. He was sick of being an orderly in the head office, serving tea and biscuits to the bosses. That wasn't what he had signed up for. Death in Orangi was preferable to serving another round of biscotti. Akbar first thought the constable was stark raving mad, but since he was the only one willing to go with him to Orangi, he had gone back into the chief's office and requested his transfer. That constable had been Aziz.

Presently they passed by a jumble of palm trees, next to which was the dilapidated local police station building. Opposite the thana was a Sufi shrine, its multicolored flags and banners fluttering in the morning breeze. It was the shrine of Mangopir, one of the oldest in the city. This one wasn't very grandiose. Perhaps this had to do with its location, here in the back of beyond. But the curious feature of Mangopir was the crocodile pool next to the shrine. Apparently, the old Pir of Mango had exercised some form of control over the crocodiles. The Pir was long gone, but the poor crocodiles remained, existing on a diet of fruit and popcorn that was thrown into the pool by visitors. They were cared for by a lone, frail old man who would descend once a day into the pool area and throw bits of meat at them. A dozen shops selling flowers, sweets, incense sticks and popcorn for the crocodiles lined the path from the road to the shrine. Akbar told Aziz to stop the car. He bought a plastic bag full of rose petals from the shop and entered the shrine to pay his respects.

In his younger days, Akbar had never been a particularly religious man. He was never regular in his prayers, and he had enjoyed the odd drink and the odd woman. Even his current conversion had been more a matter of professional convenience. But he was a superstitious man, and he did believe in a higher power. The kind of life he had led made him believe that there had to be someone up there looking out for him. And so he had become an avid visitor of Sufi shrines. He always went to a shrine before any major raid. Akbar had no one patron saint, but he patronized them all, believing in a policy of insurance just in case any one was truly closer to God than the others.

He came back out and stared absently at the crocodile pool. The creatures were all lying on the sandy bank, waiting for stray morsels to be thrown at them. The animals were endlessly patient. They reminded Akbar of himself. All these years, he had waited patiently for a morsel to be thrown his way. Just like the crocodiles.

Constantine observed him from his pickup, which was parked behind a nook of the police station wall. He shook his head and cursed himself. He wasn't quite sure what he was doing here. After Akbar had left the prison, Constantine had been consumed by a strange feeling of guilt and responsibility. Guilt, for having turned Akbar down when he had asked him to go along to recover the American; and a nagging sense of responsibility for Akbar's well-being.

Constantine had always felt guilty about the fact that he had escaped unscathed from the death of Nawaz Chandio. He had often wondered at the fact that, but for the hand of fate, he could so easily have shared Akbar's fate. After all, it had been Akbar who had dispatched him on the fool's errand to the interior. Otherwise he would definitely have been on the scene of Nawaz's death. And Akbar had done it to save him.

Something about the way Akbar had asked him to come along had triggered these pent-up emotions in him. The minute Akbar's jeep had left the prison compound, Constantine had felt compelled to go after him. Acting on a whim, he had climbed aboard his pickup and begun to follow Akbar's jeep, but at a distance, to avoid detection. He had left so quickly that he hadn't even bothered to take Ashraf or Saeedullah with him. He felt stupid about that now. How did he expect to come to Akbar's aid without reinforcements?

He thought about turning around and driving back. But as Akbar's journey continued towards Mangopir and at the edge of the city, Constantine's curiosity kept growing. He knew the sheikh had a madrasa in Mangopir, so he assumed that they were close to their destination.

It would be silly to turn back now. But this was a dangerous neighborhood, and it would only be prudent to take precautions. He saw Akbar get back into his jeep and drive away from the shrine. So he took his pistol out of his holster and cocked it.

Aziz drove a little further until a fork in the road took them onto a narrower path, which led into a neighborhood of small, closely clustered houses. At the end of the street, an elaborate mosque complex with whitewashed walls and marble tiles stood in stark contrast to the grim-looking buildings that surrounded it. Quranic inscriptions were written in large letters on the high walls, and mounted security cameras guarded the complex.

Akbar ordered Aziz to stop the car in front of the gate. He got off and shoved his gun under the folds of his shirt. The gate of the compound opened as though someone was expecting him. A tall, strapping man carrying an ancient shotgun led Akbar through a maze of darkened, interconnecting corridors that led into the inner sanctum of the complex. Students, some as young as seven or eight, rushed to their first study sessions of the day wearing white prayer caps. The guard held open a door at the end of the longest corridor, while Akbar took off his sandals before entering. The room was a small office, richly carpeted but with no chairs. Two men sat on comfortable cushions on the floor, while a third man, a clerical assistant of some sort, sat at a low table, typing on a computer.

Upon seeing Akbar, one of the men rose from the floor to greet him with a hug. He was rather corpulent and seemed to rub his protruding belly repeatedly. He wore an unusually flamboyant maroon turban and had wrapped himself in an expensive cashmere shawl. The whole room was filled with the overpowering, musky scent of attar. This was the mighty Sheikh Noman. There was a slight unease in his manner as he greeted Akbar.

The computer typist wordlessly left the room, but the other man remained. He made no effort to greet Akbar. He wore a more orthodox green turban and was far more simply dressed than the sheikh. His beard was closely cropped, but his most striking feature was his cold, dead gray eyes and stern expression. His gaze was fixed on Akbar, and it was far from friendly.

Akbar ignored him as he sat down on the cushions. "Sheikh, how have you been? It has been a long time since I saw you."

"Yes, Akbar. Mashallah, but you look good. Prison hasn't affected you at all, it seems." The sheikh nervously stroked his beard.

"It is God's Grace. He has watched over me." Akbar looked at the other man, who seemed to be eyeing him intently. "Salaam alaikum, brother, I do not know who you are."

"Uh, Akbar, this is Qari Saif. He is a highly respected scholar from the north. Qari sahib took part in the jihad against the Russians when he was a young man. He has been, uh, visiting us for some time here at the madrasa."

"Ah yes, I have heard your name. People say you are a very powerful man, Qari sahib. You have become a very famous man in our city in a very short time. My compliments to you."

"I have heard many stories about you as well, *Sheikh* Akbar. Tell me, is it true that you became a religious scholar during your period of incarceration? I find it hard to believe that you could accomplish such a task without any proper instruction, without a learned Qari to guide you to the correct path. There are so many *imposters* in our religion, it is hard to decipher whose message is the true one."

"Well, heh, I just opened my eyes to God's truth. It had always been there, but I had never bothered to look. We all end up on the path of righteousness sooner or later. I would love to spend some time discussing theology with you, but, alas, I have some pressing business with Sheikh Noman. Perhaps we can meet another time to discuss, heh, how shall I put it, how to decipher false messengers. Sheikh sahib, I have come to pick up the package that was left in your care. The appointed time is coming closer, and I must deliver it to its owners."

"Uh, Akbar, actually, Qari Saif is also here for the same, uh, package. It's not that simple for me to give you the package. Qari sahib has . . . well, he has a different view of these things."

"Oh? And what view is that?" Akbar remained perfectly calm on the outside, but his heart started thumping loudly in his chest.

Qari Saif remained impassive, twirling his silver rosary, as Sheikh Noman, now more nervous than ever, furiously stroked his beard.

"Well, uh, he believes that, uh, since the original plan had been to, uh, get rid of the, uh, package, uh, maybe we should continue to do that."

"There is no doubt about it. There is no maybe in it. The American unbeliever must be executed. Thousands of our followers will exult in what we do! It is the Will of God! He delivered this unbeliever into our midst, and so his purpose was for him to die here for the sake of our cause!" For the first time, Qari Saif grew animated, his dead gray eyes displaying a fiery passion and his eyebrows arching high into his forehead.

Akbar looked sharply at the sheikh. "This was not our agreement. I explained to you the consequences of such a move. You know what will happen. The police and the Agencies will figure out your link to the American. They have already arrested some of those idiot boys. They will crack in two minutes. And you know, in a case like this one, none of your supporters or their street protests will be of any use to you. Everyone will abandon you, sheikh. This is the best way to solve this problem. Give him to me, and the rest is my responsibility. That's what I promised you. Are you seriously agreeing with what this man is telling you?"

Rivulets of sweat poured down Sheikh Noman's forehead. "Akbar, I, uh, I see your point, but—"

"There is no room for doubt in the matters of God, sheikh! There can be no return for the American. He must die! So what if the boys have been arrested? The agreement with them was anyway going to expire on this morning. For all they know, the American should already be dead by now. They will never know. And no one can link it directly with you, or me. Even if they do, I have many friends who will hide us in the tribal areas. No one will be able to touch us there."

"Uh, in the tribal areas? You mean we would have to leave Karachi? And what about my madrasas?"

"Of course. You did not expect to be able to stay here, did you? You have done good work here, sheikh. You have served Allah's cause well. But you too have profited. You have grown rich on the word of Allah. Now, it is time for you to sacrifice a little and serve in a different capacity. All of the things that you surround yourself with are merely worldly possessions. Your life will be very different from now on, but it will ultimately be far more rewarding. You will be able to openly resist these unbelievers."

Akbar stared incredulously at Sheikh Noman, who looked more per-turbed than ever at the prospect of losing his worldly possessions. "Listen sheikh, this is madness. You cannot seriously be thinking about going through with what this man is saying. He has nothing to lose. On the other hand, it would be suicidal for you to contemplate this. There is no way you would be able to run from this. Come on sheikh, let's be reason-able and go get the American. Your role in this matter is done. Let's wrap things up. You have already cut a deal, the police will be on their way. There is no other option."

Qari Saif had worked himself into quite a frenzied state. "How dare you blaspheme like that! We are not concerned if the police are on the way! We are not answerable to them and their corrupt system. We are answerable only to Allah. You are going to go through with the execution of the American, sheikh. If you do not, your followers will never forgive you. I will not let them. The only thing standing in our way is this man. He is not one of us, he is a police officer, and his loyalty is suspect! He is the only link between you and the police. We need to investigate his real motives. Any man who tries to stop us from carrying out God's work is an unbeliever! And if someone is an unbeliever, then we must deal with him accordingly."

"Oye, who are you to question my loyalty! Ask the sheikh who has been a loyal friend of his all these years! So what if I was in the police? Does that make me any less of a true believer? I have heard many things about you, Qari Saif. I have heard, for instance, that before you became a man of God, you were a pimp selling women in the bazaars of Peshawar! I wonder how that affects *your* piety. Or did selling whores somehow give you a greater insight into the ways of God?"

Akbar noted with satisfaction that his outburst had had the desired effect. The color had drained from Qari Saif's face at the mention of his past. Akbar hadn't been sure if his allegations were correct, but the Qari's reaction confirmed their veracity. Akbar had checked up on him after Constantine had mentioned his name, but he hadn't realized that he was blackmailing the sheikh. And the sheikh, in turn, was so paralysed by the Qari's threats that he was now unable to take any decisive step regarding the American. Akbar would have to resolve this on his own.

As the Qari sat there, ashen-faced, Akbar signalled to the sheikh to join him outside.

As soon as he exited from the room into the corridor, Sheikh Noman wiped his perspiring brow with a silk handkerchief. Akbar lit a cigarette and took a long drag.

"Arre, sheikh, what's this new film? This is not what you and I had discussed. Where did this punter come from?"

"My God, Akbar, you do not know what I have had to put up with these past few days. This man is horrible. I assure you, I did not invite him to be a part of this. One of the boys from the group who kidnapped the American contacted him after they had deposited the journalist with me. He approached me a couple of days later and congratulated me. And then he came over and has been sitting on my head for the past week. He has been pushing me to kill the American. What's worse is that he has convinced most of my other supporters that this is a good thing to do. They have all been carried away with his fiery rhetoric and his stories of fighting in the jihad."

"Sheikh, this fool doesn't know how things work in this city, but you and I do. I have stuck my neck out for this case. Everyone—the UF, the Agencies, the bosses—are all counting on my ability to recover this Friedland fellow. I will be going straight back to solitary if I don't bring him back. You and I had a deal on this."

"Yes, I know, Akbar, and I don't want to do this, but this bastard has my people eating out of the palm of his hands. They do not understand the complexities of the situation like you and I do. They just want to follow any idiot who starts shouting 'Death to America.' I fear that I will lose my supporters, my madrasa students, if I do not acquiesce to his demands."

"Sheikh, do you think the Americans will ever forgive us if this journalist does not come back alive? Forget about me, you will be finished. Your madrasas, more importantly your gambling dens, that are so profitable for you? Everything will be gone. The Agencies and the Americans know that you have a role in this kidnapping, but I have convinced them that it was a positive role and that you were trying to get Friedland back. If something happens to him, that's it. You won't be able to survive in the city. You won't be able to go abroad. You think your Saudi friends will take a risk on you and keep sending you funds if they find out you are linked to this? And what about the religious learning centers that you have set up in America? I know you visit them so eagerly every summer. What's the name of that city you like to go to, the one with the naked dance bars and twenty-four-hour brothels? Las Vegas? No more of that, sheikh. Listen, maybe Osama bin Laden and this chutiya in your office can live in a cave on the side of a mountain and be quite happy about it, but do you think you'll be able to do that? Come on, you and I live in the real world. This bhenchod has nothing to lose, but we have everything on the line here."

The sheikh was contemplative for a moment. Perhaps it was the thought of never going to Vegas ever again that convinced him. "Okay Akbar, but how do we solve this problem? How do we shut this bastard up?"

"I have a plan. We'll go back inside and you just go along with whatever I say. I'll take care of him. Does he know where you've kept the American?"

"Yes. He went and saw him there a couple of times. He has a couple of his own people there on guard duty. But Akbar, what will I tell my followers later on?"

"You can tell them that he was a CIA spy who helped the American to escape."

They went back into the office, where Qari Saif now stared at them malevolently. He kept twirling his rosary, but he held it so tightly that his knuckles were white. Akbar sat down directly in front of him and looked straight into his eyes, his hands clasped together in supplication.

"Qari sahib, I apologize for my outburst. I did not mean to insult your dignity. It's just that I have become so devoted to our cause that my blood boils every time someone tries to cast aspersions on my faith. Sheikh sahib took me outside and told me of the error of my ways. Perhaps it was because I have spent so much time in prison, I think I have forgotten how to interact with great men. You are right, and Sheikh sahib is right. The American must die. But we must do it immediately. The police will not be too far behind. And I ask of just one thing from you."

The startled Qari looked at Sheikh Noman who, in spite of his own confusion, was nonetheless able to muster a sharp nod to confirm what

Akbar was saying. Then he turned back to Akbar and, in a wary voice, asked, "What do you want?"

"I want to be the one to kill him."

The silence in the room was broken by the gasp that emanated from Qari Saif. "You? But I don't understand. Why?"

"No one has questioned my faith like that. I am going to prove to you that Allah's cause means more to me than anything else. And I want you to witness the execution, so that there can be no doubts ever again in your mind."

"There is no need for that. I am convinced of your faith and devotion—"

"No, this is the way it must be. I insist upon it. You know where the American is kept? Come, take me there, and let's do it now."

"No, no, but there is no need for me to . . . what I mean is that there is no need for us to do this ourselves."

"No, it is better if we do not involve anyone else. We cannot vouch for their dedication. They may contact the police, or let the American live. You and I must do it, Qari."

Sensing the Qari's bewilderment and apprehension, Sheikh Noman spoke up. "Qari sahib, I think you have to go with Akbar. It is the only way of ensuring that this thing is done correctly. Besides, he has a right to impress upon you his commitment to our cause since you did so openly question it."

"There. We are all agreed. Where have you kept the American, sheikh?"

"We kept him isolated in one of the houses near the complex. Qari sahib has been there, and will take you. We don't keep more than two guards on him at a time, to attract minimum attention. He is quite comfortable there, though we do keep him blindfolded."

The matter was obviously closed, so Qari Saif did not make any further protest. He got up from the cushions and gestured for Akbar to follow him. They descended into the dark corridor and made their way through the labyrinth of passages to a side door, which led out onto a very narrow street. Qari Saif led them through the street to a group of undistinguished-looking buildings. The houses looked dilapidated. The bricks and mortar had not been plastered over, and rusty old iron bars covered the window openings. Garbage lay outside the front door, creating a nasty stench around the place. A solitary man sat on a stool outside the house. Akbar could see no weapon on his person.

"Is he one of your people, Qari sahib?"

"No. He is just one of the sheikh's normal retainers. He doesn't even know what is kept inside the house."

"Who else knows about the package?"

"Well, one of my men keeps watch inside, bringing food and taking the kafir to the toilet."

"Get rid of him when we get inside." Akbar gestured to the guard outside and told him to return to the madrasa to report to the sheikh.

"What? But why? These are trusted men and, besides, we will need them to help us in our undertaking."

Akbar snickered. "Heh. Qari sahib, you may be a very learned man and a great orator, but it is obvious that you don't have too much experience of such matters. The fewer witnesses there are the better. The police are closing in on us. Would you like any of these men to reveal where you are before you get a chance to get away?"

"I know my people. They are completely trustworthy and would never reveal anything, even if they were captured."

"Your mistake, Qari sahib, if you trust any of your people. I am sure a couple of them already report your daily whereabouts to the police or the Agencies. As you said, I was a police officer, and I know how these things work. If you think any of your people can last more than five minutes when they are hung upside down by their balls in a thana, then you're sadly mistaken. You may want your followers to know of your involvement in this case, but your followers cannot help you if you become a martyr to the cause. It's no fun fighting a jihad from inside a jail cell. No, we will do this ourselves, just you and I. Heh, I know you may not want to get blood on your clean clothes, but you have to get your own hands dirty if you want to further the cause."

Qari Saif looked at Akbar apprehensively. "Do you intend to join us in the mountains?"

"But of course. Where did you think I would go after killing the American?"

Qari Saif muttered under his breath as the two of them set foot in the house. It was pitch-dark, with the only light coming through the iron bars of a high window. The half-cemented floor was littered with droppings, and the only sound was the flapping of wings. Pigeons had nested near the window, entering through the gaps in the iron bars. Akbar drew his gun from under the folds of his shalwar.

"Do you have a weapon to kill him, or should I just shoot him?"

"I had left a sword with my man over here. I had thought it would be nice to behead him on camera."

"That's perfect. We can tell your man to go get a camera and while he is gone, we'll finish the job."

Qari Saif's retainer emerged from the shadows at the sound of their voices. He was sitting in front of a cast iron door that was bolted shut with a huge padlock. The man bowed his head to them and handed over the keys to the padlock. As he unlocked the door, Qari Saif ordered the guard to fetch a video camera.

"It is a pity that we cannot make a proper production out of the American's death. But perhaps what you say is correct. Better to finish the job and be on our way. I'll be glad to be rid of him. He's been quite a handful as a prisoner. He always tries to talk to the guards, trying to discuss theology with them. The kafir even quotes from the Quran."

As he spoke, he bent and pushed back against the heavy iron door. The door budged only slightly, letting in a sliver of light into a dark, dank room. Akbar peered over the Qari's shoulders into the darkness, trying to accustom his eyes. The room was freezing, and their breath turned to mist. In the furthest corner, Akbar could just about make out the shape of a man sleeping on the ground. He was huddled up in a tattered old blanket, with one hand shackled to the wall. A steel jug of water and a steel glass lay by his side, while fast-food wrappers from McDonalds and KFC littered the floor. His captors obviously wanted him to feel at home.

"Heh. Looks like you are the one he seems to have unnerved, Qari sahib. What, you don't like anyone else sermonizing in front of your men?"

"No. I don't want my followers getting confused and corrupted by anyone else's views, especially a kafir. I have to keep them focused on our mission. Besides, he was just telling them lies, lies created to divert people from the true faith, by the Jews and the American—"

The words hadn't finished coming out of his mouth before his brains splattered against the iron door.

Constantine had followed Akbar all the way to the mosque complex. He could see the jeep, with Aziz and the bodyguards in it, parked at the front of the madrasa. He was looking pretty conspicuous just sitting there in his own pickup, so he decided to scout the area on foot. It was still early, and the neighborhood was quiet. Trying to look as casual as he could in a uniform and with a gun in his hand, he circled the madrasa complex.

He was scared. This was just the wrong sort of place for him to be in. If any of the locals were to spot him, their response to a police super-intendent wandering around in their colony would not be a particularly welcoming one. And heaven forbid if they were to discover that he was a Christian.

Constantine swallowed hard and self-consciously raised his hand to cover the gold cross round his neck. At the back of the complex, the street narrowed so much that barely one person could walk in it at a time. As he rounded the corner, Constantine saw a man holding a Kalashnikov rifle step out of a door. The rifle was slung over his shoulder, and he was holding something shiny and metallic in his hand. The only audible sound was the cooing of the pigeons.

It was at that moment that the sharp retort of the gunshot echoed in the alley. The man with the rifle rushed towards the door, dropping the metallic object and unslinging his rifle in one efficient maneuver. Con-stantine looked around to see if anyone else had reacted. In the distance, he could hear men shouting. He was sure they were coming this way.

Akbar cursed himself for having shot Qari Saif at such close range. His blood and bits of his brain had splattered on Akbar's nice white shalwar-kameez. He shook his head. Five years of inactivity really threw off your timing.

The inert figure lying on the floor had woken with a start at the sound of the gunshot. Akbar could see that a very tight blindfold had been tied over his eyes. With his unshackled hand, the prisoner tried to feel the space in front of him, trying to guess how close his assailants were.

"What, what is it? Who's there? Please, someone answer me!"

Akbar had never had a very good grasp of English, but he could understand the gist of what the American was saying. Friedland began to shiver uncontrollably as he heard Akbar's footsteps.

"Please, Khuda ke liye, don't kill me!"

"No, no kill. I, uh, I police. Come to help. No worry."

"Oh thank God. Thank you, thank you so much." The American began to sob in relief.

Just as Akbar started undoing his shackles, he heard footsteps behind him and the voice of the guard, calling out for the Qari. He cursed his haste. The guard must still have been in earshot and must have heard the shot. He signalled to Friedland, whose blindfold was now off, to wait, and walked towards the open door, his gun cocked with his finger on the trigger. But the guard had already reached the outer chamber and his Kalashnikov was pointed straight at Akbar. Hands trembling, he pulled back the bolt, cocking the weapon on full automatic, as he stared disbelievingly at what was left of Qari Saif's skull. Akbar knew he was outgunned and there was nowhere left to run. Any second, the guard's twitchy finger would touch the hair trigger of the rifle ever so slightly and the Kalashnikov would spit out a burst of hot lead. He half closed his eyes and pointed his own pistol at the guard, hoping to get off a lucky shot.

The next thing he heard was a single fire. The guard fell to the floor, his head landing in the mushy mixture of blood, brains, and pigeon droppings that surrounded the Qari's body. Akbar instinctively dropped to the ground to avoid any ricochets. He imagined a posse of bearded madrasa students bursting through the door, baying for his blood. He tried to think of how he could talk his way to safety and take the American with him. Dozens of thoughts and plans raced through Akbar Khan's mind in that nanosecond, but the last person he expected to see walking through the door was Constantine, with his pistol still pointed at the inert body of the guard.

Akbar's face broke into a wide grin. "Heh. That was always the great thing about you, Consendine. Your timing."

"Shut up and move. We have to get the hell out of here. The fucking madrasa students are on their way."

Akbar turned around to see where the American was. He had stuck his head under the blanket, bewildered by this turn of events. His body continued to shake uncontrollably, still not sure whether he had been rescued from the jaws of death only to be restored to the same jaws a moment later. "Consendine, let me introduce you to Jon Friedland. But I'm not too sure whether he's figured out what's going on. Speak to him in English and calm him down."

Constantine approached the blanket gingerly. "Uh, Mr. Friedland, we are police officers. Please do not be afraid, we are here to take you from this place. Please come with us."

At the sound of Constantine's words and the sight of his uniform, the blanket came off. Friedland, his blond hair caked with dirt, his filthy face streaked by tears, and wearing a shalwar-kameez, was unrecognizable from his photographs in the newspapers. As he stepped out of the darkness of the inner chamber into the outer room, he inadvertently stepped into the wet slick that had been created by the blood and brains of the Qari and the guard. At first he didn't comprehend what had happened, as his eyes still adjusted to the light, but when he stared down at his feet and saw that he was standing in the Qari's skull, he collapsed. Akbar was close enough to catch him before he dropped on top of the guard's body.

"He's passed out. Probably better. Easier to get him out of here. Consendine, get me his blanket. We'll wrap him in it and I'll carry him like a gunny sack."

"What's your plan to get out of here, Akbar?"

"Well, heh, I hadn't really thought this whole thing out that far ahead."

The two of them could hear the voices getting closer. Constantine thought for a moment. "Akbar, call Sheikh Noman, he must be close by. Tell him to call his students into one of the lecture rooms for some kind of special sermon, to distract them. Tell him he should also call the local police and inform them that there were some shots fired and for them to come in force. If the sheikh calls them, the locals won't have a problem. You and I will carry the American out like this, wrapped in the blanket, and we'll dump him in the back of my pickup. If anybody sees us, they'll think we're disposing a body or something. Which is better than them finding out about the American."

"The prison has made you sharper, Consendine." Akbar took his phone from his pocket and dialled Sheikh Noman, giving him instructions in a hushed tone.

The two men wordlessly covered Friedland with the blanket, and Akbar tossed him over his shoulder while Constantine led the way, peering out of the door with some trepidation. Three alleys converged at the point where the quarters were. Constantine could see a small crowd approaching them from one of the alleys. But it was still early, and a slight mist hung over the area. The men were still far enough to not be able to identify him and Akbar properly. His pickup was parked at the end of one of the other alleys. Keeping his pistol in one hand, he helped Akbar carry Friedland, and the two of them stumbled into the shadows of the second alley just as the crowd came into full view. Constantine could hear an announcement being made over a loudspeaker, and then several men turned back towards the madrasa. Evidently, Sheikh Noman's call to prayer had worked.

The two men hustled and stumbled through the narrow alley, until it finally widened out and they could see Constantine's blue Toyota pickup. By now, both men were breathing heavily and, with one final effort, they dumped Friedland into the back of the vehicle.

"Akbar, what about Aziz?"

"I'll call him and tell him to drive away as casually as possible, after ten minutes."

Constantine revved the engine and reversed the pickup onto the main road. His heart didn't stop thumping until they were back on the road leading to the shrine of the crocodiles. Akbar was much calmer, lighting a cigarette and staring out the passenger window at the shrine.

"I came here in the morning and prayed, you know? I even threw some popcorn as an offering to the crocodiles. And God sent you as the answer to my prayers."

"Shut up, you fucking maulvi." But Constantine couldn't help smiling as he said it.

Epilogue

It was a busy morning for Constantine in his office. The paperwork was stacked high on his desk. His workload had greatly increased recently. The start of a new year was always busy, with the Home Department having a voracious appetite for annual reports. Additionally, Constantine's inspector general had developed a new fondness for him in the past couple of weeks. He now demanded Constantine's input on all issues and refused to make any decisions without checking with him. Perhaps the IG thought that he had intervened with Pakora to save his job, but whatever the reason, Constantine could do no wrong in his book.

He was almost finished with his correspondence. He picked up the last piece of paper in front of him. It was an order from the sessions court, confirming that the case against Akbar Khan had been withdrawn. He was a free man now, in letter and in fact. Constantine acknowledged the receipt of the document with a flourish of his pen. He put aside the stack of files and stretched his arms. His orderly, who Constantine was convinced had some sort of telepathic ability, wordlessly entered the room and replaced his cold cup of tea with a steaming hot one.

He finally glanced at the morning paper, which had been lying unread at his side. The American president had just concluded a successful state visit to Pakistan and had praised the country as a "bulwark in the War on Terror." He had made special mention of the Friedland kidnapping, and had cited the professionalism and dedication of the Pakistani law enforcement agencies in bringing the case to a successful conclusion. It was just what the government had wanted: a nice, firm pat on the back by Uncle Sam. In the second story on the front page of the paper, the Don, in a special message from his New York headquarters, had also given his congratulations to all of those who were involved in recovering Jon Friedland. He had singled out Pakora and referred to him as a "brilliant, incorruptible individual," and had vowed to maintain him as Home Minister for as long as he remained the head of the United Front. The Don's unequivocal declaration had poured water on the hopes of all the other aspirant UF ministers who were hoping to unseat Pakora.

The same article went on to say that Deputy Superintendent of Police Akbar Khan, the newly installed head of a special investigations unit, who had reportedly played a key role in the recovery of the American, had been recommended for promotion to the rank of superintendent. The writer did not dwell upon Akbar's stay in prison or the UF's enmity towards him. The past, it seemed, could be whitewashed quite easily.

Constantine had heard that everyone connected with the case was being rewarded in one way or another. Hanuman had been nominated to receive a medal for his contributions and would be promoted to head the provincial police as its inspector general when the current IG retired in a couple of months. Constantine hadn't spoken to Tarkeen since that night in Orangi, but Rommel had called him a couple of times just to chat. Through him, Constantine had discovered that Tarkeen too had been guaranteed a promotion and a plum new assignment on the president's personal staff in Islamabad, also to take effect later in the year.

Rommel had proved himself to be a singularly good friend. He was an honorable man learning to survive in a dishonorable world. Constantine had grown fond of him. Tarkeen's departure, and Constantine and Akbar's counsel, would allow him to grow into his role.

The other major story in the paper was an article written by Jon Friedland for the *San Francisco Chronicle*, and syndicated around the world. Under the headline "My Karachi Kidnapping," Friedland had recounted his ordeal and claimed that his captors were surprisingly good to him. From his writing, at least, it seemed as if the kidnapping had not had any permanent ill effects on Friedland. In fact, he was set to profit from it tremendously. A book deal was naturally in the offing and the entertainment pages were ablaze with rumors that both Bollywood and Hollywood were vying for the movie rights. Friedland hadn't publicly commented on these rumors, but he had heaped praise on the courageous officer who had dramatically rescued him from his captors.

News of Akbar seemed to dominate the papers these days. Judging by the comparative column space that crime reporters were devoting to them, it was clear that Akbar's fortunes were on the rise, while Maqsood Mahr's were unquestionably declining. Akbar's new unit had been conducting raids and making arrests all over the city, while Maqsood had been handed an official censure from the inspector general for his poor investigative record.

Constantine was about to put the paper down when he spotted a small news item hidden away inside the second-to-last page of the paper. A man named Ateeq Kapadia had been killed in an armed encounter with personnel from Akbar's unit, when he had attempted to snatch a motorcycle the previous night. The report noted that he was found to be in possession of a handgun as well as large quantities of heroin, causing speculation that he may have been a drug dealer. The report noted that Kapadia was reputed to have had a prior criminal record and was wanted in several cases. The report did not mention him by his more familiar name, Ateeq Tension, or his connection with the UF. Constantine's face morphed into a mask of serenity. So Akbar had finally got him.

Constantine could not express the relief he felt. He had brought Mary and the girls back from the naika's on Christmas Day and, though there had been no fresh threats, Tension's presence had remained a worry for him. Other than that, normalcy had slowly returned to the D'Souza household. Constantine had expected Mary to make some reference to Salma Begum, or at least question him about his past. But she had not. A strange bond had formed between the women in those two days, a bond based on mutual concern for the man they both cared deeply about. Constantine did not know whether Salma had told Mary about the past, but he noticed that Mary showed no signs of insecurity about Salma. On New Year's Day, Mary had sent over a cake to Salma, something that Constantine knew she only did for family and close friends. Two days after that, Salma had come over to visit Mary and the girls. It was the first time she had set foot in Constantine's home. He had not been there himself, but he had heard that she had sat there for several hours, chatting and playing with the girls.

Putting aside the paper, Constantine got up from his chair and strolled out of his office. He couldn't figure out if he was happy or resentful at the rewards that everyone else was reaping. To be perfectly fair to them, they had all offered to take him along in their ride. It was he who had turned them down. So if there were no plaudits for him, it was his own doing. He could still cash in if he wanted to. It would take one call to Akbar or Hanuman and he would be back in the Karachi Police. But did he want to jump back into that life? The thrill of the chase, constantly living on the edge. Or was he now content to watch others from the shadows?

Constantine had been a keen sportsman in his youth. As a hockey player, he had nearly made it to the national team. He remembered something an old coach once told him during practice. For a sportsman, the time he spends at the peak of his best years is the apex of his life. It can never get any better than that. The feeling of exhilaration, the intoxicating nature of youth, the belief that nothing is beyond your grasp. Immortality. There is no feeling like it in the world and, once it is gone, you spend the rest of your life trying in vain to recapture it somehow. But it would never come back. Sometimes Constantine felt as if his years in the police had become like that as well. What you did in the few years that you had power, position, and ability could never be matched with anything you did the rest of your life. Everything that followed inevitably felt more mundane, less fulfilling. The trick, just like in sport, was knowing when to quit. Boxers kept coming back for one last fight, one more shot at greatness even though they had become punch-drunk. Cricketers continued to play even after the reflexes slowed down and the eyes lost their certainty, desperate to cling on, unwilling to bring the curtain down on themselves. Police officers were the same. One more case, one more medal, one more dramatic encounter, one more narrow brush with death. But ultimately, if you didn't take your bow and step off the stage at the right time, either the enemies that you made in a lifetime of pissing people off caught up with you or your own colleagues stabbed you in the back. It was all about the timing.

Constantine walked through the prison gates into the sunlight of the outer courtyard, to the same spot where he had met Rommel three weeks ago. The weather was warming up. This was welcome relief for a Karachiite like Constantine. The soft, warm sunlight felt good on his face. As he stretched again, a man approached him from the outer gate. The man walked up to him, salaamed him, and handed him an envelope. Inside it were 100,000 rupees and a note from Akbar. The note simply said, "There's a place waiting for you. Akbar." The messenger indicated that the amount was Constantine's weekly share, courtesy of Akbar's bookie friend, and that he would deliver a similar amount every week.

Akbar had made his decision when he walked out of those same gates. What would Constantine do? He smiled as he thumbed the money. What was it Akbar had said? In the end, we are all prisoners of our own destiny. And so it was.

Glossary

aalim: Islamic scholar

adab: a form of highly formal traditional greeting, used in the Moghul royal court, where the supplicant raises his or her palm to their face and bows in front of the person they are meeting. Used to portray deference.

afsar: officer

arre: colloquial term; the closest English term to it would be "Hey"

aur: the English equivalent would be "and"

ayaash: someone who likes to party, especially with regard to booze and women

baba: colloquial term, equivalent to saying "Hey man"

badmashes: street thugs, gangsters

badshah log: literally, "royal people"; colloquially used to describe someone who has a casual, devil-may-care attitude, with no care for consequences, similar to royals

barey mian: old man

beater: official at the police station who collects all the illegal payments from the area's vice dens, on behalf of the police station in-charge

bhai: brother; often used by representatives of political and religious parties to address each other

bharwa: pimp

bhenchod: expletive meaning "sister-fucker"

chutiya: expletive, literally translates to "cunt"

chowkidar: night watchman

crore: ten million rupees; approximately 100,000 USD

Defence, Clifton Defence: Posh upscale residential neighborhoods in Karachi, known for their very liberal and Westernized outlook

dupatta: scarf, part of traditional dress, often draped across the chest or shoulders, but can also be worn more conservatively to cover a woman's head; less conservative than a hijab

fatigue: colloquial term used by the police to describe an unwanted task that is dumped on to a junior subordinate by a senior

fauji: Army personnel

ghazal: traditional ballad

goonda: gangsters

gora: white person

gully: side alley

harami: literally means "bastard"; used colloquially to imply someone who is sneaky and conniving

haramkhor: bastard

hari-pagri: green turbans; colloquial term used to describe members of the Tableeghi Jamaat, who go around proselytising and inviting people to become born-again Muslims; very similar to Jehovah's Witnesses

hijira: hermaphrodite

Hum Don se pyaar karna chahte hain: literally, "We want to make love to the Don," though when said in Urdu the term "make love" isn't meant to be sexual

imam zamin: amulet worn or given by Shias to someone for their protection

izzat: honor

kana: colloquial term for a one-eyed person, someone who can only use one of their eyes

khas-o-khas: colloquial term to describe someone who is in the inner circle or who has a special relationship

Khuda Hafiz: Urdu term which means "good-bye"; literally, "God protect you"

khokha: colloquial term used to describe one crore; equals 100,000 USD

kya: what

kya karoon: What can I do?

kyun: why

kyun re: colloquial term meaning "why"

lakh: 100,000 rupees: approximately 1,000 USD

mai-baap: mother-father; colloquially, someone to whom everything is owed, like a patron

madarchod: motherfucker

madrasa: religious school

masjid: mosque

maulvi: Islamic scholar

meter: crazy or angry; going off the scales, or off the "meter"

mohalla: neighborhood

munshi: police station clerk who is responsible for all the administration of the station

naika: chief madam, as is explained in the text. Prostitution is illegal in Pakistan, but a very established and lucrative trade has thrived for a long time in spite of this. The police often extort bribes or regular payments from brothels, and often corrupt police officers even become active partners in the business.

Napier: the traditional red light district of Karachi

Orangi: Karachi's largest slum, know for its influx of criminals, ethnic political parties, and various religious extremist groups

oye saale: mild expletive, equivalent to "Hey, idiot"

paisa: money

pakora: literally, a fried snack, but people with large and bulbous noses are often referred to as having a "Pakora nose"

peti: street term for one lakh, or 100,000 rupees; approximately 1,000 USD

phadda: a fight, used colloquially to denote something that becomes an issue

the police lines: residential area for police officers which is usually attached at the back of or in the same compound as a police station, so that officers and men can reside close to their place of work

Preedy: The city center, or downtown area of Karachi, known for its various markets. Preedy police station has traditionally been considered one of the city's most lucrative police stations due to the plentiful opportunities for corruption.

randi: prostitute

reader: a term from the old British colonial nomenclature, a reader is basically the office assistant, or PA

reti bajri: silt, sand and pebbles. In Karachi, police stations on the outskirts of the city often allow builders and truckers to illegally fill trucks with reti bajri to aid in construction projects in the city. This is considered an extremely lucrative source of revenue for the local police.

saala: mild expletive, equivalent to "idiot"

saala bharwa: idiot pimp

saale: same as saala

salaam[ed]: to greet somebody

sardar: head of a tribe

setting, do a setting: make an arrangement

sifarish: requesting favours from politicians or other influential people

Sohrab Goth: an area in Karachi notorious for the presence of drug dens and illegal activities

sone ki chidiya: literally, "golden bird"; same as golden goose

tableegh: spectacle

tamasha: the process of preaching conversion to Islam, done by missionaries who are similar to Jehovah's Witnesses and who also advocate born-again Muslims.

tandoor: a traditional oven, used to bake naan bread.

tapori: street tough

thoko: colloquial term meaning "to kill somebody"

thulla: derogatory street slang for police officer

tick off: to mildly admonish someone

wadero: Sindhi word for rural landowner

wardias: members of a city ward

ward boss: head of a ward, the basic administrative unit of the United Front Party, usually organized at a neighborhood level, same as political wards in the US

YaAllah: translates to "Oh God"

yaar: friend

Acknowledgements

This book was conceived one evening when I was in the middle of one of my complaining rants to my wife, Samar. She was the one who encouraged me to put pen to paper (or fingers to laptop) and thus began a new chapter in my life. To Samar, who has stood by me through rain and shine, the good times and the bad, and without whose love and encouragement this book would never have been possible.

To my mother, for putting up with me for thirty-six years: I am who I am because of you.

To Chaudhry Aslam, Mushtaq Mahar, Shahid Hayat, and Irfan Bahadur, for teaching me how to be a cop.

To Fayyaz and Nadeem, for telling me all the true stories that could only be told by converting them to fiction.

To my mother-in-law, for poring over the edits of this book, despite crashing computers and Karachi load shedding.

To my son, Suleyman, who is the only person in this world who can make me laugh at will.

To my agent, Jessica, for believing in me as a writer, and to Cal Barksdale, and the rest of the team at Skyhorse Publishing for making this book possible.

To Bina Shah who was that critical link—thank you!

To my friends who read my first and second and third drafts, and gave me the confidence to continue: Saad, Faisal, Asad, Ateeq, Adnan, Daniyal, Amanda, Alexia, Nazish, Samar Zia, Adeel, Kulsoom, Saugata.